W9-COM-546

IN HER BLOOD

IN HER BLOOD

Caro Ramsay

SEVERN
HOUSE

First world edition published in Great Britain and the USA in 2023
by Severn House, an imprint of Canongate Books Ltd,
14 High Street, Edinburgh EH1 1TE.

severnhouse.com

British Library Cataloguing-in-Publication Data
A CIP catalogue record for this title is available from the British Library.

ISBN-13: 978-1-4483-0676-3 (cased)
ISBN-13: 978-1-4483-1194-1 (e-book)

All Severn House titles are printed on acid-free paper.

MIX
Paper from
responsible sources
FSC® C013056

Typeset by Palimpsest Book Production Ltd.,
Falkirk, Stirlingshire, Scotland.
Printed and bound in Great Britain by
TJ Books, Padstow, Cornwall.

For Alan

PROLOGUE

The girls skipped through the field, holding tightly onto each other's hand; the hem of the red dress, the scalloped border of the lace skirt, brushed the long grass. When the little girl stumbled and was swallowed by the green, her older sister helped her up.

They had been left behind, but it was too hot to hurry. There wasn't a breath of air, a stillness settling with the heat.

The girls tripped and fell, rolling down the embankment, laughing, then dusted themselves off before climbing through the hole in the fence. They were crossing the tracks at Church's Pass to get to the den. Forbidden fun.

The rest of them were already up the hill on the other side with their picnic; they were shouting and shrieking. Happy kids on the school holidays.

Then the girl in the red dress heard her friend call to them.

She waved. Her friend waved back.

The hand slipped free. The train thundered past.

Her sister had gone.

ONE

Death isn't so bad, it's the life before it that's bloody awful.

Killagal Blog, 2021

The bubbles detached themselves, soaring to the top of the glass where they floated free. The Taittinger was ignored for the moment as all heads turned to watch the Friday night news on the big screen in the pub. The barman of the Ben Nevis Hotel, knowing who the six well-dressed drinkers in the corner were, obliged by turning the sound up. The scene was a familiar one; recorded on the court steps immediately after the verdict. Marilyn Lovell, the mother of the victim, was giving a statement to the camera, her strong features determined to achieve some closure. Her face was haggard, her hair scraped back, her skin pitted and lined with a life of hard knocks and abuse. Her eyes were red-ringed, tears flowing freely, but whether they were tears of fear or anger was difficult to tell.

DCI Christine Caplan put her hand over her glass when the bottle came her way; any more bubbles and she'd explode. Listening to the chatter, she looked over the team she'd worked with for the previous three months: no stress, no strain, pulling together the evidence. The team had gelled quickly. It didn't happen often, but when it did, it made investigating the horrors and depravity of the human mind almost tolerable.

This team would go far. Caplan hoped they would stay together, but she wouldn't be their senior officer. Tonight was her last night here. In five minutes she'd get in her car and drive away.

As cases went, it had been one of the easier ones to solve; millennials with all their tech-savvy should know to turn their phone off when they are strangling their girlfriend in the kitchen before relying on an alibi that necessitated them being in a pub thirty miles away.

DCI Caplan sent up praise that criminals were rarely clever.

At ten-thirty she stood up, said her goodbyes and left the murder team to their celebrations.

An hour later, she drove through Kilnlorn and then pulled off the track outside her cottage, bouncing the Duster along the rough, potholed stretch of grass and brick that passed for a driveway. Caplan did a quick U-turn so the car was facing the water, not the tumbledown project they had bought as a house. Stepping into the still night air, she zipped her anorak up fully. The Duster heater had lost its long battle against a west of Scotland winter a couple of months ago. Now, she was never sure if it was colder inside or outside the car.

Sitting on the bonnet, hands snuggled in her pockets, Caplan breathed in deep, listening to the silence, watching the waves of the sea loch twinkle darkly in the moonlight.

Thinking.

It was preternaturally peaceful here. Despite the state of the cottage, the weather, and the hundred and one issues of being here, she could, sometimes, think that she – that they – could be happy. It was a wistful feeling, sad because it was so rare. It was the briefest glimmer of how lovely life might be.

She opened her phone; some emails had arrived during the drive home. One was from the builder. Taking a deep breath, ignoring the tweak in her stomach every time somebody mentioned the cost, she opened the attachment. It was supposed to be good news, but in reality it was merely fewer degrees of awful. Being left unoccupied for eighteen months plus damage sustained in the winter gales – to say nothing of the prevailing wind and the copious rain – had wreaked havoc on the cottage. The builders thought she hadn't noticed the absence of glass in the front windows. But she'd gone ahead and bought Challie Cottage anyway.

Their two children were over the water somewhere, on the island of Skone, both still in recovery. It was nearly midnight. Emma would be fast asleep by now, ready to be up at dawn for her physio and yoga. Kenny? She could imagine him sitting out on Honeybogg Hill, thinking. He'd be ruminating on his self-worth while staring at the stars. Caplan looked up; the night sky was a carpet of ebony velvet and diamonds. Her son had the capacity to think too deeply about everything. Where did that ever get anybody?

Aklen would be at home, asleep on the sofa. Like her finances, Caplan knew she was pushing her marriage harder than it could take. The cottage had been marketed as a 'project'. According to Constable McPhee's mother, the previous owners had bought it as a holiday home. Caplan had seen the photographs of it before it fell to ruin, when the family had staycationed here, when the loch and the mountains shimmered in the sunshine, when kids swam in the shallows, dad went fishing and mum sat on the yellow-cushioned swing seat sipping a glass of chilled Pinot.

Caplan had spent more than a few hours on the swing seat herself, wrapped in her duvet, her fingers warming round a mug of soup. She'd buy some yellow cushions too, if and when Aklen joined her.

In its prime, Challie Cottage had five bedrooms, beautiful views across the water and bountiful silence. It had cost the previous owners less than a tenth of their two-bedroomed flat in London. It was rumoured the family had used it for a fortnight in the summer for the last four years. McPhee's mother said they had tried one Christmas at Challie and been back in Islington by midnight on Boxing Day. Now it was home to a feral cat christened Pavlova.

Caplan scrolled to the end of the builders' report. She shouldn't have. It was a graphic of what the house could look like; moving the living room upstairs and installing a wall of glass with a wraparound balcony that would take in the view.

It was beyond beautiful. Now she had that vision in her head, she wouldn't be able to settle for less.

She looked over her shoulder at the caravan. It'd all be solved by a good night's sleep.

The caravan was not old, but everything felt damp. Caplan hadn't quite mastered the timer on the heating yet, and the April day had been laced with a bitter chill. The duvet was cold as she slid under it in her cotton pyjamas, lying there chittering for ten minutes before she gave up, got out, got dressed again and lay down on top of the duvet, watching her breath clouding in the air. The chill pervaded every surface; her bones were getting old living here. Years ago, more years than she was happy to remember, when she had been at her dancing weight, they had told her that she'd always be susceptible to 'cold', something about the fat cells not forming properly in adolescent girls who maintained a low body mass through diet or exercise. But her body knew the difference between 'cold', and 'too cold'. It seemed to her that the latter had become more of an issue since she'd been submerged in the icy waters of the Sound last summer, that period of time – it had seemed like hours – when she'd barely survived, and she'd seen people die. Since that horror, she felt the cold of that night was always within her. It could be tamed, mollified, warmed and cosseted, but at moments like this, the cold ate through her soul.

She got up, slipping her anorak over her shoulders before filling a kettle with water and turning the gas on, holding her fingers above the blue flame in an attempt to warm up. She listened to the familiar, cheerful hiss from the cooker, soon to be accompanied by the chuckle of the boil.

Preparing the Lovell case for court while wrapping up another three for the teams she was supervising had kept her busy. She'd have a long-awaited weekend off now. Out to the island to visit the kids, then head home to Glasgow and see if Aklen had bothered to chase up a final valuation for the house they needed to sell. Or *she* needed to sell.

Work was over for forty-eight hours. It'd be Monday before she could get to grips with the builders. She leaned her forehead against the cupboard, aware of the hush and roll of the waves outside. The wind must be getting up; the caravan was rocking gently. Heavy rain was forecast for the early hours of the morning. She could hear sheep bleating on the hill behind her, the rattling of loose tiles on the cottage roof beating out a tattoo over the night air. They were rocking her to sleep, slowly and gently.

Her mobile rang.

They had a situation at Cronchie.

TWO

Killagal is getting death threats.
Where are you?
I'm here. I'm waiting.

As Caplan was approaching the bridge, the weather turned. The forecast stiff breeze had pushed the dark clouds in from the west, bringing their gifts of heavy rainfall.

For most of the drive, the sky had possessed that infinitely intense darkness of a cloudless night on the west coast of Scotland. It was a constant reminder to Caplan of how insignificant she was. A minuscule blip on a tiny peninsula of a little country on a small but very precious planet.

Somebody had jumped from the Connel Bridge into the freezing water. Had they felt too insignificant to go on, had they endured an intolerable day? Had they lost their job, were they unable to heat their home or feed their kids, or to push back the darkness until the sun shone for them again? Too beaten down to enjoy the simple pleasure of a walk in the rain or a cuddle from the cat. But then, that presumed the wherewithal to afford a waterproof jacket and the cost of a family pet.

A poor soul had taken an extra punch that they couldn't bounce back from. How easy had it been on this dark, starry night for them to climb onto the rail of the bridge, to stand and think for a moment and then . . .

Such thoughts had crossed her own mind, times when she was too tired, too cold, too mentally exhausted to care if she ever took another breath. But she had.

Yet there had been times . . .

Inwardly she shuddered at the sight that greeted her as she drove round the bend: the huge iron span of the Connel Bridge. Beyond that, an area of churning water was highlighted out on the Sound, the beams of bright searchlights emphasising the darkness. A lone patrol car was up on the bridge, lights flashing. She drove along the access road and indicated as a uniformed cop flagged her to pass before recognising the vehicle.

She presented her warrant card; he waved her to a small car park on the bank where the River Etive met the Sound. There were a lot of vehicles. This, plus her being summoned to the scene, suggested it might be more than a tragic suicide. Caplan glanced at the dashboard clock; it was quarter to two. She wondered how the night would have ended if she'd stayed with the team in the pub.

She got out of the car and stood for a moment, getting the feeling back in her numb feet. Pulling up her hood, she rammed the toggle to her chin to keep the rain out. This might take time. Her colleagues at Cronchie had taught her to always carry an overnight bag in the back of the car, especially after she'd bought the remote cottage. She'd texted Betty's B&B to leave a key out. No matter how long this took, there'd be breakfast and a hot shower waiting for her in the morning.

God, it was cold. The clouds were scudding across the sky, threatening now, pushing away April's warmth, inviting the chills of March to have a reprise. She took a moment to get her bearings as the roaring water sucked at her guts and the pressure pulled at her ears. Mother Nature in the raw. The bridge lay to the north, arching over the mouth of the Sound. The disruption and anger of the water at this point was caused by the rolling wave, the Falls of Lora. Caplan had never witnessed it with this power. Twice a month the height disparity of the incoming tide and the outflowing river created a tidal race between the two potent and opposing currents. She could hear the thrashing suction of a whirlpool at the river's edge rendering the raised voices of the recovery unit barely audible.

People. Lights. Rescue teams. The frantic activity was now stilling. Looking across the fractious water, she could see two kayakers paddling furiously into the wave, getting spat out of it then burrowing back in, being tracked by the powerful search-lights as the beams of the head torches were lost in the dark. They looked as if they were already towing the cradle, which explained the slight lull in activity ashore.

Was the jumper a local? Someone who knew about the tides and the times? There was no way of swimming to safety, no danger of them being hauled out and saved against their will. They'd get caught in that current for eternity.

She showed her warrant badge, signed in and was directed round the back of the short line of shops, a GP surgery, a pharmacy, a dental practice and café. There was a small bin area sectioned off by both wooden and wired fencing, now cut open revealing the steep drop of twenty feet to the water's surface.

The river below sounded like a caged animal, thrashing for liberty. There were fifteen personnel at least present, all facing out over the Sound. Somebody up on the bank in the garden next door, the furthest promontory of the land, had the strong spotlight. He and his colleague were fighting to keep it focused on the kayaks in the strengthening wind. Caplan climbed up onto a low wall, looking over the heads of those in front of her, seeing the long wave that rolled over on itself, never advancing to the bridge and the sea, or retreating into the safety of the glen. The kayaks were still wrestling with the current, struggling to keep hold of their cargo, lining themselves up, then passing by with another hook in case they lost contact. It was medieval jousting on water, in the dark, using one hand. A radio flickered to life, barking commands.

She listened without hearing what they were saying, not wanting to interrupt the operation, still wondering why she was called out to a suicide.

'DCI Caplan?' shouted a voice she knew. Young McPhee, always pleasant and enthusiastic; his smooth face was swamped by a woolly hat with ear flaps, his thin body bulky in his padded jacket and trousers. She still had on the clothes she had slept in.

'DC McPhee, good to see you again. What's brought us out on a night like this?'

'A jumper, from the bridge. We're still trying to recover the body but it's proving difficult. Terrible weather.'

She nodded and looked around her, then leaned forward and shouted as quietly as she could, 'Why am I here? Something untoward?'

McPhee smiled, backhanding rainwater from his forehead, and gestured to the small figure in an overlong red kagoule, his hand on top of the hood to prevent it being blown down. 'Craigo suggested we call you in.'

'Is he filming a remake of *Don't Look Now*?'

Caplan took another look at the kayaks, then walked down to the centre of activity where she tapped the small figure in red on the shoulder.

He spun round quickly, causing his hood to fall down over his face, splattering Caplan in spray as it did so.

'DS Craigo?'

'Oh, hello, ma'am. Yes indeed,' he shouted, his little raccoon eyes darting left and right, as if their meeting was somehow unexpected.

'You called me out for a suicide? Why?'

'It's the bridge, ma'am.' DS Craigo was pointing, answering with that logic that brought him close to being punched on many an occasion.

'Yes, I know what it is,' Caplan said slowly. 'We've a bridge and a dead body in the water. Why do you need me?' She side-stepped to a spot a little more protected.

'Well . . .' He followed her.

'Well, what exactly?' she asked.

'The roadworks – and the jumpers' car park's empty.'

'Explain. As quick as you can.' Caplan blew down her gloves to warm her fingers.

'Well, ma'am, jumpers tend to park either in that lay-by there or in this one here. During the day the lay-bys are usually busy with tourists stopping to photograph the bridge. But at this time of the morning, with plenty parking space, we've a jumper but no car. Taxis aren't allowed to let people off near here, for obvious reasons – they take them to the phone box instead. There's a helpline there.'

'And the roadworks?'

'Oh, it's going to be an issue, ma'am. First jumper for a long time.' He pointed to the bridge. 'The construction company have left machinery at the side. See it there? It makes the top of the fence accessible. They could be liable. I thought I'd get you out.' His finger turned to point at her. 'And congratulations on the Lovell case, ma'am, that was very quick.'

'Thank you,' she shouted back, her words snatched by the wind. Caplan was thinking it through, looking out over the water, feeling the cold in the breeze. Her forty-eight hours off was receding with the tide and here was Craigo with his small-village politics and theories, and his unerring instinct for relevant trivia. The jumper could be local, he would be known. There would be an inquiry, of course; the construction company might have made suicide an easier option than it should have been.

'Okay, but he could have walked from the Bridge B&B over there. As soon as the body is on dry land, we're finished here. Whatever's up on the bridge will be there tomorrow,' said Caplan, wriggling her toes to keep her circulation going.

'Not that B&B, ma'am, Toni phoned them and asked. Their guests are all present and correct. But the contractor, ma'am. That's bloody disgraceful.' He pointed with his chewed pencil.

'Do we know for definite he fell from the bridge?' Caplan shouted. The longer she stood there, the colder her ears were getting, the louder the roar and the rush of the water seemed to be. 'Could it be accidental, falling in from here, from the bank?' She was aware how slippery it was underfoot.

'Then the body would be here at the side, ma'am.'

Caplan looked down, felt dizzy and stepped back. 'It's impressive, the bridge.' She nodded at the dark imposing structure, huge when seen from this angle. She had seen many a photograph of it, pretty in autumnal colours, on calendars of the Scottish Highlands, but never, ever in such hostile weather as this.

'Yes, cantilever, built in 1904 and it's a—'

'Yes, okay, but a common place for suicide?'

'Not recently due to the new, higher fence. Folk are finding things tough, and Felix Construction made it easy to jump in a bad moment.'

'Get the body processed as an unexpected, unexplained death. I'm going to have a look around before I go.'

The noise of chatter rose over the wind as the land crew leant over to lift the cradle with the body from the water and lay it on the bank, the body lying, one leg hanging out, like a little kid who couldn't stay still in bed. The group parted to let the photographer and the DCI have a look. After a few initial flashes, the photographer said it was okay for the limbs to be placed in the plastic body bag, ready to be zipped up. The body looked more human suddenly, having been assigned the position of sleep.

'Pockets?' asked Caplan.

A gloved hand appeared with an evidence bag. There was a quick look through the anorak, the dark shirt, the pullover, a pat-down of the sodden cord trousers.

'Nothing. Mugged? No sign of a struggle. Emptied his pockets and jumped?' suggested McPhee.

'Well, someone took his watch.' The gloved hand rolled back the cuff of the anorak sleeve. 'A Fitbit, from the look of that mark. Might be worth a few bob.'

'We might be able to track it,' said McPhee, straightening up.

'Okay, forget what I said earlier, get the area around here searched.' Caplan looked up into the night. 'We'll leave what we can to daylight, it'll be cheaper and easier, but for now start with the slipway. And the shore while the tide decides if it's on its way in or out, anywhere within throwing distance. The approach road and car park can remain secure until the morning.'

She regarded the body, so much information absorbed by sight alone. He was in his thirties, she guessed. Well-dressed, well nourished, neatly trimmed moustache, dark-eyed, dark-haired. Dressed for being out in this weather but not for the hills. He had good, solid, rather strange-looking shoes, reminiscent of the ortho-paedic ones her friend wore in school. He'd been a thin-faced young man, maybe going a little prematurely grey. In this light, and with the temperature of the water, the skin round his closed eyes was white compared to the nose, the right cheek and the right ear, which were reddened by impact with the bridge or by the turbulence of the water.

Caplan thought he looked like a geography teacher.

A geography teacher who had nothing in his pockets. If he had emptied them with a view to taking his own life, then somebody would be waking up to a small pile of personal effects, and a note. There would be recriminations and guilt. She looked up at the bridge, closed her eyes and sighed. Life would never be the same again.

She turned her attention back to the body. 'Can you take that off? Bag it carefully,' Caplan said, pointing at the gold band still on the third finger of his left hand.

'Don't want to lose any evidence, ma'am,' said a disembodied voice, just loud enough to hear. There were a few answering snorts of laughter.

She shrugged it off. 'How long do you think he's been there?'

'Not long. It was phoned in an hour ago. The body would've been seen if it had been there in daylight. Lots of tourists here today watching the seals play on the Falls. My guess? Anytime that it was dark enough. It looks to me like he fell in the water,' said Craigo.

'Really?' replied Caplan, light on the sarcasm.

Craigo didn't notice. He pointed with the leg of his glasses, his hood tipped up to hide his face completely. 'Some folk on the bridge have been hit by wide vehicles, toppled off, but they have visible injuries. This poor man has nothing. A jumper might empty their pockets. Locals know well enough to stay away from the water . . .'

'Except mad canoeists and the odd surfer.'

'The ring has an inscription.' The officer kneeling at the body had taken a picture of it on his phone and opened up the image to read it. '"To CB from EM", and the date 3 November 2013. Wedding day?'

'Well, that's a good lead.' Caplan was suddenly very tired. 'What do we think? A drunk on a stag weekend, a pub crawl? A golfers' outing? Accident, suicide or crime? First thing, call round the hotels. There's no key card on him? Then a B&B? Is that really an easy place to jump from?'

'It is at the moment because of the roadworks,' repeated Craigo, back on his favourite subject. 'There's a ledge to step onto the rail now. That's the whole bloody problem, ma'am, as you see . . .'

'Cameras on the bridge?'

'Disabled due to the roadworks. We'll request dashcam footage, as well as CCTV,' said Craigo.

'Take your time with this, we don't want anything coming back to bite us on the bum.'

'No sign of foul play. Just no ID?' asked McPhee.

'Doesn't make sense. But they never do, do they?'

When daylight came, it was still cold and bitter, with the harsh, chilling sun of spring bracing through the clouds. Caplan's decision not to tackle the long drive back to the caravan had been justified. She was in need of sleep and a hot shower. This was going to be a hard day that might entail another long drive. Once again, she was – she inwardly grimaced at her choice of phrase – in at the deep end at the start of a case.

But today she'd be detailed with something new. Craigo and McPhee, the local team, could deal with the bridge man.

Caplan was glad of the arrangement she had with Betty

Medhurst, the owner of the April Farm B&B. Betty had left a small breakfast out for her when she'd eventually arrived at ten past four. She'd slept lightly, had her shower, dressed and pulled her hair into its trademark chignon, four pins to hold it in place, no more. Then she was ready to eat.

Betty was used to her staying here. She'd slept here many a time before she'd put the caravan on site at Challie Cottage. She hoped to be heading back to Glasgow today, to Abington Drive, to her husband. The graphics from the builder might cheer him up a bit, enough to get the family home valued. She needed Aklen to share this vision. He was conjuring up objections to coming back north, back to his birthplace. It wasn't that Aklen didn't want to be in Glasgow. Or in Kilnlorn. He didn't want to be anywhere. She gave a thought to the man who had jumped off the bridge. Somewhere there was a wife waiting for him to come home. Was that tragedy the result of another man losing the long battle with depression?

Turning on her laptop, Caplan tucked into the banana, two yoghurts and a cup of tea made from the Clifton's raspberry and pomegranate teabag that Betty had left out for her. She checked the news headlines. More madness going on in the world, young men being sent to slaughter other young men that they would have enjoyed a pint with, had they met in a pub in Spain rather than on opposite sides of an inconstant and dubious border. Some celebrity engaged in the mud-slinging of a bitter divorce, accusation and counter-accusation of domestic violence. A brief report on the Lovell verdict. Investigations ongoing as to the identity of the vigilante who had uncovered the whereabouts of 'Britain's Most Evil Woman' and set fire to her flat. She was now reported to be recovering in a safe location. The article was less about finding the arsonist and more about the public money being spent on keeping the child-killer, 'Girl A', safe now that she had turned eighteen.

There was nothing about the man in the river.

Caplan sat on her bed, eating her yoghurt with one hand, and texted Aklen. *How are you today? Something has come up, should be over within a couple of hours, I'll get back asap.*

That wouldn't go down well. Still, he could amuse himself in the meantime by doing some packing. He hadn't actually said he was remaining in Glasgow; he was just doing nothing about moving. They had argued about it intermittently for the four days before she had come up to Fort William to work the Lovell case. What Aklen really wanted was to be moved from their Glasgow four-bedroomed detached house in suburbia to Challie Cottage, minus any hassle. Or as their daughter had put it, he wanted to be transported from one sofa where he could sleep all day to another sofa where he could do exactly the same. Both their kids were within twenty miles of the cottage at Kilnlorn, over a hundred from Glasgow. It was Aklen who was slowly annexing himself. As he had been over the last eight years.

She understood it, she empathised with it, but good God it was tiring. It was difficult to see the young man he had been, incredibly handsome, witty, intelligent, falling to nothing, his vibrant colour fading to sepia. He was disappearing. His PhD, his career, his marathon medals, all testament to what he had lost. He was a shadow of that man now.

Maybe the man on the bridge had had similar thoughts, standing above the water near Cronchie. That might explain the jump.

That morning, about half-three, Caplan had left DC Toni Mackie, her bushy blonde hair escaping from her woolly hat, bossing cold, wet men around, telling them to get a hot drink, placing warm blankets over shivering shoulders. Every team had a member like that, and it was usually a woman. DS Craigo had been busy doing whatever Craigo did. Mackie would go back to Cronchie to write up the preliminary reports before going home. Caplan knew that PC Mattie Jackson would have an incident room ready for them when they got back to the station, but she'd have a new case by then.

Despite it being past nine a.m., the car park at Cronchie police station was still half empty when she drove in. Mattie Jackson was behind his desk, as usual.

'Got it all sorted for you, ma'am, they're upstairs,' he said, going back to his monitor as if he had only seen her the day before rather than a gap of a few weeks.

DC Toni Mackie was pleased to see Caplan, even though they had acknowledged each other's presence at the bridge in the early hours of the morning. She was her usual noisy self, pinning up a photograph of the deceased, case number on the top right corner, and pounced when she saw Caplan come in. 'Hello, pet, how are you doing? Did you get any sleep, have you had something to eat? Are you going to be warm enough in that jumper? Do you want a coffee? Oh no, you like that weird stuff. We still have it in the cupboard from the last time you were here, I mean no other bugger'll touch it.'

DCI Caplan swore that Mackie was getting more like her own mother.

A map of the roads around the bridge and a timeline were already on the wall. On a small scrap of paper was written *12.25, Bevan McDonald, a couple on the bridge*. They had traced a witness already? Two people? It could be something. Equally it might not be connected at all. It might have been a perfectly innocent couple walking back after going out to take photographs of the complex wave patterns. This was a tourist hotspot, the bridge was an iconic landmark, the tidal flux was a natural, impressive phenomenon. Normal rules might not apply. DS Craigo was on the phone, the amount of A4 paper covered in scribble on his desk suggesting he might have been there most of the night.

They didn't need her.

'Good to have you back, ma'am,' Craigo said when he ended his call.

'Good to be back. Do we know anything from this witness?'

Craigo looked around him, as if a pantomime horse had appeared out of nowhere.

'Anybody?'

'It was Bevan McDonald, the Bevmeister. He likes a drink,' admitted Craigo.

'Was he driving drunk?'

'Oh no. Probably. Yes.'

Caplan looked from Craigo to Mackie. There was something she wasn't being told.

'He saw a big monkey,' said Mackie finally.

'A big monkey?' Caplan repeated slowly.

'A big monkey.'

Caplan let that go. She pointed to the ghostly image on the board. 'The man in the water – do we have an ID yet?'

'We've called him Mr Bridges, for . . .'

'For clarity?' prompted Caplan.

'For the moment,' nodded Craigo.

* * *

Caplan was in her office, hoping to get on with some paperwork and waiting to have a quiet word with DS Craigo about the monkey and the Bevmeister. Mackie knocked on her door, telling her she was wanted downstairs.

Caplan closed her file. 'Any leads on the identity of the body?'

'Things are coming in, but it's a bit early yet. What do you want us to do with the *Express*? They're annoying Mattie.'

'What do you think? What's the local grapevine saying?'

'I'd leave it to word-of-mouth for now. We've already had three landladies on the phone saying that they're missing a guest. News about a body in the water'll get round soon enough. We don't need the media to do anything for us.'

'Anything useful in those three?'

'Two of them were at the same stag night and are probably lying drunk in a bed different from the one they are supposed to be in, but we did get a call from Happy Harris at breakfast that might be of interest. He's downstairs, hence why Mattie wants a word. Some chap didn't come back from his conference last night.'

'What conference?' asked Caplan.

'Well, we can't find one . . .'

'Really?' Caplan got up and slipped her jacket on. Then picked up her rucksack as well, in case she could get away. 'What about the man who saw the monkey on the bridge? Where's he? Narnia? Mordor? Remaking *Planet of the Apes*?'

Mackie shook her head. 'He just said it as he saw it, ma'am. I think Bev's going to come in later to give us a statement now that he's . . .'

'Sober.'

'To be fair to him, he thought there was a man and someone who looked like a big monkey. It was dark. As soon as he heard about the commotion, he got his wife to call in. He was going across the bridge at half-twelve or thereabouts and there was defo somebody up there with Mr Bridges; they might have been talking him down . . .'

'Or mugging him before throwing him over. We'll see if the PM comes back with any signs of a struggle.' She looked down at a scene photo of the bridge that was stapled onto the front of the file, the dark struts looking like fine wire highlighted by the flash in the night. 'A large monkey? So maybe a big man, bulky jacket, dark trousers?'

'Maybe a fluffy hat, and a big scarf and he couldn't make out the neck,' added Mackie helpfully. 'It'd be a glimpse in the headlights, just an impression, that's all.'

'We're lucky he didn't see green fairies.'

'Not at this time of year,' said Mackie seriously.

As Caplan went through the secured door into reception she bumped into a couple, barely recognising the man until he said hello to her. She looked from the man to the woman then to PC Mattie Jackson, who was slightly amused at the DCI's discomfort.

'If I didn't know better, I'd think that she didn't recognise you, Happy,' said Jackson, sliding back to hide behind his toughened glass partition.

'Dave Harris, I recognised you of course but I didn't think you were working here. How's the arm? How are you doing?'

'It's getting there, slowly.' Her ex-colleague looked at the ground.

Caplan now saw that the hand of the woman beside him rested on his forearm. Mrs Harris she presumed.

'The bed and breakfast at the end of our road, Kerrera View, has a guest who didn't come home last night. Jen, the owner, wants to know what she should do.'

'Was he up here for a stag do?'

'No, for a medical conference. She didn't quite catch which one. I think she's already phoned it in, but I thought I'd pop in and see what's what.' Happy Harris smiled, something he did very rarely.

'Mattie, can we get a photo of the deceased round to the B&B as soon as possible?'

'Do you want to go yourself, ma'am? In case it's him?' said Jackson, peering from his glass cage.

'Is there a reason why I should?'

'Just that you've been away. Will I get Craigo down? He'll be wanting to say hello.'

Caplan got the feeling that Jackson was pushing an agenda, but she couldn't figure out what. But as Craigo and Jackson had rowed out in the dead of night to save her life, Jackson could manipulate any situation he wanted.

'Why don't you wait outside,' Jackson suggested to Caplan. 'The weather's good. Happy, come and see this, we've got a new buzzer system in since you left.' And Happy was taken away, shooed into the cage by Jackson.

Caplan was left with the woman she had assumed was Happy's wife, who was now standing a little too close to her, waiting for something. 'Is your husband always so interested in door-entry systems?' Caplan asked as they walked out the back door of the station towards the Duster. 'Sorry, I don't think we've been introduced.'

'Marie Harris. But I know who you are, DCI Caplan.' It was an accusation. They walked into the sun together, like colleagues leaving the office, their matched stride making it awkward. 'My husband really misses being on the force, he's desperate to be back.'

'Why isn't he back? He looks fine.'

Marie stepped forward and stood in front of Caplan. She was a small woman, close-cropped black hair, almost shaved at the back, two long feathered earrings swinging against the curve of her cheek. She was either older than she appeared from a distance, or maybe a real worrier, the lines around her eyes deep and creased. 'He failed his fitness, the service is only obliged to find him a job if he was injured in the line of duty, but he wasn't, was he? You went off into the water with DCI Fergusson. That was official. But you didn't sanction the actions of those that followed you. That was what the service lawyer said. The Federation argued the point. It didn't work. He took a bullet.'

'Yes, I know. I was there.'

'I thought you might've cared, might've known what happened to those who got hurt that night.' Marie Harris's eyes narrowed with bitterness.

'Mrs Harris, I, like your husband, was in hospital. I was assured that he was making good progress. I presumed, wrongly, that he had either returned to active duty or was on light duties elsewhere until he made a full recovery. Why would I think otherwise?' She shook her head. 'Police Scotland has a whole HR department to deal with these issues. I suggest you talk it over with your husband and seek a legal answer and I will support him in any way I can, but for now, I have a job to do. Excuse me.'

Marie Harris didn't move, so Caplan sidestepped her and walked over to where the Duster was parked.

'He could have died, you know,' she shouted.

Caplan stopped. Turned round. Then walked back. 'Yes. But he wasn't supposed to be there. Do you understand that? They intended to kill him. I'm very sorry about that but it was his decision to get on that boat. He shouldn't have been there. As far as his job goes, he was not acting as an officer of Police Scotland. That's why the service made the decision they made. I'm sorry.'

THREE

Catch me if you can.
I'm here, in plain sight.

Killagal Blog, 2021

Unlike Betty Medhurst's B&B, Jen O'Neill's establishment was a modern house in a small estate of eight or nine houses. The road was long, well-paved, bordered by short grass and daffodils. One of the nicer developments on an old hill farm and as such it was out of the way, its height affording a good view out to the water and the island of Skone. Harris had lived here for most of his married life. His wife sounded local, although Happy Harris was a soft-spoken islander, dour by nature.

Caplan's conversation with Marie Harris had troubled her, and she was still mulling it over when she accompanied Craigo up the path of the large bungalow. A sign showing 'Vacancies' swung on a well-oiled hinge in front of a beautifully tended garden where colourful gnomes clambered over a rockery, and an ornamental pond undulated with black koi looking for food.

Jen O'Neill was waiting for them, the door opening before they rang the bell. Something about her guest had made her suspect he'd come to some harm. Caplan had learned that was a 'thing' in this part of the world, an instinctive way the locals read those who entered their small community. It was a resource to law enforcement that didn't exist in the anonymity of big cities.

'Do come in. Is it true that you've found a body?' she said, stepping over a plastic truck and some Lego that had been aban-doned in the hallway. Caplan suspected Jen was a single mother, working from home and making the business fit round her life as a mum. Caplan noted the lock on the door into the living room, an attempt to keep the business part of the house separate from her private life, and her children. There was a white-bricked fire-place, photographs of a young boy and two girls, all under seven, on display. The central wedding picture spoke of a separation that was more final than a divorce. The picture of five young men standing next to a fishing boat added some tragedy to the tale.

'We understand that one of your guests didn't come back last night?'

Jen nodded, a little nervous. 'I'm not sure, it might be nothing but with Marie being next door, I mentioned it. They said they'd let you know. Mr Maxwell still hasn't been in touch.' She shrugged, and her untidy ponytail bounced.

'Did you get his first name?'

She shook her head, her forehead wrinkling in concentration. 'I don't think he gave it. He was in and out really. Sometimes we don't speak much until breakfast the following day.'

'What age would you say?'

'Anything from late twenties to late thirties.' Another shrug, another bounce of the ponytail.

'Did he pay by credit card?'

'No, cash.'

'Is that usual?'

'Some do, some don't. He offered me payment in advance.'

'Is that usual?'

'Some offer, if they're sure of their plans. He explained it was a last-minute thing, three nights. The Friday, Saturday, Sunday. He phoned up – most people book online nowadays.'

'Description?'

'Taller than me but not much, dark hair, moustache, a wee bit grey. Thin-faced. He answered his phone Dr Maxwell. It went as I was showing him to his room . . .' She stopped in her tracks. 'One thing was a bit odd.'

'Yes?'

'He had two mobile phones. He went out to the garden, I told him the reception was better out there. He was walking up and down with a phone to his mouth holding it flat like a plate. But when it rang in the room, it was a smaller phone. Silver.'

'If you had to say, Jen, have a guess: if one phone was work and one was his personal phone, which was which?'

'The one he used outside was personal. He laughed into that

one. He was serious and Dr Maxwell on the silver one he answered in here. Do you want to see the room?'

'Yes, please.'

'Of course.' She led them down the brilliant white hall, laminated floor that smelled of pine cleaner, and opened a door with a black '1' painted on it in italic script. 'He came in, took a phone call, did some dictation, then went out. I haven't seen him since.'

'When did he arrive?'

'About five Friday, late afternoon anyway.'

'Dressed?'

'Anorak, jumper, trousers?' She shrugged. 'Nothing out the ordinary. He was very nondescript.' She looked out the huge window. She certainly gave her paying guests the best view. 'He was quiet and polite, very well spoken. I'm sure he was dictating something into his phone that evening, about teatime. You could hear his voice, you know, not like half a conversation, only him talking.'

'You're very observant,' encouraged Caplan.

'Later, I asked if he was hungry, and I made him a cheese sandwich.' She faltered a little, realising that might have been the man's last meal.

'Did you catch anything he said.'

Jen shook her head. 'I tried not to listen, sounded medical to me.'

'Did he bring a car?' asked Craigo.

'Yes, dark blue hatchback. No idea what kind.'

They looked round the room. Every item of furniture was a result of a trip to the Ikea in Glasgow. Craigo pulled on a pair of gloves and started opening drawers, the small wardrobe, the door of the ensuite. All he found was an overnight leather holdall. Craigo had a quick rifle through the bag, nothing much. There were two phone chargers but no phone, a tablet charger but no tablet. They'd need to get his wife to confirm that nothing else was missing. Or if anything was missing at all.

'Did you see him go out?'

'No, I had the kids at soft play. But the car had gone.'

'Do you know what he was doing up here?'

'He said something about a conference. He talked about nice walking weather, nice coffee and where to buy the best whisky.'

'Did he mention his wife's name?'

Jen thought but shook her head. 'He had two kids.'

'He didn't ask for a specific recommendation to a good pub, or a restaurant, as if he was going to meet somebody?'

She shook her head again. Wrinkled her nose, thinking hard. 'He mentioned a few places that he intended visiting, the Standing Stones, the Falls of Lora, the Folly at Oban, you know, the normal tourist things. And a few out-of-the-way places, a mountain . . . Ben Otty? That was all. He might have been a climber, but if he was then his gear was still in his car.'

'Never said where he was going last night or anybody that he was meeting up with?' Caplan asked, looking around. Apart from the bag, the room looked as if nobody had been here.

'Did he commit suicide?' Jen asked.

'Did he seem the type?' asked Caplan, knowing that there was no type, it was a roll of the die, a hard strike on a row of hard strikes. It could be one harsh word, that's all it might take. That thought had struck her many times with Aklen, when she had said more than she'd intended. 'Though all of us could be the type in the wrong circumstances.'

'It wouldn't appear so. I mean, when he talked about his boys, the pride just oozed out of him. I think he'd plenty to live for. So no, I don't think he would have jumped off a bridge.' She sighed and looked around. Looking at the belongings of a man who might never come back to collect them. 'But you're right, you can never tell, can you?'

FOUR

People don't like it if you kick puppies.
They don't like it if you kill babies either.
So don't get caught.

Killagal Blog, 2022

It hadn't taken Toni Mackie half an hour to track down the Dr Edward Maxwell they were looking for. She'd found a picture of him on a Bluebank Clinic website which was enough for an initial identification. Records showed that the date of his

marriage matched the date engraved on the wedding ring, and
he had two boys. Caplan, with Mackie on board and armed with
a file, did the two-hour drive from Cronchie to Glasgow, and
now they were standing in the hallway outside Flat 3, Callworth
Road, Blanefield, a small village to the north of the city,
professional commuter belt.

This was a four-bedroomed apartment, the upper right quarter
of what must have been a grand Victorian dwelling in its day. The
common entrance hallway smelled of expensive wood polish and
tobacco Yankee Candles. There was an old-fashioned mahogany
hat and cloak rack with a mirror. Light filtered through an ornate
stained-glass window, a yellow corn and green-leaved pattern
marked in triangles as it rose to the ceiling dome, defined by black
wrought iron.

During the quiet moments of the drive, Mackie had been busy
informing Caplan of the little snippets of information pinged
through to her phone. Two members of the uniformed branch in
Glasgow had already been at the house and had confirmed that
Dr Ted Maxwell hadn't been at home the previous night. His wife,
Cordelia, thought that he was away at a conference in Leeds for
three nights, the same three nights that he had booked into Jen
O'Neill's B&B. She still thought he was away on business, but
with the presence of the police, she had presumed that he'd come
to some harm.

'What the fuck are you going to say? He's been shagging elsewhere? I mean, how do you tell a wife that?' Mackie whispered,
more loudly than her normal voice. 'And with a monkey?' She
rolled her eyes in mock horror.

'Let me do the talking. Two boys?' confirmed Caplan as they
reached the top of the stairs, the open hall behind them over the
banister. An old clock, high on the wall, ticked ominously.
'Maxwell' was written in thick red Mackintosh lettering on a
well-polished brass plate in the centre of the heavy oak door.

'Sebastian and Troy. Bloody stupid names.'

'Maybe a classics thing going on.' Caplan raised the brass
knocker and let it fall.

'Wouldn't have survived at ma school with a moniker like that,
it's asking for your kids to get a slap.'

'Not familiar with the song "A Boy Named Sue"?' Caplan asked
as the door was answered by a female who looked young enough

to still be at school. She identified herself as PC Margaret Owen, family liaison officer.

The central point of the apartment's hall was a large black fireplace filled with dry wood, showing that in its original formation this had been a room in its own right. Off the hall, closed doors hinted at the family rooms beyond.

'They're through here. Mrs Maxwell doesn't know any more than that we've found a body and it resembles her husband. That's all.'

'Does she know where?'

'She's presuming Leeds.'

'Okay, are the boys there? In the same room?' asked Caplan in a low voice.

'Yes, I'll take them to their bedrooms.'

'No, bring the mum out. Leave the kids where they are. What's she like? Upset? Angry? Suspicious?'

Margaret's answer was interrupted by a cultured female voice from behind one of the doors, asking who was there.

'They're in the living room. Why don't you go into the dining room,' Owen pointed, 'and I'll send Cordelia in. The boys have had some soup for their lunch. They were at their grandparents' for dinner last night, then home. Met the neighbour out with her dog, so Cordelia was here. I've confirmed that.'

The two detectives entered a tastefully decorated room with dove-grey carpets, dove-grey walls and elaborate cornicing painted the colour of oatmeal. Soft duck-egg-blue curtains hung at the window; every surface was highly polished, devoid of any ornaments. The table was gleaming walnut with a display of daffodils and tulips in the middle.

Caplan looked at the table, the carpet, thought of her own two kids and wondered if the boys ever had free run of the place. She doubted it. Then she caught sight of the framed photograph of them, the complete family. The man, moustached in this picture and smiling, looked very like the body they had pulled out of the Falls of Lora. A slim, dark-haired woman stood beside him, the woman who now appeared at the door. Caplan guessed Cordelia was a little older than her husband, or maybe Edward Maxwell was youthful-looking for his age. It added to the bigger picture.

There were tentative 'Hello's' and 'Pleased to meet you's.'

Cordelia's hazel eyes were wary. Caplan knew that her own height, the well-fitting suit, the severe hairstyle, all spoke of officialdom. Sometimes it worked for her. Here, in this nice grey comfortable room, it screamed. She was making Cordelia Maxwell panic.

Cordelia was the image of the woman in the photograph: small, Ugg boots, long black cardigan wrapped round her, as if she was chilled and had given up hope of ever warming up. She nodded a little to both of them, indicating that they should take a seat round the table and get this misunderstanding sorted out as quickly as possible. Shutting the door behind her, she turned the knob with one hand, the palm of the other on the fingerplate to make sure it was closed, giving it a final push, blocking off the hall.

Caplan thought Cordelia paused a little, composing herself with a deep breath before she took a seat, a quick glance at her ring finger.

'I'm not really sure what's going on here.'

Caplan sat down, listening to the dull tones of the clock ticking, some low voices from the room next door, a burst of children's laughter.

'Can you tell us the last time you heard from your husband, Mrs Maxwell?'

She swallowed hard. 'Something has happened to him, hasn't it?'

'I'm sorry to say that we suspect so. When was the last time you spoke to him?'

'He called before teatime last night. On my mobile; I was at his parents'. Ted's mum was doing eggs in a cup for the boys.'

'With soldiers?' asked Caplan gently, sharing common memories of a Scottish childhood.

Cordelia smiled. 'Sometimes that's all they'll eat. He called about six I think.'

'Have you tried contacting him since?'

'Yes. No response. Nothing. Texting. Calling. Emailing him. His mobile's off.'

'Is that unusual?' asked Caplan.

'Yes, for this length of time.' She took a deep breath. 'And Karl, Karl Rolland, called this morning, saying that he was supposed to be meeting Ted at breakfast. At the Marriott. In Leeds. Ted didn't turn up, Karl thought he might still be here, he wanted a word with him. I guess that means he's—' She shrugged '—elsewhere?'

'Cordelia, can you have a look at this picture, please? I hope it's not too upsetting for you.' Caplan pulled out a numbered picture in a plastic sleeve of the anorak the body had been wearing. 'Do you recognise that?'

'Yes, that's his. Or one very like it. Please tell me what has happened. Was it a car accident? That motorway's busy, he usually takes the train, he can always work on a train.'

'To Leeds?'

'The Marriott. The conference. He was looking forward to one paper in particular, "The Moral Compass of the Adolescent Mind". That'll be at three o'clock today.'

'Mrs Maxwell, there's no easy way to say this, but the body of a man who closely resembles your husband was pulled out the River Etive very early this morning.'

Cordelia smiled and her shoulders relaxed. 'Ah well, that explains that it can't be him. He'll be in Leeds.'

Caplan pulled the small evidence bag from the file and placed it slowly on the table, unfurling her fingers so that the gold wedding ring enclosed was obvious. Cordelia froze.

Caplan and Mackie sat quietly, waiting.

'Is there an inscription on it?' Cordelia almost breathed the words.

'Yes.' Caplan read it out from the photograph on her phone.

'Does it look like him?'

'Yes. We'd need a formal identification. We'll also do DNA if we can have a toothbrush or a hairbrush. We need to know if there's anything we're saying that makes you think we're wrong.'

'But he's in Leeds. Where's Etive? Is that not up north somewhere? I doubt it's him. I presume you have a picture?'

Again, Caplan slid a plastic sleeve over to her.

Cordelia's finger rested on the photograph inside but didn't dare to pick it up. Then she closed her eyes, remaining still and silent. The other two women let her have her moment. 'Yes, that's him. I don't understand.'

'Does he have family up near Oban? Or Cronchie? A work colleague? Anybody he might be visiting?'

But Cordelia was now looking beyond them, out the dining-room window, over the rooftops to the hills. She was deep in thought, calm, no hysterics, but she was mulling the question over in her mind. It was starting to rain, large droplets spattering on the windowpane.

'He's in Leeds, at a conference. He'll be at the Marriott,' she repeated dully.

'He didn't book in there. He booked a bed and breakfast in Cronchie. Would it be in his nature to get drunk and . . .?'

'No,' Cordelia smiled at that. 'He'd written a well-reviewed paper on foetal alcohol syndrome and development of the adolescent brain. So, no. He was looking out for a special whisky for his dad's birthday. He drinks a bottle a year, my father-in-law.'

Caplan didn't meet Mackie's eyes. 'I have to ask this, but is there any reason, any reason at all, that might have led your husband to take his own life?'

The colour slowly drained from Cordelia's face; she looked down at her hands on the table, her fingers turning white as if she was holding onto some kind of normality. 'No, no, he wouldn't do that. He would never have done that.' She was shocked, then the colour rose in anger. 'He had the boys, he had me. No, he'd never leave us. What's happened to him? You need to tell me.'

'He was seen on top of a bridge. Then we recovered a body from the water.'

'Then somebody pushed him in. Was there anybody else there? I assure you, he didn't take his own life.'

'That's useful to know. I know this isn't easy. There'll need to be a post-mortem.' Caplan waited to see how that was accepted before she continued. 'And that might tell us more. He could have been taken ill, got disorientated.'

Cordelia glanced round, making sure the door was still closed. 'Why wasn't he in Leeds?'

Caplan took her time, waiting to see if Cordelia was going to say something else, her cop's instinct now sensing that there was more to this. But Cordelia remained quiet, looking out the window again, tears gathering.

Caplan offered her a tissue, considering the next words to come out of her mouth. 'I know this is very difficult, but what kind of man was your husband? Do you have any idea why he might not tell you the truth?'

'Not the kind to have an affair,' Cordelia snapped.

Silence again.

Caplan heard Mackie shift beside her and shot her a glance to say nothing. 'Plenty of reasons without it being an affair.'

Cordelia took a deep breath and spoke very quietly, her eyes narrowing. 'He'd got himself into some kind of trouble.' She shook her head. 'Not trouble, but a situation. When he was worried, he kept himself to himself and that's what he's been doing recently. It was all patient confidentiality, he'd never talk about his work, but he was concerned about . . . something or someone.'

'Very conscientious? I know the type.'

'He was on the ethics committee, he had very high standards. I think he was concerned about a situation he had uncovered.' Cordelia looked out the window again. 'I'm not sure, he was troubled though . . .' A small shake of the head. 'Maybe I'm being naive. Maybe he did have another woman. Though God alone knows how he found the time.'

'Did he ever mention a name?'

Cordelia was now starting to cry fully. Caplan handed her another tissue.

'Do you have anybody that could come to stay with you? A sister?'

Cordelia was crumbling in front of them. The horror, the shit-show that her life was about to become, was slowly dawning on her. 'There was somebody, though, maybe not romantic but more . . . oh, I don't know . . . pestering him. Not a patient, he would have said if it was. He has dealt with some very unstable people, but this was different.'

The room fell still, only interrupted by the ticking of the clock, the noise of one of the boys shouting 'Mum' from next door. They heard Margaret's hushed tones telling him to be quiet for a little longer. Cordelia straightened in her seat and her hands emerged from their sleeves, almost punching the table. 'Sorry, I've just found out that my husband may be dead. How long will it take to get confirmation? I need to have something concrete to tell the boys.' Her chin was up, she was angry now and wasn't totally sure where her anger was best directed.

'We'll arrange to bring you in for a formal identification, if you are willing to do that. Hopefully tomorrow. Margaret will let you know.'

'I'll do it. What do I say to his mum and dad? This will devastate them.'

'We can inform them if you wish. Whatever works for you, Cordelia.'

She nodded, accepting the logic, but still something inside her was struggling. 'But that ring? That's his, that's our wedding day. Did you take it off his finger? It wasn't in a pocket? He couldn't have lost it? Somebody picked it up, somebody who happened to look like him, he has one of those faces – you know? Lots of people look like him.'

'Cordelia, I saw it being taken from his finger.'

'Do you think he met somebody, they pushed him, and he fell? For God's sake.' Cordelia shook her head, as if shaking loose a thought. Her eyes narrowed. 'He had an accident a few years ago, hit by a vehicle at the airport. He has a plate in his leg, left leg. Above the ankle. You'll be able to identify him through that. Because of it, he wore handmade shoes.'

Caplan recalled the slightly odd appearance of the footwear and thanked God that her face was always serene at times like this. 'We'll leave you with Margaret. Here's my card if you need to get in touch, for clarification or a chat. Or if you remember anything, anything at all, give me a call. Okay?'

Caplan nodded at Mackie, the sign to go and get the FLO.

Mackie, too long behind a desk, simply nodded back, leaving Caplan to say, 'DC Mackie, could you ask Margaret to pop in for a moment.'

She left the room.

'Sorry, what was your rank, your name?'

'DCI Caplan, Christine.'

'Are you married, Christine?'

'Yes, I am,' she answered, hoping that Cordelia wasn't going to ask if she was happily married.

'I need to know what kind of man I was married to. I don't think I got him wrong. What happened to him?'

Caplan let a breath out through pursed lips. 'It's early days. As soon as I know something, I'll let you know.'

'He didn't leave a note? An explanation?'

'Not one that we can find.'

'Well, make sure to look hard,' said Cordelia, making her way past. The words hung in the air, a trace of a silent threat.

FIVE

Some days weren't total pish.
Picnics with Mum's apple pie.
And that day got better when the crotch pixie was hit by
a train.

Killagal Blog, 2021

'Have a seat.' ACC Sarah Linden was behind her desk in her spotless office on a Saturday. Something was up.

'I think you wanted to see me. I presume that's what the text meant, quote "Get your arse into my office right now." Do you have a new case for me?'

Linden didn't look up from her screen.

Power play. The three of them had been friends for over twenty years. Sarah Linden, career cop, married three times and now assistant chief constable. Lizzie Fergusson, still a PC juggling work, three kids and an absent husband, struggling with them all. And Christine herself, the lucky one, lovely husband with his own career, two great kids, no money worries. How were the mighty fallen. Sarah went to a warm bed with a bottle of gin for company. Caplan was sleeping in a damp caravan, both her children injured in the line of her duty. While Lizzie tucked her kids up in bed at night and went to sleep, alone, with a good book and a clear conscience.

It was Lizzie's ex-husband, a DCI on the drug unit, who Caplan had nearly got killed last year in the same incident that had injured Happy Harris. Since then, Lizzie's ex was paying more maintenance and attention. Every cloud had a silver lining. She wondered how much of that Sarah knew. The ACC had always been good at keeping secrets, a good friend to have on board. Caplan would have hated to make an enemy of her, but when Emma and Kenny had been rushed to hospital last year, both injured in a hit-and-run, it had been Sarah and Lizzie who had been there for her. They had dropped everything for their friend. Caplan was sure Aklen had tried, but his anxiety had meant he couldn't bring himself to leave the house.

The senior officer hadn't looked up yet.

Caplan could wait. Linden dealt with all kinds of scum in the police service these days, some of them her colleagues; she needed her way of coping. Caplan looked out the window to the new tenements across the road, the slums of the future. She felt bad about putting Mackie onto a train back to Cronchie, but her DC hadn't seemed to mind at all. Caplan considered the Maxwell case over, the niggling aspects could be left to the team. They'd been tasked with digging into Maxwell's life, especially the phone calls made by the one phone registered in Maxwell's name. Craigo was getting a statement from Bev the drunk about the sighting on the bridge. Maxwell's GP said that there was nothing in his medical history, then added that the stress on any health-care professional at the moment was overwhelming. Mackie had sent somebody up to collect the belongings left at Jen's B&B. A good search had found no notes, nothing work-related, nothing at all. A blue Vauxhall Corsa registered to the address at Callworth Road had been found in a pub car park a twenty-minute walk from the bridge. Margaret, the FLO, was asking Cordelia about a set of spare keys.

Caplan looked at Linden's desk; the laptop, two screens, phone, mobile phone and the digital Dictaphone. What had Ted Maxwell been dictating into, and where was it? His phone? Thoughts tumbled round her head. She didn't have any real ideas about Maxwell yet. Suicide after being found out messing with a young and vulnerable patient would fit the bill. Except for the drunk man's vision of a second figure on the bridge. Just a passer-by? A local going home from the pub? It didn't matter, it wouldn't be her case much longer. She was here in the ACC's office, waiting to be given something new.

And she waited. Linden needed her roots touched up to match the streaked blonde of her short, neat hair. Her roots weren't as dark as they used to be, the boss was going grey. They had been friends for a long time and the longer this silence went on, the more Caplan suspected that this was not a reunion of old pals but a professional conversation between two police officers. This power play was something Linden did, it had helped preserve the friendship, establishing very clear lines re what basis they were communicating on. Caplan sneaked a look up at the clock on the wall, she had better things to do than wait here; if she was staying on the case then she had leads to follow up. If she was being moved onto another MIT, then she'd like to get on with it. Caplan made a point of crossing her legs and smoothing down the top of her trousers as noisily as she could, being as obvious as possible.

Sensing her disquiet Sarah Linden closed the file in front of her and opened up another. 'Yeah, hold on a moment.' Linden ran her finger down a long list of names and figures. Then asked, 'What was going on up at Connel Bridge?'

Caplan told her, concisely, stating all the unknowns as they might develop into actions and avenues of enquiry. 'We need to trace the other person on the bridge. The witness said it was a monkey.'

'Such levity.' Linden didn't flinch. 'Is that all?'

'That's all.' Caplan decided to call her bluff. 'Well, if that's it then, cheers, ma'am.' She stood up.

'Oh, one more thing.'

Caplan sat back in her seat. 'You're starting to sound like Columbo.'

'Have you seen Lizzie lately?'

'I was hoping to pop in today as I'm down here. Why?'

'And have you seen her husband, the lovely John?' asked Linden mischievously.

'Not in the way that you mean,' answered Caplan calmly, 'but yes, we have been in touch. He has been doing a bit better on the absent father front, paying more money to her, so Lizzie's having it a bit easier. Not before time.'

Linden leaned back on her chair again. 'So, you and Lizzie?'

'Like I said, I'm popping in to see her for a couple of minutes today. I was thinking of organising a get together for the three of us. What about next time I'm down?'

'That would be very nice, Christine.' Then that hard look came back into her eyes. Caplan knew what was coming. 'The missing evidence on the Brindley case?'

'Yes, ACC Linden, what about it?'

'Just wondering if you had any brainwaves, DCI Caplan. Now

that time has passed, now that you might have some idea where it might have gone.'

'If I had any idea where it was, I would have mentioned it to the inquiry at the time. Indeed, I may have actually gone to find it. I have nothing to add to anything I have already said in relation to that matter.'

'Nice to see that you are sticking to that version of events.'

'The truth you mean? It's a habit I have. ACC Linden, I do believe I solved a fairly complex case and yet it's the minor matter of a little piece of material, with no great evidentiary value, which keeps following me around.'

'Yes. Then in your last case you nearly drowned, as did John Fergusson. The guilty party got away, including those who tried to kill your children, and a police officer got shot. I might measure success differently from you. You got very wet, and I had a shit-load of paperwork to do, so we'll have none of that *I'm good at my job* crap.' Linden had always excelled at the put-down. 'When's Aklen moving to the frozen north? I'll come up and smash a bottle of plonk on the new front door.'

'I'd be happier if you smashed it over his head to be honest.'

'Is the feeling mutual? That's how my marriages usually end.'

'My marriage's fine,' said Caplan, staring out her superior.

Linden relaxed. 'I'm glad to hear it; if you and Aklen split up it would be the end of what little faith I have in marriage.'

'Why did you want to see me? No bullshit. Just tell me.'

'No issue, only keeping tabs on you. I feel a responsibility for you keeping your job.'

'Cheers.'

'And well done in the Lovell case. Try and solve this one as quickly.'

'So, I'm in the good books? I thought you might want to review Dave Harris's medical retirement?'

'No, I don't,' Linden snapped.

'So you brought me here for no reason?'

'I never do anything without a reason, Christine. You have found the car in the Maxwell case, haven't you?'

'Yes, a dark blue Corsa, but we've not opened it yet.'

'What was Maxwell's profession?'

'A doctor.'

'Oh shit.'

'But not a doctor of medicine.'

'Thank God for that.'

'He was a doctor of psychology. Specialised in troubled adolescents.'

'Christ.' Linden closed her eyes for a long time. 'Okay, I'll need to take advice on this. But, and this goes no further than this room, do you know anything about Girl A? Apart from the fact she's an underage child-killer and therefore protected under Tollen.'

'The one whose flat was set on fire?' asked Caplan.

'That's her. We can still only refer to her as Girl A, nothing identifiable. She climbed out the window with her dog to escape the flames then disappeared from the hospital in Dumfries. She was getting treatment for severe burns on her right hand.'

'I thought it said on the news she was safe and recovering?'

Linden shook her head. 'That's so the country doesn't panic. I can't emphasise how secret this is. She has a new identity, but somebody has found out who she actually is. She's now on the run from vigilantes. She needs to be found for her own safety.'

'Yes, I get that.'

'If I tell you her new identity, you'll keep it to yourself. If you come across her, you will tell me and only me. I'm only giving you this information because it might help us.'

'I didn't think it was from the goodness of your heart.'

'No, I'm doing it because she's an evil psychopathic bitch. You spent last night fishing a body out of the Falls of Lora? Right under the Connel Bridge?'

'This morning actually,' Caplan corrected.

'Well, the media, therefore the public, have all kinds of theories about Girl A. They lacked solid information because the crime she was guilty of was subject to restriction, but it happened not a million miles from Cronchie. And the new name she chose to live under was Lora Connel.'

SIX

Then the crotch pixie arrived, Rachel mark 1. The rest of the family liked her. Me? Not so much. As soon as I get rid of that one, another wee bugger comes along. Rachel mark 2 and I'm like WTF!

Killagal Blog, 2022

B ack in the Duster, Caplan tried to get her ducks in a row, second guessing what Linden and Linden's bosses were thinking. Girl A's chosen name and its association with the location of Dr Ted Maxwell's body had clearly spooked them. She phoned Mackie, who from the sound of it was eating crisps, answering the phone with a 'Hang on a mo, ma'am' followed by a slurp, a burp and then, 'How did you get on with the big boss, you still got a job?'

'I think I'll be on this for a while, Linden's not happy.'

'Well, can you be at Pimento's by half-three? Ted's colleague, Karl Rolland, the one he didn't meet for brekkie, wants to chat,' said Mackie.

'Interesting. He moved pretty fast.'

'No, not really. Ted had called him and told him that he couldn't make the conference, but he didn't want Cordelia to know. That's why he wants to talk to you. One story for him, one story for the missus. Men are such arseholes.'

Caplan rang off then looked at her watch. She'd time to meet Rolland, then Lizzie Fergusson, and would still be able to nip round Aldi's. Being a desk-bound uniform, and a good gossip, Lizzie would get all the intel buzzing around the service. She'd know about Girl A and what had been rattling Sarah Linden's cage while Caplan had been tying up the Lovell case.

Aklen would be expecting her home to make something for tea, so she rang him to ask what he wanted to eat.

He replied that it would be nice to have his wife back. No guilt-tripping there. She nearly replied that Ted's family would be glad to have a phone call, but she didn't want to put any idea of suicide in Aklen's head.

She rang off.

Karl Rolland was waiting at Pimento's in Glasgow city centre, a trendy café and deli situated in the middle of a mall. He was eating an expensive mozzarella pizza and drinking espresso so strong Caplan got palpitations just smelling it. He waved his arm, offering her a seat. If Ted Maxwell had been adhering to the librarian dress code, then Karl Rolland had more of an interior designer vibe: black suit and polo neck and a few pieces of hand-made Celtic jewellery on his wrists and fingers. Rolland and Maxwell were odd bedfellows.

She took a seat but refused his offer of a drink.

'So, how well did you know Dr Maxwell?'

'I was best man at Ted's wedding actually, so close friend as well as a colleague. That's why I'm a little conflicted.' He took a sip of his coffee, looking like he wasn't going to say any more.

'We think that he has taken his own life so there will be an inquiry. Now is not the time to hold back.'

'It might be nothing, but Cordelia was on the phone telling me the news. I immediately drove up, went round to the flat, you know. Felt helpless, wanted to do anything that can be done to make the situation easier.'

'Of course you do. She needs all the help she can get right now.' Caplan wished she had ordered a coffee and could take her time to drink it, let the silence do the work for her. The café was busy. It was noisy. There was room for the senses to be distracted rather than build the pressure that could force somebody to fill the void in conversation. 'Why did you wish to speak to me? Is it something that you didn't want Cordelia to know?'

'Firstly, he cancelled Leeds on Thursday, saying he had something to research, something very important and last minute, he didn't say what. He said nothing about Cronchie. He's said nothing to Cordelia.' He dabbed at the corner of his mouth with a napkin. His eyes were soft, the colour of treacle, and he did look upset. He also looked worried. 'There was an incident at a mental-health conference at the Hilton in Edinburgh a few weeks ago. It was a whole day thing, a professional development event. And, well, Ted left after the first session, which was not like him at all. I went out for a walk at the lunch break, I walked past a restaurant and there was Ted talking to a woman.'

Caplan felt a rush of relief, having suspected all along that it would come down to something as mundane as this. As Mackie had said, all men were fundamentally arseholes. 'Talking to a woman or eating with her?'

Rolland held up his hand, reading her thoughts. 'I don't think it's what you are suspecting. He was eating, she was talking.'

'Really?'

'We are psychologists. I read body language pretty well. It wasn't a happy exchange. Ted didn't come back for the afternoon session. But after the conference I saw the same woman corner him in the car park.'

'Did you get a sense of the relationship between them?'

'Like I said, I'm a psychologist, I should be able to answer that but . . .'

'But you think maybe they were involved with each other? Is that why Cordelia doesn't know?'

'I doubt they were involved in the way you mean. I want to be clear who this woman is before we upset Cordelia. In the car park, she looked angry. And it crossed my mind that she might be a student, or a young colleague of Ted's who was harassing him. Maybe a disagreement about a research paper. After last night, I mentioned this woman to Cordelia, very vaguely, and she'd no idea who the woman might be. When I heard about Ted my first concern was that she was an ex-patient. Young women, the type that Ted would deal with professionally, can get fixated on their therapist. Often, that's the only person in their life who ever listened to them but then . . .'

Caplan thought about it, wishing again that she had ordered a coffee, anything to play with, anything to fill the gap in the conversation. She needed to know who this woman was. A suspect? A patient? An unwelcome thought crossed her mind. Was this Girl A? 'Who was she?' Caplan prompted. 'You must have some idea?'

Rolland put his arms out in surrender. 'I don't.'

'Young? Attractive?'

He pulled a face. 'Yes, I'm sure she'd appeal to a certain type of man, but not to Ted. She was young, very short dark hair, slim, well-dressed. That was the impression I got.' He paused. 'She was angry.'

'Did you make out what she was cross about?'

'Not really, but I got the impression she'd tracked him down after he had given her the slip.'

'That way round?'

'Oh yes. Again, as I was leaving, I walked past them to get to my car, and she was saying "You're going to have to speak to me about it one day." Or words to that effect.'

'Did Ted see you?'

'Yes, he waved at me, I said hello and kept walking to my car.'

'His demeanour?'

Rolland shrugged. 'He wasn't spooked by seeing me, not like I'd caught him out in something that he'd be ashamed of. He was relieved to see me if anything.'

Caplan nodded again. 'But you didn't speak to him? Didn't ask what was wrong?'

'No, their conversation was private. And there were about forty of us coming out the hotel, I was chatting to somebody else. Ted raised his hand up to his ear indicating that he was going to call me. He did, the next night. I asked about her then and he moaned, saying that she was very persistent and "a bloody pest".'

'And you took that to mean?'

'So maybe she was a recent graduate? Doing their clinical year, a tenacious student who thought she warranted a better grade than he had given her.'

'Could you give us a better description?'

He didn't need to think. 'Skirt, blouse, very made-up face, dark brown eyes, big eyebrows, big lips, gold chains round her neck. Dressed for work, I think.'

'But he didn't tell you her name?'

'He didn't mention it.' He took a sheet of A4 out his pocket. 'So I got this list of delegates for that one-day conference and compared it to the society website. There were only about sixty people there, allied health-care professionals. Ten of them I know well, I've put an asterisk next to them, she's not any of them. But the rest? Except the men of course . . .'

'Did he mention the Falls of Lora or the Connel Bridge?'

Rolland shook his head. 'I know that's where he was found.'

Caplan thought. 'If you are totally sure that Dr Maxwell wasn't having an affair, then why do you think Cordelia didn't know about this annoying woman?'

'Because she was a patient? But dressed more like a colleague. The interaction was professional, I think. You see, Ted was very bright, he'd be a good mentor to study under. He only took the best. I don't think that young lady impressed him, whoever she was.'

'Thank you, Dr Rolland.' Caplan looked down the list.

'Mr Rolland, I've not got the PhD. That was Ted, he was the clever one.'

Caplan pulled the Duster round the corner into the car park outside the small semi where her friend lived now, the same house where she had lived with her husband until Lizzie and Christine met each other face to face after a few years and realised that one was having an affair with the other's husband. They had stayed friends after that, and since then had referred to Mr John Fergusson as 'The Bastard'.

She took a moment to check her emails, then looked at the headlines for any update on Girl A, getting nothing but the fire in Dumfries and a lot of comments from 'outraged citizens'. She spent another ten minutes checking her text messages. Emma was coming over to the mainland on Sunday. Her daughter's timing was, as ever, totally hopeless.

Caplan was texting back when she noticed Lizzie's front door opening. Her friend appeared, head out first, the body following, looking for somebody, her blonde curly hair catching in the wind, dressed in a sweatshirt and jeans. She then retreated inside the hall. Another woman appeared, saying goodbye. Lizzie placed a hand on her shoulder as she passed, a touch that lingered longer than it needed to.

Then there was an incline of heads, towards each other.

Very close friends. Intimate even.

Caplan studied the woman, although she didn't need to; she had the long limbs and sharp features that were typical of her family.

It was Grace Brindley.

Caplan felt her stomach tighten.

What the hell was Lizzie up to after all that had been said? Caplan slipped down on her seat, seeing Lizzie close the door. Brindley stuck her hands deep into the pockets of her duffle jacket and made her way down the road, crossing to the other side, and disappeared behind the hedge of another garden, walking normally and not like a fugitive.

Which, at the moment, she was not.

And that was due to DCI Christine Caplan. And then this. This put a different perspective on it all.

If Sarah Linden ever found out . . . there'd be no coming back for Lizzie. There couldn't be. Lizzie was dancing with the devil here; she was mum to those boys, a single parent working and trying hard to make ends meet. Why should she want to embark on a liaison with that woman? But then, why not? Lizzie was human. She'd developed an attraction for a witness in a case. Sometimes you couldn't help who you fell in love with.

But still, a member of the Brindley family? One of the biggest crime families? Grace herself might be a halfway decent human being; many criminals were. But her family were a danger to Lizzie's job, Lizzie herself and maybe even to her children.

Maybe her friend's type was mad, bad and dangerous to know.

If the Bastard ever found out, everybody would get their fingers burned, especially Caplan herself. She couldn't rely on Linden to keep that secret. Not after the investigation in which Caplan had lied by omission.

When she finally drove into Abington Drive, Caplan felt that she was visiting rather than going home. The house looked even more abandoned than the one next door, and that had been empty for a week. Their old neighbours had left, the new buyers hadn't taken possession yet. They had purchased a well-maintained modern house and were no doubt going to make something more homely out of it. Caplan herself was starting that process for Challie Cottage. Both estate agents who had visited to do an initial valuation for 27 Abington Drive, after a slow and deliberate look at the overgrown trees, the patchy lawn, the flaking window frames with their grimy panes, had warned them not to put it on the market until the one next door had sold.

Yeah well, the woman next door didn't work and was handy

with a paint brush. Caplan, with a full-time job and a husband to look after, felt the criticism was directed at her.

Walking up to the top step, she was surprised to hear a familiar rustle in the large rhododendrons at the side of the door. Pas de Chat popped his head out, then rushed forward, winding round her leg, mewling loudly before head-butting her.

She opened the front door with her key, and the cat rushed straight into the kitchen. Caplan was used to Aklen being too sick or tired to be up, so she was pleasantly surprised to see him placing a knife and a fork down on the dining table. He looked up and smiled at her, and for a moment her heart soared. He was there again, the young lecturer at the university who had swept her off her feet, with his jet-black hair and Alain Delon eyes.

He looked at the cat, who was now arching his back against the cupboard where the Dreamies were stored.

'I never know when you'll appear so I thought I'd set the table. How are you? You look tired.'

'Yes, didn't get much sleep last night.' She looked at the table. 'Oh, that's very nice.' It was more than he'd managed for a while.

'It's been a difficult day.' It appeared that Aklen had made a step forward, and while they couldn't afford it, she felt the need to mark the occasion. 'I'll tell you what, instead of me cooking something why don't we get a coffee and some food at a drive-through, get some fresh air. I was going to pick some groceries up but got side-tracked.'

'We could phone something in, why not share a curry?'

Her hands were still on her jacket on the back of the chair. She knew that she was pushing him to get outside, further than he might want to go, but somebody had to. 'Do you not fancy going out? Not out the car, but outside?'

'Could you not cook us something nice?' He bent down to stroke the cat. Pas head-butted the cupboard door with greater vigour. 'I haven't seen him around for a while.'

'Do you think he's run away? Surely the McGuires took him when they moved out?' asked Caplan, looking at the top shelf of a very empty fridge. Everything there was 'use within four weeks of being opened' and had been there since Christmas at least.

'I presumed he'd gone, I've not seen him. I know cats like to come home but good God, they moved to Chester.' Aklen gave Pas some Dreamies. 'He does look very thin.'

'He normally appears when the front door opens. Have you been out recently?'

'Not for a while. The new people are moving in tomorrow.'

'Sooner than we thought.'

The way the cat scoffed the Dreamies showed how hungry he was.

'I hope they're nice, the new folk,' said Aklen.

Caplan thought, but didn't voice, that it didn't matter as they wouldn't be living here much longer.

Aklen stood up as if confused. The cat and the new neighbours were two more things he couldn't really cope with. 'Do you think Pas is okay?' He stroked the cat along his spine, the coat dull and harsh. 'They've abandoned him, haven't they?'

'Poor thing, there's a few pouches of cat food at the back of that cupboard if you think he needs meat.'

The pouch wasn't opened fully before Pas was stretching up the height of the worktop, getting his nose as close to the saucer as he could. He'd eaten most of the contents before it reached the floor.

'Well, nobody's been feeding him. Arseholes. I'll leave it an hour then give him some more. Don't want to overload his wee stomach.' Aklen waited until the cat had licked the saucer clean then sat down at the kitchen table, whispering to Pas about how terrible it was to be abandoned. It might have been Caplan's paranoia, but she was sure he was saying it out loud so she'd know he wasn't talking only about the cat. The lament went on.

She ignored it. It was all part of Aklen's background noise.

Caplan rechecked the fridge, the cupboards and the freezer, taking care to close each door, one after the other, really quietly.

There was no food.

She wished she'd bought the mozzarella pizza while she had the chance.

SEVEN

Was my life's ambition to become a serial killer?
That depends on the spud buckets who investigate.
I'm on like number four, maybe five.
I got nabbed for one,
but still . . .

Killagal Blog, 2022

Caplan slept the sleep of the dead. Aklen had not come to bed. He had been up most of the night watching reruns of an old programme about refurbing properties, which was ironic as there were two such properties in the family and he showed absolutely no interest in doing up either.

They had been talking last night, and it had been going well until she had pushed too hard about him getting the home report instigated. Or a loan.

And he had retreated inside his shell.

Instead of getting angry, Caplan had gone upstairs and emotionally said goodbye to a house that had not been the happiest for them. Emma's room in the loft space, remnants of a studious, hardworking childhood. Kenny's room was more of an IT showroom with elements of jumble sale. The photographs of family holidays, diving in the waves off Arran, posing on a viewing platform over the Canadian Rockies. Kenny had broken his leg later that day. No family snaps within the last eight years. The kids had marched on, without their dad.

Emma's high-school prom picture, her graduation photographs, were mum and daughter. Kenny at the football, passing his driving test, it was Kenny on his own. Caplan closed the door on her past and went into their bedroom. The bed was neat. It had been this way since the last time she was here.

Aklen was sleeping on the sofa, too tired for the stairs.

Caplan fell asleep immediately, dreaming of the mysterious Ted Maxwell and Lizzie, apparently the best of friends, who laughed at Caplan behind her back, until they all decided to go for a swim across the loch at the Connel Bridge, where the water became thick with bodies, and a dark-haired woman with a gold chain round her neck watched from the bank and judged them.

When she woke, she didn't need Karl Rolland to tell her what all that was about.

Sunday morning for her was like any other. As was her habit, she got up early, showered, did her stretching and put on a quick load of washing before opening her laptop, keeping an eye on what had been going on in the Ted Maxwell case. She was pleased to see that very little was being reported in the media. 'Enquiries are ongoing with regard to a fatality in the vicinity of the Connel Bridge in the early hours of Saturday morning.' There was no more news on the whereabouts of Girl A, just a small item that she'd suffered severe burns in the fire and her wounds had needed specialist medical attention; nothing to say that she'd walked out the hospital. Nothing polarised people like a child-killer, a child-killer who was a child herself. Maybe the vigilantes had caught up with her and she was lying dead in a sack somewhere.

The weather forecast was chilly but sunny. Caplan decided she needed some fresh air and had a quick cup of herbal tea on the garden seat outside, her anorak pulled tightly round her, warding off that early morning chill that could hang around all day.

She checked her work emails. The FLO looking after Cordelia had said that the widow was requesting to be kept informed of all developments and that her father-in-law was accompanying her to formally identify the body. The next email made sense of that. Ryce, the pathologist, had worked the late shift and the post-mortem had been completed. McPhee emailed to say that Maxwell had not been at any conference within travelling distance of the bridge, and his dark blue Corsa was being brought to the station car park as in itself it was not a crime scene. The only thing visible through the car window was a bottle of whisky, wrapped in loose tissue paper. The guy who served him in the shop Jen O'Neill had recommended recalled serving him, seven-thirty Friday night. Enquiries at clinics where he worked were reporting back with stories of a pleasant, quiet colleague, a dedicated professional with a stellar career.

Cordelia had asked about his clothes at the bed and breakfast, but they had found nothing that gave any sense as to why he was there. His tablet was still missing, the traced phone had nothing that was work-related. The man kept his professional and private life very separate, but there should still be some footprint. The absence of such gave weight to the theory that this was work-related. Why was Maxwell flying below the radar? Why had he been on the bridge at midnight? It wasn't the weather to go out for a midnight stroll.

Another good friend of Dr Ted Maxwell, a Peter Biggs, had been in touch with Cordelia and she'd asked him to contact the police. He was also a psychologist and he too was at the conference in Leeds. He said that Maxwell had hinted that he wouldn't be there, he had something else to do. McPhee emailed to say that Biggs was happy to have a video interview after the post-mortem. Was this another story of 'The Pest'? Biggs might have better insight than Karl Rolland had been able to offer, like a name.

Caplan's work mobile rang, Cordelia herself, her speech thick with lack of sleep.

'I've been awake all night, thinking.' Cordelia's voice was clipped. She was not quite controlling her anger. 'I think it might've been a patient.'

'Do you think he was involved with somebody in his care?'

'In some way. But not romantically. Not him.'

'He was a psychologist, it's common for their patients to get fixated on them.'

'He knew that, he was careful. He had to be. He consulted on difficult cases: the Priory, the Nuffield, St Margaret's in Aberdeen, the Bluebank. His opinion was important. So, his patients would be at the more challenging end of the spectrum.'

Like Girl A?

Caplan asked her to note all the places her husband had worked in the last two years. McPhee was on it anyway. She could hear Cordelia breathing, imagine her retracting her hands into her sleeves, and swiping her forearms across the polished walnut of the table. 'He wasn't the type to have an affair. But somebody had got to him, in some way. He wasn't himself.'

Caplan said very quietly, 'Cordelia, was he a specialist in any field?'

'Adolescents, like I said. Criminal behaviours.'

'If he was involved with a patient, then that patient would be
. . . young?'

Cordelia's voice hardened. 'Yes, young and vulnerable. Do you
think he took advantage of one of them? And that made him throw
himself from a bridge?'

'Cordelia, I'm not thinking that at all. You've just lost your
husband, your mind will be going at a hundred miles an hour,
especially in the small hours of the morning. You'll be torturing
yourself with all sorts. In these cases, we need to pull people's
lives apart. It's not pleasant. If Ted was involved in something,
we'll find it. But so far, all evidence points to a dedicated professional, highly regarded and respected. I'm just looking for answers.'
She heard a sigh. 'I'll be seeing you later for the formal identification. Do you still feel up to it?'

'Yes, of course. Ted's dad is coming with me. The children are
over there at the moment. Thank you, DCI Caplan.'

Caplan swiped the phone off. It was time to leave. There was
still no noise in the house; Aklen was fast asleep. She gathered
her clothes drying on the radiator and got ready for the drive north.
She placed her dishes in the sink, looked at the mirror, making
sure her hair was neatly in its chignon. Her make-up hid the tiredness in her eyes, nothing more than that. She seemed to have aged
about ten years since going to work at Cronchie. She was getting
old, being put out to grass like an aged horse.

EIGHT

Drowning bastards is hard fucking work.
Cleaner than using a ScotRail Express as a blunt instrument.
Whit a fucking mess that was!

Killagal Blog, 2021

Cordelia Maxwell entered the hall of the post-mortem suite
on the arm of an older man whose facial features were
simply those of Edward Maxwell advanced by thirty years.
Margaret, the family liaison officer, had driven the Maxwells

down to the mortuary on the south side of the hospital. Caplan nodded her acknowledgement of them, noting that Cordelia was clutching a photograph of her husband tightly in her right hand, as if by holding on to that, she was holding on to him.

Caplan let the mortuary assistant explain what was going to happen, as Margaret stood by and was reassuringly sympathetic. Cordelia trembled a little, but Mr Maxwell senior remained strong and steadfast, his jaw fixed and tense. There was nodding, all in agreement that they were ready – well, as ready as they could ever be. It was not a situation that anybody could prepare themselves for.

Is this the body of your son?

Caplan looked away, recalling standing at Emma's bedside, her daughter lying in a hospital shroud, in a sleep so deep she was more dead than alive. Emma had hovered there for a few long days and nights, stretching into a week after the successful surgery. But Caplan had hope, there was light in the darkness of the tunnel. Now, ten months of physiotherapy later, Emma was walking and talking, a limp on the right leg, a little difficulty with her balance, but she had her future back. She was going to return to university; she had simply taken a little detour.

Edward Maxwell had hit a dead end.

The two visitors walked into the viewing room, warm with soft carpet, softer music, pastel blue fabric flowers. Caplan followed them in, standing well to the back and to the side to monitor the reaction of the wife when the electronic curtain opened. It might have been her on the bridge, throwing him to his death, maybe after finding out that he had not been in Leeds after all, and that he was involved with another woman, or even worse, a patient.

An underage patient.

Cordelia's alibi was cast iron. She'd been at her in-laws', then home with the boys. It was the first one Craigo had checked.

Was it a suicide? Caplan thought those men who took their own lives had a different mindset to what she knew of Maxwell. He had a supportive, loving family. Here was Cordelia, holding on to the father of the man she had loved. Caplan couldn't see it.

Cordelia looked genuinely grief-stricken, an impression that was backed up when she saw the body lying in the white shroud, facing the ceiling, head on a soft pillow. The dark eyebrows and brown moustache emphasised the pallor of his skin under the subdued light. It was the father who reacted first, withdrawing his face as if he had been slapped, the palm of his hand raised to his lips as if he was about to utter words that should never be voiced. Cordelia's reaction was more measured. Caplan watched carefully as the widow leaned forward, peering through the glass at the inert figure of her husband, then looked down at the photograph, then back at the figure. Her tired, grieving eyes searching for any sign that it was not him, any little tell-tale clue that this man was a stranger with a passing resemblance to the father of her children. She peered for a long time then she stood back, biting her lip, the tears falling. She turned around and was swallowed by the arms of her father-in-law.

Life would never be the same.

Margaret asked a few questions of legal protocol, then, patting the widow on the shoulder, asked them if they wanted a cup of tea.

Like all professionals involved in delicate situations, there was a well-known, silent tic-tac that Caplan used to instruct Margaret to take the Maxwells to the relatives' room and keep them there until she joined them.

Dr Ryce looked harassed; her desk was a mess, as if she'd been frantically searching for something that remained elusive. The pathologist had a congealing coffee sitting on a pile of files, its collapsing froth making it look like a melting ice-cream cone.

'You here about Edward Maxwell?' asked Ryce, popping a digestive biscuit in her mouth whole, and chomping away. 'Sorry, I've had bugger all to eat today. And we have a really busy day ahead of us . . . short-staffed and underfunded yet we are expected to do our job as diligently as ever.'

'And you are telling me that? Why? Do you think the police service are immune to such things?'

'I think you've better biscuits.'

'You could be right there.' Thinking that with Mackie about they never lasted long. 'How was the PM on Edward Maxwell? The wife and the father have given us a positive identification.'

'The plate in the ankle matches the plate that was surgically implanted in 2009. The serial number traces back to the factory in Italy and they did supply this hospital. He wore an orthotic lift in both shoes, the left one higher because that injury had left him with a slightly short lower extremity on that side, but it was nothing remarkable. He ate a cheese sandwich, white bread, three or four hours before he died. And the DNA confirms that he is exactly who you think he is.'

'Cause of death?'

'The initial findings on site were that he probably died of drowning, and there was water in his lungs. The water has both marine and freshwater quality which makes sense as he was pulled out of the Falls of Lora.'

'He was breathing when he hit the water?' asked Caplan for confirmation.

'He was, but not for long.' Ryce dug around in the papers on her desk, finding a file and flicking over a few pages, another biscuit hanging from her teeth as she found what she was looking for. 'Here.' She handed a photograph over to Caplan: a naked torso. It looked perfectly normal apart from the small diagonal line a few inches under the left nipple. Ryce handed over a magnifying slide without being asked. A small, angled rule had been photographed next to the wound for scale. The sides of the cut were slightly flared and uneven; even in the monochrome print, the curves at the edges were white and obscene, dead already.

'He was stabbed before he went in the water?' asked Caplan.

'He was indeed.'

'Would that have been fatal if left unattended?'

'I think it would have been fatal even if he had received medical attention straight away. It pierced his heart. Somebody wanted him dead. In every other way he was a perfectly healthy young man.'

'Was this a mugging that went wrong?'

Ryce shrugged. 'There's no signs of a struggle of any kind. My guess would be he was stabbed, then relieved of his belongings, but if you have another scenario, I'll listen. How our perp went through his pockets, I don't know. Stab, search, heft the body over the railing. With no signs of a struggle? If he fell to the ground, it'd be a bloody hard job to lift him up and punt him over the railing. He'd have been a dead weight. But there are two things you will like.'

'Good.'

'There's an abrasive line below Maxwell's ribcage. And I think

– well, I'm making an educated guess – that the killer was left-handed, from the angle of the wound. The route of the blade tracks from the midline out laterally. When facing each other, that tends to suggest a left-handed assailant, but all other options will still be on the table. You think the incident took place on the actual bridge?'

'Yes. So, a left-handed assailant or they had an injured right hand?'

'That might do it,' nodded Ryce. 'Does that help?'

'It could do. There was another party on the bridge.'

Ryce pulled her glasses down to the end of her nose then peered over them. 'Well, I was going to say that you need to look at it carefully, you might need to re-enact it and see how you replicate that injury taking into account the build and height of both participants. He could have been stabbed, propped against the rail as his pockets were emptied, then all they needed to do was pick up his legs, momentum of his body weight would do the rest.'

Caplan stared into space, biting her lip, nodding absentmindedly. 'So, a leftie. Could be a woman?'

Ryce nodded.

'Yeah, I'll do a re-enactment, once we find a suspect. The left-handed thing's interesting when there's a proposed perpetrator with a very sore right hand.'

Ryce looked at her colleague, raising an interrogative eyebrow.

'Can't say any more.'

'You do look more than a little conflicted, but knife-wound evidence is solid if interpreted correctly.'

Caplan went quiet, then asked, 'How well do you know ACC Sarah Linden?'

'Well enough. I've got rat-arsed with her a few times. Thought you and her were besties?'

'It varies. I was called into her office for a non-conversation. Something above my paygrade.'

'Were you now. Years ago, we did a post-mortem on a thirteen-year-old, Poppy Anstruther, who had been drowned by her friend. The case of the midnight feast and the unidentified shoe-mark. Seemingly the friend is out now, having been in hospital for injuries to her right hand.'

'You are sharp, Dr Ryce.'

'I'm sure you have those cases that you don't forget. Girl A is a tragedy all round.' Ryce thought for a minute and nodded. 'But before you finish the paperwork, get the mechanics of the body going over the rail correct. How old is Girl A now?'

'Eighteen.'

'An adult then. She could be tall, strong.' Ryce nodded again. 'Go up there and try it out. It'll tell you something about the strength of whoever did it. I've the exact measurements for you, plus photographs. Maxwell's short leg was on the left; even with the best orthotics there'd still be a muscle imbalance so if my theory is correct . . . you should be able to work out easily where his centre of balance was when he was stabbed, and then you might get an idea of what kind of person could *not* have done it.'

'What do I do, take a few of my colleagues up there and chuck them off the bridge?'

'I can give you some of mine if you want.'

'Could you not rather give me an idea of what kind of person *did* do it?'

'I think we both have an idea about that.' Ryce looked her in the face, smiled and said very slowly, 'Somebody who wanted him dead?'

'God, eight years at med school and that's all you can come up with?' Caplan glanced at her phone. 'Are you going out for a bite to eat now?'

'Why, are you offering to treat me?'

'No, I want to use your office and your wifi for a Zoom interview.'

Ryce picked up her handbag and her jacket, making for the door. 'No respect for the dead, some people.'

McPhee, with the efficiency of youth, had already set up the meeting. All Caplan had to do was dial in. Peter Biggs looked more like an accountant than a psychologist, dressed in a neat suit, open-collared. He was still at the conference and had a navy-blue lanyard round his neck. The framed picture and the wallpaper behind him were courtesy of his hotel.

They made their introductions. Caplan let McPhee, who managed to look fresh-faced on very little sleep, do the questioning. He needed the experience. Biggs was free and easy with his answers once he was assured that none of this would get back to Cordelia until they had found out exactly what was going on. It was the same story as Rolland.

Then Biggs confirmed that Maxwell had said he wasn't able to go to the conference as he had to do some research for a project, but that he wanted it known he was going to Leeds if anybody asked.

Caplan saw the hesitation in Biggs. What he said wasn't quite the full story. She indicated to McPhee to be quiet, leaving silence on all three screens, then asked, 'Did he tell you he wasn't going to be there, but that he was telling his wife he was?'

'Not exactly.' Biggs was starting to squirm now.

'Can you enlighten us as to "exactly"?' asked Caplan, cutting across whatever McPhee was going to say.

'I'm not sure I can,' said Biggs.

'Your friend has been murdered, the PM put that beyond all doubt. Tell us why Dr Maxwell wanted it known he'd be in Leeds when he knew he wasn't going to be.'

Biggs took a deep breath. 'I'm honestly not sure. But this is what I think. He was working on something that was very confidential. I knew about it, Cordelia knew about it, but all we knew was that it was confidential and asked no questions.'

'Something to do with his work, and I'm guessing something to do with a patient?'

Biggs made a left to right nodding gesture with his head. 'Something to do with his work, yes, but I'm not sure if it was with a patient of his. But something had gone wrong, I think he had pissed off somebody, professionally I mean, and he was a bit nervy about continuing. I'm thinking whistleblower. He was that type of guy, not the type to capitalise on someone else's illness or misfortune . . . And I think he was in Connel in relation to that. Anybody who knows him professionally would think that he'd be here. So he was free to go elsewhere and chase down whoever it was he really needed to talk to.'

Caplan nodded, understanding. 'And you think that'd be around Oban, but he didn't actually say?'

'No. Cordelia knew bits of it. Maybe the person he was whistle-blowing on was dangerous. That was the way I took it. Maybe they got to him instead.'

Caplan nodded, thinking of the way her own family had been targeted, the crime-scene pictures of their blood on the grass. But she was a police officer, involved in something with very high stakes. Those perpetrators had been professionals. She looked at Biggs in his good suit. 'Sorry, have we stumbled into a James Bond film?'

'My friend is dead. I'm telling you what I know. What I think. Reputations are everything. If he had found something out . . . well, I don't think anybody would go to these lengths to protect their reputation, but in light of what's happened?'

Caplan leaned into the screen, seeing her own face distort in the upper corner, not really wanting to believe what she was hearing. Biggs might be very close to the truth but had the wrong enemy. 'What had he discovered? Any ideas?'

'I'm not sure.' Biggs thought, then said, 'Some kind of abuse in an establishment? Mistreatment of patients? Inappropriate treatment? Inappropriate billing of insurance? Sometimes these small units can become playthings of nepotists. And . . .'

'And would he keep that a secret from Cordelia?'

'Yes, I think so.'

'But what was it that you wanted to tell us, but not her?'

Biggs took a deep breath. 'Something Karl said, about that woman? She was here on Friday early afternoon, at the tea break. Karl said she seemed more than a bit annoyed that he wasn't here.'

'Name?'

He shook his head. 'Sorry, didn't get it.'

'But she was a delegate, right?' Caplan could see McPhee already typing onto another screen.

'Well—' He gave that slight wobble of his head again '—after I spoke to Karl, I had a walk-about trying to find her. I spoke to a few people she had spoken to. Nobody knew who she was. I've looked through the delegate list, asked about. She was here on that Friday afternoon but then left. She was looking for Ted. And nobody knows her name.'

'Was she young and attractive?'

Another slow beat. 'Young, well-dressed, suit. I thought she worked for the hotel at first.'

'Scottish?'

'English, no strong accent one way or the other.'

'Uninjured? Nothing bandaged? Could walk and talk, use her hands and her feet okay?'

Biggs nodded. 'Of course. And had heels on.'

Caplan closed her eyes and hoped the 'For fuck's sake' that left her lips wasn't picked up by the microphone.

But the psychologist was talking: 'And Ted was writing a book, not a textbook but a book about a patient, a difficult patient followed through from . . . well, their life story really. You've seen the film *We Need to Talk About Kevin*?'

'Yes, I have.'

'He said it was that type of scenario. A disturbed soul not getting the support they needed, with tragic consequences. It's something that we were both interested in. In fact Ted and I had been writing a book together on the same theme. I'd found the ideal subject. For the last two years we've been meeting, patient's happy, parents are happy. It's a story that needs to be told, underfunding and failure leading to, well, tragedy. Even the victim's parents were willing to talk to us about the terrible impact it all had on them. Then Ted shelved the plan. We were thirty-five thousand words in, and he said he had another project and it was time-critical.'

Caplan felt something close to panic. 'Did he say what or who it was, this project?'

'Nothing, not a word. He went stone cold on me. If I hadn't known him as well as I did, I'd think that he was cutting me out because of the money. But if this lassie was something to do with it . . . she knew about me . . .' He shook his head. 'I don't know where that gets us.'

Caplan said nothing.

'It's not glamorous talking about death and failure, not glamorous at all. Ted would be doing it to highlight the issues. If he dropped our proposed project for this, it must be really something.'

'Okay, I'll bear that in mind. I'll arrange for somebody to come down and get a statement from you.' She texted McPhee again, asking him to see Biggs, tighten up on times, get a description of the woman, talk to others who spoke to her, hotel register, the security footage, get a name then track her down. Find out when she realised Maxwell was avoiding her, and if she had time to meet him on a bridge at midnight, 310 miles to the north. And: 'Mr Biggs, do you know where Ted kept his academic materials? We can't find his tablet. No papers, no research?'

'Really? That's odd. He'd done a fair bit of work into his project.' Biggs narrowed his eyes. 'Has somebody taken it?'

'We're assuming so.'

'But knowing Ted, I doubt he'd keep anything confidential up in the cloud. We've suffered security breaches in the past. Believe me, if something was important to his research, he'd have hidden it well.'

NINE

They called her Poppy. I called her Poopy.
She was a stuck-up cow, a right fanny dancer.
She took a long time to drown.
I was bored by the time she stopped breathing.

Killagal Blog, 2021

Caplan couldn't recall the last time she had visited Sarah Linden at home. Five years, maybe more, and Sarah had moved flat since then. Most of those occasions had been for a dinner party, never in the afternoon, never on a Sunday. Or occasionally, drinks with the three friends, herself, Linden and Lizzie Fergusson. Sarah was the richest, the most married, the most competitive. But she still thought that she was twenty-five. ACC Linden never suffered a moment of self-doubt. Which was either supreme confidence or a lack of self-awareness.

Her flat was on the seventh floor of Plantation Wharf, one of three modern blocks of flats, colourful outside with darkened windows and wrap-around balconies which would be useful once every ten years. There was a gym on the roof and a swimming pool in the basement. The view from the upper floors would be an impressive mountainous landscape to the north, the city to the south.

Caplan pressed a red switch; there was a responding buzz followed by a click that signalled the door was open. She only advanced as far as the foyer, where a barrier of glass stopped her going any further. She heard the quiet hum of security cameras swinging to focus on her and resisted the temptation to smile at them. After a brief wait, a second buzzer sounded, and the glass door released from its lock.

It was easy to forget that Linden, as ACC, did put her head above the public parapet every now and again. She could easily become a target; there would be those outside who would have her in their sights. Caplan had tasted a little of that in the Devil Stone case. The perpetrators had targeted Caplan's children, Emma had ended up in a medically induced coma, and Caplan had been told she had got off lightly. If they had chosen to use a gun rather than a car, it would have been fatal. She couldn't fault Linden's belief that being a parent left you vulnerable. It was not something Caplan would wish on her worst enemy, the thought of your child lying bleeding on the road, the noise as the car shattered their young bones. She knew what it was like to be hunted down. They didn't need to get to you, they only needed to get to those close to you. The thought of it made her hand linger on the glass door, making sure it had closed properly, a backward glance over her shoulder to ensure nobody had followed her in.

Caplan got into the lift, scented sweetly and with a soundtrack of an audio book she couldn't really place, a classic anyway. The name Carton as she pressed the button for the seventh floor brought to mind *A Tale of Two Cities*. 'It is a far, far better thing . . .' she said to nobody at all, except maybe the security man who monitored the activity of any visitor to the building. Caplan looked as if she might be a bank manager, cop, lawyer, or doctor. Her mum had always taught her to be well-presented.

Sarah Linden opened the door of her flat. She was a drunken mess, still in her pyjamas, a light housecoat hanging from her shoulders, the belt trailing behind her, hair like a nest made from old straw. A cigarette hung out the corner of her mouth. She stood back and fluttered her hand, inviting Caplan in.

'I thought you'd finally given up,' said Caplan, pointing at the cigarette as she passed.

'Not lit, is it?' Linden flopped her way down the hall to a vast open-plan lounge, triple aspect, as the estate agents would say. The kitchen was an offshoot, dark grey, looking not unlike the control room of the battleship *Potemkin*.

'Shall we? Here?' Linden indicated the island that doubled as a dinner table. The view out the floor-to-ceiling glass was incredible, up over the Campsies to the Ben over to the west.

'This is a huge flat.'

'Apartment, dear, we have apartments now.'

Caplan looked out the wall of glass. 'It's really lovely.'

'Chris, you live in a fucking caravan, you'd think a blanket in the car park was luxurious.'

Caplan thought about the warm cosiness of the lift, the words of a classic novel drifting over her. She couldn't argue. 'I've always had my doubts about the flow-through living room, dining room, kitchen thing. But this layout kind of makes sense.'

'It's crap. This country's too cold for it. And I like onions. I need to section off the kitchen or the whole place stinks.' She moved a couple of files around, plugged her laptop into a socket on the table leg.

'So, this isn't all one room?'

'Nope. There are concealed dividing doors. It's great for parties but as I hate people, I'm not inviting anybody round.'

'Except me.'

'This is business and you invited yourself.' ACC Linden stood, shrugged her dressing gown over her shoulders and pulled a briefcase up from the floor.

'Ryce thinks Maxwell was stabbed by a leftie. I thought you needed to know that.'

They had been friends for a very long time. Linden closed her eyes in something like gratitude, her fingertips drumming along the tabletop. She was recalibrating.

Linden said, 'I don't think we have any concept of the shit-show that might be coming down on us.' She passed Caplan a photograph, evidence-coded from Dumfries. 'From the hospital, for any future arrest re the arson, but look at that damage.'

It was hardly recognisable as a hand, more like burnt steak and corned beef.

Caplan repeated what both Ryce and Biggs had said. 'So I think we're looking at Girl A, aka Lora Connel, and somebody I'm calling "the Pest".'

'With regard to Girl A, keep in mind that we're looking at somebody who has not been convicted in a court of law. She was detained under a mental-health order, she was protected by her age and by patient confidentiality. And we have a duty of care.' Linden paused. 'Everything we need to know, we're not allowed to know.' She handed over a photograph of a young teenager, her neat brown hair in a bob, standing against an exterior whitewashed wall where three old horseshoes hung at odd angles. She was dressed in faded jeans and a long, crumpled t-shirt. The slight squint, the uncomfortable smile was typical of those crippled by shyness. The disembodied elbow at the side of the picture was proof that it had been cut from a group photo. Although Linden was still sitting down, Caplan could feel her eyes boring into the top of her head. She heard the metal clasp click on the main file of photographs. Caplan took her time.

Linden got up and padded across to the kitchen. She leaned over the worktop that formed the barrier with the living space and emerged with two glasses and a bottle of white. Caplan glanced at her watch; it wasn't two o'clock yet.

'Yeah, but it's a Sunday, God, you can be so prissy and disapproving at times, Christine. Did your mother make you like that?'

'No, I was like that anyway. And drinking at this time of day is good for nobody.'

'It bloody well is, I was up most of the night.'

'Working?'

'Entertaining a friend.'

'Single?'

'Who cares. You can ask him if you want, he's still in the bedroom.' Linden poured a glass for herself, then returned to the kitchen and got Caplan a bottle of expensive spring water, chilled to exactly six degrees. 'And you're a fine one to talk. Did you ever ask John if he was married?'

'I did. He said he wasn't. The Bastard lied. Thanks,' she smiled at her friend, her boss, the photographs still lying in between them on the table: 'Girl A. Lora Connel'.

Linden's eyes flickered down to the thick envelope labelled with a case number and 'Do Not Bend' printed on the upper right corner. Caplan lifted it up, feeling the slipperiness of photographs in plastic sleeves, images that were going to be scrutinised many times and needed protection.

Caplan took her time looking at the scene of devastation caused by the fire. She'd stepped into such hells before, when the world was still hissing, the heat that singed bones, a smell that could never be forgotten. Her eyes started to water by association. 'Do we know where Connel is?'

'Not a clue. Keep looking.'

'There's a fridge, freezer, a small dog bowl, or a cat bowl, half-melted onto the carpet.' Caplan flicked over again. 'More pictures of the same, a living room, a carpet charred, an open window, and lots of soot on the ceiling. It looks nasty.' The magnolia walls were covered in blackened tongues, where the ever-hungry flames had licked, tasting their quarry. Caplan had seen it before, even the pictures could bring that taste back to her mouth. 'This looks very nasty.'

'Fitting for Lora Connel. She's known online as "Killagal". Dark-web stuff. Killagal saying she kills children and enjoys it.'

'Can we not arrest her for that? She's eighteen now.'

'We don't know where she is. But let me give you this before I forget. You might need to contact this guy from the Cyber Crime Unit.' She handed over a business card. 'They've tracked Killagal down to a social-media platform called Banned Box. Killagal blogs on that, he'll send you the full bhuna, but I got some hard-copy highlights, read them on an empty stomach, they are vile. And she has a lot of followers, only been going since June. Since her day release. Last post was the first of April.'

'And was there a TV documentary . . . ?'

'I'm ahead of you. I'll send you the link. Watch it, it's no better now than it was five years ago.'

Caplan nodded, looking at the damage. 'What if the vigilantes have caught up with her? From the look of that hand, she's unable to look after herself so she's either being protected, or they got to her.'

'She was stupid enough to make it easy for people to find her. She was warned to be cautious about her past and move on with her new identity, her new back-story. She was told to keep a low profile, so she blurts it out all over the net.' She handed over a slim file. 'Print-outs of the blog highlights for you. She taunts the trolls to find her, and guess what – they did!'

'Okay, let me get this straight. Connel is released as cured from a secure facility. Hospital rather than jail. She's given a new identity as she was Britain's most hated child-killer and when out she goes online as Killer Girl . . .'

'Killagal, all one word.'

'And taunts folk to find her.' Caplan flicked through the pages of the file. The word Nith jumped out at her, the river in Dumfries.

'Very stupid thing to do for somebody who's not stupid. It took our cyber unit a good while to get at it, the signal bounces all over the place and they are still not back at her IP address. Somebody was on her trail and decided to set fire to her flat, a secret address to match her new identity. The new identity that cost the British taxpayer a fortune.'

'And this is her?' Caplan tapped the picture of the girl in jeans. 'Looks so normal.'

'The only picture I have, very out of date. Every report you read will be heavily redacted. But she's eighteen now, different rules apply. It'd seem that she's very proud of her past.'

'Do you want to look away while I take a snap of that picture on my phone? Then you can deny you knew I took it. I can say that I did it when you were refilling your third glass of Chardonnay.'

'Please go ahead.' Another long sip, a look across the top of the glass to Caplan.

Caplan took a picture and put her phone down, then looked at the rest of the photographs in the file, noticing the time-stamps and the codes. 'How did the trolls track her so-called undisclosed location?'

'She left clues on the blog. But who cares? If she was moving into my street, I'd put a bullet in her forehead and not think twice about it.'

Caplan smiled. 'That's what I've always admired about you, ACC Linden, always supportive of those with mental-health needs. And Connel must have had a long history of mental-health problems. Maybe Maxwell was thinking along the lines of "if she'd received the right help . . ."'

'She got all the help she bloody needed. Most of her life was in care and in receipt of medical, psychiatric and psychological help. She has a supportive family, she's not the product of a horrific childhood. I can't recall, but I think her dad worked for the forestry and her mum worked in the hospital. I don't care she was a juvenile, I don't bloody care if she's Joan of Arc.'

'Where is the dog?'

'Don't know. Don't care. That was why she left the hospital, she was worried about her dog.'

'What kind of dog?'

'Who gives a fuck? What type of dog do serial killers usually have?'

'She's not a serial killer yet.'

Linden gave her a raised eyebrow. 'Wait until you've read the blog. The dog was with neighbours for two nights. Elizabeth Bathory and Lassie had never been parted before so she limps out the hospital into nowhere, about the fourth of April. Maxwell's dead on the eighth. But her mad friends on Killagal, her followers if you will, may be supporting her. And you're right, she's too badly hurt to be living independently. Someone's helping her. If you find out who, serve them with an Osman notice. With a bit of luck she's dead.'

'How badly was she hurt?'

'Not badly enough. And the big question is, was she on the Connel Bridge?'

'Where a man who treats disturbed youngsters was stabbed by a leftie. The fire was last week?'

'It was ten days ago.' Linden leaned back in her seat, one hand holding her unlit cigarette, the other her glass, cradled in her palm like she was warming a hundred-year-old brandy.

'Who reported her missing?'

'Her case-worker did. Arlene McCaskill, she's back in Glasgow now. Arlene reported it to Anna Scafoli. Scafoli contacted us. I think she's the only one who sees it as we see it, that Connel is dangerous. Everybody else wants to hold her hand, her left hand obviously.'

'Who is Scafoli?'

'Some unit manager at the Rettie Centre, background in forensic psychology. She's worried that Connel's phone is down.'

'That is worrying in an eighteen-year-old,' agreed Caplan. 'While Connel is dangerous, I hate to think of her lying in a ditch somewhere.'

'I hate to think of the paperwork. She was still technically in the care of the authorities. But hey-ho,' she snapped, 'Ted Maxwell's dead, a man committed to the healthcare of troubled adolescents, a loving dad to his wee boys. I'd hate to think that we were getting focused on the wrong person here. Don't worry about Connel. She's a survivor.'

'Unless she's dead.'

'She had a chance, unlike her victims.'

'Plural?'

'You're smart.' Linden pulled a face. 'Things we're not allowed to know. But evil. Killing puppies kind of evil. The only body you have is the dead man in the river. Do you have any other reason why somebody would toss him in the water?'

'A few ideas. A pest of a woman? A patient he's crossed? A mental-health issue but the killing seems planned.' Caplan shrugged. 'It's early days.'

'Shit. But we can't ignore the commonality of the troubled adolescent.' Linden's face went rather pale under the tan she had caught on a recent trip to South Africa. The glass thumped down onto the table, a little tsunami of Chardonnay washing up and over the sides of the glass. 'Fuck!' Linden wiped it clean with a side swipe of her pyjama sleeve. She rubbed her face. 'Connel's past is another planet, we can't touch it. Not unless you busy yourself getting me some good, preferably incontrovertible evidence. The sort that would nail Mother Teresa for GBH. But in the aftermath of the James Bulger murder in '93, there was a huge swing to treating children who kill rather than incarcerating them. It's how we arrived at the Tollen Protocol. Connel is protected by law, I can't tell you or release any photograph that could lead to her being identified. Because I'm not allowed.'

'Hence why "Lora Connel" was classified.'

Linden nodded. 'On the Banned Box blog she talks about the crimes, things that only the killer would know. She boasts, I quote, "I'm on like number four, maybe five. I got nabbed for one." End quote.'

Caplan frowned. 'What?'

'We're not allowed to know. And now she's in the wind.'

Caplan's eyes dropped back to the photographs.

'Find her. Make sure that she's nowhere up here.'

'Because?'

'DCI Caplan . . .?'

'ACC Linden?' she replied, their code for being strictly back on professional terms.

'I don't want to be placed in the most difficult of positions, I would resent it. It's not my bloody job to babysit psycho bitches caught between the care system and the judiciary. She chose the name Lora Connel. We have good relocation and new identity programmes that cost a very large sum of money for those who are considered rehabilitated, but she couldn't manage that. And she calls the police a bunch of c-u-next-Tuesdays.'

'Nice.'

'And because of her age, if she commits—' Linden waved her glass in the air '—or has already committed another crime, she'll be tried, convicted and will go to jail for the rest of her life and there will be a recommendation of no parole at all until hell freezes over and they can hold the Winter Olympics there. Do you understand?'

'Oh, I understand.'

'I can see it in your face, Christine, wanting this wee psycho to be rehabbed, but there'll be a tipping point when the law will run out of nanny duty and when that happens, I want her sorry arse in jail where she belongs.' Linden sat back in her chair. 'Do some reading, I've requested clearance for more intelligence to come your way, but fuck knows when that'll happen. The powers that be want you to find a link between her and Edward Maxwell. I'm presuming, given his job, that would be at her care establishment. The Rettie. They're not happy about talking to you. I pointed out you were good, but you did need to know vaguely who you were looking for. They didn't budge. So, without knowing who she is you have to keep her on your radar. How's the cottage? How far is it from this bridge we're talking about?'

Caplan knew it wasn't a change in topic. 'In ruins and the caravan is crap. It's about twenty miles from the River Etive. Has somebody established a definite link between Dr Maxwell, Connel and the Rettie?'

'Not that anybody'll tell me.' She took a sip of her Chardonnay, giving Caplan another long hard look across the top of the glass. 'Think about the families of the victims. Keep flicking through those lovely photographs I got for you.'

Caplan did as she was told. She had seen things like this a hundred times, a home burnt to cinders. 'Is that what's left of her laptop? Bloody hell, it's melted.' She went to turn the page.

'Next photograph, have a look at the top.'

'We have a corkboard, a few pictures.'

'A few photographs but one pencil drawing – well, charcoal but who gives a fuck, black and white anyway. This was in the bedroom, least affected by the fire being furthest away from the door.'

Caplan began to get a creepy feeling up her spine. 'The only drawing?'

'I spotted that, I don't think anybody else has yet.'

Caplan looked up at her friend who was now staring out the window, biting her lip. 'Is that a drawing of the Connel Bridge?' 'It's a drawing of *a* bridge. The date on the drawing's 21 March, just before the fire . . . I'll look away while you take a little pic of that. If you can get it to somebody who knows the area really well, like your little friend PC Tufty? McSquirrel . . .?'

'DS Craigo?'

'Yeah, him. Who's the other one up there who's useless but knows everybody?' Linden tapped on her laptop.

'I've a select team with excellent local intelligence.'

'Bunch of sheep-shaggers confused by contactless credit cards. McPhee, get him operational. He's applied for promotion, see how he does. See if he can confirm it's a picture of that bridge, and drawn from where? For somebody who's been incarcerated for so long it might have been drawn from memory?'

'Or a postcard?'

'She's a fucking child-killer, who sends her postcards? It's a long shot, the only one I have. And keep your team small and close. An interview with this young lady is worth a fortune to the media. You've been warned, you'll be approached by some arsehole waving money at you.' Linden pointed her unlit cigarette across the table. 'You'll get no help with this, officially. And to be honest, I think you'll get a wall of silence wherever you go. She's a pariah. Then she'll kill again, then there'll be a government review and it'll be our fault, your fault, the hospital's fault. But nobody will tell us anything about her, because of the age and the state of her mental health when she committed these crimes. She's untouchable and the little bitch knows it.'

'But somebody is after her.' Caplan took a snap of the picture, such as it was.

Linden sighed, taking a deep breath. 'Don't read that blog file with a full stomach. Just find out where she is, without anybody knowing that you are looking. My phone lit up like a Christmas tree when the news of Ted Maxwell came down the wire. If she's not responsible for Maxwell, then prove it and we hand her back to those that deal with new identities. If she is, then we'll put her away for the rest of her sorry little life. She's eighteen, an adult. No smart lawyer is going to pull at anybody's heart strings. Not this time.'

Caplan nodded. 'Where are we legally?'

'On ground as sticky as a stick covered in Superglue.'

Caplan looked at the picture. 'I wonder what she looks like now.'

'Let's hope we never need to find out.'

TEN

This complete munter at Retts was saying I should get fit,
go for a run to the village.
That's what fucking buses are for!

Killagal Blog, 2022

Caplan grabbed a herbal tea and a hot, fresh croissant at Happy Beans just before it closed, and parked at the seafront at Cronchie, her car facing north so she could see the huge span of the bridge in the distance. She wondered what had happened up there exactly. The day had turned rather warm, humid and dark, with low cloud rolling in from the sea. But she kept her jacket wrapped round her. The reality of Lora Connel being at large, if she was as evil as her alter ego Killagal made out, was biting in deep. She opened her tablet and started scrolling through the document that ACC Linden had sent her. It had been compiled by Anna Scafoli, so a medical document, Caplan presumed, not a legal one.

There was a lot of information, well ordered, making Caplan wonder if Scafoli had this to hand and had merely tweaked it to suit. To suit what? For an occurrence that she foresaw, that Lora Connel would strike again?

Much of it was redacted, thick and thin black lines making a barcode of the pages. The first page had been left intact, a Word attachment of warnings and caveats that the information was not for public use. There had been leaks of various documents and records that pertained to Girl A in the past through a psychiatric nurse at the hospital who was subsequently disciplined and 'let go'. Because of the status of Girl A as a juvenile offender incarcerated under the Tollen Protocol, the document also stated that there would be a lack of clarity about the injuries the victim had suffered. Scafoli hoped it would be kept in mind that Girl A was a patient, not a convict. As she read the words, Caplan could hear the moral majority being outraged: *Try telling that to the mother of the girl who had her head held underwater until she drowned.*

The next paragraph reiterated that Girl A had the right to confidentiality both over her medical past, and to her whereabouts. At the time of writing, she had the right to live in peace as a free individual.

At the time of writing? Caplan deduced that Scafoli suspected she might have to defend her decisions in court. She read on, keen to find out what the official version was, then she would make up her own mind.

Girl A had gone to a residential centre for seriously disturbed children after she had murdered her friend Poppy Anstruther during a stay at Sugar Loaf Camp. Caplan read the name again, the one Ryce had mentioned: Poppy Anstruther. She could recall the case five or six years before, at least a picture in a newspaper came to mind, a soundbite on the news. And Sugar Loaf 'mountain' was familiar to her, nothing more than a large rock in the middle of a field. Emma had been there, a camp for Scouts and Guides, all tents and huts, campfires and singalongs. Caplan remembered with some amusement that every other mother had sent some home baking with their child; Emma was the only one whose mum didn't bother. Thinking of it now, she could have cut the neat edge off a Sainsbury's fruit loaf, wrapped it in tinfoil and nobody would've been any the wiser.

Sad that Sugar Loaf would now be associated with the murder of a young girl.

Girl A had been placed in the Rettie Centre for residential care, considered to be suffering from a severe personality disorder. Caplan couldn't recall Rettie on the list of where Ted Maxwell had worked, but the field of speciality was definitely apposite. In June 2021, Girl A, having always responded well to treatment, had been considered safe to be released. For hours, then days, with decreasing levels of support and judging that she had grown out of the horrors she had witnessed as a child, there had been a gradual release back into society.

Caplan read on. Girl A had been incarcerated previously, aged nine, after the death of her younger sister. Again the report failed to give details but no doubt they were horrific enough to have damaged a young and fragile psyche.

Anna Scafoli had added that, despite Girl A living as Lora Connel within the constraints of her new identity, somebody had tracked her down. So Scafoli knew nothing of Killagal, or that Connel had been seduced by the dark web, had exploited her notoriety, and had followers, kids who wanted to be like her.

Caplan looked at the bridge without really seeing it. She was casting her mind back through the years, thinking of the big cases that had disappeared from the media because the perpetrator was underage and entitled to anonymity. And Linden was right, in the last thirty years there had been a determined movement to get dangerous children rehabilitated, as understanding of the development of the human brain improved. The Tollen Protocol was supposed to ease the tug of war between law enforcement and mental-health care. Could those children, who were so damaged that they were compelled to damage others, ever be healed? It was the old argument of nature versus nurture, the rights of the individual versus the rights of society.

Connel must be from round here or spent time here, maybe on her holidays. The Connel Bridge connection had sparked Linden's interest. The girl knew it well enough to draw it from memory. Or she may have been doodling from the calendar picture in front of her. But that little sketch had meant enough to her to put it on display.

Caplan knew the Sugar Loaf Camp was about forty miles away, and was about to confirm it on Google maps when her phone pinged. Craigo sending her a drawing of 'The Monkey'. She closed her eyes. Had they seriously spent money on getting a likeness of what a drunk man had witnessed on a dark night while driving across a bridge?

She flicked open the attachment.

And was pleasantly surprised. It was a drawing of two rectangles, one on top of the other. Bevan McDonald's 'impressions' were written in handwriting that was worse than Craigo's. The figure was as tall as the man on the bridge, with a long coat, very long, that swirled in the wind. A high collar was noted, giving the impression of no neck, just a big round head. This was dark, something covering the face. And the impression of bulk, width – the figure was a lot wider than Maxwell, who was slim in his anorak and trousers. No hat. And the figure had moved easily.

Bev had got a fair impression of Maxwell; he might have got a fair impression of the other party as well.

She flicked between that and the skinny young teenager that Linden had identified as Connel, and the slim build of the Pest in the suit. She had no idea what she was looking for, but nothing struck her.

Nibbling at her croissant, she opened the link that Linden had sent her. The opening credits of the TV documentary 'The Rage' appeared on the screen. It had been broadcast when Girl A had been sent to Rettie after the death of Poppy, part of a season called *The Child Killers of Britain*. Anonymised witnesses shown only in profile spoke about how evil she was. Girl A had once tried to throw a puppy from a cliff. She was present when her wee sister was struck and killed by a train. Another younger sister had had to be hospitalised with suspected poisoning, before her death at the family home in tragic circumstances. Then the programme moved towards the murder of Poppy Anstruther. It was reported, over a filler shot of woods, that the leader of the Guide camp had, allegedly, been drunk on the night of the murder, when three girls had gone out to visit boys while the others had a midnight feast.

Poppy was later found drowned.

Caplan placed the remains of the croissant on the dashboard. One child hit by a train, another dead in unspecified tragic circumstances, then Poppy.

The most chilling thing for Caplan was the normality of the short film clip of the family at home. The kids running through the woods, faces blurred, a conga-type dance round the garden, the adults holding a glass or bottle. The soundtrack faded in, much laughter and merriment.

They could have been any family, anywhere.

She closed down her tablet to watch the horizon and the island of Skone, looking for the ferry. It was late so she retrieved the file with the hard copy of the blog, opened a page at random. The writing style was adult and engaging, the narrative about the excitement of watching a young man die, the writer seemingly obsessed with the amount of blood. Caplan stopped reading at the

lurid description of a spaniel puppy being shot in the head after
it had bitten her. The writer was pleased about that.

Linden had said there was a supportive family behind Connel
– maybe they knew where she was. How would she track them
down? If Anna Scafoli knew, would she be permitted to tell the
police? How much of Connel's life had been incarcerated? How
prepared was she for life outside?

Caplan saw the boat bringing Emma over from the island. Too
much looking after other folk's kids, now she needed a bit of time
with one of her own.

Emma was smiling as usual, laughing with her friends, the three
of them walking slowly along the harbour. Moving gingerly with
her two elbow crutches, Emma picked her way over the rough-hewn
surface, looking like she had gained a little weight. Her hair had
thickened up, and was pinned over to the side, hiding the scars
that reminded her of her little dance with death. The two friends
from the Allanach Community walked beside her; one Caplan had
met before, the other probably one of the many students who
passed through the community at Skone, trying the hard reality of
an eco life in a cold climate.

Caplan at these moments felt an overwhelming urge to scoop
Emma up and take her home, look after her until she was fully
recovered. That was emotion, not practicality. At home, Aklen
would start a subtle game of who was suffering the most and
have Emma limping around to make him cups of tea, as she
fought her disability as much as Aklen seemed absorbed by his.
Caplan knew that was unfair. But it was a little too close to
the truth.

'Hey, Mum,' Emma yelled, her hands waving, her elbows still
in the clasps of the crutches, 'I've got Jens and Elsie with me, can
you take us for lunch?'

Caplan did a quick calculation of the credit left on her card,
smiled and shouted back, 'Sure.'

Some things never change.

By five-thirty, Emma was safely back on the ferry to Skone, and
DCI Christine Caplan was walking into the station at Cronchie.
Mattie Jackson was on the desk as usual. He seemed to live behind
that Perspex screen.

'Good afternoon, PC Jackson. Anything come in about Ted Maxwell?'

'McPhee has it all upstairs, ma'am, but nothing has come over this desk.'

'Was wondering if you could tell me anything about this Girl A? Her flat in Dumfries was set on fire a few days ago?' Caplan unwrapped the scarf from her neck casually, posing the question as if she'd been listening to the news on the car radio.

There was a definite but minute pause before Jackson replied. 'Read about it, yes?' he asked, not committing himself to giving anything away.

'So has anything else come down the wire about her, news of her whereabouts? I believe she might have links with this area?' Caplan knew she was being awkwardly casual.

He was awkwardly casual in return, shaking his head, reminding Caplan of Linden's warning about the wall of silence. 'As far as Girl A is concerned, we've no idea of her current whereabouts,' he said, not even looking up from his keyboard.

Caplan paused for a moment. There was something off in the way he was responding. 'We' the police service, or 'we' the community? He was normally respectful, informative and good-humoured, but not today. She wondered if she should ask him something about the Connel Bridge, or a fatality by train, or the death of the girl at Sugar Loaf Mountain.

She spoke naturally, as if merely passing the time of day. 'We've all been told,' she said, utilising his vague 'we', 'to keep an eye out for her. Because, as far as we, the police, are concerned she's the victim of a crime, of wilful fire-raising. She's lost her home, and we need to ensure that she's safe. She left hospital with a terrible burn on her hand.' Her voice was conversational now. 'If you hear anything, let me know so I can pass it on up the chain.'

'Sure, and that's us to a T, always vigilant, keeping people safe.' He quoted the motto of Police Scotland. He turned his back on her, reaching for the phone, but didn't dial. He was making a decision.

Caplan's shoulder started to hurt; she moved her rucksack from one side to the other, or maybe it was the weight of the crap she was putting up with at the moment.

'The incident at Church's Pass wasn't a million miles from here,' Jackson said. 'Maybe that's what they're thinking of.'

'What incident?'

He shrugged and started keying in a phone number. 'Ask them upstairs but if you go up there, don't use a satnav, take Craigo and an Ordnance Survey map. In his vehicle, you'll need it. And be careful.' He started speaking down the phone, something about a back-actor that had been borrowed without permission. Their conversation was over.

Keeping the words 'Church's Pass' in her head, she climbed the stairs, hearing Toni Mackie loudly recounting some incident from the train journey from Glasgow, some guy who had chatted her up. She was excited.

As she went into the toilet, Caplan wondered if it had been a novelty for Mackie, the train ride from Glasgow up to the station at Oban. Would that be the same for her, if, when, she finally got her family to come together and settle this far north? Get away from the eight years of hell since Aklen was bullied at work, was lied to, suffered thinly veiled accusations in the press, so vague and obscure that they were difficult to refute. Such a slippery eel, the near-truth. It had killed him inside. He had walked away, mentally unable to stay and fight, to face the legal action he was entitled to take. And would have won. But at what cost? He was defeated before he even started.

He needed to move north to get away from the memories of that hurt.

Caplan stood for a moment, looking in the mirror. She'd presumed, wrongly, that Aklen would then get well, as it was 'over'. They had got some closure, a line had been drawn in the sand. She'd presumed he'd walk into another, less stressful job. She had presumed a lot. Although he was well liked and respected in his field, the lies seemed to follow his reputation like a dark cloud.

She checked her hair, her make-up; she needed to look efficient. She thought her face was thinner, but her hair was the same as she had worn it when dancing: chignon at the back of her head, worn low, just above her neck. It had been cold in Glasgow, and late afternoon here had brought a temperature drop. There was a rumour about a storm being on the way. She needed to check what outdoor gear was in her car, her boots, hillwalking jacket and trousers. Her life as it was now. What had Lora's life been like up here? From the little she knew, school and the Guides, a supportive family; but some malevolency was lurking in the shadows, making her grow into a monster.

People change.

Caplan took one last look in the mirror, ran her finger round her jacket collar, and was set for whatever the discussion would bring. She wasn't going to walk away from her band of merry men until she had whatever grapevine gossip they possessed on the board. It was up to her to decide what was important or not. It wasn't up to them to tell her what they thought she might like to know.

The incident room was quiet apart from Mackie, the early shift gone. Those present said hello then busied themselves. Caplan wondered if Jackson had phoned up, warning them. She looked at the wall, recapping for herself. Somebody had lured Dr Edward Maxwell, a clever, cautious man, onto the top of the Connel Bridge. There was a description and an unflattering drawing of the other figure on the bridge labelled 'Bev's monkey'. Why did Maxwell go there? Obviously, something to his advantage. There was a brief description of the Pest and a list of institutions scored out – not known as a member, didn't work there, not part of the governing body. Maybe she was from another part of his work or his life. Security footage had been requested to aid ID. Girl A may or may not be relevant, but Caplan owed it to Cordelia and the boys to focus more on this incident and find out who had stuck a knife into the soft flesh of their husband and father's chest and thrown him from the Connel Bridge.

She turned. Craigo smiled at her, a look of relief passing through his usually confused features. He too must have heard the storm warning, as she saw his all-weather jacket over the back of his chair. Mackie had her matching jacket hanging on a hook. She was some relation of Craigo's, a cousin who wasn't really a cousin.

Mackie was having a good scratch, her nails leaving white weals on her forearm that quickly streaked red. Her short-sleeved t-shirt was a little too tight.

Caplan knew her team were good. And that Mackie excelled at being the centre of attention when she wasn't supposed to be. But when the spotlight was on her and she was tasked with something important, her lack of self-confidence came to the fore. She had great potential, yet it was McPhee going for the promotion.

Caplan cleared her throat. 'From here in, this is a murder inquiry.

Maxwell was stabbed before he was pushed. Okay, Toni, do you want to recap?'

Her DC got up and waddled to the front, pointing to the photograph. 'This bloke—' She thought for a moment '—Max? Mac? Ah shit, I've forgotten his name already.'

It was McPhee who rescued her, gathering some papers to outline what was going on with Dr Edward Maxwell. To Caplan's mind, this was the way they were supposed to work, search out and investigate their own little pieces then feed it into the system. It wasn't only possessing the knowledge, it was the understanding. Caplan knew from long experience that it was new eyes looking at that intel that worked, moving it around and getting a new picture to emerge from the same pieces. And often the detective pursuing a single line of investigation could get focused on that, and only that.

Mackie had fallen quiet, which was unusual in itself. She was staring at McPhee, who was on his feet, rubbing his forefinger along his hairline, looking at the wall. He could have been analysing a very complex bank statement with a massive hangover.

Caplan coughed lightly and McPhee looked up as if he'd got a fright, swore slightly under his breath. 'Of course, of course.'

Caplan waited. They'd been working on the case all day, they must've moved forward somehow. Craigo sat like a garden gnome, staring up into the light bulb above his head, a small smile on his face, content with the world and totally oblivious to the tension that was building in the room.

McPhee finally started talking: Edward Maxwell, his wife, the two boys, his mum and dad, his current places of work – the Rettie was not one of them. His movements the twenty-four hours before he died. They'd been busy on the phone, summing up the short life of Dr Edward Maxwell in more detail. Edinburgh Uni, masters at St Andrews, then three years to do a PhD, interested in adolescents, troubled adolescents. He'd written two well-received textbooks. No money issues, no controversy. He'd earned praise for whistleblowing on one abusive clinic.

Was it Caplan's imagination or did McPhee pause slightly for effect before he said: 'He had a special interest in youngsters who kill.'

Silence dropped on the room.

'He was a man of merit in that area, well-respected, published in academic journals. He seemed a popular guy, a hard worker and a decent sort, not one to shirk or make waves but he wouldn't shy away from a situation that he thought was unjust.'

'With reference to patients or colleagues?' asked Caplan.

'Within the NHS that could be either,' muttered Mackie.

'There's no obvious patient causing him grief on an initial look, but we need to go deeper. You know, thinking about the nature of the disorders he deals with, mental health covers a lot of ground.' McPhee flicked a few pages on his tablet, repeated that Maxwell's wife had mentioned he was working on a project. What else was he researching? They had found no documentation on that, nobody seemed to know. 'He was scaling down his NHS work, doing one clinic a week in the Queen Elizabeth. He was consulting round the big private clinics but they're less forthcoming.'

'And nobody knows what this big project was, there's no electronic footprint?' asked Caplan. 'That takes some doing in this day and age. He said to a colleague, a project like Kevin, in the film? Where a mentally disturbed youth is let down by the system. Maybe, more broadly, the non-demonisation of those patients. Those I've spoken to, they all knew there was something.'

'We were hoping that his home computer might tell us,' McPhee said. 'Cordelia Maxwell knew the password, we have his personal emails, and his academic work where there's no patient identification. There's nothing on his cloud storage, which is the obvious place for it to be. The legal guys are seeking permission to access his patient files and any other secured storage, but as they're mental-health patients and juveniles we've to jump through a whole load of hoops.'

'Have you found any reason why he should come north?' asked Caplan.

'None that I can find, ma'am.'

She stood up. 'Thanks, McPhee. If you can indulge me for a moment, do you recognise this?' She opened her phone up so the charcoal drawing of the bridge filled the screen, then passed it to McPhee who passed it to Craigo.

They answered in unison: 'It's the bridge.'

'The Connel Bridge? Do you know where that view's from?'

Craigo considered for a moment. 'Up on the hill, over to the west I'd say. It's drawn from a height though.'

'Thanks.' Caplan took her phone back. She pinned up copies of the post-mortem pictures, Maxwell's clothes, his shoes, the shirt with the cut from the knife as well as pictures of the insults on his body. She talked them through the plate in Maxwell's leg and the positive ID by his wife and father, and by DNA. And that he wore heel lifts, the left bigger than the right in his handmade shoes.

'With a lift in both feet?' asked Craigo, his pen pointing in mid-air.

'Yes. Any thoughts why he was there? Anybody? Come on.'

'Those who know him well tell the same story. He had something on his mind, something big, so I conclude the something big was up here. No one thought there was a third party in the marriage. He got to the B&B about five-thirty p.m. and was dead around half-past midnight.'

Caplan tapped at the road map. 'Where are we on sightings? Bevan saw him alive with A. N. Other 0037 hours approximately, is that still correct?'

'We've had a few more sightings, ma'am.' Craigo went to a badly drawn map on the wall. 'The Afghan hound walker was on the south bank on the west side of the bridge. She saw the large figure, dark, moving south off the bridge and walking up to the Osprey. Both parties were walking quickly due to the weather, but they were in sight of each other for a few minutes.'

'The Osprey?' asked Caplan.

'That's the restaurant to the west of the bridge near the slip road.'

Caplan nodded.

'Afghan walker is not clear on time but thinks closer to 0030, or later. Nobody seen on the bridge then. We're hoping for good dashcam footage from a Stevenson's lorry as it came off the bridge going south. The air brakes gave the dog a fright, so the owner noticed it. It was going in the same direction as the large figure. Once we get timings, we can request some footage from the village. So, A. N. Other didn't go in the water with him.'

'Good work. Ryce wants a re-enactment to test a few things. Any volunteers?' Caplan was aware of the two DCs looking at her, waiting for some kind of decision. 'Right, Mackie and McPhee, you two are volunteered to get soaked on a windswept bridge.'

'The guilty party knew about the tidal race, knew the body wouldn't be swept out to sea or washed upriver,' said Craigo.

'If he had survived the stab wound, he would have died in the wave. So why stab him? To search him? Did he resist?'

'There're no signs of him resisting. Only a bruise where his flank hit the rail. The killer might have used the top rail as a fulcrum to punt the body over.'

'It could still be a mugging gone wrong?'

'Could be, but I doubt it.' Caplan got back to her feet and turned to the squad, talking calmly and persuasively. 'There's something we must consider here, it has the potential to threaten the entire case. It's an avenue of investigation, that's all.' There were murmurings of anticipation. 'Craigo and I are going to investigate this angle, the rest of you follow the leads on Maxwell, and stay absolutely focused on him. I know you've found nothing so far, it doesn't mean it's not there to find.' Caplan could imagine the wrath of Linden breathing down her neck, but having seen the documentary, she doubted it was safe to wait any longer.

She was grateful to pause when Mackie appeared with a tray of tea and coffee, some biscuits.

'We need the hive-mind here. This is a very sensitive topic, and I'd like your cooperation. You may have heard, read in the media, that Girl A was recently released, judged as sane and able to live a normal life with the rest of us, with a minimal amount of support. You may also know that her flat was set on fire and Girl A was badly injured.' Caplan saw a quick look flit between Mackie and McPhee. These were the local cops. God, they might have worked on that investigation. 'Basically, she needs medical help, and we'd like to ensure that she gets it. If her real ID is known, then it's imperative that she's reprocessed through the new identity scheme but needs to be safe while that's ongoing. So, if any of you are familiar with Girl A, or know anything about her, know anybody who might talk to me, or to one of you on a totally confidential basis, then please let me know. I've nothing but a redacted report and a name that she may or may not be going under. Can anybody help me?' Caplan looked around the room, expecting a stunned silence.

DS Craigo said, 'Oh, you mean the Halliday girl?'

ELEVEN

Some clatty bitch has died of too much happy hormone.
OD'd on Irn-Bru and Maltesers.
Found naked, dead in the park.
Not one of mine but seriously? Murder by happy hormones.
What a way to go.

Killagal Blog, 2021

Caplan kept calm; she knew her face never showed it but sometimes she did wonder about her colleagues.

'Oh, is she old enough to be out now?' asked Mackie in a tone that suggested a troublesome but loved puppy was on his way home from the kennels. 'That's nice.'

'I should think so, she'll be what? Eighteen?' Craigo did a bit of mental arithmetic, his round little head bobbing from side to side, the two tufts of hair that stuck up jiggling this way and that. 'Yes, ma'am, she's eighteen if she's a day.' He sounded happy. 'Is she coming home then?'

'You know who she is?' asked Caplan. 'The Halliday girl?'

'Oh, course we do, we all do, well, those of us from round here. There was the other investigation and that was up there.'

'Craigo?' Caplan tried to keep the impatience from her voice. 'Do you know where she lived when she was here?'

'Near enough,' said Craigo cheerily. 'The old loggers' cottages, ma'am, I mean that's what they were called long before young Gillian came on the scene, and that was where—'

'Gillian?'

'Gillian Halliday, ma'am, killed her wee sister when she got a fright in the storm, she was sleepwalking, you see—'

'But nobody knew where she got the knife – I mean nobody ever worked that out,' said Mackie, offering the team some insider knowledge. 'There was a lot of folk in the house that night, but oh my God . . .'

'That's right, ma'am, woke up covered in blood and no memory of any of it.'

'Well, that's not quite accurate according to the—'

'Well, that's what Jeannie McColl said. That's right, isn't it, Toni?'

'Oh aye, and she's not often wrong.'

Caplan caught McPhee nodding. The power of the Cronchie gossip machine.

'Okay, can we accept for a moment that the power of the forensic science unit might have uncovered a few things that Jeannie McCann can't . . .' She stumbled at the awkward assonance.

'McColl, ma'am, Jeannie McColl,' corrected Craigo, 'as in the song.'

'Indeed, but your intel may be slightly awry here.' Caplan took a very deep breath. 'It would be helpful if you could confirm for me the crime that placed Gillian Halliday in a secure unit.'

'Oh, that'd be the Anstruther girl, Poppy Anstruther at the Sugar Loaf Camp.'

Mackie nodded.

They were talking about the right girl. 'Okay, let's just establish some ground rules here.'

Caplan reviewed the Tollen Protocol for them. McPhee immediately saw where this was going, wriggled in his seat and looked uncomfortable. As far as Mackie and Craigo, both older, were concerned, she could have been reading out her shopping list.

'If I can just reiterate that nothing said here goes outside these four walls. What would make me and ACC Linden happy is if we can engineer, in a legal way, contact between Gillian Halliday and her care-worker. She's gone off-grid and because . . .' Caplan stuttered. 'Well, because she seems to be able to draw the Connel Bridge, for that reason alone, it has fallen to me to locate her and put a protocol in place for her to remain safe and well.'

Craigo almost clapped. 'That's very nice of you, ma'am.' Then he added, with the tone of congratulation still in his voice, 'Do you think she might have pushed Dr Maxwell off the bridge?'

'No, but you can see why we want to locate her,' said Caplan carefully. 'She might come to harm if somebody thought that.' But she could see their minds were racing. 'Right, back to Poppy Anstruther, that was at the Sugar Loaf Camp.'

'Yes,' Craigo nodded, pleased that he knew the right answer.

'And the other fatality, the one with the knife?'

'That was at her house, ma'am.'

'So,' she kept her voice very low and quiet, 'it would be very useful if we could talk to the family. Do you, any of you, by any chance know where the Hallidays are now?' She emphasised, 'If I wanted to speak to Gillian Halliday's mum and dad, today . . .'

'Gillian's mum and dad?' clarified Craigo.

Caplan took a deep breath. 'Yes. The arson attack was an attempt on her life. She was given a new identity that you are not privy to . . .'

'Laura, wasn't it?' said Mackie. 'Lora, spelled with an O rather than AU and it was . . . err . . .' They waited while Mackie hit the side of her head with her own fist. 'Connel! Was it not Lora Connel?'

'Oh, that's rather clever, ma'am, isn't it? Lora-with-an-O Connel.'

McPhee was sombre. 'So she knew the bridge and the Falls.'

'Yes, it would appear so.' Caplan felt slightly sick, feeling the same panic that ACC Linden must have felt when she heard that the body of a psychologist had tumbled from the top of the Connel Bridge into the Falls of Lora. Then was told that Girl A was no longer in her secret accommodation. And the drawing on the wall. 'She was Lora, she had a new life, her flat was set on fire. We need to know where she is now. Her case-worker has not heard from her. Vigilantes may be targeting her and her own mental health may be suffering while she's away from her support team.'

Craigo screwed his face up again. 'Do you want me to ask Jeannie if she knows where she is?'

'Can we not ask her parents?' suggested Caplan, anxious to keep the intel as tight as possible.

'Well, Miranda's still at Ben o' Tae, but the dad? I think he went a bit off the rails himself, as you would. I don't think things were the same up there since the accident, the one on the railway I mean.'

Caplan tried to recall what the blog had said. The incident in the house, Poppy Anstruther and the accident at the railway were three, but the blog had said four, maybe five.

'It all went wrong for them then, Jim disappeared sharpish anyway after Rachel. Bloody men. Rowan's still there I think, he's a dad himself now. The wee one will be about a year old. Little Ann . . . Anna . . . something like that.'

Caplan looked at McPhee and was rewarded with a subtle eye roll. 'Where do they live?'

'They live up at Ben o' Tae too.'

'I've heard of that.' Caplan was thinking where she'd heard it before. Somebody had been looking for it.

'Tiny cottages,' said Craigo. 'Like I said, old logging place up on the hill.'

'Where the residents interbreed and they think eggshells give you warts. Not very far from here. Three miles as the crow flies, a lot longer by the road,' said McPhee, scrolling through Google maps.

'What are you thinking, ma'am?' Mackie asked. 'Do you think she might be there? Is this connected to the dead psychologist? I presume Lora has been under the care of a psychologist.' Mackie was proving that she was not as daft as she looked.

'Not Lora. Just Girl A for now, Toni, we're simply ensuring that she's safe. I have my instructions, it's a welfare check. She was nearly killed less than two weeks ago.' Caplan shook her head. 'Now, let's act like the proper investigation team that we are. We visit the family home and ask them. Girl A, as we'll call her for clarity, had a new identity, but she wasn't living in witness protection. She was able to communicate with her family; she may have said something about where she intended going after she got out of hospital.'

'I was at college when the incident at Sugar Loaf happened. A lot of folk were unhappy she wasn't locked away for good,' McPhee said. 'It caused difficulties up here, incomers, the press, bloggers, podcasters. They weren't welcome.'

'Well, the law is the law.' Caplan wanted to take the team to one side and find out about the other activities of Gillian Halliday, the other murders she had boasted about committing. How many were they looking at here? 'We go and talk to them, starting with where she might think of as home. The information that you hear in this station stays in this station. We are keen to realise the whereabouts of Girl A to ensure her well-being. And that is as far as it goes.'

'Yes, ma'am. But we're looking for Gillian Halliday,' Craigo nodded.

'Girl A,' reaffirmed Caplan. 'Nothing that will identify her to a third party.'

'No wonder after the train thing, and the stabbing thing, her wee sisters . . .'

'Is this all public knowledge?' asked McPhee, concerned about the accuracy of the local telegraph. 'I was still training when this was going on.'

'Well, yeah, we were the closest station at the time, when the shit really hit the fan, when it all came out,' Craigo said. 'But you know, it didn't pull the community apart the way it might have in some places. But you can't help your children, can you? Everybody has a lot of time for Miranda. The way she's coped has been remarkable.'

Both Mackie and Craigo shook their heads. 'Soupy Campbell was a great cop but I think he was glad when the Fiscal took the case from him.'

Caplan made a mental note: DI Soupy Campbell. 'As I said, nothing of this leaves this room. We have to keep this quiet. Do you all understand that?' she reiterated.

There were various murmurings.

'And I mean really quiet. I don't want more vigilantes catching wind of it and putting two and two together, making five. We may be bringing Girl A back to this station. I don't want any of you spat at, or the station burning down when we are all in it. Craigo, do you have your car with you? We need to get to Ben o' Tae.'

He shook his head.

'I have mine,' said McPhee.

'What do you drive?'

'A Toyota Prius,' he said proudly.

Mackie shook her head and lifted the phone. 'I'll see if the Land Rover is available. You'll need it for Ben o' Tae. But it'll be better left to tomorrow. With the weather, and the dark.'

'Is the place cursed?' asked McPhee under his breath, looking at an empty page of Google maps. 'It's no man's land.'

Caplan ignored him. Ben o' Tae? She was still wondering where she'd heard that name as she watched Mackie go to the phone.

She wanted peace and quiet to look up the files. Now they had a name, she could secure the permissions she needed. Mackie shouted across the office that a large vehicle was moving north and needed police escort, roadblocks and controlled traffic flow.

It was using a lot of resources, so no Land Rover available. Craigo then offered to go home and get his Hilux but repeated it would be better left until tomorrow.

McPhee came over to her desk and said quietly, 'I'm not long out of Tulliallan.'

'Hence why you're the only one who knows about Tollen.'

'And Craigo just blurts out her name—' He snapped his fingers '—just like that.'

'As he has every right to, as he knows exactly who she is. I think most of the folk in Cronchie know. She didn't appear on the planet when Poppy Anstruther died. The locals know who she is, and I agree that we need to have a gatekeeper on that. I need somebody to work on Maxwell and what he has been doing. I need a connection between the two. You need to look closely at him, everything needs to be worked from the Maxwell end. It's his murder we are investigating. It's too coincidental that he ends up where Girl A started. I need somebody with a young head.'

He nodded and smiled. 'Oh, I get that.'

'No problem. One thing is, there could be a digital aspect to the crime, stuff on the dark web. Here's the number of the man who knows. Find out exactly where the investigation into the IP went. Mackie's wasted in the office, she's not as daft as she appears. She can be a good wingman for you while you dig about into Ted Maxwell. There's something under the surface. Something to do with work, and that lassie who kept pestering him.'

Caplan picked up her rucksack and looked at her watch. 'Where does time go?'

But McPhee moved closer to her, almost whispering. 'What was Ted Maxwell doing? He's squeaky clean, a straight-down-the-line husband and father.'

But then that was exactly what John Fergusson, the Bastard, purported to be. 'Any other time he had been away recently? Anything to suggest that he wasn't where he said he was? Look into his colleagues. Had Maxwell reported them? Made an accusation against them?'

'Cordelia seemed to be suspicious of "somebody at work"? Do we think that was the woman, the Pest? The constable we sent down got a good statement from Biggs.'

'Oh yes, the Pest.' Caplan tapped the desktop with the tip of her pen. 'That relationship was professional, in the sense that it wasn't personal. She was looking for him. He was very keen to keep out her way. Maybe he knew something about her, something that he didn't like. The timing seems correct for that. Maybe it was the thing that Cordelia suspected was on his mind. Maybe the subject of the book that we can find no evidence of.'

'Yeah, where are his notes, his drafts? That's puzzling me.'

Caplan nodded and sat back in her chair. 'Yes, it bothers me as well. Ask for Cordelia's permission. But his professional records will be subject to all kinds of caveats of confidentiality. You've already checked his devices, haven't you?'

'Only the one phone, but the tablet and second phone are still missing.'

'Because whoever killed him took them?'

'Maybe. Or because Maxwell was smart, he hid them too well. That's what I think. He was a PhD, he'd be used to taking notes and was, in all other parts of his life, careful and meticulous. Why would this be any different? Some secret research that nobody else knows about and there's nothing to be found? I deduce that's because he didn't want them found. He ring-fenced his new project for a reason and that same reason might have got him killed.'

'Patient confidentiality might explain it?'

'I know, but there'd at least be anonymised notes, but there's nothing. He was keeping something secret from everybody, colleagues included. Mackie's been chasing that down, so far everything has come up a blank.'

'I think he knew something about one of his colleagues. Was that why he came up here? For proof? Keep digging.'

Caplan retreated into her office, emailed Sarah Linden and said that she was going to interview Girl A's mother the following day. That wasn't a job she thought she could do with such little know-ledge of the issues that had taken the girl to a secure unit for her mental health. If Linden wanted her to wait, she'd wait. If Linden wanted her to find out where Girl A was, and expected her mother to tell her, then Caplan needed to know a wee bit more about what their daughter had put them through as a family. Craigo knew. They all knew more than she did.

And if Craigo advised not going to Ben o' Tae in the dark, then she'd take that advice. Craigo wasn't the type to be scared, but he did know the roads and the hills. And who knew what horrors they might find up there?

It would all look better with a new dawn.

For now, she needed to arm herself with as much knowledge as she could.

She typed in Halliday and Cronchie and watched as thousands of results came back. She looked at her watch, pulled over a new A4 pad, and sighed.

She was looking for anything, anywhere that Halliday and Maxwell would meet, just two tangential lines in the sand. Not enough for a threshold of evidence for a charge of murder against her. If it would stick, with her background. Or maybe it'd be culpable homicide. They'd wait for the Fiscal to sort that out. Caplan felt she was on a mission to find Gillian and to make sure she was safe, and that the rest of the world was safe from her. Once she had done that, she could refocus the investigation on Ted Maxwell, knowing even as she thought it, how much she had come to believe that the two situations were interwoven.

As soon as she had tracked down Gillian, she'd get Linden off her back and then try to ascertain where the teenager was when Maxwell was murdered. McPhee would be digging deep into the psychologist's background as she was digging into Gillian's and she had no doubt that the major incident system would run its program and spit out a time, a place, a person that had commonality. She could do with Harris back, inputting information.

Caplan lifted her pen and began scrolling through a world of 'Sources close to' and 'A commentator reported'. Much of it was rhetoric and vitriol, but once she got to articles from respected sources, she did vaguely recall some of the incidents.

The first was regarded as a tragic accident, the death of three-year-old Rachel Mary Halliday in the summer of 2011. Then another story about the death of a Rachel Halliday in 2013. She reopened the first one, thinking that somebody had got the date wrong.

It was a simple story, village kids bored in the summer holidays. The ten youngsters were excited that they were going over the railway up to Church's Pass. Two older boys said they had a really good den up there that the youngsters could use. They had taken sandwiches, juice, crisps, chocolate, and it seemed that they went with their parents' blessing – a long hot summer day in the middle of the holidays, village kids, all from this close-knit community, going out to have a picnic. Nobody knew they were going to Church's Pass. They weren't allowed that far.

Then wee Rachel Halliday was hit by the Oban train.

Caplan sighed. It was as simple as that. As beloved of local newspapers, there was a family photograph: the mum, the dad, three kids. And then a separate picture of the very young girl, blonde hair starting to darken, baby-toothed smile. She was holding something that looked like a fluffy dinosaur. The caption said 'Rachel Halliday, three years old'.

Could the death of the wee girl have triggered some psychosis that had haunted her big sister? Were they out together? A child that young couldn't have been out on her own. And who bore the guilt? She read down the article. Her big brother and her sister had both been present. Caplan hoped to get access to the family tomorrow, especially the brother and then the other kids who had witnessed the incident. The article didn't say who else was there, only that the children of several local families had been involved. She skim-read the rest, eventually finding the names Rowan and Gillian Halliday. What had the death of the wee sister triggered? Was that the basis for the soft-shoe approach that the teenage Gillian had received?

That made sense.

But then the reality of it struck her, sending a cold shiver through her. Killagal's boasting on the internet. She had killed three or four times but only been found out once. Surely even thinking like that was a sign of some kind of mental illness or a personality disorder. Or was it taking advantage, taking the chance of being a celebrity even on the darkest corner of the web?

Linden had said that Girl A was clever. Caplan looked around on the net again, getting more and more frustrated. The second 2013 article used a lot of words to say very little: tragedy strikes family for the second time. But another Rachel? The big problem with this case was the total lack of access to official documentation. She looked out into the incident room, seeing a valuable source of the information she needed: the office gossip. She knocked on the window and beckoned DC Mackie to come in. The constable looked rather alarmed and trudged her way slowly across the office, stuffing a half-eaten custard cream sideways into her mouth.

'Okay, Toni, tell me your version of what happened to Gillian when the second wee girl died. I know about the first instance, the one with the train where wee Rachel was killed.'

'Yes, ma'am.' Mackie sat very upright.

'What was the other Halliday girl called?'

'Rachel.'

Caplan closed her eyes. 'I know about Rachel, she was killed by a train. It's the other one I'm after.'

Mackie nodded, her blonde curls bouncing. 'Yes, ma'am. She was also called Rachel.'

'Okay, two daughters both called Rachel? Why?'

'She lost her once, then maybe thought, you know, replace her?' Mackie shrugged. 'But then George Foreman called all his sons George Foreman . . .'

Caplan raised an eyebrow. 'And they say boxing doesn't damage the brain. The Hallidays? One son Rowan and then Gillian.'

'Rowan's the eldest, yes that's correct.'

'That railway incident was accepted as a tragic accident, a wee girl wandering onto the track. What about the second, the one you and Craigo were talking about out there?'

'I'm thinking, ma'am, but at the time we were told not to say anything about it, no matter who asked us. Because of her age. Because of the mental-health issues. It's a terrible thing to have that in the family.' She made a strange fluttering motion with her fingers. 'Is it okay to talk now?'

'To me, yes. But still not to the outside world. I'm your senior officer, and I need some information from you.'

'Yes, I know that, ma'am, but if you were meant to have it, then, well, you would have it, DCI Caplan. Wouldn't you? What you said out there about Tolkien.'

'Tollen.' Caplan closed her eyes. Took a slow count to ten.

'I was thinking that it could be an awkward situation.' Mackie coughed lightly. 'If you were entitled to it, you'd have it.'

Caplan opened her eyes and looked at Mackie again. She was Craigo's cousin right enough. With their DNA came the ability to be both wonderfully helpful and incredibly obstructive at the same time.

'I understand your concern. It's a matter of paperwork, Toni.

ACC Linden's bosses have set the wheels in motion for me to access the medical and criminal records, but with the age of the perpetrator, the sensitivity of the crime, the publicity around the situation, it's going to take ages. They're going to have a lot of meetings. Gillian had to escape from a fire, she's scared, she's badly hurt. Bearing in mind somebody cocked the release plan up, they might use this delay to cover their tracks. Well, my back's against the wall. So, what do you know?'

Mackie was silent. Caplan smiled at her colleague, at her sunburst blonde hair, her freckled round face, the crumbs of the biscuit on her lower lip. She could see the outline of the lace of her bra, and the large sweat stains under her arms.

'Toni? If anything terrible happened to Gillian, I'd feel responsible. So would you. Anything you know will be about her past, and nothing can change that. But somebody poured petrol through her letter box, then a petrol-soaked rag, followed by a lit firelighter to make sure the flames wouldn't go out.' She waited for that to sink in. 'Somebody wanted her to die, to burn to death. It was a one-bedroomed flat. A single door. One floor up. She was lucky to wake up and get out. She climbed onto the roof of the adjacent property taking her dog with her. People are after her, and she's scared. I need to find out where she is. Tell me about the second incident. I don't want any curve balls thrown at me by the family when I go to talk to them. You know these people, I don't.'

'Oh, they wouldn't do anything like that. They're really lovely people. It'd be much easier if they were a bunch of bastards, but the Hallidays are nice. Miranda's one of those calm women, you know. Always has homemade shortbread, goes to church, never loses her temper. It's sad, all that tragedy.'

Caplan, hating Miranda already, added mentally: and has a daughter who could be a triple murderer.

'Talk me through the tragedies in that house. I don't want to put my foot in it, like thinking there was only one Rachel, and the date was wrong. Do you know them well?'

'Oh no, never met her until the incident with wee Rachel Susan, but that's what everybody says, Miranda's lovely.'

'I know what happened to Rachel One,' said Caplan casually, now she had Mackie talking. 'What about the second incident where Rachel Two died?'

'Ahm, let me think. Rachel two was only eleven months old when she passed away.' Mackie paused.

Caplan asked quietly, her eyes fixed on the junior officer, 'And what happened to her?'

'Gillian slit her throat.'

TWELVE

I tried to be better with crotch pixie 2.
I folded her over, put her in a suitcase and out with the bins.
Would have worked if she hadn't made such a racket.

Killagal Blog, 2022

Caplan had been glad to get out of the station on Sunday night; her head was spinning. Her job was horrible at times; sometimes it was difficult for her to think there was any hope for humanity. An eleven-month-old baby had had her throat slit by her older sister. She couldn't shake that from her mind during her normally restorative drive home.

After feeding Pavlova, Caplan sat in the caravan waiting for the kettle to boil. She started to re-read some of the Killagal blogs, now that she had a better grasp of the context. If she'd just read it as a piece of fiction, it would have been funny, adolescent but amusing. The truth behind them was very disturbing: nobody sane would boast about murder and animal cruelty in the same tone as saying they had a cold and were going to bed with a Lemsip. Killagal had described the view from her flat over the River Nith. Dumfries town centre wasn't a large area, and she had made it easy for those who meant her harm to find her. The last blog was dated 1 April. Was that significant?

Caplan closed the laptop, thinking about Gillian's mum keeping the family going while knowing what kind of monster her daughter was. As if there was some intuition between them, her mobile pinged with an email from Emma. Attached was a video of her standing on one leg, then attempting to stand on the other. They had spoken about it at lunch, the next step in her physio.

Caplan dabbed the tears from her eyes. She watched the video again with the sound turned up, hearing the shouts of encouragement from the onlookers. Emma, in fleece and shorts on the sand, standing on one leg easily, then changing over, or trying to. The other foot came an inch off the ground and she lost her balance; there was a 'no!' of disappointment from the crowd, a one, two, three of encouragement before she tried again . . . slightly better, then she lost her balance and had to put the good leg down again. And again, the crowd shared her disappointment, but the third time she lifted the good leg and the bad leg took her weight, slowly, with the encouraging crowd noise getting higher and higher. Emma leaned forward, her arms out like an aeroplane, and held the position as her audience counted to three. Then she fell over onto the beach and her friends rushed forward to cover her in soft golden sand, Emma laughing as she was buried.

It was a small thing but showed the extent of her recovery. The leg that had sustained all the nerve damage was slowly regaining power and control. That had been an exercise they had practised at home when the kids were wee. When Caplan, the ex-dancer, could bend forwards and place her forehead on the front of her knees.

Back in the day.

Emma was thriving out on the island, her new friends looking after her well. Under the wing of the Magus, Christopher Allanach, she intended to campaign to rid the community of the stained reputation left by the Devil Stone case. With the experience her father had been through, which Emma was old enough to witness, she would be well aware of what a falsely tarnished reputation could do to a man of principles, and how lies and falsehood left a smell that nobody could ever trace back to the source.

While Emma was earning her keep, Kenny would be skiving off his duties a little earlier than he should, charming his way out of it. He had his father's charisma. Emma said her brother was working at the micro-brewery on the island and was probably involved in some tasting capacity. He was still getting monthly assistance from his parents, at a time when they could little afford it. Kenny was the cheeky chappie with charm by the bucketload. If he fell in the Clyde, he'd emerge with a grin and a salmon in his mouth. He'd made bad choices, he'd nearly got himself and his sister killed, but he was still Caplan's wee boy.

And Gillian was still Miranda's wee girl.

People couldn't help the mental illness that afflicted them, any more than they could help having diabetes or the flu.

Mental illness was easier to accept than the concept of evil. Caplan always said she was a cop not a priest, but she wondered how conflicted Miranda had really been when she had heard about the death of her youngest daughter at Church's Pass. Did she feel any resentment about Gillian's lack of care? Then to give birth to another daughter, call her the same name, giving the same soul another chance, and to then lose that child so violently . . . Miranda and Jim had handed Gillian over to the authorities with dignity and had always provided support.

Then it had got too much for Jim.

The inability of the press to print the names must have afforded the family some protection from the worst of it all. Those who knew would only know because they were close to her or had been known to her. And, if Craigo and Mackie were anything to go by, the local community had rallied round. Whatever night terrors that wee girl had suffered had been an early indicator of a troubled psyche. In short, the girl was ill.

Caplan turned the gas off; the need for sleep was greater.

She was woken with the gentle light of dawn creeping in through the thin curtains of the caravan.

By ten o'clock on Monday morning, she had parked the car and was pulling her wellies onto her feet. It had been raining during the night, the long grass and the ferns were drenched with their bounty. She checked the map, mindful of Jackson's words, and made double sure that she was in the right location. Church's Pass was a nowhere place, a steep slope up through the woods to where the railway was. The place where three-year-old Rachel Mary Halliday had died.

The two girls, Gillian and Rachel Mary, had left from Ben o' Tae. Not wanting to go near there until she had company, Caplan was following the route the kids from the village would have taken, setting off from the main road and walking up the first of the long slopes on foot. As she went, she crossed the Forestry Commission track where Gillian and Rachel Mary would have joined the path of the others who had gone ahead, including their brother. It was normal for Gillian to join them, not so normal for Rachel Mary.

Caplan made a note to check out why she was there, guessing a lack of childcare might be the answer. It'd be the same old story, the mother was to blame.

Was it a one-off, and on that one occasion she had been hit by a train? There was a lot about it that didn't feel right to Caplan. A three-year-old near a railway track, so close that nobody could get her out the way when the train approached. The reports of the rest of the kids were typical, too shocked to speak, their brains protecting them from one of the most awful things that a human being could witness. Most of them had already been at the top of the opposite embankment, or further up the hill, except for one boy who had stood on the slope, filming the train.

The small child had been decapitated. Had witnessing that set something off in Gillian? Inspired her to slit the other Rachel's throat? Why did the teenage Gillian kill Poppy Anstruther? A taunt that was taken too far? The death of Rachel Susan had been Gillian's own doing. She'd never denied it. She was in the same bedroom with the knife on her bed, her wee sister dead in the cot next to her. Her throat slit. Nearly decapitated.

A good psychologist would be able to tease some sense out of that. A good psychologist had been stabbed and thrown off the bridge a few miles from here. Not very far at all as the crow flies. Was Gillian Halliday his 'Kevin'?

Caplan walked on, up through the trees. This was a creepy place. No wonder they didn't allow the kids to come up here and play no matter how bright the sun had been. She'd ask the mum, ask Rowan, ask Gillian herself if she ever tracked her down.

She crested a gentle slope, coming upon the railway track that ran round the contour line of the hill at this point. There was a large chain-link fence covered with yellow signs warning 'Track In Use', 'Risk of Loss of Life', 'No Entry', 'Trespassers Will Be Prosecuted'. It looked recent, but it was about ten years too late.

Such a fence had been there on the day of the tragedy, but somebody – no doubt one of the kids – had cut a hole in it earlier in the summer. There were regular reports from train drivers about older teenagers hanging around the track, but in the early summer of 2011, drivers had spoken of early teens, even younger. It was thought they were the Ben o' Tae kids. There was good vision north at this part of the track, and the trains here were not fast. They were quiet though, so they often sounded their air whistles when they left Cronchie Station. Caplan had heard it herself at night, working late in the quiet of the office. She looked along the line, peaceful just now, recognising it from the documentary.

What was that rhyme? 'Piggy on the Railway Line'?

The report said that Rachel Mary had been hit by the southbound train. Surely there had been some mistake? The track was straight here, running north before swinging out to the coast. They'd have a good view of the train coming, enough time to get the girl off the track. It was the northbound train that would come round the corner, through the trees and take them by surprise.

Or did nobody want her saved? Had nobody wanted her there in the first place?

An annoying wee kid forced to tag along because their mother had told them to all go out to play and to play nice because she was busy.

After parking the car, Caplan looked at her phone. It had taken her fifteen minutes to drive down the coast, the bridge diminishing in the distance, in and out of sight, to the lay-by where she had agreed to meet Craigo for the journey up the hill to Ben o' Tae. She closed her phone and sat in the Duster, thinking about the eighteen-year-old Gillian. How disturbed she must have been as a child. How little time had passed for her to get better. She was faced with a world as an adult, a world she'd only known as a kid.

She began to feel a degree of empathy for the entire family, loss and more loss.

She looked around the lay-by. A motorhomer had stopped to take some pictures of the view. While she waited for Craigo, Caplan checked the road map again. She was parked at the bottom of a steep hill with the words 'Historic Railway, Narrow Gauge' running on the contour line. It would take another ten or fifteen minutes for them to get up to the logging cottages at Ben o' Tae. Most of that would be vertical.

Caplan got out, opened the boot and once again pulled on her wellies, scrutinised by the couple in their motorhome who were now enjoying a bacon roll. It had stopped raining but it looked as though darker clouds were gathering. She knew there was a storm coming, the media was full of weather warnings for the south, the southwest and then the west. Caplan hoped it would have blown itself out by the time it got up to them. She had some vague memories of spending the night in a caravan during a storm, the carcase of the van lifting with the wind. A six-year-old Christine had been terrified they'd be hurled over the cliff, like the house in *The Wizard of Oz*, twisting and turning in the great wind. She'd been unable to sleep but too scared to get up in case she woke her mum and dad, got a row and was sent back to bed. Eventually she'd got up to go to the toilet and found her parents sitting at the small table at the front of the caravan, playing Scrabble.

Closing the car boot and looking out over the dull grey water, she wondered where that holiday was. Dornoch? It had been a day like this, waiting for a storm.

She glanced at her watch, knowing that she'd hear the loud engine of the Hilux when it arrived. Walking out the lay-by, she started up a track that forestry vehicles used. The sign, relatively new, said no unauthorised vehicles beyond this point. Under that was a very small slate, hand-painted in white lettering, that announced that Ben o' Tae was up the hill.

She started to walk, keeping her hood up against the rain still dripping from the trees. She had only walked for a couple of minutes, and she was deep in the woods. Pine trees on either side, battalions of them lined up over the hillside. She walked on slowly, aware of how quiet it had become. The road was very close below her but she could hear nothing. The paths parted, the Forestry Commission road turning along the contour line of the hill, away from civilisation. She noticed a flattening of the way. The old railway marked on the map? The track to Ben o' Tae she presumed; it was grooved by generations of tyres over the years. Looking through the corridor of trees, she could see nothing. She was glad she hadn't tried to bring the Duster up here, that would be a new suspension job that they could ill afford at the moment. She turned onto the easier forestry track. The trees, pine trees so tall they seemed to join over her head, cut out the daylight until the path took on the hue and tone of an early summer dusk. It was deadly quiet. She stopped, hands in pockets, listened to the noise of the drops falling from the trees. She pulled the hood down, her head hot from the climb. Taking a deep breath, she could smell the pine resin, the minty and sweet-scented air.

She looked round her, the carpet of pine needles under her feet reminding her of the chase after a murderer that night in Glen Coe, the hollow thud of their shoes as they ran. They had been chasing the wrong— She heard a gentle crack. She turned round slowly, thinking she saw movement in the wood. A forestry-worker? She called out but nobody answered.

A couple of steps and she was at the edge of the trees, and saw something moving away from her, brown and camouflaged. Too tall for a deer, it had been upright. A man walking? She pulled out her mobile, ready to take a picture. It was hiding behind a tree. She waited until it sidestepped then she took a few pictures of it on rapid shoot.

It could be perfectly innocent. Why did they not answer her call? Why should they? Why would anybody reply to a mad woman walking along a logging track in the drizzle of a Monday morning?

Then she heard the low growl of a vehicle making its way up the hill, a large engine working hard. She caught sight of an old Landy as it passed, windows covered in splattered mud. There was an impression of a red-faced, tired-looking woman in the passenger seat, her head rolling with the movement of the vehicle, her hair covered by a dark bobble hat. The driver was indistinct but the young woman in the back was holding a baby, her head turned towards Caplan, staring.

So they were going home, a good time to pay them a visit.

She turned round and started walking quickly down the hill, back to the car. Somebody was up at Ben o' Tae, and all she needed was Craigo to join her then they'd drive up after them and ask Miranda Halliday a few questions about her daughter Gillian.

As Caplan waited beside the Duster, she looked at her phone, opening up the images she'd taken. The first two were unclear, a tall brown shape in the trees, maybe with a glimpse of red jumper at the neck that showed this was not an animal.

She swiped through, catching stills of a man as he moved in and out of position. She got to the last one. The subject had indeed hidden themselves behind a tree. But Caplan could make out something pointing her way.

It looked like the single barrel of a shotgun.

She shivered and swiped her phone closed, telling herself that shotguns were commonplace in this part of the world. Scotland had incredibly tight control over firearms of any kind; Caplan wasn't used to seeing guns, certainly not one being pointed at her. She put her phone in her pocket, reminding herself to allow a time-limit here. She'd call into the station before they went into the house up at Ben o' Tae, and call again when they came out. Just in case it wasn't safe.

Just in case there was a little too much inbreeding.

THIRTEEN

My best memory was watching a young man die. This guy, smashed up by a motorbike.
All these doctors and nurses, machines beeping and tubes going everywhere.
Then they made a decision. It was over.
One of the doctors slipped on the blood on the floor and fell on his arse.
Poor bastard. He was the same age as I am now. The dead bloke I mean, not the doctor.

Killagal Blog, 2021

As the Hilux bounced up the hill, rocking and rolling like an old army truck, Craigo gave Caplan a short discourse in the life and times of Eric Arthur 'Tonka' Thomson, decorated soldier. He'd pulled a child to safety during a landslide. He'd lifted a huge fallen tree to rescue a colleague trapped underneath. And much more. He was Gillian's maternal grandfather and viewed these hills as his own. Craigo spoke as if it was his right to do so, and to do so with a shotgun.

Caplan half-listened, wondering how much the passage of time and consumption of whisky had embellished the tales as the vehicle ground through the gears. 'So he lives up here. Who else is with him? Sounds like he shouldn't be left on his own?'

'Well, they've knocked the cottages into one so Tonka lives with them all. His daughter Miranda married Jim Halliday and had Rowan, Gillian . . .'

'And the two Rachels.'

'But Jim left. Next door were Duguid McCleary and, can't recall his wife's name. She died in an accident up here with some farm machinery, and they had just the one daughter, Gail. So Duguid and Miranda got together, then Rowan and Gail.'

'Not sure if that's lovely, weird or lazy.'

The surface of the track had been neglected, gravelled then grassy with huge potholes which would have been fatal to normal vehicles, and sheer drops on the far side that needed careful navigation. Caplan appreciated why Craigo had preferred to visit the Halliday residence in broad daylight, as she held on to her seat belt and the handle on the door, wondering how long this roller-coaster ride would last. And how long the Hilux could continue on the rapidly deteriorating surface.

'Any more of this and you'll be claiming Police Scotland for new suspension.'

'Wouldn't be the first time,' Craigo said with no trace of humour, his eyes fixed on the path in front of him, his small ferrety mouth a fine line as he concentrated on negotiating a large, exposed boulder that caused the vehicle to clatter and bounce, forcing Caplan to hold onto her seat belt a bit tighter. The track was winding higher into the forest. It now resembled the approach to a culvert, the surface running with the current rain. The treeline was thinning out to bushes and grasses, the odd bit of heather. The track disappeared then re-established itself. The sides grew higher and steeper, heather and scrub took over. White wisps of cloud ghosted over the greenery. They passed a wooden sign saying 'No Journalists Beyond This Point' beside a few bits of curled barbed wire.

The faded lettering on an older sign read 'Ben o' Tae', patchy but legible.

'I'm feeling a bit uneasy about this,' said Caplan.

It wasn't like Craigo to be so quiet.

He then said, 'Jen.'

'Jen who?'

'It was at Jen O'Neill's, at the bed and breakfast, ma'am. I think Ted Maxwell asked her if she knew where Ben o' Tae was, except he pronounced it Ben Otty.'

Caplan nodded slowly. 'You're right, Craigo. She thought it was a hill, that he might have been a walker and had left his gear in the car.'

'There was nothing in his car, and he wouldn't have got very far with those handmade shoes he was wearing.'

'No.' Caplan looked out the window; the terrain was getting rougher. Who could live up here? And yet here they were, as she had done many times before, walking in dead men's footsteps. 'Do you know the exact story of what happened at Sugar Loaf Camp? The details were subject to restriction.'

She knew Craigo gave her a sideways look. Not as green as he was cabbage-looking.

'Why do you ask? Do you think she got away with two other murders? That was being said at the time. We thought it was daft rumours but now, looking back . . .'

'She said it herself on her blog, but did she mean it? Poppy Anstruther was found drowned in the early hours. Gillian seems responsible for that one.'

'Midnight feast, the summer solstice, at the Guide camp. It's the one with the stone that looks like a Sugar Loaf.'

'I know. I'd always wondered what a sugar loaf looks like and turns out it looks like a rock. Emma was there once. The camp's a big place, tents, woods, toilet blocks, ponds. That night they had a party, it had been the Family Day. A group of girls, including Gillian and Poppy, got up at midnight. They woke the leaders up to join in. Some had arranged to meet boys, the rest were messing around. And then Poppy was found face-down in the lochan. She was thirteen. Then Gillian's past emerges. She'd been in residential care, on and off, after the death of her sister. The Guides were an attempt to socialise her. Then another girl ends up dead, surrounded by Gillian's footprints. It all had to be hushed up, or as we'd say, subject to restriction. Then she's out for a few days and somebody else dies. Funny that.'

Caplan's statement hung in the air of the Hilux.

'A weird family, held together by tragedy,' muttered Craigo, guiding the vehicle round another nasty rock in the track.

Coming from Craigo that was rather a telling statement, thought Caplan, as he was well on the weird scale himself. There was a brief parting of clouds and weak sunshine glinted off the windscreen as they gained more height. The track was better maintained now, and the Hilux picked up a bit of speed on a gentler slope. There was a slight bend in the road and then a long straight track rolled out in front of them.

Craigo explained. 'This is the path of the old railway.'

'Yes,' said Caplan dryly.

'Used by loggers back in the day. Closed many years ago now, but that's why there're a few cottages scattered around the hillside. I think the idea was to get logs here by rail, then down the hill to the harbour. The woodsmen lived up on the hill. Over the years the old places have been converted, some are very basic, some rather luxurious. Be interesting to see what they've done with this one. Here we go.'

Caplan had noticed the view: the sea, the islands, the harbour as close as the crow flies. Spectacular didn't cover it. Then the vehicle turned and a fence came into view. Another sign, 'Beware of the Dog'.

Craigo pulled the Hilux to a halt beside the Land Rover she'd seen while she was walking, then started to reverse.

'What are you doing?' she asked.

'Turning round.'

'Try to do it without plummeting over the edge. That's some drop.' She looked at the short distance between her door and the fence. 'Do you want me to get out here?'

'I wouldn't do that if I was you.' Craigo pointed to the rear-view mirror.

Caplan adjusted her own mirror to see a very large, concerned-looking German shepherd watching them, daring them to get out the vehicle. She looked over her shoulder at a small terrace of cottages painted cream, the dark blue of four front doors exactly matching the blue surround of the windows. A large pane of glass replaced part of the roof in the middle of the terrace. She noticed the three horseshoes on the wall – this was where the teenage Gillian had been photographed.

Craigo pumped the horn gently.

The dog started barking very loudly, hackles up, interspersing bouts of noise with glancing at the front door of the nearest house, wanting his master to appear and give him permission to sort the intruders out. Caplan and Craigo stayed exactly where they were. Warrant cards at the ready, they waited, watching the blue snake of the Sound to their left, the grey smoke swirling from the chimney of the house to their right. Caplan noted two other smaller cars tucked round behind the old Land Rover, a red Corsa and a white Stepway. At the front, there was no garden, just the occasional flowerpot and a few tubs scattered here and there on an area of grey flattened stones. Old white garden furniture was tied down to protect it from the constant wind. The drystane dyke in front of the house was incomplete. An old, abandoned doocot was overgrown by hardy weeds.

The dog was still barking. The front door opened and a tall man in oily jeans and faded sweatshirt appeared, his tanned thin face framed by long scraggly black hair. He was followed by two springer spaniels; a grey speckled one running around, the other limping badly, the white feathering on its legs blending with a muddy bandage on its front paw. Caplan told Craigo to show his warrant card at the side window. The man gave it a look as if he was going to get a gun and chase them from the premises, then waved to say *Wait until I get the dogs in.*

As Caplan unclipped her seat belt, Craigo said, 'According to the council records, Gillian's mum lives in the first house, the grandad and her brother Rowan live in the other bits. Rowan married the McCleary girl. I think that might be her father, Duguid. The two families grew up here, the girl next door marrying the boy next door, nice when that happens.'

'This is the guy who now lives with Miranda? Is there not much on the TV up here?' whispered Caplan, as the man clicked his fingers at the German shepherd, who immediately trotted off after him round the corner of the house, leaving the two spaniels at the front, sniffing.

'You tend to forget about Rowan, Gillian's brother. He was that bit older, more mature, but he was right there at all the tragedies. He's been so supportive of her and his mum, easy to forget that he was, in the scheme of things, just a lad himself. He's lost two wee sisters, then his dad and his sister by separation. He's never said a word against her.'

'Does he work?' Caplan asked, looking around. There wasn't much evidence of a steady income, everything looked jaded and worn.

Craigo looked out the driver's window, searching for the answer on the drifting clouds. 'How old would he be now? He went to school with my cousin's daughter, so he'd be what? Twenty-two, or twenty-three or . . .'

'He's married, old enough for that.'

Craigo scratched his head in that annoying Stan Laurel way, then took off his glasses and started cleaning them.

'Where's the nearest unrelated human being?' asked Caplan, looking around the remote landscape.

'Miles away, ma'am. Bit like the place you bought.'

Maybe for very similar reasons, thought Caplan.

They waited, watching one spaniel run around like clockwork. The fatter of the two, the one with the bad leg, lay down and panted, looking up at them in case they had biscuits.

'I wonder what they're doing while he pretends to put the dog away? Hiding the remnants of their human sacrifice?'

Craigo glanced at his watch. 'Bit early for that, ma'am.'

'What happened to Gillian's dad? Had a breakdown and left?'

'Yes, rumour was he ran off with another woman but he just ran off, had enough. And Duguid lost his wife. What was she called now, Mrs McCleary? She was very badly hurt in an incident up here, died from her wounds, right there where the doocot is. Finola? Fiona I think.'

'And Rowan married her daughter, Gail? Was Gillian at home at that time?' whispered Caplan, the chilling words of the blog floating into her head. 'Should we be whistling the theme tune to *Deliverance*?'

'Oh, very good, ma'am,' said Craigo, 'not the first time that's been said, but it's too easy to put blame when sometimes bad things just happen. The McCleary guy's a mechanic. John Deere, that's a dangerous job. He usually works onsite but he brings the odd thing here, faulty machines lying all over the place. Here's the man now.'

The tall man was back, stooping as he came towards them to look in the side window of the car. His hands were black with oil. He must have been working on a machine when interrupted. He had the smiley eyes of a Billy Connolly lookalike. He could have been the brother with a wise face or Gail's father blessed with good genes.

The look on his face drifted from greetings to suspicion.

'Can I see the warrant cards again? We don't like journalists here,' he asked, putting his hand out.

Craigo opened the door, judging that the spaniels posed no threat. One was sniffing around, nose to the ground and following a scent, grunting. The fatter one with the bandage was lying in a puddle.

The man examined both warrant cards carefully then regarded each one of them, taking in their features. He was polite, educated, and certainly spoke much slower than the average west-coaster.

'We're not journalists obviously. There's nothing to be concerned about,' said Caplan getting out the Hilux, stepping in front of Craigo, drawing the eyes of the man. 'DCI Caplan, and this is Detective Sergeant Craigo, here to see Miranda Halliday.'

'Duguid McCleary,' he introduced himself. 'Ignore the dogs. Miranda?' He made a quick nodding movement of his head. 'She's ben the house.'

'We need a word about Gillian? After the incident ten days ago we're checking up on her welfare.'

He shook his head. 'That concerned? Should've been here nine days ago.'

'Believe me if I'd known we would've been, but the police are like the secret service these days. Getting information from the moon is easier. Do you know where Gillian is, Mr McCleary?' Caplan asked casually. 'Her hand needs medical attention, she needs to contact her support-worker.'

'We spoke . . .' He nodded in understanding rather than answering the question, walking towards the house, his long stride causing Craigo to jog. 'She's okay. Nasty burn on her hand. A sore leg, all that blood seeping out. She's moved on, she'll have a life of moving on, that one.' When he approached his own front door, he called out, 'Miranda? The polis. Again!' he added, with a wry look over his shoulder.

A voice shouted from somewhere deep in the house, bouncing off the narrow hall. Duguid tilted his head, saying *Follow me* and Caplan stepped into the darkness. The floors were uneven, the house oddly jointed together, with doors plastered over, walls that stopped, changes in ceiling height for no apparent reason. The air smelled of damp and fried bacon with a top note of fresh baking. One dog bumped them on the back of the legs as it trotted past, the other limping quickly to source the good smells.

At the end of the passage was a sudden sharp turn to the left leading to a conservatory which served as sitting room, dining room and drying room from the amount of clothes on the racks at the radiator, a pile of dry laundry on the end of the sofa. Caplan spotted the baby clothes straight away, confirming what she had seen in the back of the Land Rover as it passed.

Gillian's second victim had been eleven months old. She wondered how old this baby was. By the conservatory door she saw a wooden plaque that signposted 'The Fairy Garden', and followed the arrow to look out onto a beautiful lawn with well-tended shrubs, fairy-lights hanging from the trees, a picnic table and a barbeque. It must have been the only flat bit of land for miles.

Miranda Halliday came into the room, rather harassed and ruffled, looking older than her forty-two years. The light-brown hair tucked behind her ears needed a good cut, she was wearing jeans and a fleece a few sizes too big for her. She was a big-boned woman, but the cut of the clothes and her sunken cheeks suggested a sudden and recent weight-loss.

She said hello nervously, a couple of cups dangling from her hooked finger destined for the kitchen, then apologised for the fact that they had been late back from their appointment, as if there'd been some pre-arrangement between them.

Or had they been expected?

Miranda offered them tea and cake, explaining that they'd finished a cuppa, and then nervously added, 'Or is it not that kind of visit?'

Caplan was about to open her mouth but Craigo got in first, saying that a cuppa would be very nice as he was parched with the drive up here.

Miranda looked round, 'I'll take them through there, Duguid, can you put the kettle back on. The shortbread is out the oven.'

They were ushered through to a small wooden structure with three walls of glass. The air was immediately fresher in here, scented with the peppery aroma of tomato plants from the previous summer and a more recent odour of plastic table covers.

They chatted a little, Craigo making a fuss of Ollie, the fatter of the two spaniels, asking if they were gun dogs or not.

'My dad tries to work them,' Miranda said curtly.

Caplan was on the point of butting in to ask about Grandpa, then noticed that Miranda, lovely and welcoming as she was, had become uncomfortable; a slight look of nervousness settled on her features.

'You're here to talk about Gillian?' she asked.

'Yes, we are. We're concerned about her welfare.'

'Oh, God yes, I've had a lifetime worrying about her.'

'When did you last hear from her?'

'What day are we today? Sunday? No, Monday. It must have been Thursday when I last spoke to her on the phone. She had discharged herself from the hospital, against the doctors' wishes. She left and found somewhere to go.'

'Where?'

'She didn't tell us that exactly.'

'Miranda, do you know what an Osman notice is?'

'No, I don't.' The skin round the light blue eyes creased up, the worry was immediate.

'Well, we have one for you. It means that while you're well aware of what your daughter has done, and why she's been incarcerated for the last few years, we feel we need to tell you now that because of recent events, the fire, she could be very stressed and a violent episode could be triggered. There's a small chance she could be a danger to yourselves and your family if you do not distance yourself from her until she's been assessed and given the support required. If she tries to contact you again, you must inform us. For her safety as well as yours. Those that set fire to her house were serious.'

Miranda seemed to deflate. 'Oh no. They'd been pleased with her progress at Rettie. She was doing well, mature enough to take on board everything that has happened in her life. She was well enough to move on.' She paused a moment. 'We knew she'd been in Dumfries but we never visited her there. We knew her flat was near the river, she likes living where she can see water.' Miranda slid the palm of one hand slowly over another, looking down at them. Then she said, talking to herself more than anything else, 'Gillian was the victim here. Somebody tried to kill her. You should be after the people who set that fire, not her. If she's hiding, she's hiding because she's scared.'

Caplan took a deep breath. 'And rightly so, she needs protection. She has to get in touch with her support-worker while the police in Dumfries are investigating the arson. We need to know if Gillian's okay. How are her injuries? Her welfare is our concern, Mrs Halliday. Her case-worker, advocacy-worker and support-worker have heard nothing.'

Miranda looked at the door, grateful when Duguid appeared with a single mug of coffee and handed it to Craigo.

'What if I remind her to call them, the next time she phones us?'

Craigo took a loud slurp of his coffee. 'That's great.'

'So remind me of your name?' Duguid sat down next to Miranda.

'DCI Caplan, Christine.'

'Gillian's done everything asked of her through her day release. She's gone on the run to get away from whoever's after her. You can understand that.'

'I do. Can I ask you both, do you know who Killagal is?'

'Who?' they both asked, glancing at each other with uncertainty.

Caplan knew it was the first truly honest thing they had said. Everything else was a little evasive. Mackie had said how supportive Miranda and her partner were. They wouldn't desert Gillian now. She looked around. On the old dresser was a haphazard arrangement of small plants, seedlings, dried flowers and photographs, some of very young children. On the wall were four very detailed charcoal drawings of crows, the same style as the picture of the bridge. From the progression of the photographs over the years, only two of the kids had grown to school age. After that, they were all of a handsome boy, fair hair, serious eyes but a broad smile when he chose to use it. A small photograph showed three kids aged ten or thereabouts, piled on top of a stack of logs; two girls and a boy. One of them was a younger version of the teenager in the photograph Linden had showed her. The older girl, laughing, was slighter, with large blue eyes and long fair hair that dropped over her shoulders. Caplan thought they were the same eyes, saddened now, that had gazed out the window of the Land Rover.

Caplan couldn't imagine staying in a house where one of her children had been killed by another. But maybe the house was too infamous and they couldn't sell it. What was the point of moving away, the heartache couldn't be left behind.

Miranda saw where she was looking.

'Do you think it odd that I have pictures of them all?'

'Not at all,' Caplan smiled, 'I can't imagine being in your shoes, what you must have gone through in these last ten years or so.'

'The seventh of July 2011 is etched into my head as the day the world changed.'

Miranda sat back into the settee, moving her wet hat which had been drying on the arm, and began talking with Craigo, who was sipping his coffee, talking about the cost of oil and how lucky they were as they had plenty of matured wood in the store, more chopped to be kept until it was ready.

Craigo was asking if they ever caught anybody stealing it, the price of gas and electricity these days.

She rolled her eyes. 'God help them if they did, the way Granda carries on.'

'Granda?' asked Caplan, 'Is he out at the moment? I thought I saw somebody with a gun?'

'He could be. There was an accident down on the main road, one deer was killed outright, a stag was hit a glancing blow. It's out there suffering. If they don't shoot it, it'll drop and die a terrible death.' She paused, remembering who she was talking to. 'We've a gun cupboard and all the right licences.'

'I'm sure you have.'

'We stick to the rules.' There was a little snap in her voice; Caplan had touched a bit of a nerve.

She made a mental note, then attempted to bring the conversation round to *Did your Gillian really slit your other daughter's throat?* But couldn't find a way of doing it gently.

'Do you get a lot of journalists and weirdos around here looking for Gillian?' asked Craigo.

Caplan almost choked but Miranda took the question as an acknowledgement of some of the difficulties that she had faced in the last few years.

'Not much now. But at first, yes, it was awful. We closed the bottom of the road with a boulder. They had to walk all that way if they wanted any juicy pictures. But they didn't really know who they were looking for. It was all gossip and mirrors. Rowan had a terrible time. I have to say that the authorities have been very good at protecting Gillian, and protecting us as a family. Our family liaison officer still keeps in touch. We get a Christmas card from her.'

'In touch with you or with Gillian?'

'With me. I think that Gillian's trying to shrug off her old life. She's eighteen, she's having her teenage rebellion a bit late. Maybe that's why she's not been in touch with her support-worker.'

'I just hope she hasn't come to any harm,' said Caplan.

'She's fine,' said Miranda with certainty. She glanced up to the photograph on the wall, the three of them on the log pile. 'She's a lovely girl, quiet and unassuming. We had no idea of the anger issues that were going on underneath. Don't know what we could've done about it if we'd known. But she's outgrowing us, she has to move on.'

'Does the name Edward Maxwell mean anything to you?'

'He was found dead in the Falls, wasn't he? But no, I didn't know him.' Miranda's voice faded a little. McCleary visibly braced himself.

'You've heard the name though?'

'Of course.'

'Some people have thought that because Gillian's whereabouts are unknown, and that man was found dead up here, there might be a connection.'

'There's not,' said McCleary, his hand resting on Miranda's shoulder.

'You seem very sure about that?' said Caplan.

Miranda looked away but McCleary looked directly at Caplan, a slight challenge in his eyes. 'We are.'

Caplan asked, rather coldly, fed up with being messed around, 'Who all lives here now? Are there three cottages?'

'Yes, but they all interconnect, so one house now, with a communal hall that runs along the back. It was outdoors in the old days but was boxed in years ago. There's me, Miranda here, then Rowan and Gail in the end, with Alice. She's a year old next week,' said Duguid. 'And Granda.'

'And you have no idea where Gillian is now?'

Duguid was silent, Miranda's eyes drifting off to the corner of the room, considering the answer to what should be a simple query. 'It doesn't matter how many times you ask that question. No, I do not know where she is at the moment.'

'Miranda, when people are scared they run for the familiar. Under the Tollen Protocol, we're not allowed to know where that might be in Gillian's case. But it took me, a Glaswegian, less than five hours to work out where you were. It might take somebody not encumbered by officialdom even less. There's a threat to your daughter's welfare, you only need to look at the mood of social media. There's no tolerance, it's the Wild West. She is hated.'

Miranda looked up, hearing footsteps come along the long hall.

The door opened, and a slightly plump young woman came in holding a baby. She looked out of place, dressed in a neat dark skirt, white blouse and ballet pumps.

'Sorry, whose big red truck is that? I need to go out.'

'These are the police, asking about Gillian. This is our daughter-in-law, Gail, with wee Alice,' said Miranda. It was Craigo who stood up and looked at the baby, making little cooing noises, stroking her face with his forefinger, as Miranda looked on with grandparental pride.

'She's lovely.'

'So, what do you want?' asked Gail, rubbing her right eye which looked red and sore.

Caplan wondered if she had been crying. 'Welfare check, worried about Gillian, worried that the fire at her flat might have provoked something. Her mental health isn't strong. And of course, anything that happens round here is going to spark rumours.' Caplan smiled.

Gail bounced the baby a little. Caplan stood up, ready to leave, but Gail said, 'Have you been up here before, this high?'

'You must get some lovely views, I saw the pane of glass from outside,' said Craigo. 'You've bought a place a bit further north for the view, haven't you, ma'am.'

'Talking about taking most of the wall out to put in glass,' added Caplan.

Miranda seemed confused by the change of conversation, but Gail happily handed the baby over to Craigo and said, 'Really? Pop upstairs for a minute and I'll show you what my very clever dad did.' She beamed a smile at her father, who nodded graciously. This was obviously a 'something'. 'Come this way.'

Gail set off via the long hall at the back of the cottages. 'Sorry for the state of me, bloody worn out with the baby, worried about all this with Gill. Hence the eye infection, sinuses,' she sniffed. 'Just back from the opticians. Come up here, there's a great view from the top of the stairs at our end.' Gail's fair ponytail bobbed as she walked quickly past an old exterior door with a fresh lock on it, then up a double-turn stairway carpeted in dark blue, a pram parked at the bottom.

They climbed the creaking, twisted stairs, not an easy task to manage a baby up and down. A small corner table sat on the first turn with an electric candle releasing scented vapour into the air.

Clary sage? The scent was an ineffective panacea for the pervasive smell of damp in the rest of the property.

'Is this what you were thinking of, for your house?'

The upper landing had been opened out and a single pane of glass replaced the wall to maximise the view. From the ceiling, an old light with a biplane shade banked slightly with the draught. Even in this murky weather, with the sky outside a churning, ever-changing palette of greys, it was breathtaking. Out to the west were the rolling hills. Then the vast expanse of water narrowing to a dark inconsistent line where the currents met. The Falls of Lora. Above them spanned the Connel Bridge. Caplan looked and took a mental snapshot.

It was the view from Gillian's drawing. As she looked at it, Gail rubbed at her eye and Caplan recognised other smells that mingled on the landing: Napisan, fabric conditioner and, she thought, cigarette smoke.

'That is truly breathtaking.'

'It's wonderful on a clear day but even on a day like this, well, you can see why I never ever want to leave this place. Gillian sat here and drew it many times. It was always her thing, drawing.' Gail took a breath then turned to Caplan. 'You are the police, right?' She stepped closer; her large eyes with their long luxurious lashes framing bright blue irises made her look like a child, a tired, exhausted child, highlighted by the redness of her right eye. She frowned, leaning forward, ready to say something quietly into Caplan's ear, but took a step back swiftly as they heard footsteps at the bottom of the stairs.

It was McCleary. 'Gail? Come down. Alice's playing up.'

It wasn't a request. Gail shot her a quick smile, and turned to go down the stairs. Caplan took a last look at the view, a quick glance around at a closed door to her right. It was partially concealed by a half-drawn curtain. Below it she saw a small line of sawdust at the skirting board, where the vacuum cleaner could not reach. Another, slightly open, door revealed the edge of a bath. A third had a Yale lock on it, the corner of a desk and computer monitor just visible, an Excel sheet on the screen. A fourth was open revealing a double bed in a cream ironed bedspread, a cot right at the bedside.

At that moment Alice started to scream.

*　　*　　*

They got into the Hilux but as Craigo turned the ignition key, the engine coughed and failed to catch. Then spluttered. Dead.

'Oh, please God no,' muttered Caplan as Craigo turned the key again and got the same result. 'Don't look round but McCleary has let that bloody dog out again. I'm not getting savaged because your car won't start.'

'It's been playing up, that's why I parked it this way round.' He let off the handbrake, and the vehicle began to roll silently off the tarmac platform down the hill. Craigo slipped it into second and then released the clutch. The Hilux bumped, then the engine caught, and they were now going down the steep slope using the engine as a brake.

Caplan looked behind them. McCleary was standing straight-legged, hands on his hips like John Wayne, the three dogs behind him, watching them go. She glanced at the huge picture window; Gail was there holding Alice on her hip, one hand on the windowpane.

'Where do you think Gillian is?'

'Me, ma'am?'

'Nobody else here, is there?'

'Well, it's all about the fat spaniel.'

'It is?'

'Yes. A fat springer spaniel. Do you think the liver-and-white one was at the vet recently getting a burnt paw treated? Two of the dogs here are very fit. That dog has only been here a short time or it wouldn't be so fat. That poor thing has never had a decent walk in its life.'

'I noticed it unnerved Miranda when you asked about the dogs.'

'They weren't honest with us.'

Caplan held on to the seat belt as the vehicle began to bounce. 'Yes, I know that. You think she's here, don't you?'

'We should check to see if the dog was picked up and brought back here.'

'If she's here, we need to take her into some kind of custody. If there's one iota of a scrap of evidence between her and Ted Maxwell, we need to find that. We can't move forward without good evidence. And Gail was definitely trying to say something to me before Duguid appeared. Asking about the Hilux, saying she wanted to go out? Living in the wild makes you plan your journeys and she'd just come in.'

They sat in silence.

'They've a gun.' Caplan looked out into the deep dark woods. 'Do you think it's safe for us to go back in there?'

'If you thought that, ma'am, you wouldn't have asked.'

FOURTEEN

It was a bit spur of the moment to use the train.
It was all about the timing. I saw the driver's face then waved.
That was that.
Looking left, nothing.
Looking right, hardly anything but a few fragments of her
    dress, and some wet, red patches on the rails.
And her head.

Killagal Blog, 2022

Back at the station, Caplan was thinking about Ollie, the dog who'd been brought home. It was confirmed by Dumfries that he was a liver-and-white springer spaniel. The vet down there had treated one of his front paws after the fire. Was Gillian brought home as well? She felt they had to strike while the iron was hot so she hastily drafted a report, and a request for further information and for firearm support.

The answering email from Sarah Linden merely reiterated much of what Caplan already knew: that Girl A was the victim of a crime, her flat had been set on fire on the night of April Fools' Day. She had saved her dog, an act that had nearly cost her her life. Both had suffered from smoke inhalation. Girl A, as Lora Connel, was taken to hospital for oxygen and treatment to a severely burned right hand. After an overnight stay, she'd discharged herself, picked up her dog who had stayed with a neighbour, and then they both disappeared into thin air between 2 and 3 April. It was easy for a teenage girl to do that, but dogs are noticeable.

Linden had included some screenshots of messages of support taken from the Killagal site, with Linden's strongly expressed opinion that there were some real sickos out there. Also attached was a more recent picture of Gillian, maybe as she had been in Dumfries. It was a bad photograph, but Linden had thought it might be of interest. Gillian had a look that would struggle to go unnoticed: Goth-plus. Lots of black eye-liner, dramatic make-up, wide black trousers, red ripped t-shirt, her black hair teased up like she'd put her finger in a socket. She wore Doc Martens, and some sort of robe draped over her back, and she was sitting on a single seat, like a queen on her throne. Except that her legs were wide open, and she was leaning forward, glaring into the camera, a cigarette hanging from the corner of her black mouth. Everything about her was vaguely threatening.

Caplan looked closely at the image, thinking how that outline would look, the spiky hair and a thick coat. Was this Bev's monkey? She closed it down, wondering who took the picture. Nobody lived in a bubble these days.

Was Gillian up at Ben o' Tae? The description of the dog matched. She loved her dog. And where else in this world would she go? Who would have her in their house? How safe was Alice? Was that what Gail was going to say? It was possible that Gillian Halliday had killed three children, one by drowning, one by slicing her throat and one by pushing her in front of a train. Bloody hell. Caplan looked at Linden's email, the words so much more chilling written in plain black and white. Her blood ran cold. If it was a man, she'd have no hesitation, so why when it was a teenage girl? Surely murder was murder. But her job, as she had been detailed to do it, was a duty of care. Caplan sat in silence, considering the darkening presence of Gillian Halliday, the awful crimes laid at the feet of one so young. Gillian was entitled to her privacy. Except for that excerpt from the blog where she sounded proud of what she had done, moaning about how hard it was to hold some-body's head under water until they could breathe no more. 'Drowning bastards is hard fucking work.' Gillian was right, it took time. A slit throat might be a spur of the moment action, a young kid with a knife, sleepwalking, or getting a fright when wakening up, lashing out. But not drowning. Carrying a knife to a bridge for a prearranged meeting to fatally stab the victim took planning. And looking at the picture, here was Gillian, a young woman making herself look as unattractive as possible, keeping people at bay. She might be responsible for *four* deaths. Rachel Mary, Rachel Susan,

Poppy Anstruther and Dr Edward Maxwell. Oh yes, the person who struck the match to set fire to her flat, starting a blaze that nearly killed her, had an understandable point of view. Wrong of course, but it was understandable.

Caplan was now faced with engaging a firearms team on the evidence of a fat young spaniel with a sore paw, and the worried expression of a young mother looking out a window. That was going to be a hard sell. Then she remembered the photograph she had of the old man pointing the shotgun at her.

She hadn't called for armed back-up the night the Devil Stone case closed. That hadn't ended well. That would be another argument: by the time you realised you needed back-up, it was too late.

Her phone rang. She was wanted downstairs. Probably Marie Harris wanting to know if her husband could have his job back.

Caplan came into the reception area to see Mattie Jackson with his jacket on ready to go, but his hands were in his pockets, his small rucksack casually over his arm. He was chatting to a younger man; everything about him, his hair, the red woollen jumper, the collar of the denim shirt curled over the top of the crew neck, his neatly trimmed beard, whispered precision.

It was Jackson who spoke. 'This is DCI Caplan, she was up at your house with Finnan, Finnan Craigo. Do you know him?'

The younger man shook his head, a small movement that didn't disturb his chiselled features. His doe eyes and delicate nose were beautifully sculpted. The beard and moustache, minimal hipster, framed a thin-lipped mouth that looked rather mean compared to the rest of his face. To Caplan, he looked like a Shakespearean romantic hero, the one that died when he got the right girl. He was concerned but guarded.

'Rowan?' asked Caplan, 'Rowan Halliday?'

'Yes.' A smile, his right hand raised to hitch the shoulder of his sweater up higher, towards his neck. He dropped his arm then stretched out a hand, soft and warm as Caplan shook it.

They went through the secure door into the informal interview room.

'Please have a seat. Thank you for coming to see us but I don't think we requested you to pop in.'

'Yet.' He gave a short sharp smile, hard on his lips but his eyes remained easy. 'You'd have come to see me sooner or later, and I didn't want you arriving at work. I've had enough of that over the years.' He sat down, placed the palms of his hands flat on the table. 'So, I came to you before you got to me, just so you can ask me the hundred questions I've been asked before, then you can leave me and my family alone.'

'After we have made sure no harm has come to Gillian. And that no harm will come to her moving forward.'

'Apart from the burns, she's fine. She's free now to live as she wants, she's not an escaped convict like social media seem to believe, and most of that is sparked by the way you guys behave whenever she breathes. She gets attacked, you are up at the house, and Mum's phoning me at work. You need to back off.' He took a long breath, slowly letting it out. 'It's a merry-go-round.'

'You work at the Coffee Café?'

'My colleagues know that Gillian is not the main talking point of my life now. As you know, my sister's identity is protected but as soon as the police appear at the shop, we've every TikTok wannabe influencer and true-crime podcaster coming in and sitting for two hours nursing a coffee, to have a look at me and try to find a new angle. I love my sister dearly but there're a lot of wankers out there.' He put his hand over his mouth. 'Sorry.'

'There's a few in here as well.' Caplan sat down. 'Gillian left hospital between the second and the third of April. Do you know where she has been since then?' She waited, forcing him to look away. 'You can tell me the truth.'

'Of course. I feel I can't trust Duguid to get the story straight. Ollie, her dog, got hurt in the fire. Gillian went to hospital, and Ollie went to some neighbours, but Gillian doesn't do friends. You'll see that when you meet her. When the neighbours said they couldn't keep him any more, Gillian walked – well, limped – out the hospital, collected Ollie. Gail drove down to pick them up and brought them to Ben o' Tae.'

'A woman with a young baby, your daughter, was happy about Gillian being in the house?'

Rowan shook his head. 'Gail was trying to keep everybody happy. I think she wanted to gauge Gillian's mood. Gail's as much her big sister as I'm her big brother. I think Mum hoped Gillian was going to stay but it was only one night, and then she left.

She's been in touch, but we don't know where she is. She's used to people not knowing where she is. Look at the arson.'

'She left hospital on the evening of the second of April. She spent the evening of Monday the fourth with you?'

Rowan pursed his lips, then nodded his head. 'Gillian's odd. She's my sister and I love her, but she's not normal, as you know. She left at some point during the night. She was gone by breakfast.'

'Gone? How?'

Halliday shrugged. 'She's always been nocturnal. You'll see that from her history. She's learned to be secretive. She says as little as possible.'

'Were you happy to have her back?'

'We're not scared of her.'

'She killed your two wee sisters?'

He flinched as the words hurt him. 'I know. Gail said that she'd leave me and take Alice if Gillian stayed. She was only half-joking. I think,' he added, the charming smile again.

'Was she?'

Another smile, the blue eyes crinkled. 'We agreed to put locks on the outside of the door. Gillian was locked in at night. Gail was content with that, and we both knew that it'd be better if Gillian moved on, better for her to be away from Cronchie.'

'Better if she stayed away from her keyboard,' muttered Caplan.

'Do you know anything about a new book that's coming out about—' Rowan made inverted commas with his fingertips '—"Britain's Most Evil"?'

Caplan's face remained impassive. 'Nothing that we've come across. What have you heard?'

'Just a rumour, folk asking questions. It raises the stakes against Gillian having a quiet life. People making money from her illness, it wreaks havoc on us. We had people up at Ben o' Tae, taking photos with their phones through the window.' He rubbed his face with his hands. 'And now Granda walks about with a shotgun.'

'He pointed it at me.'

'Sorry about that. I hope he didn't scare you.'

'He's a brave, brave man from what I hear, quite the hero. But your sister is missing. A man has died. I'm under pressure.' It was her turn to shrug.

'She'd already left town when the man on the bridge was killed.'

'With all due respect, you've no idea where she was when the man died. As you said, she'd already left by then.'

Halliday nodded. 'Have you found any connection between the man on the bridge and Gillian?'

'Not as yet.'

Halliday hitched the shoulder of his jumper up again, his little tell. 'He came by the café on Friday afternoon, the man on the bridge. He was one of the folk asking questions.'

Caplan was grateful for her poker face. 'Why did you not tell us before?'

'I'm here now.' His doe eyes could be beguiling. 'It was only when his picture was in the paper that Sean, my boss, said he was the guy who had been in asking about me. I wasn't there, I was at the cash-and-carry. Sean told him that I didn't work there any more. The guy had a cup of coffee and left.'

'Did he leave a card or anything?'

'Not that I know.'

Caplan nodded. 'Rowan, do you know where your sister is?'

'I know how she is. She's okay, that's why Gail called me to let me know that you had been up at the house.' He shook his head, 'Well, she was returning my call as I'd left a message to see if she wanted anything brought home from the chemist for her eye. Gail said that you guys had paid a visit, that you were looking for Gillian. I think she suspects that I've been in contact with my sister more than I've told her and she's right.' He shrugged, the beautiful nose twitched slightly. He was almost pretty; the features that should have gone to his sister were wasted on this face. 'Gail didn't sleep at all the night that Gillian was in the house.'

He put his hand into his pocket, pulled out a mobile phone, not state-of-the-art. They had a new baby, Gail was the breadwinner, they still lived in the parental home. His jumper was good quality but well worn. He turned the phone to her.

'There you go, lots of text messages back and forth. Gillian's well. She got a bit of a shock with the fire. Gail thinks that Gill might have said something on that stupid blog thing she does, you know, given too much away.'

'How does she know about that?' asked Caplan.

'Gill told her,' Rowan responded, as if the answer had been obvious.

'Whose phone is that? Her mobile has been silent since she left hospital.'

'It's an old one of mine. She ditched hers. She's put this one off as well now.' He shrugged. 'She said she'd found a place to stay where nobody would find her. If you're concerned for her safety, the best thing you can do is leave her alone. The media will get a hold of her whereabouts if you don't. And while it's unlawful for them to say anything that identifies who she was then, they don't care. She's mentally fragile and social media is toxic.'

'And if I think that she might be guilty of causing Ted Maxwell's death?'

'Well, you're the detective. You need to find out where she is. Look what happened when they found out she was in Dumfries. Forgive my reticence in not telling you more. Gillian knows how this works, she keeps us out the loop. She only came to us because of the dog. Please respect our privacy because once that door is opened, any bloody journalist can get in. I don't want them, or podcasters or media influencers up at Ben o' Tae. So please . . .' He arched his eyebrows, pleading. Then nodded his farewell, got up and left, closing the door quietly behind him. Caplan, still thinking what an attractive young lady he would have made, heard a brief conversation between Halliday and Jackson outside, their voices fading.

She looked at the closed door, thinking about Rowan, wondering how bright he had been at school. He worked in the Coffee Café; it was Gail who had the career. They were a strange breed up at Ben o' Tae, the earth-mother, the father, having no joint kids but looking after each other. The son marrying the daughter, the grandchild. The grandad. One mother dead, one father away, the other daughter incarcerated. It had all been very neat.

The image that came to mind was one of shedding skin; they had shed the other family members like an unwanted hide. Gillian had bounced back, been sent away, then bounced back again. She thought of the way Halliday and Jackson had been exchanging pleasantries before and after Halliday had spoken to her; maybe Jackson went to that café for his caffeine fix.

Instead of the family being pulled apart by Gillian's actions, they had closed ranks. Her dad couldn't live with what she had done. There should be four Halliday children; Rachel Mary and Rachel Susan had gone before they had a chance to grow up.

Gillian had been removed. The family dynamic was odd to put it mildly. Caplan made a mental note to get Mackie to look into it.

It was all something or nothing, but it could have been Gillian on that bridge. If they proved that, then it would be case closed, and it would all start to unravel back to where it started with Rachel Mary at Church's Pass. Piggy on the railway . . .

FIFTEEN

Puppies appear cute.
Not so cute when their brains have been blown to pieces.
Whit a mess.
It bit me so what did the wee fucker expect.

Killagal Blog, 2021

Caplan quickly wrote up the report that Rowan Halliday had given a voluntary statement to the effect that Gillian had moved on. She ruminated on that as she typed. Gillian had grown up at Ben o' Tae, it was the one place that she'd think of as safe. Her dog was there. Gillian had been thinking about the view out that top window, thinking about home maybe, knowing a release date was coming. Gail had seemed keen to show Caplan that, she'd tried to tell her something. And the image of the young mother at the window, her palm flat to the glass, clutching her baby, her sad eyes watching them as they silently rolled away. What dynamics were at work there? Gail with the precious Alice. Miranda playing happy families with another baby to dote on?

Medically, Gillian was ill when she committed those crimes. *What would you do if it had been your Emma?* Craigo had asked her in the Hilux as they came down the hill. He'd looked over at her with those sandy-coloured eyes that could look cold and calculating. They'd been fixed on her then, like a feral animal sensing prey.

Caplan thought about the cigarette smoke, the way Gail had led them upstairs, the way McCleary had called them back down again.

Maybe there was a reason they could say so definitely that Gillian wasn't on the bridge, because they knew exactly where she was. They needed to return. She'd taken advice from Rettie. Anna Scafoli, the case-worker, had offered to come along and talk to Gillian if she was found on the premises.

She got to her feet, lifting a stack of photographs, went through to the incident room and started pinning them on the board. The first was the smiling face of a three-year-old girl with her Sunday-best hat on. Caplan started talking, the other occupants of the room listened. '2011, Rachel Mary Halliday is fatally hit by a train at Church's Pass. Two and a half years later, Hogmanay 2013–14, eleven-month-old Rachel *Susan* Halliday – think the 'm' is before the 's' – has her throat slit. That was the year of the bad storm if you recall. For that incident, Gillian Halliday, aged nine, is sent to the Hollows residential centre. She makes good progress, is let out, then four years later, June 2017, kills Poppy Anstruther at the Sugar Loaf Camp.' Caplan banged her fist on each picture. 'Gillian Halliday, can we place her on the bridge?'

Craigo put his finger up in the air. Caplan felt like asking him if he needed the toilet.

'Good CCTV footage, ma'am, and dashcam footage from the Stevenson lorry, and Leo Greene, a local farmer, coming home late at night across the bridge.' They walked over to Craigo's monitor, Caplan wishing for the large wall-mounted screens they had back at Glasgow. 'I've put it together as much as I can. I think that's Maxwell walking towards the bridge on this CCTV camera. We don't see the other figure, but look at this, a couple of minutes further on. Maxwell's leaning on the rail almost at the midpoint of the bridge. He's relaxed, looking over the water, then here he turns as if somebody is behind him. He glances over his right shoulder, then takes a step back.'

They watched the replay, looking closely at the image. It was very clear. Ted Maxwell walked under the first camera, hands in pockets, not hurried, any rush in his step due to the weather and the chill of the night. His shoulders were slightly hunched. He didn't seem to be carrying anything.

'He's picked up again here at 0025. He's about five minutes' walk from the bridge here.'

'So, looking at Bev's timing, he was attacked a few minutes later?'

'But Bev wasn't too sure of the time, too drunk. He got home about 0040 hours and worked out the time backwards, so what does that mean, timing wise? Maxwell walked onto the bridge and was stabbed as soon as he got there?'

Craigo raised his finger again, looking like a determined Boy Scout doing a task badge. 'We also have timed dashcam footage right here.'

McPhee pressed play. 'Here's the dashcam footage of the log truck. There's Maxwell on the bridge, 0037. What did he think he was doing? There's nothing on the log of the phone we can trace. The other was a burner. Who innocently buys a burner phone?'

'For secrecy?'

'So an affair?'

'More like patient confidentiality in this case.'

'Don't know him well enough, ma'am. But look here, a glimpse of the other person as they are caught in the headlights.'

'They?'

'This figure, large, wide, either man or woman?'

'Is it Gillian? Nothing about it says it isn't Gillian. From that clip it's very difficult to tell. We could get it cleaned up, I suppose.'

'That'll cost.'

'Well, Maxwell seems to be standing at the Cronchie side of the bridge. He's waiting beside the storage boxes.'

'Bloody roadworks,' moaned Mackie, with heartfelt emotion.

'Then Maxwell starts to walk onto the bridge and this dark shadow follows him but we can't track it. Until we see it on the road, we have no idea where it came from, or where it went.'

'Keep looking. What is it wearing? Can we blow that up a bit?'

'A long black coat. We see it in this camera here a minute before. A glimpse of the shadow as the car slows at the roundabout, then this van catches sight of it from the back. And it walks out towards Maxwell, who's now on the centre of the bridge.'

Caplan sat down, feeling her stomach tense. What was Maxwell there for? What was he expecting? He didn't look nervous, he looked relaxed, but there was something else. Caplan tried to think where that posture belonged. He was waiting, like a reception party at the airport.

'Anything we can get's good. Anything to prove it's Gillian's better than good.'

'The timeline fits, this is at 0034 hours.'

'Are they waiting for the lorry to go past?'

'I'm not being sexist, ma'am . . .' said McPhee.

'That's what every man says when they are about to say something sexist, but go on,' said Caplan.

'Was a woman capable of flinging a man like that over a bridge? I know there were roadworks, as Mackie said, she might have encouraged him to stand up on a platform to see the rolling wave, and then what? Tipped him over? Stabbed him then tipped him over? Stabbed him, held him up, then went through his pockets? It doesn't really make sense, thinking through the mechanics of it.'

There was silence in the room. Mackie pointed with her pen and opened her mouth to say something, then shut it again.

'Ryce had a theory about that, not sure it was convincing,' said Caplan.

'The figure in the dark coat was seen walking away, it has a flash of something white, maybe a bandage? You see it from the car footage three or four minutes later, but after that, no more sightings,' said McPhee. 'None at all.'

'They disappear into thin air?' asked Caplan, sitting back, the figure still on the screen. When the first frame came from the next car, Dr Edward Maxwell was gone. She rewound the video. The steel stanchions of the bridge framed the picture, the dull light created a halo around the black spiky hair. Caplan tapped the screen. 'Hello, Gillian.'

Caplan sat in the Hilux with Craigo. He was annoying her by drumming his fingers along the top of the steering wheel. They were gathering in the lay-by at the bottom of the hill, waiting for the convoy to set off up the small winding road that led to Ben o' Tae.

McFarlane, the tactical response manager, had been very efficient in putting a team together. Caplan, with very little interaction with firearms, had been surprised when McFarlane had swung into action. In her head, she had been imagining FBI and SWAT teams going through the trees, armed with assault rifles. But he said that he and his associate would accompany them up, discreetly armed, to deal with this situation as Caplan had reported that a firearm had been pointed at her. They would take it further, review the mental health of the person who held the licence ASAP, but for the moment it was softly softly. Tonka Thomson had never put a foot wrong.

She had her warrant, she had back-up. She was wearing a radio and a camera, something she'd not done for a long time. They were going to go in with two uniformed officers detailed to keep an eye on Grandad, and another two to help search the property.

In the eyes of both Craigo and Caplan it would've been better to leave it until they knew Grandad and his shotgun were elsewhere. But the image on Caplan's phone had been blown up and clarified. It did indeed show a single-barrelled shotgun, not broken, ready to fire, being pointed towards the lens of the phone camera.

And towards Caplan herself.

It was past five o'clock when the small convoy set off, Craigo constantly interrupting Caplan's thoughts by muttering the instructions they had received at the briefing over and over.

Nearing the top, she snapped and told him to shut up. In her mind, two sensible adults, Christine Caplan and Finnan Craigo, were going to look round the house of another two sensible adults, Miranda Halliday and Duguid McCleary. It was Granda and Gillian they had to be wary of, and Caplan didn't think that Gillian would be any trouble. As long as she wasn't cornered. Caplan had taken a mantra of Scafoli's to heart: be calm, be yourself, don't corner her. And never give her bullshit, she's too clever for that.

The presence of the police cars as well as the Hilux confused the German shepherd. It didn't know who to bark at. There was a brief moment of tension when McCleary appeared at the front door, popping his head out then closing it, only to emerge a few seconds later with an anorak. Again, the dog was put in his kennel, they all got out their respective vehicles.

Caplan let McPhee read the terms of the warrant out loud. McCleary looked over his shoulder at the police van with the other two officers, who remained seated but vigilant. He glanced at the Hilux, then nodded and took a step backwards.

'I'm starting upstairs,' said Caplan, moving quickly through the rabbit warren of the hall to the upstairs landing, where the candle was still scenting the air with clary sage – an aromatic oil that helped with pregnancy, and warded off evil spirits, Caplan had

read. How apt that it was situated here on the stairs. She heard
McPhee and McFarlane engage Miranda and McCleary in conversation, no raised voices, just Miranda sounding a little distressed.
McCleary comforting her. Somewhere deeper in the house, Alice
started to cry. Rowan appeared from the far side of the long hall,
casting a glance at Caplan. The doe eyes flitted to look upstairs,
the right hand hitched up the shoulder of his jumper, his tic
confirming what she already suspected, but she took her time to
look him in the eye and try to read that expression. If she had
to sum it up in one word? Relief.

Not trusting Craigo, Caplan asked McPhee to look in the three
rooms on the upper floor: the office, the bathroom and the
bedroom, adding that he might need a key for the Yale lock on
Gail's office.

Then she pulled back the curtain that concealed the fourth
door. Two new bolts were drawn back, the padlocks hanging
open with the keys still in them, the door slightly ajar. The smell
of cigarette smoke wafted out. Caplan gently knocked on the
door, and loudly introduced herself as DCI Christine Caplan from
Cronchie police, and could she have a word.

Slowly, she looked into the room. It was a riot of white and
pink, a baby's room, except for the single bed underneath the
window and a tub armchair in the corner, under the eaves. On it
sat a large woman dressed in black, her booted feet up on a stool.
Ollie the spaniel lay at her feet, chewing at a toy. The woman's
black hair was short and stuck out, gelled into spikes. Sitting on
the chair, as calm as the Buddha, she looked as round as she was
tall. The back of her left hand was covered in tattoos that proclaimed
'Fuck' and 'Hate'. If there were any tattoos on the right, they were
covered by the bandage – apparently clean, although the sweet,
sickly smell in the room told its own story. Her lips were ebony
to match her eyes; Cleopatra she was not. She had a small tusk
pierced through one eyebrow. If this was her being inconspicuous,
no wonder she had given away her location on Banned Box.

But everything about her screamed a search for identity, any
identity. She was putting herself out of the reach of normality as
that was where society had put her. She couldn't lose if she didn't
play the game.

Caplan noted that Gillian's outline, without doubt, was a dead
ringer for Bev's image of the figure on the bridge.

Gillian Halliday was no longer a child, and the world would want to know who she was.

Now she was public property.

Their eyes met.

There was a moment of stillness, then a voice said, bored with resignation, 'Well, hello, fucking arsewipes.'

SIXTEEN

Yeah yeah. Did you see that in the papers?
Two planes had a near miss?
No, they didn't. They had a near hit.
Plane crashes smell like barbeques, so I'm told.

Killagal Blog, 2022

By nine o'clock on Tuesday morning the incident room was buzzing. Everybody was typing, on the phones, planning ahead. The case had broken. Caplan, who was waiting for permission to interview Gillian once the infection in her hand was under control, rearranged the pictures on the wall, adding wedding photos of Gail and Rowan. And she pinned up a report on somnambulism, how it could be used as a predictor for a stressed mental state, for them to read.

She had phoned Cordelia the night before, both of them awake at two in the morning, offering her a police officer at her front door to keep the press away. Cordelia said they were going to stay the night with her in-laws at their holiday cottage.

True to form, McFarlane had been very efficient with his copious paperwork. Craigo had let it all pass by him. At Ben o' Tae, Caplan had been strangely touched by the way Miranda had hugged her daughter, the way Rowan had taken his sister in his arms and held on to her, as if he had let her down. The only pause was a quick conversation about Ollie's medication.

Craigo had interviewed a sobbing Miranda before passing her back to McCleary. Gail had stood in the corner with the baby, rocking her gently, Rowan in the no man's land in between. Caplan thought she could sense her relief. How concerned had she been about the safety of her child, how much did she feel she could say in that house? To her husband?

It was Gillian's response that had puzzled Caplan. Nothing. A mere shrug of the shoulders. She didn't shout, scream or protest her innocence. She had walked out to the police car and got in, no resistance at all.

The atmosphere was good when Caplan started the briefing.

'Thank you, everybody who was involved last night.' There was a good-natured round of applause that Craigo took, nodding in appreciation.

Caplan ignored him.

'Now the work starts. Gillian spent the night in hospital. They'll give us the all-clear as to when I can interview her. There'll be a psych assessment obviously. But after all the excitement, what now? A huge sense of relief, that she's safe and everybody else is safe. Now we've to get a body of evidence together that will put the identity of the person who stabbed Edward Maxwell beyond all reasonable doubt.'

'Should she have been let out at all?' asked McPhee. 'That's another shit-show we might have coming our way. Maybe Soupy's investigation did the right thing – just pass it on for the Fiscal and mental-health services to argue over.'

'Maybe somebody in her care team foresaw this,' Caplan said, 'but were powerless to stop it. Hindsight is always precise. But in the end, Gillian's safe and was apprehended with minimum fuss. There'll be a statement for the media, something to keep them at arm's length.'

'How did she address you when you went in the room?' asked Mackie, knowing the answer.

'Miss Halliday took a deep draw of her cigarette, released it slowly through her nostrils and greeted myself and the two accompanying officers with "Hello, fucking arsewipes".' Caplan allowed them to have a giggle at that. 'I've spoken to Miranda and Cordelia already today. Be aware of the emotional, legal and medical tightrope we are on here.'

At the hospital, Caplan straightened her jacket, ready to talk to Gillian. ACC Linden had been delighted about the result of the 'operation'. Caplan had smiled at the terminology. All they had

done was walk through a house and up the stairs to a bedroom
door with two locks on it. McPhee had pulled back the curtain,
the door hadn't even been closed, Caplan had knocked on it out
of politeness, and walked into the room.

Linden was preparing a press conference in Glasgow, keeping
a physical distance from the story. That would hold the media off
for a while, as the lawyers disagreed over who was allowed to
know what, and whether Gillian warranted protective custody.

Caplan thought of the two dead sisters. The mental-health team
at the hospital had said Gillian was a self-harm risk but could
be interviewed with caution. Caplan was trying hard, if not to be
neutral, then at least to try to understand. That could be Emma,
her own child sitting there. The hunter was now the hunted,
the law was the law.

Craigo was as ready as he ever was. Caplan had her job to do.
And Ted Maxwell was dead. She had to forget that Gillian might
have carried out her first kill aged six or seven. More to be pitied
than scorned. But that did not make Ted Maxwell less dead,
Cordelia less a widow, Sebastian and Troy less orphans.

Five minutes later they were at Gillian's hospital bed. A plain-
clothes officer sat outside, reading a computer magazine. Gillian
had been offered and refused to have a responsible person
with her. She had also been offered and refused a lawyer. As far
as she was concerned, she had done 'fuck all'.

Caplan knew this was the game. And to Gillian it was a game
she'd played all her life.

But for now, she was a patient on intravenous antibiotics. This
was merely a chat, to make sure she was okay. Everything else
could wait.

It also meant that Gillian was ahead in the game.

Caplan smiled, looking at her, taking in the hair, the attitude,
the Black Death t-shirt.

Gillian saw her look and sneered, 'Are you gay? Do you fancy
me? If you do, fuck off.'

'No on both counts.'

'Are you shagging yer wee chimpanzee?' Gillian tilted her spiky
head at Craigo.

'Again, my answer is in the negative but just cut the crap,
Gillian. You need our help or you're dead by the end of the
month; you are still Britain's most hated woman. People would

have celebrated if you'd been toasted in that fire. Do you understand that?'

'Are you allowed to say that to me?'

'I thought I just did.'

'I'm not thick but what's your point?'

'Well, I for one don't really give a shit but I have a whole load of paperwork to do. So we're going to have a very brief conversation about what happened on Friday eighth, the night that Dr Edward Maxwell met his death.'

'I was fucking pole-dancing, wasn't I.'

'One-handed?'

'Fucking talented, me.'

Caplan sighed. 'What were you doing, where were you?'

'I was at home. I don't have a fucking car, do I. Can I have a fag?'

'No. This is a hospital.'

'Spent my whole fucking life in hospitals. Can I go back to Retts?'

'Nope.'

Gillian threw her substantial weight back on the bed. It creaked loudly. 'Why can't I have a fag?'

'Lots of things in life you can't have.'

'What's with the wee chimp?'

'He's the brains of the outfit,' replied Caplan impatiently; it was like talking to Kenny when he was in one of his moods. 'He's the one that says nothing but sees everything. Where were you Friday night?'

Nothing. The black-eyed Cleopatra stare.

'Please, ma'am,' asked Craigo, holding his pencil up like he was still at school, 'can I ask Gillian a question?'

'You should ask her what hairspray she uses, you could use some to stop you looking like Oor Wullie when the wind blows in the wrong direction,' said Caplan, never taking her eyes off Gillian, who was watching them carefully, second-guessing their relationship, considering her next move.

'Well, Miss Halliday?'

'Polite little fucker, isn't he?'

'I have him well trained.'

'It's about the keys, and the locks on the door, your bedroom door,' Craigo said.

'Aye.' Gillian shifted in her seat. 'What about it?'

'Well, they didn't trust you did they, your family? It was okay to have you home, but they wanted you locked up.'

'I sleepwalk.'

'Yes, I know. You were sleepwalking when you killed your little sister, Rachel . . .'

'Rachel Susan,' offered Caplan.

'Yes, thank you, ma'am,' replied Craigo.

Gillian shifted uncertainly as Craigo turned round in his seat, talking to Caplan. 'You see, ma'am, the family were rather scared of Gillian here. They still are. She's not in control of her somnambulism, sleepwalking, ma'am.'

'Yes, I know.' Caplan knew he was getting at something, she knew the signs.

'What time did they lock the door on you? One floor up at the front of the house where the land slopes away. Small windows, your bad hand, a door that was locked at night.'

Caplan turned to Craigo. 'What happened if she needed to go to the loo?'

'Oh, Miranda was very specific. The door was locked between eleven at night and seven-thirty in the morning. Maybe she peed in a bucket.'

'Oh, fuck off you two.' It was a teenage tantrum, and not a very convincing one.

'Gillian, you're in hospital, with a cop on the door. You have an ensuite, and the minute you're back at Rettie, you can have a ciggie.'

'Well,' said Craigo, right on cue, 'she won't be though, ma'am, will she? She'll be put in the mainstream prison population. That'll be a first for her.'

Caplan nodded.

'But she couldn't have done it.' Craigo looked from Caplan to Gillian and back again. 'She was locked in her room.'

Gillian smiled sweetly, 'Too fucking right, I was.'

As they left the hospital to drive back to the station, Caplan didn't know whether to strangle Craigo then, or later. But it was a point that any half decent defence council could pick up on, equally a point that indicated her own family thought that she was dangerous, and she had, against the odds, got out of the flat at Dumfries by climbing through a window and onto a roof next door.

Caplan dropped her colleague off at the station and told him, in the most sarcastic tone she could muster, that it was all worth looking into and to come back to her when he had a result. It was something that had to be explored, but it should have come up in the briefing, not in front of their main suspect.

Craigo in his defence muttered something about only realising the significance later, although Miranda had mentioned the timing of 'lock-up' when they were escorting Gillian out of Ben o' Tae.

Caplan checked her phone to see a text from Linden instructing her to go straight to the Rettie Centre for half-past eleven to attend a meeting, to 'help' them. So the ACC had got them to agree to talk, no doubt after she'd pointed out that it may be proven they had released a dangerous young woman into the community, a triple killer. Or worse.

Caplan, sensing a way of gaining more access to restricted information, texted back that similar charges could be laid at the door of Police Scotland.

A single emoji pinged back. Two fingers.

The Rettie Centre looked like an expensive clinic from the outside, mostly because of its location in the rolling hills and the attentions of a team of gardeners consisting of both staff and residents. Through a double set of locking doors, it quickly became a non-subtle mixture of hospital and prison. Everything was secure, either obviously or covertly.

It was lunchtime when Caplan and McPhee arrived, and there was 'free association' in the canteen. At a glance it was difficult to determine residents from staff; inmates from health-care professionals.

A radio chuntered quietly in the corner. There was a sense of busyness, food being prepared and served, chattering. Caplan noted a girl, early teens, staring into space, moving her mashed potato round and round with a plastic spoon.

There but for the grace of God. She had always thought that her kids were healthy; the damage to Emma's brain was still uncertain, but from their recent meeting, nearly normal . . . and Kenny, well, he just needed to get his act together.

Caplan and McPhee were eventually signed in and given lanyards to wear, which were then deftly tucked out of sight, making Caplan wonder what their purpose was. They were escorted efficiently to a blue-carpeted room which was large and airy, a light wooden table in the middle with six or seven people sitting around it. Each one with a folder in front of them, two of them with tablets. Everybody had a glass and a small pitcher of water.

Welcome to Operation Whitewash.

At the top of the table was a rather stuffy, grey-haired lady, plump-cheeked, a multi-coloured scarf decorating the top of her jacket. Mrs Deborah Blane carried an air of authority. No doubt she'd be chairperson of loads of committees, endlessly good at getting things organised.

Her presence suggested this was going to be a PR exercise.

Mrs Blane introduced them to Dr Peyton, chief psychiatrist of the Rettie, who was dressed in an expensive dark blue suit, as neat as a pin. At the same time she pointed out that Dr Peyton had never been in any kind of therapeutic relationship with Gillian Rose Halliday.

'Can we speak to the person who was, then?' asked Caplan smartly.

A stressed-looking young red-headed woman in a loose yellow jumper put her pen in the air and introduced herself as Anna Scafoli.

Caplan nodded. 'It's nice to meet you at last, you've been helpful.'

Another woman in a good suit was not named, but was taking plenty of notes, as Peyton gave Blane the side-eye.

With a slightly ironic look, Scafoli explained that Peyton was also the clinical director.

Caplan turned her gaze on him as he started to speak. Dr Peyton was an expert who loved the sound of his own voice, evident in the condescending way he explained the difference between psychopathy and psychosis.

'Yes, I know,' said Caplan. 'Does Gillian Halliday have a precise diagnosis? One that would be robust in court?' she asked.

'Mostly a severe form of borderline personality disorder.'

'Which can't be diagnosed until she's eighteen, from what I've read?' queried Caplan.

'Mental health is fluid until the brain development is complete,' smiled Peyton.

'She's an adult now. You must have had a well-cooked hypothesis of a diagnosis when she was seventeen and eleven months.'

Caplan swore she saw Scafoli smirk.

'Gillian was an interesting case from the start.' Peyton's fingers came together; he was in condescending mode again.

'Cutting her wee sister's throat kind of interesting?' enquired Caplan.

Peyton smiled kindly. 'Our patients are young, most of them have never developed a normality of mental health that they can then be abnormal from. They have grown up in chaos, no stabilising influences at all, nothing. Well, I guess you see that as well in your line of work. This patient is "interesting" in that no adverse childhood episodes – ACEs – actually happened to Gillian herself. She didn't grow up watching her mum being beaten to a pulp by her dad. There was no alcohol or drug abuse, there was good moral teaching. Instead she suffered, and was maybe affected by the accident when the woman next door was killed, or by the death of her sister by the train and the slight isolation from society. Did Gillian slip into an aberrant pattern of stress-management techniques? Many of our residents try to fool us, hearing voices one minute, having tics and spasms, thinking they can pull the wool over our eyes. Gillian has always been more . . .'

'Direct?' offered Caplan.

'Let's be clear. There was no psychopathy, she's capable of love and responsibility. We put her on a programme to nurture that and she was doing so well that we started the release programme.'

Scafoli added, 'She scores high in compliance. She takes her meds, her antidepressants, antipsychotics and mood-stabilisers. As she matured things got easier for her, bearing in mind how young she was when she came. She doesn't have the impulsivity, the aggression that others have. All reports of her violence state it's episodic, controlled and targeted. Triggered, you might say, but by what? Stress is too vague.'

'And the sleepwalking was a symptom of the stress?' asked Caplan.

'And the younger sister may have been the trigger of that stress. It's not unusual for a newborn to spark stress in an elder sibling. Cure the stress and cure the sleepwalking is simplistic but you get the drift. We talk a lot about lifestyle, safe environment, the development of good interpersonal relationships, shared experiences of well-being, learning together. Gillian was—'

Peyton interrupted. 'Much of the success of that depends on what they are returning to, what environment is waiting for them out there. In this aspect, Gillian scored very well with her supportive family and extended family, but we do still need to manage her because . . .'

'Because she may have killed Dr Maxwell?' suggested Caplan.

'Because she's an overeater with no sleep pattern,' said Scafoli. 'She mistakes burying her emotions for managing them. She can be very controlled, but she's smart and talented. I was really . . . well, I can't deny I was concerned when I heard about Dr Maxwell.'

Caplan bit her tongue, thinking how Cordelia's view may differ somewhat.

Peyton cleared his throat. 'Her neighbour was killed in an accident at the cottages. It is something she remembers well, one of very few things she remembers. With that degree of amnesia, it could be she has a PTSD scenario. More usually seen in children born into war zones, those who have seen what no child should see. They have episodes. Then normality.'

'Was killing Poppy Anstruther an episode?'

'Temper? Uncontrollable anger? She could recall very little, but others present said there was bad feeling over a boy, just a teenage crush but they can seem the most important thing in the world at that age.'

'Maybe we got her wrong.'

Scafoli got a scowl from Peyton, a cough from Blane, but continued.

'She managed fine on her day and weekend passes. Never went back to her house, which might have been too much of a trigger. She never displayed any of that behaviour when here, even when her brother visited. Or her sister-in-law. Under supervision, they brought the baby. It was fine.'

'DCI Caplan, the media are often after a particular diagnosis, a box to put the patient, the client, into. Gillian didn't fit.'

'And we did look hard at her identity. She's a loving daughter, looked after Granda, was in tears at the thought of being taken away from them. But a trigger sets off her violence. We never witnessed it in here. Not once.'

'Was Dr Edward Maxwell ever part of her treatment?'

'Absolutely not,' said Peyton. 'With this visit in mind, I cross-referenced almost everything in her file. He's never been consulted. Maxwell and Halliday have never met, not even as a file across a desk. It never happened. There's no connection between them. He should have no knowledge of her.'

McPhee leaned forward, smiling. 'If Gillian had been unfit for release, then should you have sought an ongoing detainment order? Would that have been the right protocol?'

Caplan smiled; somebody had been doing their homework.

'But there was no sign, nothing. Or there was and we missed it. I missed it,' said Scafoli.

'What's your qualification, Anna?'

'Psychologist, involved in the day-to-day treatment and care of the residents.' She shrugged as if her time here now might be limited.

'Gillian Rose Halliday could make the Rettie famous for all the wrong reasons,' mused Caplan, just to be annoying.

'Who was the outreach support?' asked Peyton.

'You should ask Arlene McCaskill, she was her outreach support in Dumfries. She'd no doubts about Gillian doing well in the big wide world.'

'One thing, if I was thinking of writing a book about an unusual child-killer . . .'

'Then she'd be an interesting one to do,' confirmed Scafoli. 'White page, you see, no ACEs, the perfect upbringing, then suddenly all hell broke loose. She doesn't fit any of the theories we have, she rewrites the book. It's hard to identify who she really is.' She paused. 'If you find her difficult, I'll be happy to come over and talk to her. She doesn't like me, but she does know me. I'm somebody separate from her family. Let me know if I can help.'

Caplan didn't think it was by chance that Peyton's pager went and the meeting quickly broke up. Scafoli and Caplan walked back along the corridor slowly, McPhee dropping behind, allowing the two women to chat quietly.

'Amongst the others in here, Gillian was a feisty ray of sunshine. She's capable of love – her dog, her dad, her mum. She's very close to her brother. Of all the atrocities that she has been associated with, the one that shocks her most was her dog being shot.

The one that sticks in her memory is one time when Rachel Susan was rushed to hospital and she was in the car that followed the ambulance. At the hospital Gillian wandered off. She saw somebody die, crash teams and all that. It would have left its mark. She cut that wee sister's throat four months later. Munchausen by proxy was thought of at one stage but Gillian's a more complex character. She loves. She loses the things she loves. Maybe she didn't have to be brought up in a recognised traumatic environment to suffer. Maybe her life has been dreadfully unlucky. If I can be of any further help, let me know.' Scafoli shrugged and added, 'Off the record, I like her. She was off the wall and funny, but never cruel.'

'But no precise diagnosis for Gillian Halliday?'

Scafoli shook her head. 'PTSD from her own crimes? That makes her an interesting subject to research and study if your victim was thinking of doing a book on her. It would be a bestseller, especially if she then pushed the writer off a bridge.'

'I read that she had no memory of the incidents?'

'She claims she couldn't really recall the first incident with Rachel Mary at Church's Pass, she's blocked that one. The second one, she was supposedly asleep when the wee sister was killed. You know both daughters were called Rachel?'

Caplan nodded. 'Weird.'

'Makes you wonder about Miranda's mental health. Rachel Susan was killed on a stormy night, there was a Hogmanay party. They put all the kids in one room.' Scafoli's eyes screwed up a little. 'She has never told me why she might have killed her. I'm not sure she knows. One theory is that she killed that sister because she had seen her other sister die, the horror of it deeply affected her. Maybe it all spirals from those two events. If she met Dr Maxwell on the bridge and he triggered her? Caused her to lose control?'

'Confidentially, whoever it was took a knife.'

'Not so easy to argue that one. Sorry.'

'Do you believe her about her amnesia?'

'No, I think she's lying through her teeth.'

SEVENTEEN

Some cockwomble was saying that everything is a matter of
life and death.
It's not.
It's a matter of death.
If you think about it logically.

Killagal Blog, 2022

The incident room was busy. Caplan had updated Linden on what had been said at Rettie. Essentially nothing. Linden replied that she was winning the argument to get all relevant documentation released. Caplan finished her daily phone call with Cordelia, then gave a brief but necessary statement about Gillian's status in the inquiry. They had played the protective-custody card. They should concentrate now on proving who killed Edward Maxwell. Miranda and Rowan were being interviewed in the station. Duguid McCleary and Gail Halliday were still up at Ben o' Tae. It was reported that everybody was being cooperative.

Caplan had left messages for Arlene McCaskill at both the numbers she had. She wrote it up on the wall then looked over her shoulder. There was a lot of activity on the sightings map, with timings going off in all directions. McPhee had asked the big question: how had Gillian got from Ben o' Tae to the bridge and back?

'We can track that figure off the bridge. Let's say it is Gillian. Here she's walking near the roundabout at 0040 hours, then up at the Osprey, the restaurant.'

'Why is she keeping out the way? Avoiding the main road while dressing in a way that attracts attention?'

'Well, nobody said she was sane. And now, past the restaurant, she disappears.'

'What's up there?' asked Caplan.

'A residential estate.'

'Have we done a door-to-door?'

'On the lower half, nothing as yet. We've checked it and double-checked the footage, and she doesn't appear again, so she must've gone into one of the houses. Do we have any intel of her knowing anybody in that area? Craigo? How's the grapevine on that one?'

'Gillian grew up here. I think we'd know about close friends. And who in their right mind would help her get away with murder?'

'Somebody who was scared of her? Anything on her mobile phone? The one she shared with Rowan?'

Mackie replied, 'No calls except to pizza take-out, curry take-out, her family. No numbers not traced, no communication between her and Maxwell.'

'But we only have one of Maxwell's phones, can we be sure?'

'All the numbers she called are accounted for. Can you access the dark web in a café or a library? Killagal posted one blog after the fire.'

'But maybe written before she hurt her hand? And is this stuff within her IT skills?'

McPhee said, 'Can't find her mobile device, can't find Maxwell's mobile devices.' He shrugged. 'That's odd.'

'I'm still working my way through a long list,' said Mackie defensively. 'I'm very busy.'

They looked at the screen, watching the figure walk smartly up the hill and to the right, disappearing out the range of the camera. 'I suspect that flash of white every now and again is the dressing on Gillian's right hand.'

'We need to pick one good image and get it clarified. But how did she get from Ben o' Tae to the bridge and back? Sorry, I'm repeating myself.'

'Drove?'

'Can she drive?' asked Caplan.

'Country girl, private roads, she'll know how to drive. She could have rolled the car down the hill at home so that nobody heard it, like we did, ma'am,' said Craigo.

'And being local, she'd know where to park without getting spied on by the cameras. But I still think a bloke would punt the doc over the railings of the bridge easier than a lassie could,' said McPhee.

'Want to try it?' asked Mackie.

'Not particularly.'

'Miranda and Rowan are still in the interview suite. Find out who locked Gillian's door. Was it really done every night?' asked Caplan. 'Though it would have been useful to know that before they had a chance to get their stories straight.' She looked right at Craigo.

'If my daughter was a violent somnambulist then I think a fair precaution would be to lock her bedroom door at night from the outside,' said Mackie.

'They did it for all four or five nights? Definitely?'

'Aye, but before you go down to the interview, has anybody talked to Miss McColl? The teacher?' asked Mackie.

'Jeannie, well her name's Jane but everybody calls her Jeannie,' said Craigo, his fine hair up on end, caught by static.

'Who's she?' asked McPhee, running his eyes down a list of names as Caplan checked those on the wall. No McColl.

'Gillian's schoolteacher, and it was for the time she was out between Rachel Susan and Poppy.'

'What about her?'

'Well—' Craigo sat down on the edge of a seat and Caplan felt obliged to follow '—we got talking in the queue at the Post Office. She was asking about the case and about Gillian and mentioned how many times she had complained to the authorities.'

'About what?'

'About Gillian, aged eight.'

Caplan nodded slowly. 'She had complained about Gillian being violent to the other kids?'

'No, ma'am. She said that Gillian would come to school with clumps of her hair missing, lots of small cuts and bruises. She reported it, the records will be there. Somewhere.'

'Those complaints would have been followed up. At Rettie, they gave the opposite impression, loving family, no abuse. Did the teacher say what the result of the report was?'

'The presumption was self-harm. But McColl knows that Gillian was in the care of a child psychologist. Even as a very little girl, it was believed she was disturbed and self-harming. There was no third party involved.'

'But what did she think, in her experience?' asked Caplan.

'That somebody was subjecting that girl to violence within that home.'

'Craigo, as a local do you think there was something odd going on up there?'

'Who knows? McColl was one of the few folk who saw Gillian outside Ben o' Tae, ma'am. I've learned to never second-guess what goes on behind closed doors,' he lied.

Caplan's phone pinged. It wasn't Aklen. It was Cordelia Maxwell again, asking her to get in touch. She slipped the phone back into her pocket.

'We chase that up tomorrow.'

McPhee spoke up. 'Ma'am, can we just focus on Maxwell for a moment? None of this is anything to do with why Gillian was in jail. The first two incidents were fully investigated. She got treatment, the family took measures so that her somnambulism should not result in any trauma or harm to any other member of the family. There's a theory that she has a deep-rooted hatred of any of her female siblings. Rowan and Gail seem to be safe. The attacks on the youngsters were from her unconscious vitriol.' The DC started tapping his pen off his desk. 'This's not about Gillian, it's about Maxwell. What if he thought there was a miscarriage of justice? Both Biggs and Rolland thought he was a whistleblower. What if there was an issue with Gillian's treatment? Listening to them this morning, what did Rettie actually do for her? For her care? About Gillian herself? She's a subject a teenage psych specialist would be interested in. And remember this mystery woman, the Pest. She's not coming forward, so what's her story?'

'McPhee, the first was a tragic accident. The second she was not aware she was committing a crime. The third she was conscious and aware. And older.'

Caplan asked them to keep going and try to find the electronic copy of what Maxwell was working on. Only Rowan had mentioned a book about Gillian. There was no reason why Maxwell wouldn't have been open with Rolland and Biggs. She had to read the reports from the uniform team who had been left up at Ben o' Tae after they had removed Gillian from the premises. Rowan had been cooperative. Had it stayed that way?

Caplan popped along to listen to Miranda Halliday who was in the first interview room. She was sobbing into a hanky, heartbroken. She looked worn out. It seemed genuine but you never knew, never assume anything. After a couple of minutes, she slipped into the room. 'Hi, I've been to see Gillian. She's well, but that hand is badly infected. She's on a drip.'

Miranda shook her head; she looked like she'd been awake for days. 'I knew it when I saw it, could smell it. She never listens to me.'

'She's a teenager, Mrs Halliday, of course she doesn't listen to you,' Caplan said, easing the conversation forward. 'I have a daughter and a son, aged in between your two. My daughter is so normal it's frightening. My son has given me a few moments though. Can't imagine what Gillian has put you through as a family.'

'It's a very difficult thing to say, that you're scared of your own child. How can that be? But believe me, she's always between us, above us or beyond us. She has always been somewhere else, somewhat other-worldly.'

'Did she ever self-harm?'

Miranda opened her hands out, pleading. 'I've said so many times, no. But she was always clumsy, always hurting herself. I really tried to keep an eye on her but . . . I really tried.'

'Nothing to reproach yourself for. You've been there for her, Miranda, you've done your best. It can't have been easy for you.'

'I kept thinking that this one would be the last, there'd be a better treatment, a better medication.'

'And your husband, it can't have been easy for him?'

'He couldn't cope. Every time he looked at Gillian, all he saw was Rachel Susan. And who can live with that? That was our family, so we thought. A boy and three girls: Gillian, Rowan and Rachel Mary, Rachel Susan. I've been reading the nonsense in the paper and online. They say that we knew Gillian was not well and did nothing about it. Of course we did, but it happens in increments. We tried to get help. I still find it very hard to believe . . .'

'Do you?'

'No. Yes. She's my daughter. She's good at drawing, hates coffee and *Eastenders*, likes mini Easter eggs, crows and Elmo from *Sesame Street*.'

'She was praising you for the apple pie on her blog; she still feels, sounds, very involved with the family?'

'We Facetimed her when she was at Rettie, about Granda and the dogs. God knows she likes her food, but the apple pie was

Fiona, before she passed away. She was the baker, I stick with my shortbread.'

'Where did he go, your husband?' asked Caplan, knowing that he had gone to Dubai, to be with another woman who did not have any murderous offspring. 'He must have known that Gillian was not well, surely?'

'Dubai was his way of dealing with it. I had Rowan to look after, he's always been a sensitive boy. He lost his sister and his dad. Jim's back now, London. He's always sent us support, money for Gillian, for me and Rowan. He comes up when he can. He can – well he could – cope better once Gillian had grown up. We thought she was better.' Her eyes filled up. 'Maybe we were wrong. She couldn't have killed that Maxwell man.' Miranda shook her head. 'She was locked in, I locked her in myself.'

'And you never forgot.'

'It was only four nights, I didn't forget. It was the price of having my family together under one roof.'

'Your daughter Rachel Susan was eleven months old when she died. What exactly happened?'

Miranda took a long time to answer. 'They think that Gillian cut her throat while she was asleep. The knife was found on the bed Gillian was sleeping in, she had blood on her hands. She was sleepwalking, there was a storm, we were having a party at Ben o' Tae. Hogmanay, lots of friends round. We don't have many friends after that night. We were very drunk and making a racket. That pushed her over the edge.'

'Takes some heart to keep looking after Gillian when you know she killed your other daughter.'

'More to be pitied than scorned.'

'Miranda? Did you think that anybody in that house was abusing Gillian?'

The denial was sincere and absolute.

In the other interview room Rowan Halliday was leaning back in the chair, relaxed in his arrogant boredom.

'Must be tough growing up with a sister like that,' said Caplan after she'd reassured him that Gillian was doing fine.

'She's always been my sister, I can't see her the way that others do.'

'But she killed one of your young sisters. Maybe both of them.'

'Technically, I'm sure that's correct. She's always been weird. I know that must sound awful for you to hear, but it has been explained to me many times by all kinds of doctors. She has different sides to her personality. She doesn't do well with rejection, attachment, obsession. When she's in control she can be rational, but when she's not in control, well, on each occasion when she's killed, something had put her out of kilter. But it's never black and white, we don't see it coming. And to be honest, because she was not named for legal reasons, that Tollen thing, it's easy to fool ourselves that the Most Evil Woman in Britain is not my wee sister who loved Elmo from *Sesame Street*.'

'What does your wife think?'

Rowan's gaze, the large doe eyes, floated over towards the door.

'Two strong bolts like that on an internal door. You weren't that confident.'

'Gail threatened to leave, like I said. A young female relative could be one of Gillian's triggers so Gillian and Gail agreed about the locks. Duguid, then and there, popped out and got two locks from the hut, fitted them.'

'And were the locks used as they should have been?'

Rowan hesitated. 'Yes, I'm sure they were, but . . .'

'But?'

'Well, Gail said that once in the four days that Gillian was staying there, the locks were open when she got up in the morning. Turns out Gillian had called Mum. She'd needed the loo and Mum had forgotten to lock her back in. They'd stayed up and had toast, a cup of tea, chatting.'

'What night was that then?'

'Saturday? Friday? It was a day that Mum wasn't working, anyway.'

Gillian may have been vulnerable, with mental-health issues. She was dangerous. She had her rights, but she generated a lot of admin. No matter how much Caplan and the team were scared to let her loose in public again, they had to stay within the law. That afternoon, Caplan and Craigo found Gillian sitting up on a hospital bed, reading a slim romance novel, judging from the lurid cover. Her hair was slightly flatter, her make-up in place but her face was still angry.

'I've brought some stuff that your mother dropped in to the

station,' Caplan told her. 'She thought you might be comfier in your own PJs.'

'Twice in one day, you really do fancy me. I was only joking, you know.'

Caplan ignored her and moved the water jug from the right to the left side of the bed. 'How's the burn?'

Gillian raised the paw of her right hand. 'Imagine being on antibiotics that give you the shits when you can't wipe your arse.'

'First-world problems, eh?' Caplan sat down. 'Now that your hand has been attended to, I'm going to ask you the same questions again.'

'Why?'

'Because I can. Do you know a doctor called Ted Maxwell?'

'Why, should I?'

'I'm just asking.'

A small smile passed over her face. 'You wouldn't believe me if I told you.'

'Try me.'

'Well, he used to work at Rettie. He waited until everybody else went home then he'd have us all into his office to snort coke and then we'd start shagging.' She looked at the black polished nails on her left hand.

'Must have been tiring.'

'Of course I've bloody heard of him. He took a dive off the fucking bridge, didn't he?'

'Did you kill him?'

That got an eye roll and a sigh.

'Make sure you note Miss Halliday's response, DS Craigo.'

Her colleague nodded.

'Do you remember killing him?' asked Caplan.

'What the fuck do you think?'

'I've noted that, ma'am,' nodded Craigo.

'What do you know of Dr Maxwell?'

'That he jumped. I can so totally get that, like imagine coming up here when you aren't forced to, enough to drive anybody to suicide.'

'Do you know him apart from what you've seen on the news?'

'Never bloody heard of him before that.' The black ringed eyes stared Caplan out.

'Do you have a case-worker?'

'Loads of them, which one do you fancy, the most recent one?'

'Arlene McCaskill?'

'Nosey bitch. Oh yeah, my release woman, total fanny. Right fucking arsehole.'

'A fanny and an arsehole, remarkable woman,' said Caplan with equanimity. 'What about Anna Scafoli?'

'She's not so bad.' Halliday shifted her bulk on the top of the bed, smoothed down the cover that had ruffled beneath her. 'Can I go back to Rettie now?'

'Nope. Why did you blog on Banned Box? Why leave yourself open to such danger?'

'What . . . is . . . the point of life . . .?' She looked at the ceiling tiles.

This was an act now.

'You didn't know Ted Maxwell and you didn't leave the house on Friday night, except for the one-handed pole-dancing.'

'Broke the fucking pole, didn't I?'

'Who let you out? You were supposed to be locked up.'

She paused. 'Yeah, how bloody trusting is that?'

'They said that you agreed?'

'I didn't want to come home, go home.' She closed her eyes and turned away but not before they had seen the fear on her face. Craigo pulled a face and looked at Caplan. 'I wanted somewhere for Ollie, then I was on the move. Can I go back to Rettie?'

'No. Why do you want to go? Surely better to be outside?'

Gillian swung her stare to Caplan. 'Don't like being out here, full of bloody weirdos like you two. Can I get a better book to read? This is pish.'

'It's a romance, what did you expect? To be clear, was it a condition of you coming back home being locked in? You needed to go somewhere after the flat was burnt. That wasn't under your control. I can't think that your family wanted you back, I mean not really . . .'

'You can't talk to me like that.' Another sly, slow smile crept over her face.

'That's why the chimp's here, to prove that I didn't. But like I say, you've the chance to get your story in first. But I'll see you around, hopefully not at the mortuary.'

'It's getting a bit busy down there at the moment, ma'am,' said Craigo.

'Well, Ms Halliday might have put one of them down there herself.'

Caplan walked back to the door quietly, with all the poise of a prima ballerina.

'Miss Halliday,' she heard Craigo's voice, 'where did you sit your driving test?'

Caplan waited for an answer. There wasn't one apart from a quiet '*Fuck off, you cunts.*'

Craigo closed the door. Caplan looked at him. 'The report said that she used to be such a nice girl.'

'Well, she got over that quick, didn't she?'

EIGHTEEN

*I've never worked out why people get more upset about killing
   dogs, rather than killing people.
It's not true. I cut my wee sister's throat.
I threw Bobo the puppy off the cliffs at Durness.
Believe me, people were more upset about my wee sister.*

Killagal Blog, 2022

A box of new documentation had arrived. Caplan blew the dust off and started cutting the security sealing with a pair of scissors. There were a lot of files to be examined and cross-referenced.

She texted ACC Linden to say 'Cheers'. The immediate answer was 'Anytime'.

Toni Mackie had gone out and bought her a sandwich – tuna, no butter, no mayo – as it was obvious Caplan was going to be there most of the night. The rumour was that Mackie was going out on a date, a first date with a new man; further rumour was that he was the man from the train and that Mackie was 'keen'. The DC had dressed in a low-cut black blouse that showed off her rather generous figure, and the grey straps of a once white bra. But she had more make-up on than usual, her brown eyes ringed by hazel eyeshadow, mascara dramatising her long lashes.

She had slipped on a bulky cardigan that went down to her ankles at the back, and a haze of perfume followed her everywhere through the small station.

She placed the sandwich down in front of her boss. 'What are you looking at, ma'am?'

'Just going through all this from the start. Question: If Ted Maxwell was interested in Gillian therapeutically, then why kill him? That's not her thing. She got Ollie, she loves dogs, dogs are a commitment, it suggests she wanted her liberty long term. We are missing something. Apart from whatever it was that Maxwell was working on.'

'It's worse than that, ma'am. It was on the radio at teatime that we arrested Gillian at gunpoint.'

'Oh Christ.'

'Aye, we arrested a mentally vulnerable teenager at gunpoint. It's all over social media.'

'Well, it's more interesting than posting pictures of their mince for the world to see.'

'Shall I put the kettle on?'

'No, you're not my mother, go out and have a nice time, I'll see you tomorrow.'

'Well, you keep your eye on the weather, it's going to turn nasty. Are you going home, ma'am?'

'Eventually. Are you?'

Mackie nudged her boss with her elbow as she went past. 'I'll be snuggled up in somebody else's nice warm bed.'

'And so will I,' teased Caplan. 'Except mine will be at Betty's B&B.'

The door closed, heavy footfall down the stairs, a few loud words, a few ribald remarks, and Mackie was away.

Caplan spent a long time looking at the board. It all pointed to Gillian. Everything. It was very neat. She pulled the file of photographs from Poppy Anstruther's crime scene from the newly arrived box. She'd leave the documentation with Mackie for cross-checking. She came across a misfiled document, a statement from an Evan Reekie from the incident at Church's Pass that had been located for Soupy Campbell's review. One line had been highlighted.

She wasn't there.

Caplan wiped the whiteboard clean and started to draw. She

could see Church's Pass very clearly in her memory. Where had Gillian been standing? Where was Evan? And she couldn't figure out why the issue of the train being southbound bothered her so much.

The Church's Pass incident had gone to a fatal incident inquiry involving a DCI Shaw. The railway was found negligent. But DI Thomas 'Soupy' Campbell had re-examined the case while he was the investigating officer in the Anstruther inquiry, and that had resulted in a medical board and the Tollen Protocol being applied to the guilty party. He was an experienced and capable officer. Had he been pressured to get Gillian off the streets? She could feel his frustration. He had passed away with Covid in 2020; she felt it would have been good to get his impression on the current situation.

Caplan pinned Evan Reekie's statement on the wall. And started arranging photographs from each scene in chronological order. She recognised the view out the back bedroom window from Ben o' Tae, dated 1 January 2014. They'd fairly cut back the trees and levelled the land to make the Fairy Garden. The cot in the picture was a bloodstained mess, spatter up the walls, the clean spot on the floor where the killer stood as a barrier to the spatter. She looked along, the plan of the room, Gillian's bed, the imprint of the knife in her blood on the duvet. And the two most shocking pictures: a set of tiny pyjamas for an eleven-month-old baby, the top half stained dark brown, and Gillian's bigger pyjamas, Elmo from *Sesame Street*, a gift that Christmas, white background, the red of the monster smeared by the red of the blood.

All very interesting, but it got them no closer to putting Gillian on the bridge.

Gillian didn't have a licence but the locals thought she could drive. How did she get out the house? Caplan had further reports on the residents at Ben o' Tae to read. Jim Halliday intrigued her; Gillian's dad, who had kept in touch. Was his leaving to do with Gillian or had the situation between Duguid McCleary and Miranda Halliday been going on for longer than they thought? Had that destabilised Gillian's fragile mental state?

Fiona McCleary, Duguid's wife, was dead by then. She was a shadowy figure throughout this. There had been a fatal accident inquiry when she was killed. The kids had been playing in the yard. A parked vehicle had slipped its brakes and set off down the slope, pinning the woman against the drystane dyke she was kneeling beside, gathering wild borage. Caplan looked at the photographs of the aftermath of the incident. She recognised the point on the wall where the doocot was, indeed it was where they had parked. No doves there because the crows had killed them all. Caplan closed her eyes, recalling what it looked like now. The plants and flowers growing, the trees of the Fairy Garden. The fatality had been on 17 May 2009, the inquiry had been eight months later and had ruled accidental death. The only recommendation made was to level the land behind the cottage if vehicles were going to sit there. Somebody had already requested the file because one of the children present at the time was Gillian Rose Halliday, the second oldest child of the family next door.

Caplan looked up at the timeline, thinking that they were uncovering a monster. Should they now be looking at all the periods when Gillian was not incarcerated in some institution? That was the logical thing to do. She'd need to pull together a presentation, ask for a task force to be put in place. How many other files had this little scribble – review, Gillian Rose Halliday was there?

And how did it start? Young Gillian was normal, so it seemed, then there was the incident at Church's Pass. Caplan flicked through and found the names, made a note, then went back to the original file, the one Anna Scafoli had compiled.

Which reminded her that Arlene McCaskill, the case-worker, had not yet called back.

Caplan opened the folder and began reading. There was a lot of background intelligence in the first few paragraphs, no names, but describing the intertwining family relationships of Girl A and the rest of those that were living, hidden away from the world, up in the woods at the cottages near the old railway line. She was now able to fill in all the gaps.

There was a map showing the cottages at Ben o' Tae, the path of the old narrow-gauge railway, and the natural gulley that ran down to the Sound. When the dwellings were sold, the four cottages were knocked into two, the Hallidays and the McClearys living there. The children lived in this tiny, isolated community. There was Girl A, her brother and her parents and her maternal grandfather. The second house was occupied by Duguid McCleary and the daughter, Gail. Gail and Rowan had married late 2020 and continued to stay at Ben o' Tae. That was all it said, not who was where at the time of each of the tragedies, and there had been many. Despite everybody being in employment, there didn't seem to be that much money at Ben o' Tae; not on the poverty line, but not that far above it. Caplan was reminded of that maxim about existing only three payslips away from being homeless. Now it was Gail who brought the money into the house, working for a firm of accountants who paid for her to study and sit for further qualifications, mostly from home to enable her to look after Alice. 'Granda' wandered the woods all day. McCleary tinkered with cars and farm machinery on a cash-in-hand basis. Rowan worked as a manager in a coffee shop, Miranda in a care home. A more interesting thing, to Caplan, was that the children, three of them at school age, had been home taught. Mostly by Fiona McCleary until she was crushed by a car that her husband, Duguid, was working on.

They were a closed community who seemed to get on well; indeed, at the time of writing, the families had intermarried. There was no sense of violence, no criminality on any part of the residents who lived there, no adverse events except for Gillian self-harming, which the teacher had reported as possible abuse.

The statements from the wider community said that the families were well known and well respected.

So, Gillian had grown up loved and adored by her family, maybe a bit protected from the outside world but was that a bad thing? Or was that what they wished people to think, safe in their seclusion?

It was reported that the kids were always warm, even if the clothes were hand-me-downs. They were polite but maybe suffered a little from social isolation. Caplan wondered if that had maybe brought about the twisted violence that plagued Gillian. The violence that started when Rachel Mary was hit by a train. She did a bit of mental arithmetic, thinking about the lie of the land. It was still the southbound train that troubled her, but she couldn't think why. Caplan checked the map then checked the report, and then resorted to Google maps. The incident had happened further along the track as the train wound its way to the coast, just before the rails went into the cover of the trees. Looking at the bigger picture, it was clear that the kids from Ben o' Tae could have considered this all as part of their garden, just a small collection of cottages surrounded by never-ending trees. Tapping the map, her phone lying beside it, Caplan tried to orient herself. The cottages, the site of the incident, the village, the town. The site of the little girl's death was close enough to Cronchie for the village kids to meet the Ben o' Tae kids. She could see her own two doing that when they were young, forming a gang, sometimes going into the village for a chippie, sometimes going up into the woods to see what they could see. On the day the three-year-old died, they had been visiting a den the way that kids do. Rachel Mary had walked down the hill, probably across the field, holding her big sister's hand. One of the bigger children would have been Gail, another Rowan. Three years was a big difference in childhood but still too young to see the danger in crossing the railway line when the excitement of a picnic in the big boys' den lay ahead.

Ten kids had gone up to the den.

Only nine of them came back.

Caplan's phone pinged. The two cops who had stayed up at Ben o' Tae had left and were on their way back. They reported that 'Granda' was a dead loss for an interview, he lived his own life, knew nothing about the goings on in the family. There was a summary from the interview with Gail. Like a bad detective story, Caplan skipped to the end.

> I've known Gillian all my life. We've been friends from an early age, we grew up living in the same house almost, there's only three years between us. Rowan, Gillian and I were the only kids for miles around. I was more often in their house than I was in mine.
>
> After the fire at Gillian's place, I drove to Dumfries to collect her and Ollie. That took for ever. She was in a bad state. Could've been the infection or the shock of the fire. We brought her in, we made her something to eat. It was lovely to see her again. Don't want to sound soppy but she belongs back with us. Things are different now, I was conflicted. I did not want her to be under the same roof as Alice. I said that to Rowan. 'If she stays, I'll go elsewhere until it gets sorted.' Then my dad said about the bolts. They all looked at me as if it was my decision, I could hardly say no, could I?

Caplan went into the main incident room, picking up the mouthful of sandwich she had left. She spent a long time sitting on the desk, looking at the timeline, the pictures of the scene in the flat after the fire, the picture of Ted Maxwell who was becoming lost in all of this. She moved his photograph centre stage. She was supposed to call Cordelia back. She looked at her watch. It had taken her less than an hour and a half to get nowhere.

There were noises downstairs, the odd raised voice, doors opening and banging. She was looking closely at the timeline, trying to get Gillian from Ben o' Tae to the bridge, when she heard footfall coming up the stairs, the click of the electronic lock. Somebody with a key card on their lanyard was letting themselves in, too heavy to be Craigo, too slow to be McPhee. For a moment she thought it was Gillian, heavy-footed.

Whoever it was went past the door, then came the sound of running water in the women's toilets.

Caplan waited for a moment, got up and walked behind the door, stayed there so when they came in she'd see them before they saw her.

The door did indeed bang open. 'Hello, missus. How're you getting on?'

'Mackie?'

'Aye, thought I'd come back and gie you a wee hand, you know, if you're stuck. I'll put the kettle on.'

There was no mistaking the red eyes and the messed-up mascara.

Caplan thought that she'd been stood up and had maybe stayed in the pub for one drink longer than she should have. She'd had chats like this with Emma when she was young. With Kenny, charming, smiling, cheery Kenny, it was usually him that did the standing up.

'Nice of you to come back, I need to pick your brains.'

'I'm here to be picked.' Mackie curtseyed in full.

'First though, I'll get you a black coffee. A strong one.'

'I think we should start at the beginning. It might be worth tracking down the kids who were at Church's Pass that afternoon. We already have the names . . . in that pile there. And somebody said that there were a few kids in the house on the night Rachel Susan had her throat slit. Something to do with the bad weather and Hogmanay. Do you think we could go through all these incident reports and find out who was there each night, see if there's any other commonality? There's one person who was at each of these incidents.'

'It was a thing at the time. You know the old rhyme, "Piggy on the railway picking up stones".'

Mackie hummed away at the little rhyme. Then creased up her eyes. 'Just give me a mo.' She ran her fingers through her mop of blonde hair. 'Nine kids in all? Gillian, Rowan, Rachel, Gail was there, the Reekie boy, the three Mitchell brothers – can't recall their names but somebody from down that part of the village – and one older boy, and that strange girl with the kidney.' Mackie rubbed her eyes, making her look like a colourful panda. 'Hang on,' she said, rifling through a buff folder which was more tattered than it should have been. 'Well, there were seven boys and three girls, plus Gillian and Wee Rachel Mary, so ten in all, Gillian and Rachel Mary were late to the party, coming down the embankment. It was the Reekie boy who had waited for them, he was still at the top of the opposite embankment. He saw the train coming and got out his phone to film it. Not the impact, he'd dropped his phone by then, but he did see what was splattered up the tracks all the way along the line and that was something he was never going to get better from.

'He struggled after that, him more than any of them. And Gail of course, she was on the hill, but well. One minute the wee one was there, then she was gone. Gillian had no real memory of it. It was the train driver and Evan Reekie who suffered the most.'

Caplan looked from one file to the other. 'We had Gail on the hill on one side of the rails and Gillian at track level on the other side. We have a clip of film?'

'It's on the system.'

'Can you get it for me? What did Gillian and Gail say?'

'Also in the file, they were interviewed by specialists. There was a big fatal incident inquiry.'

'Yes, I read the recommendations of that. Seemed to blame the rail company more than anything else. And the Halliday kids and the McCleary kid, they're all like one family.'

'Of course, they all lived in the same house.'

'Mmm.' Caplan rubbed her face with her hands.

'You're very tired, ma'am, you should go home. There's nothing to see in this. It was a tragic accident.'

'But it was where it all started, Toni. Up to this point, Gillian is normal. What was the name of the boy at the top of the embankment? The one who witnessed it, filmed it, the Reekie boy. Could we talk to him, he seems to be the one who was right there.'

Mackie slowly shook her head. 'Only through a medium, ma'am. He passed away himself a couple of years back.'

Mackie was snoring now, her head down on McPhee's desk, dribbling over his paperwork. Caplan took her heavy jacket and placed it over her shoulders, muttering about bloody men. Ignoring the regular rise and fall of Mackie's sleep, she went back to the report of a young Evan Reekie's statement. She didn't even know what she was looking for. She was tired. She closed her eyes, picturing a young boy standing on top of the embankment, seeing in her mind's eye how it might have been that day. It had been sunny, high summer, more foliage on the trees. The rest of his friends had already gone on ahead. Evan had looked back, the embankment was steep, he would have been looking down. Gail's somewhere below him, and he'd be able to see Gillian on the other side of the track.

He'd said that he saw 'her arm'. A young child recalling what an arm was doing? Who did the arm belong to? The arm that had reached out to try to pull Rachel back from the path of the train? It was the only detail young Evan could recall. She started an electronic search for the footage from his phone.

Piggy on the railway line picking up stones.

He'd said, 'She wasn't there.'

What did all that mean?

Option one: Gillian had been so disturbed by the traumatic death of Rachel Mary that she had subsequently killed the replacement sister. Then killed a 'friend' over some boy. A brain so young had developed hard-wired in an aberrant and deadly pattern.

Option two: Gillian had pushed her wee sister into the path of the train. She'd stabbed Rachel Susan. She'd drowned Poppy.

The decisive incident was the initial one.

Caplan knew exactly how unreliable memories could be. Even if someone were a hundred per cent sure about what they thought they saw, how reliable was the memory that had been formed at the time? The brain was clever at adapting scenarios, making sense of things that make no sense at all.

But there was some film.

Option three? Something made Rachel Mary move forward. Gillian tried to stop her but couldn't. Everything that had unfolded from then was a result of the guilt that she could not save her sister. Did somebody shout for Rachel Mary? She was very young, three years old, nearly four. She might have responded to a shout, a call maybe meant for Gillian. Had the wee one merely heard a greeting, 'Hello', or 'Over here', and taken a couple of steps forward onto the line?

Who else had gone over the embankment? Out of sight? She read down the list of names, stopping at Rowan. Why was it only ever Gillian who got injured? Sibling abuse? What was Gail scared of when she'd taken Caplan to the top of the stairs at Ben o' Tae? What was she going to say? Was the caring and contrite Rowan merely an act?

Rowan, the lovely brother, the quiet voice in a house full of shouting.

Rowan who had the precision, the clarity of mind. The caring brother who had inserted himself into the investigation.

She walked up to the whiteboard and looked at the picture of Rowan on the log pile, getting the feeling that she was starting to see what Dr Edward Maxwell had already suspected.

NINETEEN

Very few people find it easy to kill.
I'm just fortunate I'm talented that way.

Killagal Blog, 2021

By the time Caplan left for the night, the station at Cronchie was under siege and she had difficulty driving out the car park without hitting a journalist. The press office was sending a specialist over from Edinburgh because the media from God knows where had descended, wanting to know where 'she' – the Most Evil Woman in Britain – had been taken. Why at gunpoint? Were the rumours true? All they were told was that she'd been moved to an undisclosed location to receive medical attention for the injuries sustained in the fire. The reporter on the local evening news was talking with the backdrop of Cronchie harbour and the islands beyond, adding his own postscript that a source close to the case had reported that, after being arrested at gunpoint, Girl A was undergoing further psychiatric evaluation and that Police Scotland were conducting an investigation into the death of Dr Edward Maxwell, a forensic psychologist whose body had been found in the early hours of Saturday morning. He added that at this point it was unclear if Girl A had ever been in the care of Dr Maxwell at any time, at any of the mental-health facilities she had resided after killing her friend five years previously.

As she left the car park, Caplan looked at the members of the public standing around. She didn't recognise them, but she could sense their wrath. They needed better protection round the station, or they might need somewhere else to work.

When Caplan walked in the back door at seven-thirty the next morning, her stomach full of yoghurt and green tea, there was a man already at reception waiting for her. She thought the concentrated look around his brown eyes and the thick black eyebrows looked familiar. This would be Jim Halliday, father of Rowan and Gillian, father of the two Rachels.

He stood up and introduced himself. She said she'd nip upstairs and then come down to get him. Once upstairs she called Anna Scafoli, asking whether it was advisable for Gillian to see her dad. It was a good bargaining tool.

After a quick re-read of the file, Caplan settled him in one of the interview rooms. Both of them had a strong coffee. She couldn't face another mouthful of green tea.

'I can't imagine what your family has been through. You've always kept in touch with Gillian?'

'Yes, why not? She's my daughter.'

'Do you think she killed your two younger daughters?'

Jim Halliday's face didn't show a flicker of emotion. 'I've lost two, I don't want to lose a third.'

'Do you think she was capable of doing that?'

'The general consensus is that she did it, so the question is moot.'

'Did she ever admit to both?'

'No.'

'Has she ever denied it?'

'No.' Jim Halliday resettled in his chair, ready to tell a story he had told many times. 'A hypnotherapist had a chat with her after Rachel Susan died. She told the whole story of how she woke up, her hands covered in blood. Then she looked down and there was a knife lying on top of the bed. But she'd no recall of killing her sister.'

'She was sleepwalking?'

'Yes. It didn't take us anywhere but she, Gillian, didn't really do it. Something inside her did. It's a terrible world to walk in, mental health. Broken arms, split lips are easy to see. But Gillian's brain? There's something very wrong there. But you can't see it, can't tell when it's going right or wrong.'

'I'm hearing stories of a fairly objectionable young woman, liable to harm and self-harm if she's not comfortable in her environment. But I quite like her.'

He got out his phone. 'Look at my screensaver, look at that.' He welled up as he showed her a picture of Rowan and Gillian, each in Santa hats, laughing. Caplan thought that it had been a long time since her own children had looked as wonderfully happy as that.

'Lovely picture.'

'Can I see her? I have photographs for her. She was told in Rettie to keep a happy book for herself, you know, something to look at on her down days. I bring her photos to put in it. Most of these are 2016 and 2017. Those were good years.' He held up a thin plastic Co-op carrier bag, a pathetic collection of memories, but he was proud of them. 'Did she lose everything in the fire?'

'Just about. We can go and see her as long as you can keep a secret.'

He smiled. 'And what would that be?'

'Where she is. We'll go out the back way. The car will take you the long route round and make sure that you're not followed. And please, tell nobody. If the press find out, she'll get hurt.'

*   *   *

Caplan let the young female constable sitting outside the room go for a sandwich, while she watched Gillian and her dad chat in the hospital room from the seat in the corridor. She glanced at her watch; she had time to call Cordelia.

'Thanks for calling back . . . eventually.'

'I'm sure you've seen the news.'

'Did she kill my husband?'

Caplan paused for a long time before saying, 'Enquiries are ongoing.'

'Has she said why she did it?'

'We're still looking into it.'

There was a deep breath. 'We came back late last night and there's been a visitor at our house today. Somebody was looking for "Ted's book", the one he was working on. I sent her away, I thought she was some kind of madwoman. I might've been wrong.'

Caplan could hear the hesitation. 'Have you ever seen her before?'

'Was he having an affair with her?' The voice at the other end trembled. 'Sebastian saw her, he said that he'd seen her before. She knew where I lived, she knew the boys. She'd been at my house. Who was she? Was he having an affair with her?' Cordelia was like a stuck record.

'Cordelia, let's find out who she is first. We've no evidence that Ted was having an affair. Why do you keep thinking that?'

'Please tell me if he was.'

'I'm a cop not a marriage counsellor. We've gone through the data on his satnav, he's not been anywhere but work, then Connel. His Fitbit app tells the same story, he goes to work, he comes home. Now, the lady who visited you, what did she look like?'

'She was young, slim, short dark hair. Very well-dressed. Early twenties, maybe.'

'Did she tell you her name?'

Cordelia thought for a moment. 'No. She said she was a colleague of Ted's. Then today, my neighbour said that the same woman had already been around the flat. Gerry saw her up at the house. Another time she was talking to the boys. Gerry called the kids in, just being careful. The boys said the woman had asked if Dad was home, they said no and that was that. The second time, she was quite different.'

'Different? What day was the first time? Could she remember?'

'It was the day the Lovell verdict came through.'

'Okay,' said Caplan, so the evening of Friday the eighth. Ted Maxwell had died very early next morning. This woman, whoever she was, had been two hours away from the Connel Bridge. 'That's the sort of thing you would recall, it was the lead item on the news that night.'

'Yes, then when the woman went down the stairs, her phone rang. Gerry thinks she heard her name when she answered it. Cheryl. This woman could be involved. She said Ted had some of her academic work and she wanted it back. Was this the same woman that Peter and Karl saw?'

'Could be.'

Cordelia said nothing for a while. 'But she did have something to do with his death, didn't she? She was here just before he died?'

'We can't be sure. But your husband's death is all over the news and she's not coming forward to help us with enquiries, so I deduce she's got something to hide. I'll get somebody to call you and get more details, like when she arrived, when she left? We'll find out where she parked her car, some CCTV, get her plate number and we get her.'

'I want to know what's going on.'

'So do I. Did she call him Ted or Dr Maxwell?'

'Ted. I said I couldn't help her about the material she was looking for, maybe she should try his office. She got very insistent. I told her that he never kept any of his documents here. Seb and Troy are getting older, more computer savvy so, no, there was never any sensitive material in the house.'

Caplan changed hands, holding her mobile phone to her other ear. Through the glass, Gillian seemed to be describing the burns on her hand to her dad. 'Cordelia, we think your husband was killed because of something he found out. He might have been about to blow the whistle on something. That fits with his personality, his moral compass, but we can't find what it was. He has hidden it well. Maybe from her. You don't have any ideas, anything he said, just mentioned in passing?'

She said tearfully, 'I should've listened more.'

'He never told you though.'

'No.'

Caplan let her talk; she was sounding less frazzled. When she eventually managed to close the phone, Caplan turned back to the interaction between dad and daughter. There was no doubting the affection between them: Jim had tears in his eyes, Gillian was beaming. But Caplan studied them carefully. Kids often loved their abusers. Caplan couldn't afford to leave any stone unturned no matter how unsavoury it was.

She entered the room, going into the corner as if she wasn't listening. Picking up the small photograph album in its Co-op bag, she asked if she could have a look through it and then got comfortable in the single seat, feeling tiredness fogging her brain. The warm room, the quiet chat of Gillian and her dad, made it a retreat from all the recent activity. She wasn't looking forward to the re-enactment on the bridge later. It would be bitter up there. She could hear footfall, phones ringing unanswered in the distance as she flipped over the photographs. Both families were there, including Granda, but she paid most attention to Gillian. As a kid, aged twelve, she seemed so very different from the woman she grew up to be. And then she noticed that darling Rowan was in every one of the photographs. Caplan wished she had liked him when she'd met him. He was obviously the one constant in his sister's life; her dad was gone, her mum had taken up with her boyfriend. Gail and the baby were a new family unit, but they were still very much at home. Rowan was the one who had been honest with them, he had stood up for her, had wanted her home. Gail had protested, as well she might, but Rowan had facilitated the move. Then Ted Maxwell had been killed.

There was a variation on the log-pile picture that Caplan had seen up at Ben o' Tae; the family group piled up on top of half-cut logs. This picture was older than the others. Two mums, two dads, four children, one of them a babe in arms. To the side, not risking climbing up on the wood, were three older people, two women and a man. The two older women must be Gail's granny and Gillian's gran. The very dark woman must be Fiona McCleary. So many deaths in a span of a few years.

There was something about the picture that made Caplan smile. Kids, dirty-handed, hair all over the place. Both Rowan and Gillian had skinned their knees, their clothes didn't fit properly. The two mums looked tired, glad of a bit of respite to get the picture taken, one with her hand resting on the shoulder of the other holding the baby, offering a little support. A spaniel was jumping up, getting in on the act. In her head, she could hear Fiona McCleary say to Miranda Halliday, *Say cheese.* And so, they turned.

Gillian was a skinny, brown-haired kid, knock-kneed, with a blunt-cut fringe that didn't quite sit straight. Her smile was broad, full of joy. Rowan's floppy fringe almost covered his eyes, and his smile was more reserved. Gail was a skinny youngster balancing on top of the woodpile, standing high, her hand up as if she'd conquered the world. There was something wholesome about their happiness, with no mobile phones or tablets in sight, only fun in the dirt.

She thought that she would have liked them if Emma or Kenny had brought them home for ginger and crisps after a visit to the cinema. It was a shock to think that the young girl with the blunt fringe might have grown up to be one of the youngest serial killers the world had ever seen. But, as was often said, they don't go around with 'Evil' printed on their foreheads. There were no clues in that impish little face.

She eased the photograph from its fixative and flicked it over. It was dated, followed by a list of scrawly biro handwriting with their names, Fiona, Rowan, Gillian, Gail, Eric, Jim, Miranda, Duguid.

The next one was taken a few years later, of the three kids, early teens, lying on their backs, feet up in the air, pretending to be dancing as they held on to the world. Caplan recognised the dance from the film *Gregory's Girl.* She looked again at the date, 2016, then behind them, noting the odd shape of the rock in the background. Making sure Jim and Gillian were too busy talking about Ollie's paw, she pulled out her phone and googled the rock at Sugar Loaf Camp. It was a year before Poppy Anstruther died but it was the same place.

TWENTY

It's amazeballs what fuckwidgets leave lying around.
Cars parked on a hill.
Unlocked.
A wall at bottom of the hill. Person leaning on wall.
Then gravity. The human body is very easily crushed.

Killagal Blog, 2021

The bridge was higher, colder, much more exposed than Caplan would have thought possible. They had a good idea as to Maxwell's location as bevved-up Bev was more than halfway across when he'd seen the 'man and the monkey'. Forensic scrutiny had revealed nothing of interest.

Toni Mackie stood in for the perp, McPhee stood in for Maxwell, being the same height and weight, with similar slightness of bone. He had a cross of black tape on his tight-fitting sweatshirt to show where the tip of the knife had entered.

'Gillian' tried to mimic the trajectory of the short knife, the correct direction and depth, instinctively using her right hand. She ended up having to do it backhanded, her right hand starting across her body and then swinging out. That looked okay but wasn't convincing. Mackie repeated the motion a few times, Craigo filming it as she did so. Then Caplan asked Mackie to use her left arm. And not to think about it. Aim for the cross on the shirt. Craigo only filmed the first attempt. As a cop in Glasgow for over twenty years, stab wounds were something Caplan was well-versed in. It looked good to her. A short blade, a sharp point, a quick jab in exactly the right place.

And Gillian's right hand at that time would have been too painful to use with the infected burn festering underneath.

The re-enactment of getting 'Ted' over the railing of the bridge proved more telling. The instructions were not to bruise the body, and 'Ted' wasn't to fight back. The construction company's bright yellow containers were sitting at the side of the railings. Mackie simply asked her victim to slump, then eased him up onto the box, the weight of his upper body on the rail. It was easy then to lift his legs, the fulcrum of the victim on his flank. When Mackie tried the 'lift', the victim moaned that it was bloody sore, then rubbed his side exactly where Ryce had found the abrasion.

But Mackie couldn't do it with one hand, no matter how hard she tried and how inventive she was.

Caplan was convinced that the murderer had it planned. The knife had been brought to the scene after some communication between Gillian Halliday and Ted Maxwell that they could not source. She'd simply lured him to the bridge, walked up to him and stabbed him, before stripping him of all his identification, his mobile devices, and punting him over the rail into the freezing waters below.

Caplan knew that Gillian was bright. Would she go into that situation effectively one-handed? She'd have thought it through.

The whole exercise had taken two precious hours that the investigation couldn't afford. Except to prove that it took the use of both arms to get the body far enough over the rail for it to topple. Even factoring in the thrill of an adrenaline rush, it appeared impossible.

She thanked her team. Mackie forgot she was on the bridge, stepped backwards and was nearly flattened by a tour bus.

Caplan drove back to the station to pick up some paperwork. Mattie Jackson was on the back shift and waved a memo at her before she'd even got in the door of the station.

'There's a phone call for you, ma'am.'

'No there's not.'

'Well, they asked for you by name. You've to call them back.'

'Jackson, I really do value you as a colleague, but we're walking a tightrope here timewise. We need to get some actual evidence that Gillian threw a young psychologist off a bridge. McPhee and I . . .' Then she realised that Jackson was waiting for her rant to be over.

'We can get on with that, ma'am, and I said that you'd visit this lady. She's only up the road, you could be there and back within thirty minutes.'

Caplan was exasperated. 'I don't have thirty minutes. What part of that don't you understand? I'm not talking to just anybody.'

'I didn't get her name, ma'am, but I know who she is. Evan

Reekie's mum, boy who was at the embankment when Rachel was killed. You requested the video from his mobile phone? It's on the log.'

Caplan recognised the look that Jackson was giving her. 'She's worth talking to?'

'Worth more than thirty minutes of your time, ma'am.'

Caplan had planned to get back to the caravan to review the case in some peace and quiet. It'd be good to establish the link between Gillian and Maxwell. She knew it was there, somewhere just out of reach.

Instead she found herself driving ten miles in the wrong direction to a small, anonymous estate down near Taynuilt, to a neat terraced house where the Reekies lived. Number five had a square of well-tended garden, an immaculate Toyota Prius in the driveway.

Gaynor Reekie smiled as she opened the door, a small woman, neat as a pin, her hair in a short plait. She was dressed as if she might have returned from a yoga class but as Caplan followed her through the house, the plastic bags on the kitchen units suggested she'd nipped to Aldi.

She unpacked her groceries while Caplan introduced herself. Gaynor's mood turned to anger, slamming the cupboard doors closed. 'Evan died, did they tell you that?'

'Mattie Jackson was the one who said I should talk to you. It was a female DC called Toni Mackie who knew about your son.'

Reekie furrowed her brow, trying to place the name. 'Don't think I know her, but so many people walk through your life at a time like this. So many people have offered me money for my story. They seem to forget that we have lost somebody, it's all about bloody Gillian.'

'Sorry to bring it all back up again. I read what happened two years ago. Please believe me when I say that I'm sorry for your loss.'

Reekie turned, gently bouncing a packet of macaroni in the palm of her hand. 'Are you? Really? Or is that what they teach you to say?'

'Both. I've a son. He was nearly killed last year. I'm sincere in what I said. It must be awful.'

Reekie smiled, nodding hesitantly and then looked out to the loch. 'He never got over it. We thought that he was doing well, it all became something unsaid, you know. We kept going as a family, we got him help. He was ten at the time, you know – Rachel, the train and all that. Old enough to know what he saw. The therapist kept an eye on him and thought that he was doing well.'

'The therapist's name?'

'Jon, Jonathan Warner. Nice man. He came to the funeral, thought that was good of him. He didn't have to do that.'

'There was something in the notes about hypnosis?'

Reekie sat down, ran her fingers through her hair. 'Do you want a coffee?'

Once settled, she told the story. 'The hypnosis was earlier. All the kids who were at Church's Pass that day were offered counselling.' Reekie closed her mouth, thinking. 'And we knew that Evan had been struggling a little. But he did well, as the years passed. He got a place at Central Saint Martins in London when he was eighteen.'

'He must have been very talented.'

'He was, very. He had an exceptional visual memory. Could look at something once, and draw it, even weeks later. Couldn't spell to save his life though.' She looked out at the water then to a painting in oil of the same view; the muted colours and brushwork gave it a magical, ethereal quality. 'Looking back, I think his work sheds some light on his state of mind. On that day – *that* day – he flew down to London, into Stansted, got the Stansted Express, something he'd done many times before. There was an incident. The train stopped. It took two hours.'

'Suicide on the line?'

'Yes. And he couldn't get away. He was stuck in the train after one person had done what he had witnessed.' Reekie sniffed. 'He called me late that night. Said that it had been a difficult journey. He asked after us all. I knew there was something off with him. He even asked—' She started to cry '—he asked if I'd put Elsa on the phone. He'd never done that before, he always said that he didn't like the bloody dog. We said goodbye. He put the phone down. He left his room and hanged himself from the banister in the flat. The Amazon delivery man found him. He was still warm.'

'Jesus.' Caplan let out a long sigh. 'Do you put it down to what happened at Church's Pass?'

'Whatever it was, it started there. At first there was nothing, a few sleepless nights. We got him therapy because he became so destructive and nasty, unsettled, couldn't sleep, pacing the house at three in the morning. It was destroying the family. He found his way again, he settled. Then, after Rachel Susan was killed, it all came back to him. He had a suicide attempt after the Halliday girl was arrested for the murder of Poppy Anstruther. All these things had a linear connection in his mind.'

Caplan was a little wary at the way this woman had it all noted, the names, the victims, each time inserting her son as part of the narrative.

'It was like he was responsible. Once we got as far as Poppy in the story, people were saying that it was probably the case that she'd pushed her wee sister onto the train tracks. Did she stab her other wee sister or was that really sleepwalking? They kept coming back to Evan, asking him what happened at Church's Pass. He tried to help. He had some hypnosis, he would have been about fifteen then. But all he could say was that the wee lassie was hit by the train.'

'Difficult time for any teenager. Why did he not say no? If it upset him so much?'

Reekie shook her head. 'Survivor's guilt. We got him more counselling. As part of that he had to think about it and desensitise. He couldn't do that, so they walked him through it in a trance, asked him to replay it in his head while in a safe place. Deep relaxation.' She wiped the tabletop with a cloth, rubbing like she could erase the memory. Then she burst into tears. 'He'd filmed the kids, then filmed the train coming round the corner, as a boy would.' Reekie closed her eyes. 'At the moment of impact – well, immediately before it – he dropped the phone. He could see what was going to happen. The police said, if he'd just managed to hold on to the phone, filmed it, it would have helped. He felt so bad that he dropped it. He felt so guilty. If he'd done that, then Poppy would still be alive.'

'That's not helpful to anybody,' encouraged Caplan, while acknowledging those words would have been spoken by her colleagues in frustration. 'Why did they think it was so important? The film?'

'Well, he said that it was all wrong, why didn't they leave him alone. That she wasn't there.'

'Who wasn't there?'

'Gillian. When the wee girl was hit by the train. You see, they were saying that Gillian must have been very close to push the wee one in front of the train. But according to Evan, she wasn't standing anywhere nearby. He was only ten, they said it was all a mess in his head. But he said he recalled it clearly, he had that type of memory. They said he was wrong. But it was them changing the story, not him. That messed with his head.' Reekie sighed. 'Nobody believed him. Gillian was getting the blame. The producers of that *Turning Heads* programme portrayed Evan like an idiot.'

Caplan recalled that – an 'unreliable witness', they had called him. 'So, he witnessed that Rachel Mary's death was an accident, but after Rachel Susan died, they tried to get Evan to change his story? Is that right?'

'Yes. No. More that he had remembered it wrongly. They said that what he had actually witnessed was Gillian pushing her sister in front of the train.'

'Okay,' said Caplan, slowly. 'Even though, when hypnotised, he said different.'

'But Evan said that she couldn't have pushed anyone.'

'I accept that maybe she didn't, but I can see what the previous investigation was thinking. She saw her wee sister die then she killed the other wee sister.'

Reekie leaned forward: 'But what I really wanted to tell you was that the doctor who died on the bridge phoned me. He asked if he could see the film. I was supposed to meet him on Sunday. He was going to finalise the time. Now he's dead. So is Evan. There's something awful going on here.'

'I think you're right. Can I see it, do you have the video?'

'It's on my phone. I've seen it a thousand times. It shows nothing. But Dr Maxwell already knew a lot of the detail that Evan had noted.'

'He'd already seen it.'

'Not only seen it, he sounded like he'd studied it, dissected it. I think he might have paid more attention than I did.'

Caplan had saved the short clips of film on her phone, less than thirty seconds. In the car, parked in a quiet lay-by, she clicked on 'play'.

From his position on top of the embankment, Evan had heard the Oban train and filmed it as it appeared on the left of the screen, round the corner through the trees. Then, to the right of the screen, on the other side of the tracks, appeared a very young girl wearing a white skirt, followed by a taller girl in red. The train thundered past.

It was very clear until the film showed the sky, then a brief flash of blurring, then a close-up of grass. Caplan sent the video clip to her tablet and watched it on the bigger screen. She went through it almost frame by frame, looking at the front, then the top of the train. She thought she could see the train driver reacting. The noise was intense, the train screaming to a halt way, way too far up the line. The train, as she inched it along, frame by frame, was almost beneath Evan when the impact had happened. Then the blurred image as the phone slipped from the boy's hand. She moved back a few frames, seeing something she thought at first was a bird, or a piece of paper, but she couldn't make sense of it.

It was very late, but Caplan couldn't sleep. Craigo had decided to stay at the office and was scrutinising the video clip. She hadn't said anything to him, just asked him to examine it closely.

The Fiscal was getting antsy. The case was going round and round, and each time it came back to Gillian. With the consternation in the media, the Fiscal was wanting to go ahead and press charges after they'd seen the dashcam footage of the figure on the bridge.

And here they were, down another blind alley, looking at something that had never been considered a crime.

Why was she resisting so much? They had evidence. But did they have enough? Why not charge Gillian? Then find out what was between her and Ted Maxwell. Both Karl Rolland and Peter Biggs had been reinterviewed, and they knew nothing of Gillian Halliday except she may have been on Ted's list of 'interesting'. But Caplan had said to the Fiscal's office that they needed more time. Any competent defence would ask how Gillian got there, from a remote hillside location to the bridge.

Any evidence was circumstantial. But it all pointed to Gillian.

It was an itch she needed to scratch. What was the relationship between Maxwell and Gillian? Where was the electronic footprint of Maxwell's work?

Cordelia, for one, needed to know.

Something about this case was annoying her. She suspected that it was the same thing that had been annoying Dr Maxwell. Walking away and giving up went against the grain. Caplan had asked Gillian that question, *Did you kill him?*

It had taken a moment; Gillian had refused to answer, rolled her eyes and given her the look of an angry tiger. *Do you remember killing him?*

What the fuck do you think?

Scafoli, who knew Gillian better than most, thought she was lying about her memory loss. Why? Well, it stopped a lot of inconvenient questions.

Gillian was younger than her years, she had been denied normal social niceties, but there was something salvageable about her. She had an ongoing mental-health disorder although had been judged stable by the time that Caplan got to talk to her.

Caplan got out of her bed and opened the laptop again. She watched the video clip, pausing it as the flash of white appeared in the lower right of the screen.

Then her phone pinged, a WhatsApp from her sergeant. It was a photograph of Craigo's hand, a slim image, his fingers straight and pointing up, the wrist rotated so the thumb was hidden behind the other fingers. The palm, viewed sideways on, was a sliver of pale skin.

Caplan went back to the clip. Yes, it was obvious now. But what was the hand doing?

What difference did it make, it was the hand of somebody on the west side of the track. Gillian was near the fence on the other side.

Then the words came back to her. *She wasn't there.* Evan's phone had stopped filming, picking up only the grass but Evan himself had watched the train go past. He had seen what was on the track, his mum had been very clear about how good his visual memory was.

And who was, and who was not there.

Mackie had also sent her a file, with the title 'Worth a visit?' She'd been typing up a brief summary on the death of Poppy Anstruther, and had read the report from the woman who had been in charge that night.

If the Fiscal had his way the answer would be no, it wasn't worth a visit.

The Guide leader, Alison Watkins, had been asleep in her tent at the camp when she was woken at midnight by two girls. It took her some time to come round. The girls apologised for disturbing her but told her she was needed. They went out and, as a surprise, the Guides had laid out cake and drinks in the eating hut. There was an impromptu party during which Gillian, Poppy and a girl called Abby wandered off. Poppy's bed was still empty when everybody, including Gillian, came back from the party. Later, two girls, Pauline and Abby, found Poppy at the small lochan in the wood at the campsite about ten minutes' walk from the tents. Her head in the water, her body on the bank.

Gillian and Rachel Mary.

Gillian and Rachel Susan.

Gillian and Poppy.

Gillian and Ted.

And the words drifted into her head: Gillian and Fiona.

TWENTY-ONE

My dad's a plank. After I saw the guy die in the hospital, he took me to Burger King as he thought I was upset. So that was a result.

Killagal Blog, 2021

Caplan woke around six on the Thursday morning with the rain drumming on the roof of the caravan. She got up, listening again to the comforting hiss and bubble of the water inside the kettle sitting on the gas ring. It brought back memories of family caravan holidays when the kids were wee. Even as tots, her kids had been out and about, nothing stopped them, not the rain, not gales, nothing.

How had Gillian grown up? Was there anything so abnormal about her upbringing? Maybe a dangerous little quirk of her personality had been accepted by the small community she grew up in, whereas it may have been noted by childcare professionals in playgroup or nursery. There were four adults, her big brother and the girl next door: the pseudo big sister. The problems only started when younger siblings came along.

After Rachel Susan's death, Gillian had been sent to a small residential unit called Hollows. Her family always kept in touch, they took her out. She had always known that she belonged. And that she was loved.

The earlier death at Church's Pass had occurred in 2011, not so long ago. Gillian, aged seven, would have received specialist treatment for the stress of the incident, then joined mainstream school. The whole idea of the Tollen Protocol was nurture not punishment.

Rowan had been at the railway that day but saw nothing; a little voice in Caplan's head immediately added 'claimed to see nothing'. He had been twelve, that bit more mature.

The kettle was singing, so she poured the water into a cup, letting the teabag drift around a little. Rowan still carried that air of quiet assurance.

She looked at her phone for the time, and thought she may as well have a shower while the water was hot.

Over her tea and yoghurt, she opened the link to the TV documentary 'The Rage'. She was going to watch it again, now she knew the players on the stage.

It covered the incident at Church's Pass. A witness – Evan, she presumed – was accused of changing his story. Not that he was too young, too traumatised, just that one of the main witnesses had lied. This time she recognised the family, even with their faces blurred, as they danced the conga round the garden. Two girls running to join the back of the line, Gillian tumbling to the ground. Gail, much taller at this age, helped her up and held her hand as they caught up with the adults, making sure she was okay.

Then a race across the lawn, still a slope in those days, a climb over the fence, first to the doocot was the winner, but the winner was brought down by an innocent-looking body block by the blurred face in second place, who then claimed victory, and was then picked up by the rest and gently thrown over the low dyke. The soundtrack faded in, much laughter and merriment, which then drifted to the usual voiceover.

But people had watched that years ago and Gillian was still thought to be 'evil'. When she'd been considered fit to return to society, she was quietly released under a new identity, but somebody had found out exactly who and where she was and had torched the place.

On her drive to work, Caplan thought long and hard about the documentary, trying to pinpoint what was troubling her about this case.

She'd only been in the incident room for three minutes when McPhee pounced.

'Can I have a word, ma'am?'

'We are having a word.'

'In your office maybe?' McPhee held out his tablet, showing a Zoom meeting.

Caplan stopped scrolling through her laptop and went into the office, trying not to show her impatience.

'I've found her.' He was excited. 'Meryl.'

'Meryl?'

'The young lady who was interested in Ted was not Cheryl but Meryl. Meryl Murdoch. There was a lot of security footage from Callworth Road, so I took a shortcut. She's not on any professional register because she's not qualified yet, but I went back through some lectures Dr Maxwell did during lockdown, the university has them online. Plus a screenshot to check attendance. This is the print-out.'

Caplan looked at the twelve faces on the Zoom meeting, not recognising anybody from the description until McPhee tapped the screen with his finger.

'I spoke to one of her clinical team leaders. Meryl has already had an official warning, blogging about clients and breaking confidence. She wants to be on the telly.'

'We shall make a detective of you yet. So, Maxwell lectured Meryl at some point. For an encore, find out where they met in real life.'

'She lives down in Dumbarton. Has a placement in Alexandria, in an assessment unit. She has the day off today. We could go and ask her?'

'Would you be offended if I took Craigo?'

McPhee deflated.

'He will annoy her, in a way you won't. We'll report back to you. Excellent work.'

Meryl Murdoch lived in a modern flat overlooking the Clyde in one of the nicer estates. After opening the door, she strolled back to her white and gold living room, where a permanent white Christmas tree stood decorated with gold baubles beside a wall mosaic of photographs in gold and silver frames, mostly of Murdoch and another woman, arms round each other, usually with a drink in their hands, celebrating. Murdoch herself, in white sweat-suit and gold jewellery, matched her flat. The over-large sweat-suit drowned her slim frame, with an ankle cuff pulled up to reveal six inches of tanned shin, the sleeves pushed up over her forearms and the snake of gold bangles. She looked relaxed and happy, reclining on her sofa. She was keen – too keen – to see the police, which was odd considering she had not come forward with any information about the death of Dr Maxwell.

Caplan suspected that Murdoch was enjoying herself.

'Before you start—' There was a casual toss of black geometric-cut hair, a few strands of deep purple running through it '—I can only tell you what is in the public domain.' She smiled at Craigo. 'Girl A's still covered by patient confidentiality and you'll need all kinds of court documentation to get me to break that with regard to anybody.'

Craigo waved his pencil. 'We'd probably just ask her,' he shrugged.

Caplan let Murdoch talk to Craigo as if he was the boss. At the moment he was standing awkwardly in the living-room doorway, looking at Murdoch and avoiding Caplan's eyes. Murdoch couldn't have been more than mid-twenties, a pointed face that was a little too smug. Caplan decided not to sit down, which meant Craigo had to stand as well. A very slight sneer passed Murdoch's face, there and gone.

Murdoch was enjoying Craigo's discomfort. She was a bully, and Craigo, a man Caplan knew had been a victim once and prob-ably most of his life, took two steps back, which in the small flat looked as though he was now standing in the hallway, blocking the exit. Murdoch watched him, sitting back, looking like the cat that got the cream and had the cake and eaten both. There was a trawl of long nails through the hair, a pout, and a stretch that was merely for show.

She was bored.

Any moment now Caplan expected Craigo to start pointing with the chewed end of his pencil. Which he did, took a deep breath, then asked, 'Can we talk about the relationship between Edward Maxwell and yourself?'

She regarded him, almost sighing with the effort. 'Police Scotland, one of the last bastions of male toxicity.' She tossed her hair again, folding her knees underneath her, smiling.

Caplan noticed her eyebrows, how thick and dark they were. Murdoch had had work done on her plumped lips, the top so much that in a certain light it cast a moustache of shadow. She could see what Rolland was meaning; this lady was not Maxwell's type. She'd have been a very pretty woman, if she'd left herself alone.

As the silence lingered, Murdoch looked from Craigo to Caplan, suddenly unsure, sensing she'd been wrong-footed. Caplan knew that Murdoch was only seeing the other woman in the room for the first time. Such pseudo-feminists didn't tend to notice other women who were doing their own thing, making their own way, getting there by being good at their job. It didn't fit the narrative, it didn't play into Murdoch's very conscious bias that all men were the work of Satan. She might now see the immaculately dressed detective with the tablet in her hand, rather than the notepad and chewed pencil.

'Oh, he's not that bad, as far as bastions of male toxicity go,' Caplan said.

'Well thank you, ma'am,' Craigo nodded, happy at the compliment though she doubted if he really understood it.

Murdoch was pulling the cuffs of her jogging bottoms down to her ankles, her mouth gaping slightly, rosy red. Caplan wondered if Murdoch was actually flirting with Craigo. He had testosterone so he was fair game.

Toxic femininity.

'Edward Maxwell, tell us about your relationship with him?'

'That's not something I'd like to talk about.'

'It's something his wife might like to discuss.'

'Ha.'

'Why were you at her house?'

'Ted has something of mine, I want it back.'

'What?'

'A piece of research that we were doing together. It's my intellectual property. I want it back,' she repeated.

'And what form did this research take?'

Murdoch wrinkled her nose; she didn't understand the question.

'Email? Hard copy? Word documents being sent back and forth?'

'All of the above.'

'You'll have copies?'

'No, he wanted everything. He asked me not to keep anything.'

Murdoch didn't add 'typical man', but it was there.

'Because what you were working on was patient-sensitive?'

'Client-sensitive.'

'Yes, and we have clients who stay with us for "Her Majesty's pleasure". What were you working on?'

No response.

Caplan typed something out, letting Murdoch stew a little. 'You and Dr Maxwell, what was going on there?' Caplan's voice was light but brutal.

Murdoch made a decision, a deep sigh. 'He became very interested in Girl A at the end of 2021. He was making enquiries about her, as a subject of study. She was a golden goose. He had a large file about her, he was paranoid about secrecy. He had newspaper clips, magazine articles, lots of comment about the Tollen Protocol.'

'To what end?'

'To write a book. We were going to write a book on it. Then he changed his mind. No idea why, he just snapped. He couldn't do it without me.'

'But he was going to, wasn't he?'

'Look, we were talking at cross-purposes. He had the impression that I was working on a literature review of cases like Girl A for my dissertation. He agreed that I could do some research for him. Then he sacks me, after I've given him some very useful data.' Her jaw set in anger, but she said no more.

'Did he suspect you were getting information you were not entitled to? He wouldn't be interested in seeing anything you were not legally entitled to have in your possession. If you did, he'd report you. You would have got struck off.'

'Not quite on, ma'am, to get struck off,' said Craigo.

'Even worse,' agreed Caplan. 'So you had access to the subject?'

'Client, ma'am,' corrected Craigo.

'No comment.' Murdoch looked down at the floor but not before she'd glanced at the wall. Caplan followed her gaze; when she looked back at Murdoch, the psychologist was looking back at her. Caught.

'We'll accept that for now. But he changed his mind anyway?'

Murdoch looked at the ceiling. 'We'd a publisher and everything; imagine the money there would be in that book.' She rolled her eyes. 'It would be my pension. Britain's Most Evil Woman. I'm still going to write it.'

'Had he ever met her?'

'No.'

'Why was he avoiding you?'

'He wasn't.'

'He was, Meryl. And you, for the want of a better word, were stalking him. So, Meryl, do you have any idea why Dr Ted Maxwell was so interested in Gillian Rose Halliday? This is a murder inquiry.'

'Nothing concrete.'

'Anything non-concrete that you could tell us?'

She looked surly; her new toy was about to be taken off her. 'He was doing a study and Gillian was part of that study. I saw him lecture about it, just after lockdown.'

'What was the study about?'

She sniffed scornfully and the spider eyes gave an eye roll. 'Children who kill.' She took a breath. 'Obviously.'

'We know that – but the kids themselves, the murders, PTSD, toxic parents, society, brain development, what?'

'Just general.'

'I could write a paper on children who kill. Unfortunately. There's nothing new in that, there must have been an angle. You told him, you can tell us.'

Murdoch shook her head. 'Nothing that wasn't in the public domain if you look hard enough.'

'So you could tell us.'

'No, you aren't healthcare professionals.'

Caplan nodded, knowing Murdoch's reticence to come forward was due to her secret, unethical source of information. If Ted Maxwell had found out how her 'insight' was sourced, he'd have dropped her like a stone. How did she react to the risk of being exposed? 'Have you ever met Gillian?'

Murdoch shook her head. 'Gillian was at Rettie, her mental health was failing, all kinds of paranoia going on.'

'How do you know that? Were you in touch with her or one of her support team?'

She shrugged; the glibness had gone. More than a little concern in her eyes now.

'Did you and Maxwell ever actually work together?'

'Not officially.'

'Did he pay you?' Caplan paused, thinking. 'Unofficially.'

'I want to speak to my lawyer.'

'Well, on you go, as long as you're quick. You seem very calm to me for somebody whose colleague – unofficial colleague – was stabbed through the heart and then thrown off a bridge. And he was a fit and healthy young man. God knows what they'd do if they got hold of you. You'd be helping yourself if you were a bit more cooperative. You could be next, until we know who did it . . .'

Murdoch laughed out loud. 'Gillian did it, of course she bloody did it!'

'I'm not so sure.' The words out of Caplan's own mouth surprised her.

'God.' A condescending shake of her head, her earrings rattling. 'Then you are one shit cop.'

Craigo folded his arms, looking at the ceiling, thinking, chewing the end of his pencil. 'Or, ma'am, it could be that Meryl here did it herself. I mean, I had a good look at Google maps and it's not impossible. She was in Leeds early afternoon Friday eighth, then through Glasgow, easily on the Connel Bridge at midnight.' He was poised with his pencil, ready to write down the next thing she said. 'Just a thought,' he went on, 'but where were you, Miss, exactly, at the time that the young Dr Maxwell was murdered? I mean, you were in Leeds on the Friday, and you were back here by the evening, but can we clarify what we mean by evening? To be clear.'

'I'm not bloody—'

'It's totally possible, DS Craigo. Her satnav will tell us if nothing else does. CCTV if she went by public transport. If she doesn't tell us, we have to presume the worst, okay? Don't get up, we shall see ourselves out. Get a lawyer and we'll bring you down to be interviewed.'

They both sat in the Duster, Craigo making notes, Caplan thinking that Murdoch was now more concerned about the ethics, or lack of, in her access to Gillian getting out, rather than the death of her co-writer. But there was another link in the chain made.

'Did you see who those pictures were of?' Caplan asked.

'Meryl and her partner, ma'am.'

'But who was she, the other woman? I've seen that face before.'

'We could go back in and ask her?'

'We could, but we won't. Get on to the council and find out who else lives there.' Caplan picked up her phone to make a call and realised there were two voicemails waiting for her.

Aklen sounding a little infirm and unsteady; something had got to him.

Then Lizzie, ranting. Caplan held the mobile away from her ear. Her friend was very angry. '*I believe you've been spying on me.*' Lizzie's voice was tight as she said it. 'Why did you not come in, why sit outside? Did you not think you'd be welcome? Well, you'd be right! Because it is no business of yours, is it? What are you going to do? Tell John? That would be just like you, tell him and then what? You facilitated this, Christine, but it's nothing to do with you. Do you think I owe you in some way? Do you now own me? Little Miss Perfect in her lovely house with the handsome Aklen who isn't everything you think he is, and the two fabulous children that could do no wrong. Well, look at where they are now. Look at you now. What the hell do you see when you look in the mirror because whatever it is, it's not what everybody else is seeing. You're so stuffed up, even Aklen can't stand you any more, you are so—'

She cut the message off.

'She doesn't sound very pleased, ma'am, does she? Is that PC Fergusson?'

'She's a police officer involved with a known criminal. Romantically.' Caplan shook her head. And then *Aklen isn't everything you think he is.*

Craigo pursed his lips. 'Oh, dearie me, that's not going to end well, is it?'

'No. And Aklen's pissed off at the new neighbours already. That was quick. I'd better go round and see what's going on. Are you okay to get the train back?'

During the drive to the train station, they heard a 'danger to life' warning on the radio, with wind and rain, an area of low pressure spinning towards the west coast.

Caplan knew she had enough clothes to do her for another couple of days but thought there might be less of Challie Cottage when and if she ever got back to it. Indeed, the caravan might have blown away.

Abington Drive was busy. A truck was being unloaded of pallets of bricks and slates, a small cherry-picker carefully easing them onto next door's lawn in a neat row.

Caplan parked the Duster in her driveway, glanced over to see if their new neighbour was going to introduce themselves, but those present, five men in all, seemed content to stand around and smoke.

When Caplan opened her front door and saw the two cards on the mat, she thought she was going to explode. Twice a surveyor had come round to do a home report. Twice Aklen hadn't bothered to even let them in.

She placed the cards on the kitchen table in front of her husband. The argument started.

Aklen shrugged. 'I never heard them. Did you know that Kenny was on the phone? He's struggling a bit at Skone. He thinks he needs specialist help, and that's expensive.'

'I think he needs to put some work in. He can't be made better, he has to want to be better.'

'Kenny needs help. You know that. If it was Emma, I don't think you'd hesitate.'

Caplan did a slow count to ten. 'Aklen, sometimes you're a real bastard. I'm not dignifying that with an answer. I love both of them equally, I would do anything for them, but you know what? We can't afford it. We can't afford to help our son. That's not my doing, I go out to work and I put money in the bank every month. You are the one who can't even be arsed to let the surveyor in.'

'I'm not well . . .'

'Well, bloody get better. It's pulling this family apart. I'm up there working my backside off earning money to keep this house, the cottage, the caravan and you. The Magus is looking after Emma, thank God, and yes, Kenny does need our help. Well, no actually, he needs your help.'

'My help?'

'He needs a better role model, somebody who doesn't say "I can't cope" then leaves everybody else to cope for them. It's not fair on us. It was you he phoned, not me.'

'And what does that tell you? You are too busy to care!'

'Or that he wanted some attention from you?'

'Actually, it's your mess.' Aklen was right in her face. 'If you had resigned when they wanted you to, then Emma would be well, and Kenny would never have dabbled in drugs, he'd never have been in front of that car. You did that, you and only you.'

If he expected a reaction from his wife, he didn't get one.

Caplan nodded and said, 'There might be some truth in that.

I'll pack my bag, I'm going home. By home I mean Challie Cottage. Even with no windows and no bloody roof I'll get a warmer welcome there than I do here.'

She went upstairs and threw a few things into a suitcase, then came down again. When she reached the front door, her husband of twenty-four years was holding it open for her.

She left without a further word.

She, Christine Caplan, was moving on and moving out. She could have paused, turned round, gone back into the house, tried to calm the situation down.

But she didn't.

She started the engine, seeing next door's cat jump onto the wall that divided the two driveways, little Pas de Chat arching his back and mewling at being ignored.

Caplan waved at him. She had her own cat now.

She selected first gear and drove away slowly, watching in the rear-view mirror to check if Aklen was looking out from behind the curtains to see if she was really going.

He wasn't.

On the two hour drive up north, through the dark and the drizzle, she tried a few CDs, none to her liking, not even *Swan Lake*. She'd danced to that, kept at the back of the stage; she was already growing a little too tall.

She drove on in silence, the hum of the engine and the comforting tick-swish of the windscreen wipers giving her company. She was already relaxing as she left the city behind and drove up the side of the loch, then on to quieter roads, turning to the coast before the Great Glen. All she could see were the shades of grey of the grass, the water and the jagged outlines of the mountains that eased into gentle contours as she neared the sea. She was content to leave the city behind and embrace the wilderness. It had been ninety minutes and she had hardly thought of her husband or her family at all. Gillian was never far from her mind.

In the distance she could see the lights of the farms and cottages she had become familiar with as she had commuted over the last nine months. Searching Rightmove, peering into estate agents' windows in Cronchie, nothing had come close to the cottage she had seen on the shore, looking over the Sound of Kerrera.

She had decided to buy it. The kids were keen, Aklen had been enthusiastic.

At that point.

Christine, Emma and Kenny had looked ahead to the family going their separate ways. Emma was going out to Skone. Kenny, once recovered, was returning to Aberdeen University. While Aklen stayed in Glasgow, watching the mounting bills and the clock ticking, receding under the duvet with each passing day.

It was up to Aklen now. She would be there if he needed her, but he had to make that decision.

He could do what the hell he wanted.

TWENTY-TWO

The best way to commit murder? Keep it simple.
Shove your victim down the stairs. Or off a cliff.
Remember to burst into tears.
Ask for therapy as you're soooooo traumatised you couldn't
*   save them.*

Killagal Blog, 2022

Nothing much had changed overnight, except Caplan's mood got worse. Aklen hadn't been in touch. She checked with Emma and Kenny, who hadn't heard from him but they both said they'd find a reason to phone home. She thought Kenny sounded just fine, telling filthy jokes to try to shock his mother.

Meanwhile the police–media liaison and the press were locked in a moral struggle over Girl A, the privacy rights of the individual versus the public's right to know. Bloggers and social-media commentators arguing over things they could know nothing about, but ignorance of the facts never stopped them having an opinion. When it was reported that Girl A had been found and escorted from her hiding place with the safeguard of an armed unit, Twitter had gone into meltdown.

Caplan was starting to have a degree of empathy with Gillian, recalling the fear that had floated across the young woman's eyes when she had talked about getting released and going out to live in the big wide world. No wonder she was scared; maybe everything else was bravado.

In her office, she looked over the short report that had come in from the uniform team who had traced Miss McColl, the schoolteacher who had reported Gillian's injuries to social services. Mackie had then traced that report through the system to find a home visit had been made. The other two children up at Ben o' Tae had no injuries, they were happy. Another two spot-checks were carried out due to the kids not being in the education system. The matter was explained as Gillian being the adventurous, clumsy, daredevil child.

The other two kids, Rowan and Gail, lived up in their little enclave, hardly seen. The GP had commented that Gillian might do well with stimulation and socialisation with her peers. Then the incident at Church's Pass happened and the phrase 'It's just Gillian' became a little more serious.

It didn't make Caplan feel any easier. It was only ever Gillian who was getting hurt.

She came out her office to find Craigo sitting at his desk, both arms folded, still wearing his outdoor jacket. He looked up at her. 'I was thinking, ma'am.'

'I see. What were you thinking about? The next tea break or something that might actually move the case along a bit?'

'Twice Ted Maxwell was working on a book, twice he has pulled out. Why? Why can we find nothing? Where is it?'

'You should join the CID. Did you come up with any answers?'

'Not at all, ma'am. Not one.'

Caplan slumped down in Mackie's chair. 'But say we're walking in the footsteps of Ted. We're both circling around Gillian, neither of us with direct access to her history. Everything's filtered by somebody, or by time. While we're thinking of attributing more crimes to her, maybe Ted found out something that caused him to rethink.'

'Something made him very secretive. He was getting the measure of her? Or he became protective, ma'am. Of Gillian?'

'Good thought.' Caplan looked at the board. 'Only one person talked about Gillian as a victim. Maxwell would respect the opinion of a teacher. Go and speak to Jeannie McCann . . .'

'McColl.'

'In the queue or wherever. Did Maxwell speak to her?'

'Yes he did, quite a long conversation, but nothing we haven't covered, ma'am,' said Craigo. 'And I've been in touch with the Fiscal that chaired the inquiry into Fiona McCleary's death. It was a Kubota landscaping vehicle, small, open-topped tray on the back. It slipped out of gear and had gathered enough momentum to smash her against the wall.'

'The gap from the house to the outbuildings is narrow but it must have come through there to go downhill,' said Caplan.

'Duguid couldn't recall, but he parks them lined up and ready. He can only think he left the handbrake off.'

'And I bet he'd never done that before.'

'It's a reflex, pulling on a handbrake. Fiona was dead long before the ambulance could get there; no surprise considering where they live.'

Caplan closed her eyes. 'I'm very tired. What're you not saying, Craigo?'

'I'm not not saying anything.'

'Craigo? Finnan? I trust your instinct, what is that instinct telling you now?'

'I don't know. I grew up on a farm, I could drive when I was ten. I was thinking about being young, the things that influence you. What Gillian learned when she was the little one. You see it in the essays she writes on Killagal.'

'We call it blogging here on earth.'

'Could I have a look at them all, ma'am?'

'Yes. While they are shocking, they are inconsistent. That night Rachel Susan fell ill? Miranda was in the ambulance with the wee one. Jim was driving behind the ambulance with Gail, Gillian and Rowan, so I presume Duguid wasn't at home. I get that, if your baby needs to go to the Sick Kids, a ninety-minute drive away, then you'd pile all the children in the car.' Caplan thought for a moment. 'But at the hospital Gillian wandered away, saw things she shouldn't see. That might've been the start of it. Life and death fascinates some people.'

'Why was the wee one in hospital anyway?' asked Craigo. 'Maybe that was the start of it in reality.'

'Okay. I'm going to speak to Gail later, she'll know.' Caplan threw her pen on the table. 'I'll get the rest of the blogs printed out for you. They're brutal.'

*   *   *

Gail put the coffee down in front of them. She sat and closed her
eyes; one finger worked its way across her forehead and back,
something troubling her. Her eye was less red, but she still looked
stressed. She explained that she'd been working up in the office
and Miranda had been delayed at work so Gail had to watch Alice
for a wee bit longer.

'I'm grateful for the interruption, to be honest, it's been spread-
sheet hell this morning. How's Gillian doing? If there's anything
she needs, let us know.'

'You seem very fond of her.'

'She was like my wee sister before she was my sister-in-law.
What do you want to know?'

'Did you ever witness Gillian being abused here?'

Gail's mouth opened, the blue eyes popped in surprise, then
she smiled and nodded. 'Oh, the mad teacher? She got it all wrong.
Gillian was clumsy and, to be fair, she was always taking Rowan
on in fights, just messing around. But she never backed down or
cried when she was hurt. She just stood up and asked for more.
Miranda was really upset when that woman from social services
appeared. We thought Rowan was going to be taken away.'

'Did you give any information to *The Child Killers of Britain*
documentary?'

She thought for a moment. 'Background stuff, yes. About the
family. Thought it was better they got it right. How wrong was I.
A handsome young researcher bought me a sandwich. It was fiction
in the end. Rowan wasn't happy when he found out. I was very
young.' She shrugged and smiled.

'Can you tell me why Rachel Susan had to go to hospital a few
months before she died? And who went with her?'

'Oh, you've got to that, have you?' she nodded. 'She was having
convulsions. An ambulance took her and Miranda, and my dad
drove behind with us kids.'

'Your dad was driving?'

'Yes. Rowan's dad met us there. The fit was caused by too much
salt in her blood. Please don't ask how that happened, but you can
see the leap I made when I was old enough to understand. I was
terrified in that car, such a long drive, it was so dark and the
flashing lights of the ambulance. The hospital was something that
we hadn't witnessed anything like before. Then Gillian got lost.'

'Are you saying that Gillian gave Rachel salt?'

'I don't know, but looking back, I have wondered a few times. Things go well when she's not here. Can I show you something? I know that when I read it, it really helped me understand how the family works. It all happens by degrees, you see. The misunderstandings become fact, the vicious truths continue. *It's not dangerous, she's only teasing.* You've no idea how often I heard that. But looking at it in the cold light of day, well, it might paint a different picture.'

She got up and walked over to a Welsh dresser on the far side of the kitchen, took out a box covered in pink flowers and brought it back to the table. Opening it up she flicked through the photographs and newspaper cuttings, every single one about Gillian.

'Quite a collection you have there,' said Caplan.

'Rowan's, not mine. I think he needs to keep tabs on things, he likes to be in control. He pays more attention to Gill than he does to Alice at times, he likes to know how his sister's being portrayed in the media. Natural, I suppose.' She found an A4 beige envelope that had been well handled, and opened it, pulling out a few sheets of folded paper. Caplan could see neat handwriting through the plain white paper, precisely lined and evenly spaced. She would have guessed that the handwriting belonged to Rowan.

'There're a few things, a few old family stories, like the time she threw Bobo off a cliff, just a wee collie puppy. He nipped her ankle, the way collies do. She just picked him up and went to hurl him onto the rocks – I mean powerfully, at the rocks. I tried to grab the pup, missed. Rowan knocked Gillian off balance but the dog still died. Then she got a fright, she didn't realise she was so close to the cliff, she didn't mean it. Her weird behaviour has been subtly normalised by the family in tiny increments.'

'Okay,' said Caplan. 'So, it didn't happen overnight. It was constant small things, and you were just too close to see how bad it was getting?'

'Drip drip drip. I think we normalised it. Miranda definitely has. She did leave the room unlocked. There you go, you can read it if you want, lots of people have. Rowan insists that we keep the original copy. Dead pets, locking Granda up, putting wee Rachel Susan in a suitcase and out with the rubbish.' Gail looked upset. 'Then my spaniel pup, Molly, pooed in Gillian's bedroom and she hit it. Molly bit her. She got her grandad to shoot it in front of me.' Tears streamed down her face; she pawed them away with an apology. 'Looking at each incident, it's just an incident, it's just kids.' She passed the box across the table. 'But if you look at it all? I'll go and let the dogs out, see if Granda wants a cup of tea. Leave you to it.'

Once she was out the door, Craigo asked, 'Is she telling us that her sister-in-law is a nasty psychopath?'

'Have you ever met a nice one?' Caplan unfolded the paper, smoothing it out on the top of the kitchen table. Then started to read it out loud, but quietly, to Craigo. 'Gillian had locked Granda in the shed and left him there for hours until Miranda came home and heard his screams. So much worse as Granda had PTSD; he's suffered from it for a while, certainly since the landslide. You told me about that.'

'Eric Thomson and the wee lassie. They were trapped for hours. They were safe but they couldn't get out. He was a bloody hero, but after that he was terrified of small spaces, wouldn't even get in a car. That's very telling, ma'am, playing on that phobia. This is very telling also.' He held up a business card. Dr Edward Maxwell.

On the drive back to the station Craigo regaled her with yet more stories of Tonka Thomson and his service in Northern Ireland and then the Falklands. It seemed to Caplan that the more she knew of those at Ben o' Tae, the less surprised she was at Gillian's mental-health problems.

Her afternoon was filled with a long and pointless Zoom meeting with ACC Linden and the Fiscal's office. Caplan was arguing that the killing of Poppy Anstruther at Sugar Loaf was an issue between two thirteen-year-olds. If they had been walking down the street and got into a fight, there would be no Tollen burden. It was Gillian's past that she carried with her. And if Caplan was reopening the case, which she reminded them had never been tried in court, the evidence never tested, guilt never proven 'beyond reasonable doubt', then a full investigation should be allowed this time.

The junior Fiscal she was talking to kept harking back to the mood of social media and asking whether this line was helpful. Could she not just pursue Dr Edward Maxwell's death? Caplan reiterated that this was the case that they were being paid to investigate, but knew she was fighting a losing battle. There was no hard evidence against Gillian, but her past made it a slam dunk.

Even within her own team, up on the bridge at the re-enactment, they had constantly referred to the assailant as 'Gillian'.

Caplan was also thinking about Evan Reekie's suicide. What had disrupted him so much, so deeply that he couldn't live with himself much longer?

Police Scotland had asked him to change his story; he had doubted what he saw with his own eyes.

Now, on her way home, she was tired and resentful. Aklen had not phoned to apologise. Not a text, nothing, and if he was waiting for her, he'd wait a long time. A quick WhatsApp to the kids, but they hadn't heard from him either. The wind was blowing a gale, the sea splashing high on the road, obliterating her windscreen, the wipers unable to keep up with it. Caplan, by force of habit, kept cleaning the inside of the window with the back of her sleeve but it made no difference, the water was all on the outside. Twice she felt the car being lifted from the road and panicked that it was a wave hitting the Duster, ready to float it out to sea, but it was merely the power of the wind howling and lashing, wanting to get inside and tear her to pieces. She drove slowly, crawling along the road with the full beams on, hearing the wind coming down the glen and the waves crashing on the shore in an attempt to catch up with it.

This was getting very nasty.

She was now inching along, peering into the darkness. She listened to the beating of the wipers and heard a terrible creaking that stopped then started again. She turned round, rotating in the seat to see what was making the noise. There was nothing out there but wind, darkness and rain. She considered her options. Going on? Turning back? Heading to the nearest farmhouse?

There was an almighty crash.

The world went dark.

Her heart missed a few beats. A tree had fallen across the road right in front of her so all she could see in the beam from her headlights was the bark of the trunk. The lower branches on the driver's side had dented the metalwork.

She had missed being killed by inches.

She leant her head on the steering wheel. She was fine. The car was trapped but the tree wasn't lying on the bonnet. The Duster would survive; it wasn't called the poor man's four-by-four for nothing. She selected reverse, and slowly the car disentangled itself with a lot of scraping and nudging of the small branches that had impacted the roof and the driver's door.

She couldn't reverse far, though, as the light was so poor. The driver's door had jammed so she climbed out the passenger's side and inspected the damage with her phone torch. The waterside trees bent and swayed alarmingly as she watched. The tree that had been uprooted had fallen across the road from the shore, the top of it now hanging, caught in the undergrowth on the opposite side.

She had driven this road many times, but now she was slightly unsure where she was, disorientated by the weather, the lack of view. The best thing to do was reverse away from the trees and try a hundred-point turn. Go back the way she came.

It took five minutes to turn, another ten along the road she had just travelled, then her headlights caught something across the way in front of her.

Another fallen tree. She swore and called the station; they must be used to this. She could survive in the car, she had plenty of clothes, she wasn't hurt. She wasn't an emergency. Jackson was at the desk, sounding a little harassed, asking her to hold on. She heard him shouting something to Mackie.

Then silence. She held on for a few long minutes of nothing. Then Jackson took her rough location and told her to hang up and get back in the car. If nothing had happened within the hour, she was to call him back. So she waited. Her brief flurry outside had soaked her to the skin, her second set of clothes was making no difference to her. She was getting colder, and it was more than the temperature dipping. It was the fact that she had to stay so still; there was no way to move and ease off the chill that gripped her muscles. She tried to get the broken heater to work; it refused. She put the blower on to circulate some air, thinking that it was the wet clothes that were chilling her. Surely April couldn't be that cold that she'd freeze to death? And then thinking of where she was, how exposed she was, and realising how wrong she was.

She must have dozed a little, wakening up when she heard a car horn and saw light blaring into her windscreen from a vehicle a good bit taller than hers.

The door of the vehicle opened and a man in a hi-vis jacket was gesturing to her to get out. She didn't need telling twice. She dragged her rucksack with her, then got up and over the tree trunk, the teeth on the bark catching her clothes and tearing her skin. A hand emerged from an anorak sleeve, the face hidden by a scarf and a hood. A voice said something, the hand grabbed her wrist to help her over, steadying her at the other side as the wind caught her slight frame and threatened to lift her off her feet.

She was pushed by him, or by the force of the wind, towards the vehicle, blinded by the six headlamps, leaving the Duster behind like a crumpled toy.

Inside the rear of the vehicle was warm, dark. It smelled of damp clothes and tomato soup. There was already a young woman sitting in the back, hood up, shivering, still not warmed through, two small children, a boy and a girl, cradled into her. They looked terrified. They exchanged tired smiles.

Then the driver said, 'You okay, ma'am? One more pick-up.'

Of course it was Craigo, she recognised the vehicle now. She sat in the back, crammed into the corner next to the woman and two children. The Hilux rumbled on. She could see nothing but the square head of the man in the passenger seat, who was looking at the satnav as Craigo watched the road. She was surprised when she recognised his voice. It was McPhee, who she'd left at the station.

She heard them talk in low tones, obviously looking for another car in distress. Then the Hilux stopped, handbrake rammed on, and both men got out, moving with some urgency.

A small Fiat had either driven off the road or, it looked to Caplan, the weight of the water had caused the edge of the road to collapse. The occupants of the car were stuck, the back end in water, the front still on the road.

McPhee and Craigo were deep in discussion. There wasn't enough room to tow the car out with the Hilux. They clambered over, McPhee getting a foothold on a thick slab of tarmac that formed a small island in the water, while Craigo tried to get between the open door and the body of the car.

Craigo stretched out his hand, gesticulating to the occupants to stay where they were until he found a better grip, then he rotated his wrist, beckoning that the figure in the car could get out.

The movement of his hand, highlighted by the beam of the headlights, stuck in Caplan's mind. Slowly, an old woman emerged, handing out her stick first. Caplan couldn't watch any longer; Craigo and McPhee needed another pair of hands. As she tried to open the door, she realised just how strong the wind was. She had to hold on to branches, inching her way along, reaching out with her arm as soon as she was close and the old lady, all six stone of her, was passed from McPhee to Craigo, then from Craigo to Caplan, who reversed back to the Hilux, along what was left of the road.

Once she was on her own two feet, the old lady pulled at the broken glasses on her face. A severe laceration over her eyebrow gave the impression she was weeping blood. How long had they been down there? Caplan slipped off her anorak and placed it round the older woman's shoulders, helping her slowly into the truck. The woman stretched out her arms to help her in. Caplan heard them say 'Margaret' and 'Helen', then something about God. Craigo and McPhee were assisting an older man, limping badly, back to the vehicle.

Caplan was still thinking about Craigo's hand gestures. *Come here. You're okay. You'll make it. Trust me.* What had Evan Reekie seen? How had that been changed and twisted and altered in his mind, along with what came afterwards? Did he have an impression? Was it right or wrong?

And nobody had believed him.

TWENTY-THREE

Dad, the plank, explained to me about death. Like I didn't know.
Wee sister, in cot, looking cute and warm and cosy.
It didn't take much.

Killagal Blog, 2021

Christine Caplan was in soporific heaven, sitting in front of a wood-burning stove on a huge soft armchair, her feet up on a matching stool and covered by two very warm blankets. She'd had a small cup of soup from the flask that Craigo had in the car. They had driven the long way round on the shore road, hoping that no other trees were down. The older lady, Margaret, had started to weep silently when they saw their way blocked again, but Craigo had reversed the Hilux then turned up a narrow muddy river of a dirt track. The vehicle bounced around, but it kept going, the engine straining when it hit underwater potholes or a steep gradient. The noise of the wind had eventually been silenced by the treeline, then returned with angry vengeance as they dropped back to sea level. Caplan hadn't cared, she was wet, she was tired, the truck was warm, she was fighting sleep. Margaret had kept her eyes closed, her lips moving in prayer. McPhee had helped Craigo with the road conditions, telling him right or left or watch this or be careful of that. Craigo worked hard at the steering wheel, competent at handling the vehicle. Caplan felt strangely secure, highlighting how vulnerable she'd felt being caught out by weather conditions that were alien to her.

Then they had gained height again on a hill road that seemed everlasting, but she'd been aware that the Hilux wasn't rolling around as much. She heard it splash through deep water, bounce a few times, then drive steadily before turning sharply and pulling to a halt. The doors opened. They had slowly clambered out, wrapped in blankets, like refugees. Caplan could smell livestock, catching sight of cows in the byre, blasting hot air out their nostrils, snorts and bellows of animals unsettled by the weather. The yard was lit up by sensor lights as the eight of them passed through the puddles.

A battered-looking door had opened onto a warm kitchen, everything soft with an orange glow. It smelled of oven-fresh bread. A collection of collies and cats lay on a large rug in front of the Aga in the inglenook. Caplan had walked Margaret into a sitting room of dark reds and wooden floors, a big dining table covered in books to one side and to the other a wood-burning stove surrounded by two settees and three armchairs, pulled up close to the heat. They removed their sodden shoes.

Craigo had dropped his hood, saying that they should sit down, and he'd get the kettle on. A voice from elsewhere said it was on the stove, nearly ready. As they wrapped themselves in warm blankets, Caplan caught McPhee's eye.

Was this where Craigo came from?

Why not? It explained the vehicle he drove.

An older man, fit and wiry, came through from the kitchen carrying a tray piled high with cups, toast, butter in wee pats, and a huge pot of tea. Craigo's dad from the look of him, in his big rough jumper, thick cords splashed with dirt round the bottom. He said very little, nothing more than 'Help yourself' and 'You're welcome.'

A first-aid box appeared, so Caplan wiped the blood from Margaret's head wound, and applied antiseptic cream. Then Margaret pointed out that Caplan too was bleeding.

Craigo had gone back out to feed and settle the animals. The wind slammed the roof; the old man saw the expression of alarm in the young girl's face as she looked up into the rafters of the old house, hearing the infrastructure creak. He smiled a toothless smile and said in an accent even softer than Craigo's that the house had been there for two hundred years, he didn't think it was about to fall down any time soon; the name in Gaelic, he said, translated as 'The house that stays standing'.

Caplan pulled herself deeper into her blanket, thinking that there was a first time for everything. The two children, Ryan and Skye, were so young they made her consider Gillian, and her absolute youth.

They chatted a little, the two police officers, Helen, the local girl with her two children, and the older couple from Edinburgh, all caught out by the storm. They heard Craigo on the landline to Mattie Jackson giving him a status report.

Then he passed them the phone. Helen called her husband, the Edinburgh couple called their hotel in Oban. They said they'd get the car fixed tomorrow. McPhee tried his mobile but there was no signal. He took the landline and left a message that he was safe. But wouldn't make it home.

Caplan shook her head when she was offered the phone, nobody was worrying about her. She wondered how the cottage was doing, whether Aklen was safe in Glasgow. As usual, she knew that Emma would be fine, holed up on the island. She didn't want to think where Kenny might be. Instead, she thought about the houses on the hills nearby, how civilised they were until the weather closed in. She thought about the night of the storm when Gillian had cut her little sister's throat open. And with the primal fear that she herself had felt when sitting in the car with the storm's fury around her, she had more empathy with the idea that Gillian's warped mind might have thought she was saving the baby from suffering at the hands of Mother Nature. There had been other people in Ben o' Tae that night, in a situation that mirrored this one, but with a celebration of the new year and alcohol. The mental-health specialist had suggested that Gillian's underlying anxiety was for the life that little Rachel Mary might have to endure, and if that life included being hit by a train, so be it. If Gillian killed Rachel Susan while she was peacefully sleeping, the baby would drift away and avoid a life of pain. It was suggested that this had been Gillian's state of mind when she fell asleep, and had carried out the deed while sleepwalking.

Had Gillian lain awake that night, trying not to doze off because she knew what was running through her mind?

Who else was in the house that night? Caplan looked over at Helen in the opposite seat, tight in her blanket, staring into the fire, holding a mug of tea with both hands, getting some heat and comfort, her children fast asleep beside her. She was staring at the flames in the burner. Caplan found herself thinking about slitting her throat; where would the blood go? The answer to that is all over the place, the spurt and spatter would be everywhere. An infant had lower blood pressure than an adult, but the effects would be much the same. The reports said that Gillian didn't wake up, she'd gone back to her bed, went under the covers, leaving the knife on top, a perfect print on the duvet cover.

Caplan looked at the spatter of mud on her own trousers, splash-back. How much spatter did Gillian have on her nightdress? Caplan tried to remember the pictures of that crime scene. The blood-stained mess of the cot, yet the blood on the pyjamas had looked smeared, vertical streaky marks over the red pattern of Elmo dancing across white cotton.

There were friends in the house, people that Gillian maybe didn't know, or didn't like. Had that upset her? The sleepwalking had been worse since the new baby arrived. There had been no warning, no overt signs of jealousy, it was all very subliminal.

Everybody thought that Gillian Halliday was guilty. She had never admitted her guilt. Who else was there? Who was another common factor?

The lovely Rowan?

Caplan slipped out from underneath her blanket, going into the kitchen and picking up her anorak that was hanging near the Aga. Wrapping herself up as warm as she could, her hat and gloves on, she glanced back into the living room where McPhee was fast asleep, then eased the back door open and slipped out into the storm.

In the barn, Craigo was looking at a young deer, last year's fawn, lying in a bed of straw. The deer looked back at him with huge brown eyes, incredibly pretty, except for the awkward angle of its leg.

'You need to go back into the house,' Craigo said. Then she noticed, folded into his other arm, a broken shotgun.

It took a while for Caplan to realise what was going on. She felt sick and backed out of the warm barn, walking into the fury of the storm. She went across to the byre, seeking out the comfort of the warmth and vitality of the cows.

She had known that there was more to her sergeant than the bumbling little guy with the Stan Laurel haircut. But this was a new level, a sense of where he came from, his family and what kind of a man he really was. She closed her eyes but still jumped at the sound of the single shot.

From the noises rolling round the rafters, the wind might be abating but it was still gale-force, the threat-to-life warning still in place.

The shed was warm, smelling of wet hair and animal dung. The cows were restive, wild-eyed and butting each other in their fear. Craigo was standing in the light thrown by two single bulbs. Each one at the end of the byre cast a weird light, and the shadows made monsters of the cows penned in, out of harm's way. Craigo had joined her, leaning on the gate, deep in thought, looking at the black beasts, one booted foot up on the railing, an oiled jacket on and a woollen hat pulled low over his ears. He was a different person here, in control and at peace with the animals, and his presence calmed them.

A bit like the way he had behaved out on the road that night, it probably wasn't the first time and wouldn't be the last.

'Do you think the worst of it has passed?'

He didn't flinch or turn. 'It'll have blown itself out by morning.'

'You can tell that by the way the animals are behaving?'

'That's the forecast, ma'am.' He didn't, hadn't, turned round to look at her. 'You'd best go in, ma'am; you're no weight at all, you could get blown over in a wind like that.'

'I saw the light on, wondered if you needed help.'

'No you didn't.' He rested his chin on the rail, looking over the shining backs of the beasts. The wind was still battering but maybe a little less intense, the noise had dropped a few decibels.

It was true. She didn't know why she had come back out here to talk to him, except for an idea that was so stupid she couldn't voice it in a normal environment. Not in front of McPhee. This wasn't a conversation for the station or in a briefing. This was too out-there.

'Are you still trying to get Gillian down to the bridge?' Craigo asked.

'She got out when her flat went on fire, she could have shinned down the drainpipe, rolled the car down the hill.'

'She's strong.'

'I'll bear that in mind if I ever arm-wrestle her.'

Craigo scratched his chin, ruminating. 'And nobody else registered at Meryl's address.'

Caplan nodded. 'That's interesting, isn't it.'

She felt a wave of relief washing over her as she heard Craigo say, 'You don't think she did any of it, do you?'

They were sitting on a couple of hay bales, Caplan with arms folded, staring at the birds sheltering in the rafters. Gillian would know what they were. Craigo was concentrating on stripping out a single stalk of straw.

'Do you realise what you're saying?'

'Oh yes.'

'That all the evidence against Gillian has been fabricated to point to a diagnosis that she didn't deserve.'

Craigo rolled the piece of straw into a ball. 'They'd only need to do it once, then everything that person does or does not do is put down to that diagnosis. Being mad is a difficult bag to get out of.'

'The "give a dog a bad name" scenario? If somebody else is doing this, then who?' Caplan went quiet. She hadn't known Craigo long, she couldn't really figure out how his brain worked but he had a secretive intelligence, one that she had grown to respect; one that others had ignored at their cost. He had a tendency to notice things, picking up little bits of evidence that lent support to a theory of his own.

'Do you think we have enough, or any, evidence to convict somebody else of these killings?' asked Caplan.

'Nope. But then nobody has looked, have they? The figure on the bridge may be odd, but Gillian doesn't walk like that. Gillian is a well-built lady and that figure on the bridge? She walks like you, like a very light-footed lady.'

'Some heavy people do walk lightly on their feet.'

'Yes, they do, but Gillian Halliday doesn't. She came down the hall at Ben o' Tae, ma'am, and I could have sworn there was a herd of elephants stalking me. She has an angry footfall. The person on the recording doesn't.'

'But we don't see much, do we? All you're getting is a vague impression.'

'A vague impression of movement is all that's needed.'

Caplan pushed back on her temporary seat. 'Right, okay, so we say that's somebody else built like that with that hair-do? There are two of them?'

Craigo scratched his head. 'Mike McGarth came to the Halloween party in the village hall last year dressed as a sumo wrestler.' He looked up and smiled. 'Gillian walks like a sumo wrestler.'

'Okay, Craigo, you've made your point. Useful to know but I'm not sure it's pertinent. Gillian was free, out and about, determined to do whatever she was about to do, for whatever reason. She was confident; that can change the way a person walks.'

'It's not Gillian on the bridge.'

'Why would somebody who wasn't Gillian lure Ted Maxwell onto the bridge?'

'We can't find a reason why she did, can we? Maybe someone else got him to the bridge. Did he take that step backwards when he realised it wasn't Gillian? It makes sense of meeting in the dark, in a place with no light. So, who else? Rowan?'

Caplan nodded slowly. Her head was starting to hurt. 'Was he in contact with Ted on the other phone? He invites him to the bridge as him? As Gillian? He had the number on the business card.'

Craigo shrugged. 'You can't tell who's texting, can you?'

'But why? Ted thinks he's texting Gillian, he expects to meet Gillian. So, a fat suit . . . that Rowan has conveniently lying in the cupboard?'

'Previously purchased because he knew this day would come.'

'How did he get away?'

'No idea. But if Gillian's been gaslighted by her brother all her life – and I mean *all* her life – think how she never said anything in her defence. Was she happier being in than out? Was she physic-ally safer behind bars than she was on the outside? Why was she the only kid who was getting her hair pulled out, getting bruised and hurt? She just kept going home, hoping that this time it'll be better.'

'It always troubled me about the southbound train,' Caplan admitted. 'Gillian and Rachel were on the east side of the track. In the blog Gillian said that she looked to her right and saw the debris of her wee sister down the track. She should have looked *left*, surely. So, who looked to the right? Who was standing there? The owner of the hand?'

'But where did you read that, ma'am?'

'I just said, on the blog. I'm not sure who's writing it. The specialist guys at work can't trace it right back to Gillian. If it's beyond them, I think it's beyond Gillian. And I have doubts that the blog is written by somebody who'd risk their life to save their dog. Killagal hates dogs. Just look at her celebration when Tonka shoots Molly. The language isn't Gillian, it's trying to be Gillian, it tries too hard. Or am I overthinking it?' She sighed. 'I just don't know.'

Caplan looked up at the light bulb, slowly swinging in the draught. 'You think Ted Maxwell had worked this out? He knew there was a malevolent mind working here? He was so very careful not to drag others into this.'

'Somebody has lost their childhood. It's not often I'd use the word evil accurately but I think that's what's going on here. It'd be wrong to let that little deer suffer much longer. But it would be evil to cause it that injury, then sit back and enjoy its suffering. That's what's going on here. Somebody is manipulating Gillian, and manipulating us.'

Caplan thought for a long moment. 'We need to go through it all again. Every little bit. I'm thinking of all the people that could be involved in this. Each murder? Were they even murder? Who was responsible? The same person? Different people? And was Gillian passed about like a whisper on the wind, each time a little distortion of the truth being added, to season the horror. We add in Fiona's death, the two puppy incidents, the salt incident. We go through each event, we get it all on the board.'

Craigo nodded in agreement. 'To rephrase a line from your favourite film, ma'am, we're going to need a bigger board.'

'That's very good, DS Craigo.'

'Yes, I thought so.'

TWENTY-FOUR

I'd do anything for Rowan. Nobody is taking him away
from me.
The sisters, though, I hated them.
These distinctions matter.

The putrid black bin bag was dumped on the desk at the front of the incident room. Caplan, who had enjoyed a huge breakfast at Craigo's farm, turned away.

Mattie Jackson had the good grace to look apologetic.

'The kitchen porter at the Osprey was moving the bins around and they found it.'

'Had we not instructed for the bins to be searched?' asked Caplan, judging the size of the bulky soft folds of material through the thin, black polythene, while holding her nose at the stench of rotten tomatoes.

'It wasn't in the bin, it was caught between the back of the bin and the fence. We're talking about these dumpster bins.'

'Do we open it? There could be all sorts in there,' asked Craigo.

'It's pink, soft and bulky.' Caplan looked closer. 'Craigo, can you put on some gloves and open it. I'll film you doing it. Don't touch anything inside, just undo the knot.'

'We should send it straight to forensics,' said McPhee.

'We don't have the time. We don't have the budget. We need to know what that is.'

'Me, ma'am?' Craigo hesitated.

McPhee's patience snapped. 'Oh, give it here.' He teased the knot open and peered inside. 'It's a lot of pink foam, held together by some binding tape.'

'The fat suit. The one thing that Gillian didn't need to do that stabbing. So where are we now? Don't answer that, I need to call Linden.'

*   *   *

The ACC was not pleased. 'What a bloody mess this is. You're making it worse.' Caplan could hear a long slow whisper escape from Linden's lips. 'They let Gillian Halliday out and she killed again.'

'It might be worse than that.'

Linden's voice snapped. 'How much worse?'

'About as bad as it could be?'

'Go on.'

'We have a fat suit. It took two hands to get Maxwell over the rail. Gillian can't use her right hand. It was somebody else on the bridge.'

Silence. Then, 'Has the DNA linked it to anybody?'

'Not yet. Let's say for a moment that she didn't kill Poppy Anstruther.'

'She did.'

'Not proven in a court of law. The evidence was not tested to that extent; the mental-health issue and Tollen swung in over the top of that in an attempt to put some therapeutic arms around her. And the mental-health issue springs from the death of her sister Rachel Susan.'

'Yeah, she slit her throat.'

'I want the blood-spatter evidence on that case re-examined.'

'I don't like where you are going with this, DCI Caplan.'

'Oh, I know, I'm walking a fine line between criminality and mental health. Err on the side of caution, unless she kills somebody again. That's what I keep being told, I've been telling others that. It's a snake that eats itself. Now we have a fat suit.'

'You'd better be serious.'

'If whoever wore it killed Ted Maxwell, there'll be DNA on it. Whatever he found out, it cost him his life. Wherever we go in this investigation, Maxwell has been there or thereabouts.'

'No. Prepare a case for the Fiscal. Their office has been on my back, let them decide.'

'It's not right, ma'am.'

'Christine, are you doing your job? Really? Or are you saving Emma again? You can't. So don't. I don't hear Gillian screaming that she's innocent. You have until Monday nine a.m., then it goes to the Fiscal. You are needed elsewhere, DCI Caplan.'

'I need a little more time on this. I'd like a log of all numbers that called Maxwell's business phone and I'd like to request sight of the documentation that DI Campbell requested on the Church's Pass incident. I want to know exactly where that blog originates, I'd like more funding and—'

'What you'd like and what you get are two different things. So, no. To both. The rest of your team seem happy that it was Halliday. Gillian will have her evidence tested this time. If she's guilty, then she goes to jail with the big girls. It's where she deserves to be. Your version of who is or is not on the bridge is supposition, so the answer to your question is no.'

Caplan and Craigo had set off early. Craigo had tracked down one of the girls who had found Poppy's body at Sugar Loaf Camp: Pauline Scott. Craigo had not mentioned their theory again, not after Caplan had relayed the phone call with Linden to him. She'd tasked DC McPhee with finding a way of proving that Gillian was on that bridge, how she got there and how she got home again. Mackie was to track down all the girls who were at the Sugar Loaf Camp. McPhee texted back some garbled report of a man being asked to move the position of his old neighbour's car seat.

Caplan called him back. 'Sorry? I didn't understand a word of that.'

'A man who lives on Ben Lawers Road, right at the top of the hill in the estate behind the Osprey, reported that his old neighbour asked him to move her car seat back. He was wandering if somebody had moved it forward. Asking around, one of the other neighbours thought they had seen the car reverse out, struck him as odd, an old lady going out at midnight.'

'Okay, weird but check it out.'

At least it got him out the office. She ended the call.

'We checked all the CCTV, the road footage, ANPR, came up with nothing, ma'am,' said Craigo.

'If we are talking Rowan, could he have used a works van? A vehicle we don't know about? And why did he do it, Craigo?'

'Because he likes being an older child, he doesn't like to share, he likes his wife, his daughter, a mum and a dad, nothing more than that. He likes being king of his small castle. He considered himself McCleary's superior. Was Maxwell asking too many questions?'

'He'd get the double whammy of getting Maxwell off his back, and by framing Gillian for his murder, she'd be back in custody permanently. But we can't put that theory together any more than we can put Gillian's. How was Maxwell lured here? We really need to find that other phone.'

Pauline Scott was now twenty-one and studying sports science at Stirling University. She was living on campus in a small flat, sharing with another girl who, having been warned of the nature of their visit, got up and exited through the front door as Caplan and Craigo entered.

Pauline was shy, slight, dressed comfortably in leggings, a Slazenger fleece over the top, her dark hair cropped close into the skull around the sides and back, a long floppy fringe at the front. Her hair was shiny, her skin glowed.

The bookcase behind her and the coffee table in front were full of books on exercise physiology and nutrition. An open laptop was precariously balanced on the arm of the sofa showing that Pauline had been working on an essay when they interrupted her. She offered them tea or coffee. They refused, and Caplan sat on the only other seat, leaving Craigo to stand at the closed door, notebook in hand, looking more efficient than he actually was.

'Is this about Gillian Halliday? We were asked to never call her that but I guess as you are the police then you know who she is?' Her voice drifted up in that teen talk that made Caplan's teeth hurt.

Caplan nodded, without actually agreeing. 'Did you know her well?'

Pauline shrugged. 'As well as anybody. We thought they were a bit of an odd family, living up there in the middle of nowhere, but once we actually met them they were perfectly normal. They had a bit of mystery about them, those from Ben o' Tae.'

'You've met them all?'

'Not really, they came down for our jumble sales in the village. So yes, I knew of them. We gossiped about them, to be fair. The way the two families were so close.'

'How well did you know Gillian?' Caplan repeated.

'Well, not from school, she was educated elsewhere, having treatment. She joined the Guides . . .' She screwed up her face. 'Looking back, maybe that was to see how she got on with her peers. I'm studying sports science and psychology and I was reading about the benefit of boxing clubs in areas of deprivation – the way the youth can get out their energy and aggression, learn

self-discipline. It gives them a club to belong to, rather than finding
security in a street gang. It serves a good sociological and societal
need. I think that's why Gillian was sent to join us. Gillian's mum
and her guy came down on Family Day and stayed longer than
the other parents. I guess they were enjoying seeing her out and
about.'

She didn't add 'like a normal person' but it was there.

'So yes, I knew her. I liked her, she was quiet and a bit weird
though.'

'In what way?'

'Didn't like to play the games, no competitive spirit. She liked
animals, used to go off on her own to look at wildlife and
stuff. She had a wee app on her phone for wild birds. She'd sit
and draw.'

'Oh,' said Caplan.

'I mean, the orienteering was time-critical, was a challenge for
points for the teams. We had to be quick and there was Gillian
staring up at a kestrel or a vulture or something.' She rolled her
eyes. 'She'd no concept of playing to win.'

'Do you remember the night Poppy Anstruther died?'

'Oh God yes. There was a plan to have a midnight feast, but
Poppy, Gillian and Abby used that as a way of leaving the campsite. They'd been drinking wine and had gone out to meet boys.
We invited Alison, the leader, to the party. I think she'd already
had a bit to drink. We ate a lot, listened to some music, danced
round the campfire, then at dawn we headed back to bed. Gillian
and Abby were back, but Poppy's bed was empty. We went out
looking for her. Alison started confusing the chain of events of
the day; she didn't take charge the way she should have.' Pauline
tutted. 'She lost her job after that.'

'Did she?'

'Failure of a duty of care, isn't it?' There was a shrug, the first
sign of unease Caplan had seen. 'We thought Poppy had gone off
with some boy who'd driven down from Cronchie.'

'Was Rowan Halliday one of those boys?'

'No, no. He's kinda cute so we'd have noticed him.'

Caplan felt a stab of disappointment.

'He'd been there during the day with his mum though,' Pauline
sniffed. 'Abby had clocked him.'

Caplan studied the young woman, realising that she'd been

exactly the same as Pauline at that age. She'd never messed around in her life, she'd been dancing, rehearsing, training, dieting, resting, healing torn muscles, taping stressed ligaments. She was doing what she loved, it had absorbed her. She would've been annoyed at a friend sitting drawing, taking time to smell the roses of life.

'And what do you think happened to Poppy?'

'I don't know. I wasn't there.'

The response was too quick, too rehearsed.

'But you were there when you were all looking for Poppy. You must've heard the others chattering. The camp isn't that big. What were they thinking?'

'Just that Poppy and a few others had gone to meet boys and Poppy hadn't come back. Abby and I were the first to the lochan and found her face-down in the water. I tried to turn her over. She was so heavy. Abby stayed there, then she got scared and came running after me. It was still quite dark and we'd not seen a dead body before. Did they ever find whose that odd footprint was? We all had to hand our shoes over.'

'No, they didn't. Where was Gillian?'

'Oh, she was already back; in fact, we didn't know at that time that she had gone out, if you see what I mean. Poppy was interested in a boy that Gillian knew so that was the reason for that.'

'What were you all wearing?'

'We'd not got undressed, just pretended and went to bed, stayed awake and then got up for the party. It was a laugh.'

'Do you have her surname, the Abby girl? We'd like to talk to her,' asked Craigo, pencil at the ready.

Pauline had a good think. 'I'm not sure I know. She was a good runner though, fast at the orienteering, I remember that.'

When they got back into the car, Craigo's level of silence was deafening.

'Well, what do you think of her then?'

'Very odd. You know something, ma'am?'

'What, DS Craigo?'

He waved his pencil in the air, a gesture that he seemed to have borrowed from his distant relative, Mackie. 'I don't think that young lady was being quite straight with us.'

'Really? I think you might be right. But she was spot on about something. There was an unidentified shoe-print. In the light of things, I think we need to look at that more closely. I'll speak to Poppy's mum next.'

Mrs Hannah Anstruther answered straight away when Caplan called at the agreed time. Craigo was on the phone to the central evidence store to track down any items that might still be held. Caplan had given him a cover story of an active enquiry, and that it should have a degree of priority.

Caplan did not have high hopes of getting anything useful from the phone call to the victim's mother. She felt the investigation was turning into a tick-box exercise for the Fiscal's office and once the time ran out, the game would be over. And she knew from the record that at the time Girl A's flat was set on fire, Hannah Anstruther had been quoted as saying she would have happily struck the match herself if she had been given the chance, and that 'that monster' had no right to a quiet life while her own daughter never got to see her fourteenth birthday.

Mrs Anstruther spoke clearly. Poppy had gone to a private school, but her mum thought it was good to meet and mix with the local children. Once she started to speak, it was difficult to get a word in. The dead girl's mum liked to talk about her lovely daughter.

'They had a day off school for her funeral. The whole school closed. The pupils stood in their uniforms on the road up to the crematorium. I had no idea she was so popular. I don't think she had any idea either.'

Or such is the popularity of murder, thought Caplan.

'When the coffin was lying, waiting to be cremated, they placed letters on the top of it. Messages they had written for her. Some of them gave me a letter as well saying how much she meant to them. I've always said what a lovely, fun-loving girl she was, so sweet, intelligent and kind. She was a wonderful daughter. I know she was the victim of a murder, and nobody ever speaks ill of them, but she really was a lovely girl. I still can't quite understand how it came about. I know that the Halliday girl is insane, but why was she out? Why was she allowed to go to that camp? Why?'

'This is a difficult question to ask, but I'd like to get to the bottom of this whole situation.'

'Yes?'

'Why Poppy? Of all the girls there, why Poppy? Was there any the stairwell. The glass shards of the landing light bulb were lying in the middle of the concrete floor, leaving the sign that asked 'Please be a considerate neighbour' deep in shadow.

As she tried to exit the door onto the long veranda that led to the flats themselves, the wind whipped the door from her hands, the bitter cold draught rushing round her feet before she and Craigo could get through and out to the open air.

It might have been cold enough to take the breath from them, but at least the air out here was fresh. Caplan looked at the metal plaque on the wall, trying to see the numbers of the flats through the bright red graffiti which proclaimed *Jamsie's is a bawbag.*

'What do they teach kids in school these days?' she said.

'Could go either way, ma'am. Either the possessive case is wrong, or there's a word missing, and Jamie does have something that is a bawbag. The item being unspecified.'

'Really,' said Caplan, checking the address on her phone. 'Do you think we're in the right place?' There was no answer. She looked at her colleague. 'Are you okay? You've gone a bit pale. Scared of Jamsie?'

'Not used to this, ma'am, it's a bit scary.'

He did indeed look unnerved, as if a fatal disease was hiding round each corner, waiting to jump out and infect him.

Caplan, the city cop, walked along to her right, shoulders hunched against the wind, guessing that there was a fifty-fifty chance she was correct. 'It depends what you're used to. You're good at scared cows and shooting Bambi. I do neds and psychos.'

'Well, we need to play to our strengths,' said Craigo, tucking his hood tight around his neck.

'I think it's along here, just show no fear. A bit of humour goes a long way, but never make them feel threatened. Oh look, it's this one at the end here. Bloody hell, what happened to her? She was a GP's receptionist, how the hell did she end up in a rat-infested shit-hole like this?'

'Maybe we should ask her, ma'am? It smells of something that isn't right.'

'This whole thing stinks like . . .'

'Dead jellyfish, ma'am, they really stink.'

Caplan knocked on the slightly worn door with flaking grey paint in a row of worn doors with flaking grey paint. This one had a slightly cleaner glass panel, the glass itself intact. There

history between them? Or between Poppy or any of the Be
Tae children?'

'Well, the rumour was that the Halliday boy was a wee bit f
of Poppy, in the way that boys and girls are at that age. Ar
think that Poppy liked him back. I'm not sure that Gillian v
happy about that. Not sure that was something she could cc
with. The doctor said that. Gillian was away and she wanted
keep things at home the same, she didn't like change. But th
couldn't live up there for ever in that wee house on top of the hi
They needed to get into the big wide world, behave like norm
people. It cost my daughter her life, it cost me my only child.
cost us everything that she was going to grow up to be. And I'v
never really been quite clear in my head why it happened. It'
been over four years. And it doesn't get easier. Is that girl stil
under some kind of protection order? She's eighteen now. I don't
understand why she gets that kind of treatment.'

'She was ill, I think that's the way we need the law to work,
Mrs Anstruther.'

'Am I still gagged about who she is? Now she's older? Her
name cannot be mentioned anywhere, but she'll be getting support,
money, a house and all kinds of bloody nonsense. I hope it's not
un-Christian of me to say that I hope she burns in hell for
eternity.'

TWENTY-FIVE

There are the normal people. Arsewipes.
And then there's people like me.
Just a bit special.

Killagal Blog, 2021

Twenty-four D Boyton Street, Glasgow G12, was the las
flat along an outdoor corridor of top-floor flats. DCI Caplar
climbed over a pile of short four-by-twos that had been lef
on the stairs. She muttered under her breath at the badly spelled
graffiti, and the stench of dead rats and cannabis that floated dow

was a spy hole, and a mat underfoot. The owner was keeping the filth outside. Through the frosted glass window of whatever room faced the car park, she could see two geraniums with early blooms, scarlet and green, thriving against the odds.

There was a noise of footsteps, an internal door opening, the sound of a television blaring then falling quiet. Caplan held up her warrant card to the spy hole and announced who she was, adding that DS Craigo was with her. A slight pause, more noises, and the rattle of a chain being pulled back. The door opened a couple of inches; Caplan smiled at the grey-haired woman inside. The wind chose that moment to gust violently and the detectives both staggered a little on their high, open corridor, willing their host to let them in so they could have the chat and get back to the car with this particular box ticked.

The door closed firmly then reopened, and Alison Watkins stood to the side to allow them in.

'Just go through the door on the left there. God it's cold. You never know with this weather what it's going to do,' she said, a faint flutter of excitement about her. She'd been looking forward to the meeting.

Caplan walked into an uncomfortably hot living room. A gas fire burning with an audible hiss was hugged by a brown three-seater couch that had seen better days. Thick fawn curtains hung at the windows, leaving a narrow opening that daylight struggled to get through. It was a dark, oppressive room, reminding Caplan of their house in Abington Drive, reminding her of Aklen, hiding away. He still hadn't phoned. She recognised that Alison Watkins was also merely marking time here; her home was elsewhere.

Watkins invited them to sit down, apologising for the non-existent mess of the place, asking them if they wanted tea or coffee or anything. She stood leaning forward, eager to please them, slightly fussing over two cushions while ushering them to the settee.

'Sorry to bother you,' said Caplan, taking a seat, turning her legs away from the intense heat of the fire. Craigo, in his very thick anorak, stood closer to the window and a welcome draught.

'Alison, please have a seat. There's nothing wrong. We want to have a chat with you.'

'It's about Poppy Anstruther, isn't it?'

'Yes.'

Watkins nodded, her thin hands grabbing at each other, her fingers entwined so tightly her skin blanched. Then she looked at the fire, pulled a slight face of annoyance, and said, 'What now? And why? Why now? It's been four, five years.'

'Five years this June. We're reviewing it with regard to another case that we've under investigation.'

Watkins' blue eyes narrowed slightly. 'What other case?'

'We aren't at liberty to say, sorry.'

'I haven't done anything.'

Caplan smiled. 'We need to go back over what happened at Sugar Loaf Camp.'

'Again?'

'Again. But this time, I'd like you to speak as freely as you wish.'

'I've always told the truth,' Watkins snapped.

'I'm sure you have, but sometimes witnesses feel shock in the moment. Time can give clarity.'

'I don't know what to say. Poppy Anstruther was so young, I'll never forget that night.'

'What was she like as a kid? You'd been her Guide leader for a while and had known her in the Brownies before that.'

Watkins nodded sadly. 'Since the day she joined, intelligent, helpful, rather lovely really. Strict parents though. Then she was in my company when we went camping out at Sugar Loaf. And, well, you know what happened there.'

'Two girls woke you up and took you to join their midnight feast? But at dawn, it was obvious that Poppy Anstruther was missing.'

'Yes. That was the first I knew about it. I think it was Pauline, said that Poppy, Gillian and Abby had arranged to meet a couple of boys from Cronchie on the main road. I see what you meant about clarity. Poppy was old way beyond her years, she'd had a strict upbringing and went a bit wild when she was away from her parents. It was awful what happened.'

'Teenagers can be so impulsive,' encouraged Caplan.

'She was found in shallow water, up at the lochan. Well, you'll know that. They were well-warned not to go there but . . .'

'What did you think about the result of the inquiry?'

Watkins started to knead her fingers into the palms of her hands, looking into the fire. 'Yes, it was a bit of a whitewash. Seemingly, it was my fault. It was even more my fault when they said I was drunk.' She sighed.

'Were you?'

'Nope. But they found my bottle of gin and all hell broke loose, everything, every little thing was down to me. They said I was an alcoholic, which I wasn't. I was an insomniac, I took a single drink at night to help me to sleep. It was a habit that I'd come to rely on. But I know I felt terrible when they woke me up, really groggy. I thought it was my sleep being interrupted. But I was never drunk. Never.'

Caplan nodded slowly, taking her time to ask gently, 'What kind of girl was Gillian?'

'Gillian?' Watkins furrowed her brow, as if it was a question she'd never been asked before. 'Well, Gillian was kind of weird, quiet. Very self-aware, self-confident? No, that's wrong. She didn't trust other people so she was self-reliant, that might be a better word for her, a loner, really. Kind of gruff and unhappy. She was thirteen and really didn't need anybody's approval or disapproval. She did her own thing quietly, nature, birds, flowers, drawing.'

'What do you remember of that night?'

'The rain had been awful in the morning. We had a family afternoon, lots of visitors and the weather brightened for that. By evening, by the time we had our cocoa I was exhausted. I had my small glass of gin and fell asleep. Then somebody shouted through the tent flap saying that I was invited to the party. I got dressed. I tried to join in the singing round the campfire but I was so tired. It was about half-four in the morning, the sun was starting to come up, not that it ever really got dark. I started packing things away, it was time to get some sleep. That's when we noticed that Poppy wasn't there.'

'You didn't call the police? These girls were thirteen.'

'It wasn't the first time girls had gone AWOL. We thought she was away with the local boys, youngsters, her own age, just kids messing about. Then Pauline and Abby found the body up at the lochan. The police came. You two will be used to it but it's quite a circus when the police turn up, all lights flashing. Gillian had been noticed walking away from the party. And that was that. Then there was gossip about Poppy, Gillian and the Halliday boy. Stupid kids' stuff. But I got the blame.'

'It was easier to blame you, Alison. Did anybody talk about the shoe-print near the body?'

'Oh, is that what this is about?' Her eyes drifted back to settle on the fire. 'I know they had a good look at the shoes I had with me. But it was when they found the bottle, when Gillian was seen walking away, the case was solved. I lost my job, I lost everything.' The hand-kneading started again.

'Why the Guides?' asked Craigo from the window.

Caplan closed her eyes in frustration. He was at it again.

'Pardon?'

'Why the Guides? We've heard that Gillian was a bit of a rebel, an individual, not the sort of person who would be drawn to an organisation like that. Well, that's what I was thinking.'

'You're right. She hated it. We didn't have much time for her. It was somebody else's idea, I think they wanted her out and socialised. Passing the buck to somebody else to look after her. It happens a lot. But my entire life was ruined that night. Not taking anything away from what happened to the Anstruthers but, it was not my fault.' She spat the words out.

'Alison, somebody else involved in a related investigation felt some pressure to change their version. Did you feel that?'

'It was all so awful.' She shook her head. 'More I felt nobody listened. They kept saying I'd been drinking and that my memory was not clear.'

'Does the name Ted Maxwell mean anything to you?'

Watkins looked at the ceiling, her eyes narrowing again, searching her memory. 'That rings a bell. Was he one of the policemen who interviewed me?' She shook her head. 'No, no, it was . . .' Standing up, she pulled some letters out from behind the clock on the bookcase beside her chair, shuffling a few envelopes of unpaid bills. There were a lot of them. She stopped at a white envelope, opened it and shook out a single sheet of A4 paper. 'This is it. He wrote to me earlier this year wanting to interview me about the incident at Sugar Loaf.' She handed it over to Caplan, who read the few lines. It was typed, the sender's address the Maxwell family flat in Blanefield. But there were no qualifications after his name, just a 'kind regards, Ted'.

'Did you speak to him?'

'Yes.' Watkins bit her lip, looking slightly wary now. 'Was he the man on the news?'

'Indeed. What did he want to talk to you about?'

She shrugged. 'No idea. I asked him if there was any money in it and he said no, just a cup of coffee. He kind of laughed when he said it, I thought he was another journalist wanting to rake over the case. I didn't meet him. It would take more than a cup of coffee for me to go through all that again.'

'Did he want to talk about Poppy's murder?'

Watkins closed her eyes a little. 'The only thing he asked was if I could remember who all came to the Family Day.'

'And could you?'

'Why, do you think I was drunk then too?'

By five p.m., Caplan was back in the incident room, feeling she was treading water. The clock was ticking, more intelligence was coming in, but she couldn't see how it fitted together. She had let it be known that they were going to have a brainstorming session and that they had their backs to the wall. Anybody with any ideas was invited.

There was still silence from Aklen, but she was determined not to worry about him. There wasn't even a neighbour she could phone and ask to pop in. In the end she called both Linden and Fergusson, talking as if there was nothing else going on between them.

She checked her phone again then looked out at the incident room. Mackie and Craigo had both stayed, as had Constable McPhee. So they were a gang of four.

'Was Ted thinking that the reasoning in one or all of the Halliday cases didn't stand up? Gillian already had that reputation, she was the obvious fall guy. How carefully did we check Meryl's alibi?'

'Already have, ma'am.'

'Well, check it again.'

'She was interviewed online last night. I didn't like the tone of it,' said Mackie.

Caplan sighed, 'The first of many such things, no doubt. She has an agent. Keen to be a celebrity psychologist giving soundbites and headshots to every Channel 4 TV documentary about serial killers, saying things she could never know. And Ted was so careful to keep this all away from his family, he was wary about bringing a monster to the door, the monster that had already killed two children. Then Meryl turns up at his flat and talks to his sons.

Cordelia thought her husband was on dangerous ground. Yet he gives Alison Watkins his home address?'

Mackie was looking at the board. 'We need to backtrack to the death that caused her incarceration, right back to point zero.'

'My thoughts exactly. I'm going to be here all night working on this. You're free to go home if you want to. We could be looking for a needle when we can't find the haystack.' Caplan's phone rang. She thought it might be Aklen until she saw the number, one she didn't recognise. She took a deep breath as she listened to the message. She swiped her phone closed and swore.

'Craigo, come with me. Gillian's been attacked at the hospital. We need to move.'

TWENTY-SIX

The last night of the year was a terrible night.
Wind and rain.
They were having a party downstairs.
Drinking, having fun.
We were all stuffed upstairs.
I could hear her breathing.

Killagal Blog, 2021

By midnight, Gillian was sitting up in bed, two nurses attending to her. One gave Caplan a dirty look as the detective slid into the hospital room. The officer who was supposed to be on duty outside the door was getting a hard time of it from a hospital official.

Gillian herself was sitting cross-legged on top of her bed, the ankles of her black leggings tugged halfway up her shins, a hospital gown on her upper half hanging round her like a thin blanket. She had gelled her hair into a spiky ball, her make-up was a couple of shades too pale, her eyes rimmed in black, red slashes across the lids. But she perked up when Caplan walked into the room. She had her left hand up at her forehead holding a dressing. The nurse was putting some strapping on her right shoulder, while the right hand was devoid of bandages, a red and bloody mass. The smell of it stank out the room.

'Are you badly hurt?'

'Nope, just my hand.' She lifted her paw of raw skin. 'Can I sue you?'

'You can probably sue somebody,' Caplan answered.

The nurse in the creased uniform scowled. 'It could've been much worse.' There followed a five-minute diatribe about hospitals, prisons, vulnerable patients and staffing levels. When she started pulling her gloves off and throwing bits of paper and dressings into different bins, Caplan went over to the bed.

'Not sure what I think of the new look, Gillian. Who taught you to do make-up like that?'

'Gail, a few lassies at Rettie.'

'I'd sue them as well. If you go out like that now, what the hell are you going to do at Halloween?'

'Fuck off.' It was said with bravado, a degree of friendliness even. But Caplan sensed that the girl was glad to see her, that the experience of physical violence against her person might have rattled Gillian Rose Halliday.

'Do you know who did it?'

'Are you not the cop?'

'First rule? Interview the victim.'

'It was some friend of Poppy's dad, he couldn't even punch straight, caught my shoulder.'

'Men, eh? They have the guilty party downstairs. He was in the ward along the corridor. Hard to punch anybody when you've got stitches on a double hernia. Most folk think he's a hero.'

'Look at the mess of my hand, the skin has burst open.'

Caplan sat down.

'Baby-sitting me is a bit below your pay grade.'

'I'm happy to sit. Happy to think about all the things you claim you can't remember. In case you go into a murderous rage, stab me but have no memory. That kind of thing.'

Gillian looked out the window, at the lights of the other hospital buildings in the darkness, then at the bleeding palm of her hand.

'It's the nothing-at-all that I don't get,' Caplan said.

And there it was, a flash of annoyance, irritation. Something else maybe.

Caplan looked at her, defiant in black, a mass of resentment for the world that had incarcerated her. At the moment her teeth were biting into her lower lip.

'It's stress, that's why I don't have any recall.'

'Even at Church's Pass?'

'Afterwards. Looking along the train track. I stepped back, I was against the fence. I couldn't get away. That's the only memory.' She looked at her hand again, a mass of blood and yellow. 'There's always blood on my hands, everywhere I go.'

'That's a good line. You could use that in your blog, your memory's much better in your blog.'

'I fucking make it up. Are you joining the thought police?'

'Your mum wants to take you back to Ben o' Tae tonight. Are you okay with that?'

'What about Dr Maxwell?'

'You're not under arrest until I arrest you. Do you want to go home?'

Gillian didn't answer. She was watching Craigo warily as he approached her and stared at her hair, peering at it, then looking at her face very closely. She didn't pull away, she stared right back at him. 'Your little chimp had better not start picking fleas from me.'

'It's all a little frightening, isn't it, ma'am,' said Craigo.

'You've not had teenagers, so you are in no place to comment. This is nothing.' Caplan turned to Gillian. 'I'm going to ask a very important question.'

'Aye?'

'Did you kill Ted Maxwell? Did you do this to him?' She held out the tablet with the photograph of Maxwell on it, lying on a slab, looking more of a ghost than Gillian did.

Gillian looked at it, then looked out the window, then out to the corridor, staff walking past.

'You ever harmed a puppy?' Caplan asked.

'Nope.'

'Thrown one off a cliff?'

'It was an accident.'

'Well, have you ever harmed Ollie?'

'No.' That was a quick answer.

'Well, you could have but you don't recall. So why would you want to harm another human being?'

Craigo said, 'Myra Hindley loved her dog, so did Hitler, and Dennis Nilsen, and—'

'Yeah, thanks, Craigo.'

'What is it with your chimp?' asked Gillian, a little nod of the head indicating the police officer.

'He's never been promoted in his life.'

'And you? Oh yes, Rowan said you're a failed dancer, a stuck-up cow with no idea what it's like to live up here, the city girl in the good suit with the posh hair-do and tight arse. Yer man's down there and you're up here. Your kids? One's a junkie and the other's a cripple. And I'm like, what the actual fuck is she doing investigating me?'

Caplan watched her for a moment. 'I'm trying to save your arse. What were you wearing on the bridge that night?'

'I've nothing to say.'

The sergeant leaned towards Gillian, raised his hand as if to pat her on the head, then lifted her hair up.

Under her wig, she was totally bald, with two tattooed angel wings behind her ears.

'I bet that hurt,' said Craigo, pointing at the tattoos.

'There's no such thing as pain,' Gillian said rather softly, pulling her wig back down. Her eyes narrowed, the long nails of her left hand cleaved at the dry skin on her forearm, the red weals cutting through the white scars of her self-harming.

Caplan spoke calmly. 'You know you should tell the truth and then maybe they can offer you support, something more effective than what you have at the moment.'

That earned her an eye roll.

'Gillian, you are eighteen now and—'

Footsteps hurried along the corridor and Miranda bounced in, stopping suddenly at the sight of her daughter talking to the detectives.

'I'll leave you to get ready. If you need anything you let me know,' said Caplan.

Miranda walked over to her daughter, casting Caplan a filthy look. Caplan and Craigo waited outside, and five minutes later the Hallidays left, Miranda clutching Gillian's elbow.

Caplan went back into the hospital room, looking around. A nurse came in and started tidying.

'What do you want me to do with this?' She held up the photo album, still carefully wrapped in its plastic carrier bag. Gillian's happy memory book.

*   *   *

'Was that necessary, Craigo? The trick with the wig?' she asked as they got into the Duster, Caplan climbing nimbly over the passenger seat. 'She could do us for all kinds of assault.'

Craigo ignored her. 'She's never alone when she kills. That's an odd thing.'

'It signposts a mental-health issue. I'm willing to go that far. If she was a cold, calculated killer, there'd be no witnesses. She lives in the middle of nowhere, all she'd need was a bit of gaffer tape and a shovel, nobody would be any the wiser.'

'I think it's odd that Miranda allowed her to go home. Would you, ma'am, if your daughter had killed your son when he was a baby?'

'That's too difficult to answer. We now have to investigate the assault on Gillian, and the press are going to love that. Of all the people who want to hurt Gillian, the big question to ask is how that guy got to the front of a very long queue.'

She checked her phone – nothing.

She turned her mobile off and snuggled back into her car seat, trying to figure out how to get some sleep before she went back to Rettie and ask again for some help with Gillian's state of mind. The alopecia had never been documented. She had an idea of asking Gillian herself for the release of any medical documenta-tion. Gillian was now regarded as an adult so she might be able to make that decision. She seemed competent to Caplan. The investigation had no time for those medico-legal arguments to reach any kind of conclusion.

Gillian, as Killagal, seemed proud of the atrocities she had committed when she was unwell, she gloried in them. To be more accurate, her blogs were reflections on how she had felt at the time of the incidents. But then, as she said, was she simply making it up to sensationalise it?

How was her moral compass now?

Caplan would like Anna Scafoli's opinion on that.

And Craigo had a point. How would Caplan have reacted if it had been Kenny, if that had been her? Miranda had lost two children to Gillian, surely it would have been worse to lose Gillian as well. Jim Halliday had taken his understandable path, Miranda had taken hers. Nobody could know what they would do in those circum-stances. They could thank God that they never needed to find out.

It was just after 9 a.m. when she arrived at Rettie, having left

Craigo at the station with a bacon roll. Anna Scafoli appeared out the building, walking swiftly to the car park where they had arranged to meet. She was clutching a coffee, her lanyard tucked away, her glasses on the top of her head.

She asked about Gillian's attack.

'It was related to the death of Poppy Anstruther, the dad of one of her friends was in the hospital recovering from a hernia operation. So, she's been assaulted and her property subject to wilful fire-raising. It needs to be investigated. She's gone home for now.' Caplan continued, compiling the argument that was swilling around her head: 'Why has she so little memory?'

'Or – why do I not buy that?' Scafoli replied. 'There's something chilling about her. She has the ability to "forget" immediately what she has done, to carry on as normal like nothing has happened.'

'Do you mean that she really saw her wee sister being hit by a train and it didn't affect her?'

'At Church's Pass, all she registered was the fact that she couldn't get away as she was backed into the fence. When she came downstairs after slitting her wee sister's throat, she asked for Rice Krispies.'

'Is that indicative of something? Not psychopathy? Not a psychotic episode?'

'Above my pay grade. I once asked Gillian if she missed being at home. No answer. I asked her if she missed her mum or anybody. She thought for a long time before she said Rowan. I hope nothing happens up there. She's a powder keg, that one.'

'If she comes back here, could we do a joint interview? I'm struggling to see what makes her tick.'

Scafoli pulled a face. 'I'll see if that's allowed, but at her age, I doubt she'll be back here.'

Caplan slipped back into her car and read her emails, glancing up every time the electric security gates to the premises opened or closed. Then a woman came out the gates and jogged across the car park. There was something about the way she was moving – quickly, clutching her handbag at her side, open anorak flapping behind her, looking over her shoulder. Sneaking out before her lunch hour? Caplan didn't get a good look at her apart from tall, thin, with curly dark hair.

The woman climbed into the passenger seat of a car in the same row as her own, about ten cars along. Caplan checked her emails as she waited for the woman to get out the car. She knew she had seen her before. When she did emerge, Caplan took a picture of her.

The car pulled out and drove across the front of the Duster, giving Caplan a clear view of the driver. Meryl Murdoch.

She sent the picture to Anna Scafoli, asking who the other woman was.

The response was immediate: 'Arlene, Gillian's case-worker.'

The one who had never called her back. The one who had been cheek-to-cheek with Murdoch in at least two of the photographs in her mosaic of treasured memories.

That was the link between Ted and Gillian, her case-worker and pillow-talk with the young psychologist. A terrible breach of confidence, something Dr Ted Maxwell would have no truck with.

What was he going to do about it?

Gillian was their golden goose.

Craigo had got hold of an Ordnance Survey map and was drawing a wavy outline on a large piece of paper, his tongue sticking out with concentration.

'What are we doing, DS Craigo? We've six hours to get this solved.'

'We have news.'

'Good news? News that will get the Fiscal off my back?'

'I phoned Mrs McGinty, then I called her son because she didn't know how she got her car, a black Fiat 500.'

'Who and what car?' asked Caplan.

'The car her son bought her on the internet. He collected it from a car park in Oban. The vendors were local, a young man. His pregnant wife was with him to drive him back. The car was registered to a Duguid McCleary.'

Caplan tried to keep her optimism down. 'How long ago was this?'

'Sixteen months. The car was sold with one set of keys. If the spare set was still up at Ben o' Tae, then say Gillian picks up the keys, drives to Mrs McGinty's street at the back of the estate in one of the cars Duguid's working on, parked it, gets into Mrs McGinty's Fiat, takes it to the Osprey at the bridge, gets changed, murders Ted, then back to the car at the Osprey, drives to McGinty's house. Reverse process.'

'Good work, guys. Simple but effective. Our suspect saved themselves a long walk. Then changed clothes in a third locus, a place we weren't supposed to find, never mind check for DNA or trace evidence from the fat suit. It kept the car driven from Ben o' Tae well away from the bridge.' She felt slightly sick. 'But can we prove who it was? It could have been Rowan? Duguid?'

'What do you want to do? Pull the car apart forensically, the foam suit would shed material. The suit is with forensics, it'll take time. Or do we look at what cars were up at Ben o' Tae and then track them through the road traffic cameras?'

'Let's ask Mrs McGinty how she'd feel about her car being cleaned. But the person on the bridge had their right hand bandaged and the left hand gloved? Too clever to leave fingerprints on the rear-view mirror or the seat lever.'

Mackie waddled off to track down Mrs McGinty.

'And McPhee, can you look at the Sugar Loaf Mountain incident, and track down those we haven't traced yet. The other girl who found the body, Abby. Try and get a sense of who was where. Like you said, there was a strange print at the scene that nobody could explain but that was all.'

Craigo tapped his biro on his forehead. 'That was the story. There was a party, more like a midnight feast, a laugh and a carry on. On the other side, some boys from Cronchie had bought alcohol and met with three of the girls, Poppy, Gillian and Abby. There's a rumour that Rowan and Poppy had a teenage crush thing going on. Rowan had been up there earlier for the Family Day and the Hallidays were staying overnight at a local B&B. Miranda didn't want to be too far away from Gillian in case she had some kind of crisis.

'When they all decide to go to bed, Gillian and Abby are back but not Poppy. It was nearly dawn. The lochan's bordered by woods on three sides. It's actually two ponds, one big enough for them to swim in before health and safety put a stop to that. The other was for fishing, whatever, it was quite shallow. The report said that Gillian held Poppy's head down and drowned her in four inches of water. It was thought Rowan and Poppy had been too pally during the day. There were a lot of shoe-prints, there was a mud shore, but this print here was never traced.' Craigo tapped the image on the board. 'I did get a good photo of the print from the archive, ball of the foot, left side.'

Caplan looked at the image closely. The sole was marred by two small but deep cuts on the outer edge. 'How hard did they try?'

'There were enough of Gillian's prints. She had her reputation. Did Poppy fancy Rowan? Was Gillian jealous? Was that her motive? It was a slam-dunk.'

'I'm going to call that Watkins woman, get her to tell me it again.'

Caplan called the number. It was answered immediately, the voice anxious when Caplan identified herself.

'Alison, nothing to worry about but reading versions of your statement at the time Poppy's body was found, and then again at the station afterwards and at the inquiry, I'm still getting the feeling that you might have been under subtle pressure about one detail. Were you aware of that?'

She said nothing, then, 'They said I was drunk, but I wasn't. I've told you, I had trouble sleeping. They didn't believe me. Not easy to deal with the dead body of a young girl. They blamed me, no help or counselling for me. I lost my job, my friends, everything.'

'You're not a stupid woman. Why did they not believe that you were sober?'

'Because they'd been told that I was drunk. So I distrusted the evidence of my own eyes. What could I say? I thought I saw somebody who wasn't there, so how can that be?' She gave a deep sigh. 'I can't forget the way that officer looked at me when I said what I saw. He was so dismissive, he asked how much I'd been drinking and said I was mistaken.'

'Who was it you saw?'

'Rowan Halliday.'

'Boss? The mark was in the mud near where Poppy's body was found. It was never traced, and Gillian's footprints were all over the place. Then all kinds of people trampled on it when they found the body. We need to look at this, ma'am,' said Mackie.

'We don't have time or the resources. If it was that easy it would have happened five years ago.'

'If we could maybe find the make of shoe, then trace it back?'

'After five years? I need to have something in front of the Fiscal by Monday.'

'I'll have something for you, ma'am,' said Craigo.

'Good luck.' If nothing else, it would keep him occupied. Caplan went back in her office, watching through the window, looking out, trying not to look at the clock. She wasn't looking at her phone either, there were only calls from Linden and Cordelia, wanting information she didn't have.

Linden was right, Gillian Halliday would get a fair trial. She'd let a jury decide. Specially if there was doubt over Rowan. Suddenly she was tired, she wanted to go home and warm her hands up over the gas burner, go to bed with all her clothes on and fall into a dreamless sleep.

Then she saw Mackie eating a cream cake, licking her fingers, flicking through something on the system. Craigo was bent over his desk, using a magnifying glass on the shoe-mark. Then he photographed the photograph and looked at the image on his laptop. Caplan was thinking through the circumstances at the campsite. The other two deaths, of both Rachels, had got them nowhere. It was all down to this. Half a shoe-print made in the mud from five years before. She started to flick through the series of statements from Alison Watkins. Had Poppy met Rowan that night? Did her brother's interest in another girl spark something in Gillian? Or vice-versa?

She was still reading when Craigo knocked on the glass, gesturing for her to come out.

'Look at that, ma'am. A man's size ten.'

'Okay, so a paramedic?'

'Could be. But it's located over here, angled that way. Somebody walking away, not by the path.'

'But they'd have examined it as evidence at the time?'

'They did not, ma'am. I've checked and double-checked and they didn't. They had Gillian, remember, the girl with the bad name. I don't think we should fall into that trap.'

'Get Mackie to look at her list of who was there, track down the boys they had planned to meet. Ask them a few questions including their shoe size.'

Caplan leaned over to pick up Gillian's happy memory album; there had been some pictures of the Sugar Loaf Camp in there. The photographs were all dated. She flicked through, looking at Rowan's footwear, until she came to the photograph of the three of them, Gillian, Rowan and Gail, lying on their backs, feet in the air. Ben o' Tae 2016, Jim had said, the year before the incident at the campsite. They were not a wealthy family; their clothes were hand-me-downs. Including shoes. Caplan reached over and borrowed Craigo's magnifying glass. And there they were, two little cracks on the outside of the left shoe.

TWENTY-SEVEN

They were there, this family.
Mum, dad, son and daughter.
Standing by the trees.
At the side of the loch.
A sight not often seen.
Happy.
Not happy.

Killagal Blog, 2022

Caplan, Craigo and Mackie sat on their desks in a deserted incident room. As far as the rest of the team were concerned, the case was being prepared for delivery to the Fiscal.

'Are there any issues with our idea that it's Rowan? Ted was looking at Gillian, he examined her case inside and out, and he found out something, and that got him killed. The mental-health professionals were wrong-footed, they were given misleading evidence and they deduced what they were supposed to.'

'Doesn't make sense. Why did Gillian never say?' said Mackie. 'Why? I've never understood why people confess to crimes that they don't commit.'

'I reckon it would take me less than half an hour to get you to confess to killing Lord Lucan if I felt so inclined,' said Caplan cheerfully. 'Gillian was mentally vulnerable, an easy target. Even then, she never actually confesses.'

'What do we do now? We're running out of time.'

'Bring Rowan in for questioning. Try to get a confession,' suggested Mackie.

'What was Rowan's motive?' asked Caplan. 'Does he want a life of Gail and Rowan, living in that house? No wee sisters around? Did Gillian put Rachel in a suitcase and put her out with the rubbish, or did Rowan do it to Gillian? The memory varies. If we knew what Maxwell knew, this case would be much easier but it's obvious he had uncovered something.'

'He was a careful, meticulous man. What if he realised that Gillian isn't the one with the issues, that she was gaslighted and manipulated. Whatever he found, it got him killed.'

Once more they drove up to Ben o' Tae, Craigo at the wheel of the Hilux, a Police Scotland Land Rover following behind. It was still early, Sunday morning. Caplan didn't know if they were right about Rowan, but she felt they couldn't afford to be wrong about Gillian. There wasn't enough to charge Rowan: he was at the Guide camp that day but as yet they had no evidence that he went back that night, except the changing testimony of a woman who may have been drunk, and half a shoe-print from years ago.

Over breakfast Caplan had called Sarah Linden and asked for more time. The ACC listened, then said, 'So you have a shoe-print of somebody who was present a few hours before the murder but not at the exact time as far as you know, a few video frames of a hand in the air, a set of pyjamas with smeared bloodstains rather than spatter stains, and a dodgy blog? Is that it? I want you to start making this case easier, not more difficult. If you go on like this we could end up arresting the whole lot of them. And is Rowan not mentioned in the blog, something like, I'd kill for my hunky big brother or some crap like that? He's mentioned in the third person.'

'I'm not sure who wrote that blog, it's a smokescreen I'm sure.'

Linden snorted. 'More solid forensics? The fat suit?'

'DNA so far is some of Rowan's, some of Gail's, but Rowan wore it when playing Santa at Christmas. And Gail helped him get it on and off. The lab have other samples to process, they have some samples that look like eyelashes but it turns out they are non-biological fibres so obviously no DNA to be collected from them. We're not testing the car for DNA as we know that Rowan and Gail had both been in it when they delivered it.'

'Nice of you to give some thought to the budget you are running up on this. Look, what you have will be made available to the defence at trial. Let the fifteen folk on the jury go for reasonable doubt on Gillian but you don't have a proven case for anybody else.' Linden abruptly ended the call.

But it didn't make it right, that look of fear on Gillian's face when there was talk about going home. What was she actually guilty of? Caplan's mind was alert as they drove up the hill, thinking about Alison Watkins' statement about feeling groggy when they woke her up. They had evening cocoa up at the camp. Who had given her that? Sleeping through situations was a common recurrence at Ben o' Tae. Was there somebody up there with a supply of prescribed drugs that induced a deep sleep? Did that point back to Gillian, the common denominator?

She could imagine Rowan putting the kettle on at night, everybody in the big kitchen for a cocoa before bedtime. All he needed to do was crush a sleeping pill into each cup, and as he wasn't stupid, he slipped a little into his own cup as well.

Rowan Elgin Halliday had no house of his own. His wife was terrified that Gillian was returning to Ben o' Tae, so Gail clearly believed Gillian to be guilty of some of the heinous behaviours, and she had threatened to leave with Alice if Gillian came back.

And what would Rowan do to avoid that happening?

Rowan, who might be a master manipulator, full of sibling coercive control, knew that Gail had nowhere to go. Could there be marital control over Gail, as she was the one who couldn't go back 'home' – her home was exactly where the problem was.

It was Gillian that had to go. Rowan wouldn't want to leave, why would he walk away because his sister was batshit crazy?

And, as he had said, they were family.

Was it Rowan who had let the brakes off the Kubota that had killed Fiona, increasing Gail's dependence on him?

That was a step too far, but she could imagine an inquisitive young Rowan, messing about with the machines that Duguid was working on.

The cars pulled into the space at the front of the house. The family were home, judging from the cars present here and up the side of the property. As they had discussed before, both the Hilux and the Land Rover turned round, ready for a quick getaway if needed. Caplan was sure Rowan would come quietly; he'd talk his way out of it back at the station.

The German shepherd trotted out, alert as ever. Then Duguid McCleary appeared, spinning a hammer in his hand. Caplan was glad to see some colourful bunting hanging from his arm and a nail in his mouth, explaining the presence of the hammer. He kneed the dog gently and it trotted back to wherever it came from.

He plucked the nail from between his lips. 'Can I help you?' asked McCleary wearily, walking away to the back garden.

They followed in silence.

The family were standing outside. Alice was rolling around on her stomach on a tartan rug. Granda was standing at the side watching Gail, mug in hand, instructing Rowan where to hang fairy-lights on the trees.

They all stopped. The relaxed mood of the coffee break slipped to one of foreboding.

'Rowan?'

'Yes?' The young man wound up the string of lights he was holding. Annoyance flickered over his handsome features. There was a small jerk of his shoulder, his tic.

He knew.

'It's okay, Rowan, we'd just like to take you to the station for a chat.'

'Do I have to? Now? It's Alice's birthday tomorrow, we were—'

'Yes, you do have to. Better today than tomorrow, eh?'

'Can it wait?' asked Miranda.

'You can get on with your decorations, Mrs Halliday, we'll take good care of him.'

For a moment there was a standoff. Caplan saw the look of annoyance on Rowan's face, verging on anger. Then saw that Gillian was smirking back at him.

Rowan's story didn't change at all, no matter how hard they pushed him, no matter for how long. He stumbled over a few little matters of the evidence, the events, the way things had happened, but overall his version remained consistent.

Gillian had pushed their wee sister, Rachel Mary, under the train. Both Rowan and Gillian, plus others, had been in the back bedroom at Ben o' Tae when Rachel Susan was killed. He'd seen Gillian get out her bed and go downstairs. Everyone else was asleep. He was fourteen, it was a stormy night, they had all gone to their bed late, it was years ago. He didn't know that she was sleepwalking, or that she was going to kill their wee sister.

Caplan wondered how much of that was memory of what he had seen, and how much memory of what he had heard since.

'But at the time, all you saw was her getting out the bed and going to the door. That was in your original statement.'

He shrugged. 'I'm sorry, I was very young. Yes.'

'You said that you didn't know she was sleepwalking?'

'Yes, I knew she did it, but I hadn't actually seen her do it before.'

'Usually where was she when she was sleepwalking?'

'In her own room, but that night she slept in my room, we all did. She was in the corner, and I was at the door.'

'Show me?' She handed him a blank piece of A4.

'All the kids were in my room that night. We had a houseful. And we, the teens, had been allowed to have a wee drink. It was New Year. I felt quite sick.'

'And what did Gillian do, apart from cutting Rachel's throat?'

'Well, she must have got up and went downstairs. Mum had left the door open, so she'd hear if any of us got a fright with the noise of the wind. They'd left the landing light on. The shade was in the shape of a biplane. It was a joke my dad always made – the landing light.' Behind the beard, Rowan gave a wry smile. It was easy to forget that, at best, he'd lost two sisters, his dad, and been separated from his closest sister. Easier to forget that it might all have been his fault.

'Why do you think your sister killed Rachel Susan?'

'Well, we were told she was sleepwalking. And the people in the house, strangers, other children? They said it all unnerved her.'

'What other trauma had she witnessed? Church's Pass obviously.'

'Well, she was there when Fiona was killed.' He closed his eyes. 'I can still hear the noise, then the silence afterwards. Yes, there's been a few things to be fair, Gillian absorbed it somehow.'

Caplan recalled the big eyes of the young deer, not unlike Rowan at the moment. Scared.

'What about when your wee sister had to be rushed to the hospital.'

'She had a fit, couldn't breathe, she needed oxygen. She was blue-lighted all the way with my mum. Gillian, Gail and I were following in Duguid's car.' He stopped. 'I think I was okay for the first few miles and then it got a bit scary, I don't recall much about it but Mum had called Dad to come and meet us at the hospital. Gillian was holding on to me so tight, she was terrified. I think that had something to do with it. I heard my mum talk later to one of the doctors, saying that Gillian might have given Rachel something. But she was transfixed by the hospital, she loved it. It was so alien to her.'

It was a good story, feeding into the Munchausen's-by-proxy idea. Or did it spark off a lifelong fascination with life? And death.

At that moment Caplan's phone pinged, a message from Margaret Owen, Cordelia's FLO: *Cordelia's been trying to speak to you about this. It arrived in the post this morning. Please find attached.*

Caplan opened the image, expecting to see Ted Maxwell in the arms of a young lady with multicoloured hair. It showed Ted Maxwell sitting outside a café, enjoying a coffee and the company of another young lady.

Gillian Rose Halliday.

TWENTY-EIGHT

Live and let live. Live and let die.
At first it seemed nothing to do with me.
Oh but I wanted it to be something to do with me.
And I made it so.
Didn't want the dog.
I said it bit me.
Dad shot it.
Simplesss!

Killagal Blog, 2021

Caplan's mobile rang at three o'clock the next morning. She had had no sleep at all, lying awake in the small caravan bed. Why had she been beguiled into thinking that Gillian was truthful in any way? Why was she so arrogant that she thought she could see something that nobody else before her could? But there was something that didn't add up, still. What difference did one picture make?

The call was a uniform from Oban to say that they had attended an incident up at Ben o' Tae, an assault. A young woman had been stabbed. He'd been instructed to inform DCI Caplan immediately.

They had taken Rowan back late last night. She could hardly get the words out for the tightness in her throat. 'Who did it?'

'Gillian Halliday.'

Caplan took a deep breath. 'And who was hurt?'

'A Mrs Gail Halliday.'

'There was a baby in the house, is she okay?'

'Nobody else was injured.'

'How bad was it?'

'Well, Gail was released after treatment. We've Gillian here, we've been told to go no further until another mental-health assessment's been carried out.'

The tipping point, there it was. The point of no return for Gillian.

Caplan put the phone down, leaning on the bed, closing her eyes, thinking that she was never going to see her way out of this nightmare. She'd just stepped into the shower before driving out to speak to Gillian at Oban, when the phone rang again.

It was ACC Linden. She was not happy.

Gillian's eyes were blackened pit-holes, her wig teased out like burnt tumbleweed. She looked defeated. Caplan asked the desk if she had been sedated but the answer was no, she had been in that state since they had brought her back. She'd refused medication; a psychologist and a doctor had been called. Gillian had shrugged her shoulders and said nothing. Except to ask how Rowan was.

It was a question she repeated as soon as she set eyes on Caplan.

'He's fine,' said Caplan. 'Before we talk about tonight, I need to ask you something more about Ted Maxwell. Had you met him before?'

'Nope, I've told you that.'

Caplan placed the print-out in front of her. 'You and Ted having coffee.'

A faint smile passed Gillian's lips, a slow breath of relief.

'Why lie to us?'

'He asked me not to say.'

'And you always do what people ask?'

'We all have fuckin' secrets.'

Caplan paused, looked at her nails, took a deep breath. 'Why're you doing this, Gillian?'

'Oh, like you'd understand.'

'Try me.'

Craigo coughed slightly. 'I think Gillian would struggle to get you to understand, ma'am, as you've never lived her life. It's like walking in shifting sand. Friends turn on you, it's all fun to them. Nobody has your back. It's terrible to feel abandoned, totally alone when everybody thinks you're the joke. When you don't fit, you do what you need to do, you become what you need to be to be accepted. To be counted. To fit in. To be seen. To be heard. The vulnerable will always run for those that can protect them, we learn that as children.'

Caplan smiled at him. 'That's very astute.'

Gillian said, 'It's a load of cockwomble arseshit.'

The report on Gail Halliday's wound was very brief indeed. So brief it was no use. But there were a couple of images that she took a photograph of.

'How bad was the injury?' Caplan asked Craigo.

'She was lucky, got out the way before Gillian could do any real damage. Gillian followed Gail into the kitchen and cornered her, made sure there were no witnesses. She, Gail, was scared that Gillian was going for Alice. Rowan was the hero.'

'Bloody hell. What kind of a mess did we make of this?' Caplan dropped her head into her hands.

'I'm sorry,' said Craigo.

'For what?'

'I'm sorry for getting it wrong.'

'You didn't. I did.' Caplan was quiet for a moment.

'Because I argued the point.'

'Yes, you did. We should have taken this to the Fiscal yesterday but thought we had it right, we had all the ducks in a row.'

'Right ducks in the wrong row. We had the right "Kevin" all along.'

'And now I've to go up to Ben o' Tae and officially apologise to them and to Rowan. Christ, they'll lynch me. I'm in deep trouble for leaving Gillian up there. Let's go and find the doctor who treated the wound, see what they have to say.'

Craigo pursed his weaselly mouth. 'I already have his statement, unofficial, caught him when he was eating an egg mayonnaise sandwich. It was left upper arm, three-inch wound. Very superficial. He thought Gail had been lucky. It went lateral to medial, it was dressed but required no stitching. Then he said—' Craigo sniffed, about to make an announcement '—"This is Girl A we're

talking about, isn't it? The gossip in the staffroom says that
lassie was lucky. I'm not usually a fan of the death penalty but
there's no cure for psychopathy.'"

'Like you said, Craigo, that statement was unofficial.'

'Is that it over now, ma'am?'

Caplan closed her eyes. 'One last throw, eh? Gillian made sure
there were no witnesses? Let's talk to a Glaswegian, they know
about knife wounds.'

The message from Ryce sounded rough. She might have been out
on the town the previous night. 'Hi, Caplan, so the wound's deeper
at the lateral edge? That's the initial incision. They were facing
each other if I read the notes right. Easy for a right-handed person
swinging a knife facing their victim, forehand if you like. But . . .
has your perp not got a sepsis risk on the right hand? There's no
grip there. So it'd be backhanded with the left. Possible but
awkward. Forehand and the blade would hit the breast before it
got to the arm and the insult would be deeper medially. Tough
call, wouldn't like to be in your shoes.' There was a chuckle on
the phone. 'But from the photo you sent, I think I see a small
hesitation mark. But to be sure, why not get the two of them back
in the room, get the victim to hold her baby and then the psycho
run free with the knife? Oh, you've already done that. Linden's
on the warpath by the way. Just a heads up.'

Caplan redialled the pathologist, asking her if she could keep
a secret.

Then she called on Craigo.

'We're going to pick up Gillian at the hospital.'

'Are you not afraid of Gillian, ma'am?'

'No. But then, I'm not related to her. She rather likes me. I'm
her route back to her life as an incarcerated person. Maybe she
did enough last night to get back to Rettie. Except she won't be
going there and she's no idea how rough her life will be when
she's behind bars in a woman's prison. They hate child-killers.
We're going to Ben o' Tae just one last time.'

Craigo pulled his ferret face again, the sand-coloured eyes darted
to his boss. 'Because we don't want the Fiscal saying that this final
incident wasn't fully investigated. And you do need to apologise.'

'I do indeed.'

*   *   *

The road up the hill that had seemed so long and desolate the first time Caplan drove up here with Craigo was starting to feel very familiar.

It was a pleasant day, warmer than the weather had been recently.

They had waited until six o'clock. They knew that most of the family would be home. Gail would be away from her desk, Rowan would be back from the Coffee Café, Miranda would have finished her shift at the care home. McCleary and Granda were around the property most of the time, one tinkering with his cars in the backyard, the other plodding his way through the woods for hours on end with his gun, reliving happy memories of a life spent up in the hills.

Caplan almost enjoyed the drive up the hill; she'd had a long day on the phone chasing up labs and samples. Tests had been completed, the results just weren't through yet. The Fiscal was wanting the case in less than forty-eight hours.

They pulled up and Craigo turned the vehicle round, the Land Rover with two uniformed officers behind following suit. Gillian sat in the back seat, her face impassive. The German shepherd appeared, turned and walked away. Caplan could hear the voice of Judith Durham, 'Morningtown Ride'. She and Craigo followed the sound round to the Fairy Garden.

They were celebrating something. The return of Rowan? The incarceration of Gillian? Then she saw the cake on the table, the balloons on the trees and the lacy pink dress and headband that Alice was wearing, and recalled it was her first birthday today.

McCleary had nice trousers on, a stripy apron and a white chef's hat. He had cleaned the oil from his hands and was getting the barbeque fired up. The picnic table was covered with a pink cloth that was piled high with paper hats and plates, all pink with 'First Birthday' in silver lettering. There were twelve candles, one for each month of Alice's life. Twinkling lights were hanging from the trees, a colourful hologram of four fairies projected ghostly dancing images on the pine needles.

McCleary was waving a spatula around, doing train impersonations to the music. Rowan stood beside him, a tray of vegetables in his hands. Miranda was holding a small, sharp knife, a roasted chicken in front of her next to a bowl of salad. Gail was holding Alice.

Against the tree was a framed charcoal drawing of Alice, the signature style of Gillian.

It was a lovely scene, the fairy-lights on, the Seekers soundtrack. Blissful.

Gail froze when she saw Caplan and Craigo step onto the lawn. She passed Alice over to Rowan's outstretched arms. Rowan was smiling with a cocky superiority. McCleary leaned over to tap Alice on her pretty snubbed nose and for a moment Caplan saw the tableau of the beautiful family that they were, the young gran and grandad, the handsome couple, the perfect baby, all healthy, all attractive, in bare feet, the women in floral summer dresses with light cardigans to ward off the early evening chill.

They saw Gillian behind Caplan and Craigo, a uniformed officer on either side. Gillian did not belong here. The tension was palpable. Caplan thought she saw a flash of fear cross Gail's eyes, a slight retreat, but there was small wonder about that. Gail looked at Rowan, desperate for him to do something about it.

Rowan took a step forward. Then McCleary placed his hand across the boy's chest and said, 'No, son, I'll sort this out. I've had enough of this. This is harassment.'

'Sorry to disrupt your meal again, but as you know there was an incident here last night. And I've been dragged over the coals for it. I've come to apologise for that and to say that I made a decision with regard to Gillian, and it was the wrong one. So, killing two birds with one stone and interrupting you as little as possible, we'd like ten minutes of your time, Gail. Then we'll be gone and you can get your party started.'

As nobody objected quickly enough Caplan ploughed on. 'We've had a good look at the injuries and the reports from the hospital. Gail, if you don't mind, can we have you in the kitchen to run through what happened, exactly.'

'Get out of my garden, now,' said McCleary.

'I've already been through it. I've given a statement twice.' Gail was angry, her mouth set in a firm line, her eyes burning into her sister-in-law.

'She's right. You can't really expect her to . . .' Miranda's protest faltered.

'You've been through the physical aspect of it. You know that there's more than one case going on here, you know what's at stake and I've to put all of it in front of the Fiscal, not only the murder of Dr Maxwell, all of it. So please, Gail, can we have a minute of your time, in the kitchen where the attack happened, then it will all be over, it will be ended. Craigo here will play the part of Gillian. She won't even be allowed in the room. My two police colleagues will have her under control.'

'Why're you doing this to us?' asked Rowan, standing in front of them.

'Because they can . . . just wait until we put a complaint in, this is harassment . . . this is—'

Caplan interrupted McCleary's rant. 'Yes, why're we doing any of this, DS Craigo?'

'Well, ma'am, the wound's difficult to produce. We've experts on these things and they're finding it hard to understand. Gillian has no memory of it. Can you show us how it happened, Gail? Otherwise they'll come back later, and again, and again. So, how about if we do it now?'

Gail shrugged. 'Okay, let me think. So, I was in the kitchen with Alice. Gillian followed me in. I think I moved Alice onto my hip, and Gillian came over to me. She was looking at Alice, then looking at me. I said something to her about putting the kettle on or something, or that's what I was thinking, then I turned round and saw Gillian pick a knife out the block and swing it at me. She said something about Rowan, can't recall what.'

'How was she holding the knife, can you remember?'

Gail turned her head to one side, her shoulders raised as if somebody had walked over her grave. 'Gillian cut me, moving her hand like that.' She waved her right arm.

Caplan looked at Craigo, who raised an eyebrow. 'Where was your arm, if you don't mind?'

'At my side. I was holding Alice on my other hip. It was awful. Why are you asking me all these questions?'

'How was Gillian holding the knife?' Caplan repeated.

'Well, like this.'

'Facing you?'

'Yes, she had me backed against the cooker. I mean, that's where I'd been standing.'

'Must have been her left hand, though.'

Gail shrugged. 'It all happened so fast, I wasn't paying attention.'

'Who did slash at you, Gail?' asked Caplan, reaching into her pocket as her phone beeped.

'She missed my baby's face by inches,' shouted Gail.

'She's just told you,' screamed Miranda, stepping forward.

'Who slashed at you? Gillian can't use her right hand. If she'd used the left she'd have hit the inside of your arm, or cut your breast, or Alice. Unless you had your hand up in the air, but why would you do that? So have a think while I check this. Excuse me.'

Caplan took her phone out and read the brief message. She tapped Craigo on the shoulder and showed the text from the forensic lab to him; they'd managed to find, and match, DNA on the eyelash extension.

Gail's eyes had drifted across, looking over her family. Then she shook her head. 'No, no. I need to have Alice, give me Alice.' Rowan handed her the baby. His hand lingered on his wife's arm, but she shook it off. 'I need to go now, I'm taking Alice and I'm going. We're not safe here. I'm so sick of all this. Nobody ever listens to me. One inch away from slashing my daughter and I get this crap.'

'It's a simple question, Gail. You must remember what happened, it was only last night,' said Caplan, taking a step forward. 'No matter how quickly it happened.'

'Keep away from me,' she screamed.

Miranda Halliday and Duguid McCleary both stepped back as Gail side-stepped to her right, crying, holding Alice very close, almost stumbling in her distress. She had sensed the change in the balance of power. Then she calmly lifted the sharp knife from beside the chicken.

She balanced Alice on the arc of her hip, twirling the knife in the palm of her hand.

Then held it to her baby's throat. 'Gillian, come here,' she said.

Miranda let out a short squeak. Both McCleary and Rowan stepped forward.

Gail flicked the knife. 'I don't think so, boys. Gill, get the keys of the Hilux. And the Land Rover.'

Gillian turned, ready to obey.

'Gillian?' asked Caplan as Gillian took the keys of the truck from Craigo's outstretched hand. 'You don't need to do this. We know it all now.'

The young constable held onto his keys until the baby screamed in pain.

'Gillian, listen to me. It's over,' said Caplan.

Gillian looked as though she was thinking about it. Then shook her head. 'It's the way it's always . . .' She shrugged.

'Gill? Move!'

'Stop, Gillian. Her game's over,' said Craigo. 'You've turned that corner. You don't need to do this.'

But Gillian just smiled, tears smudging the black eyeliner down her face. 'Ah, but I do.'

Rowan stepped forward again. Gail put her arm out, halting him. The tip of the blade twitched. Caplan saw a trickle of blood roll down Alice's neck, spreading on the lacy pink birthday dress.

McCleary approached, arms out, ready to take Alice.

Gail smiled at him. 'You take one step nearer, Dad, and I'll cut her. Gill, you follow me. If anybody gets near me, well, you know . . .'

'You don't need to do as she says, Gillian, we know about it all. We have her DNA, we know it was her. She has no power over you now, no power at all.'

'Gill, come on!' Gail screamed, keeping a tight hold of the baby and the knife. Alice started to scream louder. Judith was singing about the train whistle blowing.

Caplan looked at Craigo, who shook his head. Gillian was struggling with the keys and her bandaged hand.

'Rowan, get the keys out the rack. You're not following us. Mobile phones, please. Leave them there, or I will harm Alice. I will.' She twisted the knife slightly, the baby screeched, more blood streamed onto the pink dress.

The phones were placed on the ground.

'Kick them towards me, gently. Gillian, put your heel through each one, nobody is calling for help.'

'No,' said Craigo.

The baby screamed again. The bubble of blood on the innocent pink skin expanded as Gail shouted at Craigo to put his phone on the ground.

But Craigo, for some reason, placed his hands, still holding the phone, up in surrender.

'What the hell are you do—'

There was a crack, a single deafening crack that reverberated through the air. Gail let the baby go, jerking backwards. Her feet left the ground. Rowan and McCleary lunged to catch the baby before she fell, but gravity was quicker than their reflexes.

A tall figure walked onto the grass, his gun broken and hanging over his arm, but the smell drifting from the barrel was unmistakable.

Then Miranda started screaming.

Two hours later, they were still at Ben o' Tae. Caplan recalled Watkins' words: 'the circus' had arrived. Alice was fast asleep in Rowan's arms, an Elastoplast over the nick in her neck, her dress spattered with her mother's brains. Miranda and Duguid were in the kitchen, giving a joint statement while drinking their second cup of hot tea. Gillian was sitting in the conservatory with a female officer, sobbing at the loss of her friend Gail, and Gail was lying on the lawn, covered in an unzipped body bag while the scene-of-crime team erected a tent over her.

One of the uniformed police officers had fainted, the other was helping him recover.

Granda had been taken away, the gun cabinet re-locked.

Craigo had been as white as a sheet. He had moved the Hilux to allow access and remained alone in his vehicle, in the quiet.

Caplan was sitting beside the cake outside, in the dark, the candles burning down. She was determined to stay there until she'd stopped crying.

TWENTY-NINE

What about you?
Are you one of the elite?
Could you take a life?
Anytime you wanted?
I bet every one of you would shit your pants.

Killagal Blog, 2022

Gillian occupied a large blue chair in a visitor's room, having spent the night in hospital and been considered fit for interview. She'd been very upset at the death of Gail, her coercive controller, her protector. She'd lost her mentor. Her tormentor. It would take time to heal from those eighteen years. Everything about Gillian had diminished. She was still in black, the wig was combed flat, the black rings round the eyes had been cried out. Slumped in the big chair, she was the personification of bereavement.

'Did you get any sleep last night?' asked Caplan, sitting down. Gillian shook her head.

'We don't need to do this now.'

'May as well, I've nowhere to go.'

Caplan heard Craigo come in the door behind her. Gillian lifted her head up and muttered something like 'Oh, it's you,' then went back to gazing at the floor.

'You'll be asked many times why you never said "I didn't do it." I'd like to ask first.'

'That Ted bloke would still be alive if he hadn't bothered his backside about me. Two wee kids would have a dad.'

'He'd still be alive if Gail hadn't stabbed him. It had nothing to do with you. Ted was alerted to your case because your case-worker at Rettie was Meryl Murdoch's partner; she was taking home all kinds of confidential information. Rettie'll try to cover it up. As you would expect.'

'Bet you Peyton's shitting his pants.' Gillian looked up and frowned. 'She wants to take me out to lunch, that Murdoch woman. I'm a celebrity now. Fucking hell.'

'No, Gillian, just don't. You're a victim of this as much as anybody else. Gail wasn't going to have any narrative other than the one she'd invented for you.'

'I could have stopped it.'

'No you couldn't, she'd programmed you that way.'

'Ted's wife? I'd like to meet her.'

'What good do you think that would do?'

Gillian shrugged. 'I'd like to tell her that it wasn't me.'

'She knows. You're a good person. You risked your life to rescue that stupid dog of yours; that takes some heart.'

'But I didn't speak out. I could've said something, even at Church's Pass. I never did. I was too scared.'

'Too scared and too young.'

Gillian closed her eyes, rolling her head back. 'There's nothing . . . fuck all. You sitting there with your nice suit, your nice life, telling me how this shit-show is going to pan out . . . My life has been nothing but other folk telling me what to do.'

Craigo made a snorting noise. 'Well, you aren't alone in that. You try being a not-very-bright police officer, I've spent my entire life being bossed about by folk. And sometimes by folk even dafter than me.'

Caplan stared at him.

'Present company excepted.'

Gillian said, 'Yeah, well, you probably need to be told to wipe yer arse. Fuckwit.'

'And what about the boss here? She lives in a caravan with no heating. Her house has no roof. Her husband hasn't seen daylight for seven years. I mean, you never know what's going on in anybody else's life. Some folk think that I'm a little odd but I know I'm perfectly normal.'

The short speech caused both women in the room to stare at him, then look at each other. Gillian didn't try to stifle a giggle.

'And in my experience . . . if you ask me . . .'

'We're not asking you,' snapped Caplan.

'But there's always something. If you don't mind me saying, you've a rather nice dog, that Ollie. He needs training. Like him, you need little steps. Find somewhere to live. Don't go back to Ben o' Tae, but you should live somewhere near the trees, near the water. That's the life you're born to.'

'Yeah,' Gillian said with no enthusiasm at all. 'Bloody midges.'

'It's probably people you don't like, so keep away from them.'

'Most folk are arseholes,' Gillian nodded.

'No argument from me on that,' said Caplan, glaring at Craigo.

'Or me,' said Craigo thoughtfully.

Gillian rolled her eyes.

'The question about why you said nothing is too hard for you to answer. But what happened at Church's Pass? The starting point.'

Gillian bit her lip, some anger playing out internally. Frustration at herself. 'I don't think I know any more. I was told that I pushed Rachel, but I don't know. Why would I do that? Gail was on the other side of the track. She shouted on us, well on Rachel. I let Rachel go, she ran towards Gail when the train came. Rachel stopped, and Gail waved at her, telling her it was okay to cross. Rachel ran onto the track. So, I saw it . . . what was left.' Tears ran down her face. 'Everybody was so nice to me. Gail told them she'd seen me try to stop Rachel. So I thought I had. But I don't think that was what happened. I'm not sure.'

'But she was sure. That's how her coercive control started, Gillian. Her power over you was so great and you were too young to work it out. She was clever. When you showed the slightest sign of slipping out of her control, she'd make sure something happened to bring you back to her, to show that you couldn't do without her. That's why she visited you more than anybody else did. I think Ted Maxwell was following the evidence, being led by Gail, but he was smarter than she was. But didn't see the danger. Nor did I to be fair.'

Gillian closed her eyes, defeated. Caplan resisted the temptation to hug her.

'No point in saying it if no bugger believes you. What's the point of talking?'

'Gillian, it's a lot to take in, you need help but you'll be fine.'

'Fuck knows,' said Gillian, inspecting the dressing that covered her right hand.

'You can go anywhere now,' said Craigo.

'God, you're as thick as pig shite if you think that. You two don't get it, do you? I don't have a life. I've never had a life. I've lived in institutions. There's no point, no point in me walking through that door. I don't understand life out there.'

'I might be thick but you're short-sighted. I'm not saying that it won't take time but you can do something to ease yourself back to where you want to be.' Craigo nodded sagely.

'I've had an offer to tell my story to the *Daily Star*, and two to write a book about being me. I'm deeply popular. I'm fucking trending on Twitter, me. Like I said, that Murdoch woman wants to buy me dinner.'

'You'd be going from one controller to another.'

'Skinny bitch with a fake tan?' Gillian gave a flutter of a smile. 'Yeah, I had her tagged as a bawbag the first time I saw her.'

Caplan was unimpressed with the amount of paperwork she was supposed to be attending to. Fortunately, a press officer was dealing with the media. The station was besieged. A search was going on at Ben o' Tae. Granda was in custody, a hero once again. He was a crack shot, positioning himself so that his shotgun took out

Gail at close range without touching Alice. But he had killed a young woman, the law was taking its course.

Caplan herself was working backwards to see what they had missed. The same thread that pulled Rowan through the investigation pulled Gail as well. Except at Sugar Loaf. What tied Gail to the Guide camp? Why did she kill Poppy? A weird Rowan–Poppy–Gail love triangle? But they couldn't place Gail there and Linden wanted answers. Caplan had been warned to square the circle.

She had been going over the documentation for three hours, fuelled by green tea.

It didn't take her long, reading the initial report from the incident at Sugar Loaf. There was a file of photographs taken at the Family Day that DC Mackie had signed for. She flicked to the back and went through them.

A feeling of déjà-vu floated over her.

A catastrophic error by a close colleague. It was her team, her mistake.

When Lizzie had messed up, Caplan had owed her a lot, and she could allow her a little slack. And now Mackie? How did they miss that?

She looked up. The constable wasn't in the incident room. A moment ago she'd been helping to pack up.

Caplan waited, mentally placing Gail at every step where they'd placed Rowan.

She was the one who had everything. It was Gail who was on a long-term prescription of sedatives after the trauma of witnessing the crash that killed her mother. Caplan wondered how many of those tablets were stashed in the house. If she so desired, Gail could have everyone in the house comatose. Gail had access to keys, the dogs knew her so wouldn't raise the alarm. Rowan had said that on early starts he sometimes rolled the car down the hill, a trick that Duguid used to jump-start engines. So, when needed, Gail did the same. Did she kill her own mother? Were two busy parents easier to control than four? She'd encouraged Rachel Mary to run in front of the train. She'd slit the throat of Rachel Susan – easy, as she was asleep in the same room – leaving the knife on Gillian's bed. Gillian had woken up later, picked the knife up, gone over to Rachel, got covered in her blood. Caplan could imagine Gail in her pyjamas feigning upset, asking Gillian to check on Rachel.

And their theory of the killer's movements the night that Ted was killed fitted well, placing Gail in the lead role. She had dislodged two of her eyelash extensions when putting on the fat suit in the confined space of the Fiat. She'd only had those put on the previous week, cutting down the exposure of the suit to the eyelashes, firming up the timeline. Caplan recalled the painful eye Gail had the first time they met. No DNA on the eyelashes themselves, but there were skin cells in the glue. No relation to Gillian, which excluded Rowan. In that moment, both Caplan and Gail had known. Gail's DNA was being retested now; no doubt there'd be a match.

They had failed to pick up any of the Halliday cars on the ANPR on the road out to Ben o' Tae. To pick up the Fiat, Gail had taken an old Volkswagen Up that Duguid was repairing, placing black insulating tape over the two 3s in the registration plates, transforming them to 8s. So the ANPR tracking of the other cars registered to Ben o' Tae had been a waste of time and resources.

Gillian was easy to imitate. Fat suit, wig, make-up, the flash of white of the fake bandage, just enough for the security camera to pick up. Was that little awkward step on the dashcam footage Maxwell recoiling when he realised that it wasn't Gillian walking towards him? Did it dawn on him then that he was in trouble? Maxwell's professional instinct would have kicked in, he would have tried to talk to her. Gail stabbed him, emptied his pockets and put him over the railing – easy with two usable hands. Then she reversed the journey but forgot to put the driver's seat of the Fiat back in the right position for Mrs McGinty. She dumped the fat suit; lucky for them it missed the dumpster. Once she'd driven home, she'd opened the locks on Gillian's door. Gail could say she was up and about because the baby was awake. If she had been seen around Cronchie, she was going to the all-night pharmacy. She had a sore eye after all.

The search of the house had found the left shoe, only the left, that had made the imprint near Poppy's body. Gail was already leaving a trail, so that if Gillian was ever proved not guilty, then Rowan would have been next on the list. The binbags in Rowan and Gail's kitchen had a tear pattern that matched the one that had contained the fat suit. Gail's DNA would be there as well.

The Fiscal was keen to complete the story by finding Maxwell's missing phones. Craigo pointed out a few facts about the Sound, the River Etive and manpower. The budget for the search was withdrawn.

At what part of all that had Dr Edward Maxwell joined the story? He'd become interested in Girl A as a killer. He'd contacted Gillian, met her, and then Gail had taken over being 'Gillian' just as she'd taken over Killagal.

The control that Gail exerted over Gillian was extreme, providing her with a phone, a life, a website, leaving clues to have her hunted so she'd be chased back home, back into the spider's web. Even now, Gillian seemed lost without her mentor, her friend, her abuser. Everything that was 'Gillian' was Gail except that one piece of evidence that Evan had, the piece of film that showed Gail's hand waving to Rachel to cross the line. His visual memory had been right, Gillian had not been at the side of the track.

How trusting was wee Rachel? Why would she suspect Gail would hurt her?

And of course Gillian said her back was against the fence on the east side of the track. To see what she saw, she needed to look left . . . Gail, on the opposite side, had blogged her own memory, of looking right, by mistake, as she had for her mum's apple pie, the varying accounts of the visit to the hospital.

Caplan closed the file on the Sugar Loaf incident, not looking, but seeing the list of names on the front, the officers who had viewed the file and whose images were in there to be viewed.

Caplan heard the door bang. It was Mackie coming into the incident room, looking dishevelled. Caplan called her through. When she'd sat her large bulk on the seat across from her Caplan slid the closed file across the desk, letting her fingernail rest on the name of the Guide who'd made the cocoa on the night of the midnight feast, then she rested back on the chair.

Mackie read the list, eyes reddening, looked up at Caplan. Her mouth hung open and the words 'Oh, I am so, so sorry' came out.

'I know we were overstretched, tired, but did you not see that? Abby? The Abby that winds her way all through the story at Sugar Loaf, was Abby McCleary, Gail McCleary, christened Abigail. You were looking through the list. You failed to spot that. Failed to check it? Even if you failed to see it first time round, why didn't you double-check?'

'Sorry, ma'am.' Her eyes were transfixed on the document, lips moving but with nothing to say.

'Pauline couldn't recall Abby's surname, we should have chased it up. We didn't. We all messed up.'

Cordelia Maxwell had called Caplan, her voice quiet but firm, in control of herself. She said that she'd like to go to the bridge, that Ted's parents wanted to come along too but not the children. They could go in their own time.

Caplan didn't like the word closure. It would all be part of the healing process, the first few steps on a journey of a life that would never be the same again.

Cordelia had the support of her in-laws to help with the boys. In the last eight years Caplan had felt like a single parent to two teens, through the last years of school then into uni. That had been bad enough.

Caplan had asked her if she really thought that was a good idea, but it was what Cordelia wanted to do. And the widow had said she had something of Ted's to give to Gillian, if that could be made possible.

ACC Sarah Linden was giving a statement to the press, sitting behind a table covered with a neatly ironed navy-blue cloth. She was dressed in her full regalia, all braided, sharp epaulettes and crisp white shirt. She was emphasising, in the gravest of terms, just how hard the investigating team had worked to uncover a monumental miscarriage of justice. One innocent person behind bars for a day was one too many and she congratulated the team for their persistence and hard work in preventing another when they could all too easily have accepted the evidence being fed to them. Police Scotland and the mental-health services involved were going to carry out a review with full transparency. Everything must be done to ensure that this did not happen again. There would also be a full public inquiry, as the investigation had ended in the fatal shooting of Abigail Fiona Halliday.

While driving back to the caravan, hypnotised by the solitude and the gentle twisting of the road, Caplan considered what she was going to do with Mackie. She'd messed up a vital part of the case, she'd not been on the ball. Neither had Caplan, but she'd tasked Mackie with it. It was how it worked. Craigo hadn't followed up on Abby's surname either.

Their error would come out at the inquiry. It would all come out in the wash. The Rettie, the previous investigations, Soupy Campbell would be made scapegoats, and Felix Construction would get a slap on the wrist. But while Caplan was in the good books, she'd put pressure on Linden to get Happy Harris reinstated.

THIRTY

Life is so bloody boring.
Except death. The endpoint.

Killagal Blog, 2021

The steelwork of the bridge groaned with the rising wind. It was a cold but sunny day in May, ready to rain again. The weather was much as it had been on the day Ted Maxwell drove up here, thinking about a ghost who had gaslighted a young woman for her entire life.

He had intended to set her free.

The evil eye had no issue taking out a tender heart. Once he had contacted Gail, thinking he was contacting Gillian, he was in danger.

Cordelia Maxwell got out the back of an old Mercedes and walked towards them. Her black coat swirled round her ankles, a loose grey scarf coiled round her head and neck.

Cordelia walked up to a subdued and emotional Gillian; a few words were exchanged. Caplan and Craigo stepped back, not wanting to overhear. Cordelia took something out her pocket. A small polythene bag containing something shining and silvered under layers of clingfilm. Cordelia pressed it into Gillian's palm, wrapping her fingers round it.

She spoke to them. 'It's Ted's work on the Halliday case, a microcard. He kept it inside his shoe, cut into his heel lift.'

Caplan let out a long slow breath. 'Hence why he wore them

on both feet, to allow the room for a protection of the card on the left, so he needed a small lift on the right.'

'It meant it was with him at all times, it was important to him. It's the story of your life Gillian,' said Cordelia.

They waited a moment, listening to the gentle lap of the waves. Somewhere high on the bridge, a seagull squawked loudly.

'I respect his decision that I wasn't to know,' Cordelia continued. 'He was keeping us safe. But it's your story, I have no right to it.'

She stepped forward and hugged an unwilling Gillian before walking towards her parents-in-law and the bridge. She turned and gave them a little wave. Gillian was still holding on to her precious package, tears rolling down her cheeks.

The Maxwells walked onto the bridge holding hands, and dropped rose petals off the side and into the wind.

Two police officers had stopped the traffic to give them some peace in their moment of reflection. The river, the Sound and the Falls were in harmony today. Both time and tide had passed.

Caplan turned to walk away.

Gillian was now waiting with Mackie up on the main road, watching the little ceremony on the bridge from a respectful distance.

'Fuck's sake, a book. Me in a book. Janet and John join the police and become fascists,' Gillian chattered, sniffing her tears back.

'Your life, Gillian Rose Halliday.'

Gillian looked down, chewing on the corner of her lip, thinking. 'Ted was nice. Shame he's gone.'

'Not your fault. That's survivor's guilt. You've a lot in your life to be angry about but Ted is the one person who stuck his head above the parapet for you. If it wasn't for him, you'd still be behind bars.'

She shook her head, sniffing. 'No, I'd be out, and he'd be alive. Gail would still be here.'

But Caplan read the doubt behind her eyes. 'Gillian, Gail wasn't going to stop. She was going to control you for the rest of your life. You came this close—' She held her finger and thumb so no light passed between them '—to going down for life for a murder that you did not commit. It was Gail who was writing the blog, you know. When it got too comfortable for you on the outside, when it looked like you might escape her grasp, she lets slip where you are and BOOM, you're under her roof again. And they'd have roasted you alive in mainstream prison. They called you the most hated woman in Britain because it was true.'

'And what am I now?'

'People have sympathy for you, a lot. Gail had so much control over you, your demon and your redeemer. She abused you then comforted you, she sent you away then welcomed you back. She programmed you from the moment you were born. You were a lifetime project for her. You need good therapy. Stick with Anna, she's got your best interest at heart.'

Caplan patted her on the shoulder and walked towards Mackie, leaving Gillian to her thoughts.

She noticed Craigo on the shore looking over the water, his face restive, sorrowful.

'What's up with him,' asked Caplan.

Mackie thought for a bit before answering. 'Gillian and Finnan have a lot in common. Do you not see it?'

'Frankly, no. What're you talking about?'

'You don't get him, do you?'

'Sorry, do I need to "get" him?' Caplan was a bit rattled by her colleague's tone.

'I don't think you really understand why Gillian stayed away from that house. She was more comfortable elsewhere than she ever was at home.'

'I understand that.'

'Craigo's home life was a bit like that when his mum was alive. He needs approval. Gillian was always looking for approval, for true friendship from Gail. Every time Gillian drifted away Gail would reel her back in.'

'You think it was like spousal domestic abuse but between siblings, in-laws, step siblings, whatever?'

'As you said, look who had it all? Gail.'

Mackie turned, her cheeks reddened by the breeze. The slight rain had soaked her fringe and a tendril veined her forehead. 'In Craigo, that need for approval has never been met, it's never over. He's been bullied all his life – the kids at school, Auntie Nora. She was a real Mommie Dearest. He was bullied at Tulliallan; since then he's been the butt of every joke going. Don't think I don't know. He's my cousin. I know how he was brought up. Then you came here, ma'am, with your good clothes and your strict ways. He likes you, ma'am. He feels he can do his job under your protection.'

'He doesn't need my protection.'

'You listen to him.'

'Sometimes I listen to him, sometimes he talks bloody nonsense.'

'You joke, ma'am, but he knows you listen to him. He loves feeling an important part of the team. He sat behind that desk filing reports of lost sheep for years before you came along. He's like a wee dog, trotting after you, bringing you gifts.'

'He's good at his job, I'm not showing him any special favours, Toni. Compared to your performance recently, he's a stellar detective. And before you say it, we all make mistakes.'

'You lost that evidence, ma'am, that Brindley case.'

'Yes I did, didn't I?'

Mackie gave her an enquiring look, then turned away. 'You never put us down to make yourself look good, we've noticed that.'

'Why would I?'

Mackie half-turned, facing her again. 'He's worried that you'll leave, ma'am, with your husband, with the caravan, with the house not being sold. He's worried that you'll go back to Glasgow, and his life will revert to the crap it's always been. We're all worried about that. We are a wee station, ma'am, it was shit before you came here. Then we solved the Devil Stone case. Then you left for the Lovell murder, but you came back. Are you going to leave again?'

'Well, you can reassure him, in a quiet moment, that I've no intention of going anywhere. Emma and Kenny are here. The division I worked with in Glasgow think I'm an incompetent embarrassment, so I'm not welcome there.'

'Hard to see you as an incompetent embarrassment.'

'Hard to see you as an incompetent embarrassment, *ma'am*,' corrected Caplan.

They both looked over to Craigo who, on cue, stepped back across the rocks and stumbled, did a little soft-shoe shuffle and righted himself, then stood and looked down, confused by the concept of seaweed being slippy.

Caplan said, 'I'm amazed he manages to get up in the morning.'

An hour later, she pulled off the track outside Challie Cottage, bouncing the Duster along the rough, potholed stretch of grass and brick that was known as the driveway. She did a quick U-turn so the car was facing the water, not the tumbledown project they – she – had bought as a house. She noticed the front door of the cottage was open and presumed that one of the many builders had been finding another way of making the project more expensive.

She cut the engine and sat for a moment looking out to the water, the quiet waves of today. There was still a very cold breeze but, out the way of the wind, the air had lost its chill. A portent that summer was finally on its way. She became aware of music drifting from the open door of the cottage. It sounded like Vivaldi to her, not one of her favourites but a piece that Aklen had always loved. She was going to sleep here and then go back to Glasgow, make peace with her husband, without losing her temper.

She got out the car, getting used to scrambling over the passenger seat. Her heart thumping, she did something she had never done in the years they had lived at 27 Abington Drive; she stood and admired the cottage. Three of the trees had come down in the storm, and there were about a dozen or so roof slates lying in the front garden. She couldn't see where they had come from; the roof already had a lot of gaps, like the smile of an old man, she had thought looking at it in the half-light.

She picked her way along the overgrown strip in the garden that used to be a path. But nothing could take away the thrill that she felt every time she looked at the view.

She'd have a word with the builders then sit out in front of the cottage, on the swing, drinking a mug of tea. She was wearing Aklen's warm anorak, so she'd sit for a while and take in the view, thinking about anything but Gillian and Ben o' Tae, not a thought of Craigo, not a thought of Linden in her apartment or Lizzie Fergusson and the affair that was doomed.

It was a dull grey day today.

And it was her birthday.

Nobody knew. The best present she could hope for was some peace and quiet.

Then she saw the swing chair, with two bright-yellow cushions propped up on the seat, still in their polythene bags to protect them from the drizzle.

The music was getting louder as she neared the cottage door, hanging by one set of hinges, propped open by an old rake the builders must have found in the garden.

She heard a voice. Not conversational, instructional. Somebody was watching a YouTube clip about roofing felt. In the damp hallway, she moved along to the old kitchen. A jacket lay over one of the old plastic chairs, the door of the Aga was open. On the dusty old table was a bouquet of flowers and beside it a cat basket with Pas de Chat sitting inside, looking rather anxious about the entire situation.

Aklen was leaning on the table, looking at her. 'Hello.'

'Hello, didn't expect you here.'

'Well, I had Emma on the phone, then Sarah and Lizzie appeared at the door like a tag team, I thought I might be safer up here.'

She looked at the phone in his hand, the man in the video cutting roof felt. She burst out laughing. 'Are you serious?'

He looked up. Part of the ceiling had come down and they could see daylight and the clouds above.

He smiled his Alain Delon smile. 'How hard can it be?'

EPILOGUE

Three months later

The hotel function suite was gently lit and a few rows of chairs had been haphazardly placed, a couple of waitresses at the side handing out summer-fruit cocktails and mocktails. The French windows were open onto the patio, the sunshine was streaming in. It seemed like a good omen.

The idea to have a press conference for Gillian Halliday, no longer Britain's Most Evil Woman, had seemed an odd one but it was definitely popular. There were journalists everywhere.

There was a keen sense of anticipation.

Caplan slipped in at the back, full of curiosity, and was surprised to see Anna Scafoli from Rettie, plus, in the corner, somebody she thought could be Alison Watkins. Karl Rolland, still immaculately dressed in black, nodded at her. Sitting beside him Peter Biggs raised his hand in greeting and motioned that they might like to catch up for a drink afterwards, maybe toast an absent friend.

Meryl Murdoch, her smile plastered on, was schmoozing the room, ready for her launch into true-crime TV.

Behind the small dais was a backdrop, a large print of a charcoal drawing of the whole Halliday family. Caplan was puzzled by the images of the two young ladies, beautifully depicted, between Gillian and Rowan. Then it dawned on her: the two Rachels as Gillian imagined they would be, had they been allowed to grow up.

It was their story too.

Wanting to appear busy, Caplan checked her emails. A good offer had come in for Abington Drive, there was a text from Emma, one from Linden, and a video from Aklen showing him knee-deep in a trench with a mug of tea. She wondered if the builders had turned up to take the photograph. Or if they were going to do any building.

Two people walked onto the small podium; Caplan felt her heart leap. There was a gentle wave of things moving, postures being adjusted, pens poised and fingers over recording buttons.

Gillian Halliday had ditched the wig. Her real hair was softer, much shorter but still spiky, with a designer touch to match her form-fitting dress and kitten heels.

The other person standing shyly, awkwardly, beside her was Cordelia, dressed demurely in a navy trouser suit. She stood with her hands clasped in front of her, nodding to the audience, then started to speak, welcoming everybody, no doubt aware of the flutter of sympathy round the room, followed by a lightning flash as cameras grabbed their image of the widow. She spoke from a prepared speech, setting out their plans to take control of the story that was theirs. And to ask for respect and privacy. Caplan felt something of a maternal lump in her throat as Gillian was introduced, standing beside her at the microphone. The young lady was holding herself well.

Gillian took centre-stage and said, 'Just to let you know that I am going to continue with the book that Dr Edward Maxwell started. The book that cost him his life. The book that is my story.' She smiled. 'I have the story, but I don't have the skill to turn that into something readable. I'd need a lot more pictures in it.' That got a trickle of laughter. 'So, I'm honoured that I'm going to co-write the project with Cordelia Maxwell, which will be bitter-sweet for both of us. The book will be called *The Fall of Lora*, as had been Dr Maxwell's original plan.'

Cordelia was talking again, eloquently now. Caplan was sure that she had come away from the script. As the audience saw the change in her, the ambiance of the room subtly altered. The journalists had sensed it as well. Cordelia allowed some anger in her voice. She continued to speak about the challenges of mental illness, the challenges of being young, the challenges of being robbed of a voice, of being dispossessed of a presence.

Ted's words, thought Caplan, capturing Gillian's entrapment in a system she couldn't escape.

Cordelia was angry, her words burning into Caplan's head, piercing her brain. She spoke about those in positions of power exploiting the weak, those in places of privilege exploiting those without a voice, those with a duty of care who failed to care, those in a position of trust who abused that trust. A few journalists shuffled awkwardly in their seats, drinks changed hands in guilty displacement activity.

Caplan looked at Murdoch, who was paying no attention. She was looking at the ceiling, pulling her fingers through her short black hair, having no idea that she and her ilk were part of the problem.

Cordelia gathered herself again. 'As you know, my husband died trying to bring Gillian's story to light. He was a good man, he was using his voice to give power to somebody who had none.' She paused, her voice quaking a little, then it sharpened and carried on resolutely. 'And for those who fail in professional care, who fail in their oath to do no harm, who try to exploit their professional position and use those placed in their care for profit—' She paused '—and for celebrity, well, this book is about your victims, and one survivor. We don't know how many do not survive.'

There was a round of applause, led by Rolland and Biggs, and the two women came off stage to do a meet-and-greet. Gillian leaned forward to say something to Meryl Murdoch, who had stood up to shake their hands and take a selfie. Then Gillian seemed to stumble slightly. Cordelia leant forward to catch her, but in the ensuing tumble, something went a little awry and Murdoch got knocked to the ground, narrowly missing being elbowed in the face.

It was a beautiful move and one that Caplan had seen before. On a family video, when Rowan and Gail had been racing and tripped Gillian up.

In the melee that followed, Cordelia and Gillian helping Murdoch to her feet, Caplan mouthed 'Nice one' to Gillian before slipping out the door before she felt obliged to arrest anybody.